The President: A Novel

Alfred Henry Lewis

Alpha Editions

This edition published in 2024

ISBN 9789362097392

Design and Setting By

Alpha Editions

www.alphaedis.com

Email - info@alphaedis.com

As per information held with us this book is in Public Domain.
This book is a reproduction of an important historical work.
Alpha Editions uses the best technology to reproduce historical work
in the same manner it was first published to preserve its original nature.
Any marks or number seen are left intentionally to preserve.

Contents

CHAPTER I .... - 1 -

CHAPTER II .... - 11 -

CHAPTER III .... - 22 -

CHAPTER IV .... - 34 -

CHAPTER V .... - 46 -

CHAPTER VI .... - 60 -

CHAPTER VII .... - 72 -

CHAPTER VIII .... - 83 -

CHAPTER IX .... - 95 -

CHAPTER X .... - 107 -

CHAPTER XI .... - 121 -

CHAPTER XII .... - 132 -

CHAPTER XIII .... - 144 -

CHAPTER XIV .... - 156 -

CHAPTER XV .... - 168 -

CHAPTER XVI .... - 181 -

CHAPTER XVII .... - 195 -

CHAPTER XVIII .... - 210 -

CHAPTER XIX .... - 223 -

CHAPTER XX .... - 237 -

CHAPTER XXI .... - 249 -

CHAPTER XXII .... - 262 -

CHAPTER XXIII .... - 271 -

CHAPTER I

HOW RICHARD BEGAN TO WOO

On this far-away November morning, it being ten by every steeple clock and an hour utterly chaste, there could have existed no impropriety in one's having had a look into the rooms of Mr. Richard Storms, said rooms being second-floor front of the superfashionable house of Mr. Lorimer Gwynn, Washington, North West. Richard, wrapped to the chin in a bathrobe, was sitting much at his ease, having just tumbled from the tub. There was ever a recess in Richard's morning programme at this point during which his breakfast arrived. Pending that repast, he had thrown himself into an easy-chair before the blaze which crackled in the deep fireplace. The sudden sharp weather made the fire pleasant enough.

The apartment in which Richard lounged, and the rooms to the rear belonging with it, were richly appointed. A fortune had been spilled to produce those effects in velvets and plushes and pictures and bronzes and crystals and chinas and lamps and Russia leathers and laces and brocades and silks, and as you walked the thick rugs you made no more noise than a ghost. It was Richard's caprice to have his environment the very lap of splendor, being as given to luxury as a woman.

Against the pane beat a swirl and white flurry of snow, for winter broke early that year. Richard turned an eye of gray indolence on the window. The down-come of snow in no sort disquieted him; there abode a bent for winter in his blood, throughout the centuries Norse, that would have liked a Laplander. Even his love for pictures ran away to scenes of snow and wind-whipped wolds with drifts piled high. These, if well drawn, he would look at; while he turned his back on palms and jungles and things tropical in paint, the sight of which made him perspire like a harvest hand. As Richard's idle glance came back from the window, it caught the brown eyes of Mr. Pickwick considering him through a silvery, fringy thicket of hair. Mr. Pickwick was said to be royally descended; however that might have been, indubitably his pedigree harbored somewhere both a door-mat and a mop.

"Rats!" observed Richard to Mr. Pickwick.

Richard did not say this because it was true, but to show Mr. Pickwick that the ties which bound them were friendly. On his side, Mr. Pickwick, albeit he stood well aware how there was never a rat in the room, arose vivaciously and went snuffling and scuffling behind curtains and beneath sofas, and all in a mood prodigiously dire.

The room being exhaustively searched, Mr. Pickwick came and sat by Richard, and with yelp and howl, and at intervals a little epileptic bark, proceeded to disparage all manners and septs of rats, and spake slightingly of all such vermin deer. Having freed his mind on the important subject of rats, Mr. Pickwick returned to silence and his cushion and curled up.

Matzai, the Japanese valet, brought in the breakfast—steak, potatoes, eggs, toast, marmalade, and coffee. The deft Matzai placed the tray on the mahogany at Richard's elbow. Richard did not like a multiplicity of personal attendants. Of the score of souls within the walls of that house, Richard would meet only Mr. Gwynn and Matzai. This was as the wisdom of Solomon, since neglect is born of numbers.

Mr. Lorimer Gwynn was a personage—clean and tall and slim and solemn and sixty years of age. He was as wholly English as Mr. Pickwick was wholly Skye, and exuded an indomitable respectability from his formal, shaven face. Rumor had it that Mr. Gwynn was fabulously rich.

It was in June when Mr. Gwynn came to town and leased the house just vacated by Baron Trenk, late head of the Austrian diplomatic corps. This leasing of itself half established Mr. Gwynn in a highest local esteem; his being English did the rest, since in the Capital of America it is better, socially, to come from anywhere rather than from home. In addition to those advantages of Baron Trenk's house and an English emanation, Mr. Gwynn made his advent indorsed to the Washington banks by the Bank of England; also he was received by the British Ambassador, on whom he made a call of respect the moment he set foot in town.

It became known that Mr. Gwynn was either widower or bachelor; and at that, coupled with his having taken a large house, the hope crept about that in the season he would entertain. The latter thought addressed itself tenderly to the local appetite, which was ready to be received wherever there abode good cooks and sound wines. Mr. Gwynn, it should be mentioned, was duly elected a member of the Metropolitan Club—where he never went; as was likewise Richard—who was seen there a great deal.

Richard had not come to town until both Mr. Gwynn and his house were established. When he did appear, it was difficult for the public to fix him in his proper place. He was reserved and icily taciturn, and that did not blandly set his moderate years; with no friends and few acquaintances, he seemed to prefer his own society to that of whomsoever came about him.

Who was he?

What was he?

What were his relations with Mr. Gwynn?

Surely, Richard could be neither son nor nephew of that English gentleman. Richard was too obviously the American of full blood; his high cheekbones, square jaw, and lean, curved nose told of two centuries of Western lineage. Could it be that Richard was Mr. Gwynn's secretary? This looked in no wise probable; he went about too much at lordly ease for that. In the end, the notion obtained that Richard must be a needy dependent of Mr. Gwynn, and his perfect clothes and the thoroughbred horse he rode were pointed to as evidences of that gentleman's generosity. Indeed, Mr. Gwynn was much profited in reputation thereby.

Richard, while not known, was not liked. He wore the air of one self-centered, and cold to all judgments except his own. This last makes no friends, but only enemies for him whose position is problematical. Richard's pose of insolent indifference would have been beautiful in a gentleman who counted his fortune by millions; in a dollarless beggar who lived off alms it was detestable. Wherefore, the town, so far as Richard encountered it, left our silent, supercilious one to himself, which neglect dove-tailed with his humor and was the precise lonely thing he sought. This gave still further edge to the public's disregard; no one likes you to accept with grace what is intended for punishment.

Matzai carried away the breakfast tray, and Richard lighted a cigar. Matzai returned and stood mute inside the door, awaiting new commands. Richard pointed through the cigar-smoke to the clock—one of those soundless, curious creatures of brass and glass and ivory which is wound but once in four hundred days, and of which the hair-hung pendulum twists and turns and does not swing.

"In an hour! Eleven o'clock!" said Richard.

At the risk of shaking him in general standing it should be called to your notice that Richard preceded breakfast with no strong waters. Richard would drink nothing more generous than coffee, and, speaking in the sense limited, tobacco was his only vice. Perhaps he stuck to cigars to retain his hold on earth, and avoid translation before his hour was ripe.

It was no pale morality that got between Richard and the wine cup. In another day at college he had emptied many. But early in his twenties, Richard discovered that he carried his drink uneasily; it gave a Gothic cant to his spirit, which, under its warm spell, turned warlike. Once, having sat late at dinner—this was in that seminary town in France where he attended school—he bestrode a certain iron lion, the same strange to him and guarding the portals of a public building. Being thus happily placed, he drew two huge American six-shooters, whereof his possession was wrapped in mystery even to himself, and blazed vacuously, yet ferociously, at the moon. Spoken to by the constabulary who came flying to the spot, Richard replied with acrimony.

"If you interfere with me," remarked Richard on that explosive occasion, addressing the French constables, "I'll buy your town and burn it." The last with a splendid disdain of limitations that was congenital.

Exploits similar to the above taught Richard the futility of alcoholic things, and thereupon he cultivated a Puritan sobriety upon coffee and tobacco.

Richard cast the half-burned cigar into the fire. Stepping to the mantel, he took from it a small metal casket, builded to hold jewels. What should be those gems of price which the metal box protected? Richard did not strike one as the man to nurse a weakness for barbaric adornment. A bathrobe is not a costume calculated to teach one the wearer's fineness. To say best, a bathrobe is but a savage thing. It is the garb most likely to obscure and set backward even a Walpole or a Chesterfield in any impression of gentility. In spite of this primitive regalia, however, Richard gave forth an idea of elevation, and as though his ancestors in their civilization had long ago climbed above a level where men put on gold to embellish their worth. What, then, did that casket of carved bronze contain?

Richard took from its velvet interior the heel of a woman's shoe and kissed it. It was a little kissable heel, elegant in fashion; one could tell how it belonged aforetime to the footwear of a beautiful girl. Perhaps this thought was aided by the reverent preoccupation of Richard as he regarded it, for he set the boot-heel on the table and hung over it in a rapt way that had the outward features of idolatry. It was right that he should; the little heel spoke of Richard's first strong passion.

You will retrace the year to the 10th of June. Richard, after roving the Eastern earth for a decade, had just returned to his own land, which he hardly knew. Throughout those ten years of long idling from one European city to another, had Richard met the woman he might love, he would have laid siege to her, conquered her, and brought her home as his wife. But his instinct was too tribal, too American. Whether it were Naples or Paris or Vienna or St. Petersburg or Berlin, those women whom he met might have pleased him in everything save wedlock. In London, and for a moment, Richard saw a girl he looked at twice. But she straightway drank beer with the gusto of a barge-man, and the vision passed.

It was the evening after his return, and Richard at the Waldorf sat amusing himself with those tides of vulgar humanity that ebb and flow in a stretch of garish corridor known as Peacock Lane. Surely it was a hopeless place wherein to seek a wife, and Richard had no such thought. But who shall tell how and when and where his fate will overtake him? Who is to know when Satan—or a more benevolent spirit—will be hiding behind the hedge to play good folk a marriage trick? And Richard had been warned. Once, in Calcutta, price one rupee, a necromancer after fullest reading of the signs informed him that when he met the woman who should make a wife to him, she would come upon him suddenly. Wherefore, he should have kept a brighter watch, expecting the unexpected.

Richard's gaze went following two rustical people—clearly bride and groom. In a cloudy way he loathed the groom, and was foggily wondering why. His second thought would have told him that the male of his species—such is his sublime egotism—feels cheated with every wedding not his own, and, for an earliest impulse on beholding a woman with another man, would tear her from that other one by force. Thus did his skinclad ancestors when time was.

However, Richard had but scanty space wherein either to enjoy his blunt hatred of that bridegroom or theorize as to its roots. His ear caught a muffled scream, and then down the wide staircase in front of him a winsome girl came tumbling.

With a dexterity born of a youth more or less replete of football, Richard sprang forward and caught the girl in his arms. He caught and held her as though she were feather-light; and that feat of a brutal strength, even through her fright, worked upon the saved one, who, remembering her one hundred and thirty pounds, did not think herself down of thistles.

"Are you hurt?" asked Richard, still holding her lightly close.

Richard looked at the girl; black hair, white skin, lashes of ink, eyes of blue, rose-leaf lips, teeth white as rice, a spot of red in her cheeks—the last the fruit of fright, no doubt. He had never seen aught so beautiful! Even while she was in his arms, the face fitted into his heart like a picture into its frame, and Richard thought on that prophet of Calicut.

"Are you injured?" he asked again.

"Thanks to you—no," said the girl.

With a kind of modest energy, she took herself out of his arms, for Richard had held to her stoutly, and might have been holding her until now had she not come to her own rescue. For all that, she had leisure to admire the steel-like grasp and the deep, even voice. Her own words as she replied came in gasps.

"No," she repeated, "I'm not injured. Help me to a seat."

The beautiful rescued one limped, and Richard turned white.

"Your ankle!" he exclaimed.

"No; my heel," she retorted with a little flutter of a laugh. "My French heel caught on the stair; it was torn away. No wonder I limp!"

Then came the girl's mother and called her "Dorothy."

Richard, who was not without presence of mind, climbed six steps and secretly made prize of the baby boot-heel. Perhaps you will think he did this on the argument by which an Indian takes a scalp. Whatever the argument, he placed the sweet trophy over that heart which held the picture of the girl; once there, the boot-heel showed bulgingly foolish through his coat.

Richard returned to the mother and daughter; the latter had regained her poise. He introduced himself: "Mr. Richard Storms." The mother gave him her card: "Mrs. John Harley." She added:

"My name is Hanway-Harley, and this is my daughter, Dorothy Harley. Hanway is my own family name; I always use it." Then she thanked Richard for his saving interference in her child's destinies. "Just to think!" she concluded, and a curdling horror gathered in her tones. "Dorothy, you might have broken your nose!"

Richard ran a glance over Mrs. Hanway-Harley. She was not coarse, but was superficial—a woman of inferior ideals. He marveled how a being so fine as the daughter could have had a no more silken source, and hugged the boot-heel. The daughter was a flower, the mother a weed. He decided that the superiority of Dorothy was due to the father, and gave that absent gentleman a world of credit without waiting to make his acquaintance.

Mrs. Hanway-Harley said that she lived in Washington. Where did Mr. Storms live?

"My home has been nowhere for ten years," returned Richard. Then, as he looked at Dorothy, while his heart took a firmer grip on the picture: "But I shall live in Washington in a few months."

Dorothy, the saved, beneath whose boot-heel beat Richard's heart, looked up, and in the blue depths—so Richard thought—shone pleasure at the news. He could not be certain, for when the blue eyes met the gray ones, they fell to a furtive consideration of the floor.

"You are to take a house in Washington," said Richard to Mr. Gwynn an hour later.

Mr. Gwynn bowed.

You who read will now come back to that snow-filled day in November. Richard relocked his dear boot-heel in the casket; eleven and Matzai had entered the room together. Matzai laid out Richard's clothes, down to pin and puff tie. Richard shook off his bathrobe skin and shone forth in a sleeveless undershirt and a pair of those cotton trousers, cut short above the knee, which dramatic usage ascribes to fishermen and buccaneers.

As Richard stood erect, shoulders wide as a viking's, chest arched like the deck of a whale-back, he might have been a model for the Farnese Hercules, if that demigod were slimmed down by training and ten years off his age. He of Farnese should be about forty, if one may go by looks, while Richard was but thirty. Also, Richard's arms, muscled to the wrists and as long as a Pict's, would have been out of drawing from standpoints of ancient art. One must rescue Richard's head; it was not that nubbin of a head which goes with the Farnese one. Moreover, it showed wisest balance from base to brow; with the face free of beard and mustache, while the yellow hair owned no taint of curl—altogether an American head on Farnese shoulders refined.

Richard made no speed with his dressing. What with refusing several waistcoats—a fastidiousness which opened the slant eyes of Matzai, being unusual—and what with pausing to smoke a brooding cigar, it stood roundly twelve before he was ready for the street. One need not call Richard lazy. He was no one to retire or to rise with the birds; why should he? "Early to bed and early to rise" is a tradition of the copybooks. It did well when candlelight was cheap at a dollar the dozen, but should not belong to a day of electricity no dearer than the sun.

Before going out, Richard crossed to a writing cabinet and pressed a button, the white disk whereof showed in its mahogany side. It was not the bell he used for the wheat-hued Matzai, and owned a note peculiar to itself. As though in response came Mr. Gwynn, irreproachable, austere.

Upon the advent of Mr. Gwynn, one might have observed sundry amazing phenomena, innocent at that. Mr. Gwynn did not sit down, but stood in the middle of the room. On the careless other hand, Richard did not arise from the chair into which he had flung himself, but sat with his hat on, puffing blue wreaths and tapping his foot with a rattan.

"Mr. Gwynn," quoth Richard, "you will catch the four-o'clock limited to New York. Talon & Trehawke, Attorneys, Temple Court, have on sale a majority of the stock of the *Daily Tory*. Buy it; notify those in present charge of the editorial and business departments of the new proprietorship. There will be no changes in the personnel of the paper so far as refers to New York. You are to say, however, that you will give me charge in Washington. Talon & Trehawke can put you in control, and forty-eight hours should be enough to carry out my plans. The balance of the stock you will buy up at your leisure. This is Tuesday; have the bureau here ready for me by Thursday evening."

Mr. Gwynn inclined his head.

"Can you give me, sir, some notion of what Talon & Trehawke are to have?" asked Mr. Gwynn.

"Their letter addressed to you—here it is—says that sixty per cent. of the stock can be had for two millions eight hundred thousand."

"Very good, sir," and Mr. Gwynn bowed deeply.

Richard pulled on his gloves to depart, whereat Mr. Pickwick yelped frantically from his cushion. Richard tapped Mr. Pickwick with the lacquered rattan.

"Old man," said Richard, "I am going to take a look at the lady I love." Mr. Pickwick moaned querulously, while Richard sought the street.

Richard, the day before, dispatched a note and a card to Mrs. Hanway-Harley and had been told in reply that he might call to-day at three. Richard decided to repair to the club, and wait for three o'clock.

Richard, during his week in Washington, had found a deserted corner in the club and pre-empted it. At those times when he honored the club with his presence, he occupied this vantage point. From it he was given both a view of the street and a fair survey of the apartment itself. No one approached him; his atmosphere was repellant; beyond civil nods, curtailed to the last limit of civility, his intercourse with his fellows had not advanced.

On this afternoon as Richard smoked a solitary cigar and reviewed the thin procession of foot passengers trudging through the snow beneath his window, he was attracted by the loud talk of a coterie about a table. The center of the group was Count Storri—a giant Russ. This Storri did not belong to the Russian legation, did not indeed reside in town, and had been vouched into the club by one of his countrymen. He had onyx eyes, with blue-black beard and mustaches which half covered his face, and hair as raven as his beard. Also he valued himself for that a favorite dish with him was raw meat chopped fine with peppers and oil.

Storri's education—which was wide—did not suffice to cover up in him the barbarian, videlicet, the Tartar—which was wider; and when a trifle uplifted of drink, it was his habit to brag profoundly in purring, snarling, half-challenging tones. Storri boasted most of his thews, which would not have disgraced Goliath. He was at the moment telling a knot of gaping youngsters of monstrous deeds of strength. Storri had crushed horseshoes in his hand; he had rolled silver pieces into bullets between thumb and finger.

"See, you children, I will show what a Russian can do!" cried Storri.

Storri came over to the fireplace, the rest at his heels. Taking up the poker—a round half-inch rod of wrought iron—he seized it firmly by one end with his left hand and with the right wound it twice about his left arm. The black spiral reached from hand to elbow; when he withdrew his arm the club poker was a Brobdingnagian corkscrew.

The youngsters stared wonder-bitten. Then a mighty chatter of compliments broke forth, and Storri swelled with the savage glory of his achievement.

Richard, the somber, who did not like noise, shrugged his shoulders. Storri, by the fireplace, caught the shrug and found it offensive. He made towards Richard, and offered the right hand, his white teeth gleaming in a sinister way through the fastnesses of his beard.

"Will you try grips with me?" cried Storri loudly. "Will you shake hands Russian fashion?"

"No," retorted Richard, all ice and unconcern. "I will not shake your hand Russian fashion."

Storri broke into an evil grin that made him look like a black panther.

"Some day you must put your fingers into that trap," said he, opening and closing his broad hand.

Richard making no return, Storri and the others went back to their decanters.

Richard might have said, and would have believed, that he did not like Storri because of a Siberian rudeness and want of breeding. It is to be thought, however, that his antipathy arose rather from having heard the day before Storri's name coupled with that of Dorothy Harley. The Russ was a caller at the Harley house, it seemed, and rumor gave it that he and Mr. Harley were together in speculations. At that Richard hated Storri with the dull integrity of a healthy, normal animal, just as he would have hated any man who raised his eyes to Dorothy Harley; for you are to know that Richard was in a last analysis even more savage than was Storri himself, and withal as jealously hot as a coal of fire. Presently Storri departed, and Richard forgot him in a reverie of smoke.

It stood the quarter of three, and Richard took up his walk to the Harleys'. It was no mighty journey, being but two blocks.

In the Harley drawing room whom should Richard meet but Storri. The Russ was on the brink of departure. At that meeting Richard's face clouded. Dorothy was alone with Storri; her mother had been called temporarily from the room. At sight of Dorothy's flower-like hand in Storri's hairy paw, Richard's eyes turned jade.

"Mr. Storms," said Dorothy, as Richard paused in the door, "permit me to present Count Storri."

"Ah!" whispered Storri, beneath his breath, "see now how my word comes true!"

With that he put out his hand like a threat.

Storri's exultation fell frost-nipped in greenest bud. It was as though some implacable destiny had seized his hand. In vain did Storri put forth his last resource of strength—he who crushed horseshoes and twisted pokers! Like things of steel Richard's fingers closed grimly and invincibly upon those of Storri. The Russian strove to recover his hand; against the awful force that held him his boasted strength was as the strength of children.

Storri looked into Richard's eyes; they were less ferocious, but infinitely more relentless than his own. There was that, too, in the other's look which appalled the Tartar soul of Storri—something in the drawn brow, the eye like agate, the jaw as iron as the hand! And ever more and a little more that fearful grip came grinding. The onyx eyes glared in terror; the tortured forehead, white as paper, became spangled with drops of sweat.

There arose a smothered feline screech as from a tiger whose back is broken in a deadfall. Richard gave his wrist the shadow of a twist, and Storri fell on one knee. Then, as though it were some foul thing, Richard tossed aside Storri's hand, from the nails of which blood came oozing in black drops as large as grapes.

"What was it?" gasped Dorothy, who had stood throughout the duel like one planet-struck; "what was it you did?"

"Storri on his knee?" asked Richard with a kind of vicious sweetness. There was something arctic, something remorselessly glacial, in the man. It caught and held Dorothy, entrancing while it froze. "Storri on his knee?" repeated Richard, looking where his adversary was staining a handkerchief with Tartar blood. "It was nothing. It is a way in which Russians honor me—that is, Russians whom I do not like!"

CHAPTER II

HOW A PRESIDENT IS BRED

Mr. Patrick Henry Hanway, a Senator of the United States, had the countenance of a prelate and the conscience of a buccaneer. His grandfather—it was at this old gentleman, for lack of information, he was compelled to stop his ancestral count—was a farmer in his day. Also, personally, he had been the soul of ignorance and religion, and of a narrowness touching Scriptural things that oft got him into trouble.

Grandfather Hanway read his Bible and believed it. He held that the earth was flat; that it had four corners; and that the sun went around the earth. He replied to a neighbor who assured him that the earth revolved, by placing a pan of water on his gate-post. Not a drop was spilled, not a spoonful missing, in the morning. He showed this to the astronomical neighbor as refutatory of that theory of revolution.

"For," said Grandfather Hanway, with a logical directness which among the world's greatest has more than once found parallel, "if the y'earth had turned over in the night like you allow, that water would have done run out."

When the astronomical one undertook a counter argument, Grandfather Hanway fell upon him with the blind, unreasoning fury of a holy war and beat him beyond expression. After that Grandfather Hanway was left undisturbed in his beliefs and their demonstrations, and tilled his sour acres and begat a son.

The son, Hiram Hanway, was sly and lazy, and not wanting in a gift for making money that was rather the fruit of avarice than any general length and breadth and depth of native wit. Having occasion to visit, as a young man, the little humdrum capital of his State, he stayed there, and engaged in the trade of lobbyist before the name was coined. He, too, married, and had children—Patrick Henry Hanway and Barbara Hanway. These his offspring were given a peculiar albeit not always a sumptuous bringing up.

When Patrick Henry Hanway was about the age of Oliver Twist at the time Bill Sykes shoved him through the window, Hiram Hanway caused him to be appointed page in the State Senate. There, for eight years, he lived in the midst of all that treason and mendacity and cowardice and rapacity and dishonor which as raw materials are ground together to produce laws for a commonwealth. He learned early that the ten commandments have no bearing on politics and legislation, and was taught that part of valor which, basing itself on greed and cunning and fear, is called discretion, and consists in first running from an enemy and then hiding from pursuit. Altogether, those eight years might have been less pernicious in their influence had Patrick Henry Hanway passed them with the chain gang, and he emerged therefrom, to cast his first vote, treacherous and plausible and boneless and false—as voracious as a pike and as much without a principle.

Patrick Henry Hanway did not follow in the precise footsteps of his sire. He resolved to make his money by pulling and hauling at legislation; but the methods should be changed. He would improve upon his father, and instead of pulling and hauling from the lobby, he would pull and haul from within. The returns were surer; also it was easier to knead and mold and bake one's loaf of legislation as a member, with a seat in Senate or Assembly, than as some unassigned John Smith, who, with a handful of bribes and a heart full of cheap intrigue, must do his work from the corridor. A legislative seat was a two-edged sword to cut both ways. You could trade with it, using it as a bribe, bartering vote for vote; that was one edge. Or you could threaten with it, promising nay for nay, and thus compel some member to save your bill to save his own; that was the other edge. A mere bribe from the lobby owned but the one edge; it was like a cavalry saber; you might make the one slash at a required vote, with as many chances of missing as of cutting it down. Every argument, therefore, pointed to a seat; whereat Patrick Henry Hanway bent himself to its acquirement, and at the age of twenty-six he was sworn to uphold the law and the Constitution and told to vote in the Assembly. In that body he flourished for ten years, while his manhood mildewed and his pockets filled.

The native State of Patrick Henry Hanway was a moss-grown member of the republic and had been one of the original thirteen. It possessed with other *impedimenta* a moss-grown aristocracy that borrowed money, devoured canvasbacks, drank burgundy, wore spotless tow in summer, clung to the duello, and talked of days of greatness which had been before the war. It carried moss-grown laws upon its statute books which arranged for the capture of witches, the flogging of Quakers at a cart's tail, the boring of Presbyterian tongues with red-hot irons, and the punishment of masters who oppressed their hapless slaves with terrapin oftener than three times a week. However, these measures, excellent doubtless in their hour, together with the aristocracy referred to, had fallen to decay.

The moss-grown aristocracy were aware in a lifeless, lofty way of Patrick Henry Hanway, and tolerating while they despised him as one without an origin, permitted him his place in the legislature. Somebody must go, and why not Patrick Henry Hanway? They, the aristocracy, would there command his services in what legislation touching game, and oysterbeds, and the foreclosure of mortgages they required, and that was all their need. The supple Patrick Henry Hanway thanked the aristocracy for the honor, took the place, and carried out their wishes for patrolling oysterbeds, protecting canvasbacks, and preventing foreclosures.

While these conditions of mutual helpfulness subsisted, and Patrick Henry Hanway kept his hat off in the presence of his patrons, nothing could be finer than that peace which was. But time went on, and storms of change came brewing. Patrick Henry Hanway, expanding beyond the pent-up Utica of a State Capitol, decided upon a political migration to the Senate of the United States.

When this news was understood by men, the shocked aristocracy let their canvasbacks grow cold and their burgundy stand untasted. With horrified voice they commanded "No!" The United States Senate had been ever reserved for gentlemen, and Patrick Henry Hanway was a clod. The fiat went forth; Patrick Henry Hanway should not go to the Senate; a wide-eyed patrician wonder was abroad that he should have had the insolent temerity to harbor such a dream—he who was of the social reptilia and could not show an ancestor who had owned a slave!

This purple opposition did not surprise the astute Patrick Henry Hanway; it had been foreseen, and he met it with prompt money. He had made his alliances with divers railway corporations and other big companies, and set in to overturn that feudalism in politics which had theretofore been dominant. The aristocrats felt the attack upon their caste; they came forth for that issue and the war wagged.

But the war was unequal. The aristocrats, who, like the Bourbons, had learned nothing, forgotten nothing, plodded with horseback saddle-bag politics. Patrick Henry Hanway met them with modern methods of telegraph and steam. Right and left he sowed his gold among the peasantry. In the end he went over his noble enemies like a train of cars and his legislature sent him into Washington by a vote of three to one. He had been there now twelve years and was just entering upon his third term. Moreover, he had fortified his position; his enemies were now powerless to do him harm; and at the time this story finds him he had constructed a machine which rendered his hold upon his State as unshakable as Gibraltar's famous rock. Patrick Henry Hanway might now be Senator for what space he pleased, and nothing left for that opposing nobility but to glare in helpless rancor and digest its spleen.

When Patrick Henry Hanway came to Washington he was unhampered of even a shadow of concern for any public good. His sole thought was himself; his patriotism, if he ever possessed any, had perished long before. Some said that its feeble wick went flickering out in those earlier hours of civil war. Patrick Henry Hanway, rather from a blind impression of possible pillage than any eagerness to uphold a Union which seemed toppling to its fall, enlisted for ninety days. As he plowed through rain and mud on the painful occasion of a night march, he addressed the man on his right in these remarkable words:

"Bill, this is the last d———d time I'll ever love a country!"

And it was.

The expletive, however, marked how deep dwelt the determination of Patrick Henry Hanway; for even as a young man he had taught himself a suave and cautious conversation, avoiding profanity as of those lingual vices that never made and sometimes lost a dollar.

The Senate of this republic, at the time when Patrick Henry Hanway was given his seat therein, was a thing of granite and ice to all newcomers. The oldsters took no more notice of the novice in their midst than if he had not been, and it was Senate tradition that a member must hold his seat a year before he could speak and three before he would be listened to. If a man were cast away on a desert island, the local savage could be relied upon to meet him on the beach and welcome him with either a square meal or club. Not so in the cold customs of the Senate. The wanderer thrown upon its arctic shores might starve or freeze or perish in what way he would; never an oldster of them all would make a sign. Each sat in mighty state, like some ancient walrus on his cake of ice, and made the new one feel his littleness. If through ignorance or worse the new one sought to be heard, the old walruses goggle-eyed him ferociously. If the new one persisted, they slipped from their cakes of ice and swam to the seclusion of the cloakrooms, leaving the new one talking to himself. This snub was commonly enough to cause the collapse of the new one, after which the old walruses would return to their cakes of ice.

Senator Hanway—one should give him his title when now he has earned it—was not inclined to abide by those gag traditions that ruled the Senate beaches. He was supple, smooth, apologetic, deprecatory, and his nature was one which would sooner run a mile than fight a moment. For all that he was wise in his generation, fearing no one who could not reach him for his injury. He did not, for instance, fear the Senate walruses, goggle-eying him from their ice cakes. They could do him no harm; he did not take his seat by their permission. Upon deliberate plan, therefore, Senator Hanway had not been in his place a fortnight before he got the floor on an appropriation, and began to voice his views. The walruses at first goggle-eyed him in wrathful amazement; but he kept on. Then, as was their habit, they set sail for the cloakrooms, waving condemnatory flippers.

ONE OF THE MOST REVEREND OF THE SENATE WALRUSES

ONE OF THE MOST REVEREND OF THE SENATE WALRUSES

Senator Hanway had thought of this, and the cloakroom move did not disconcert him. He seized on one of the most reverend of the Senate walruses, one festooned with the very seaweed of Senate tradition, and, casting him, as it were, on the coals of his hot rhetoric, proceeded to roast him exhaustively. The cloakroom walruses smelled the odor of burning blubber and returned eagerly to their cakes of ice, for there is nothing so pleasing to your true walrus as the spectacle of a brother walrus being grilled. It was in time understood that if the walruses placed an affront upon Senator Hanway he would assail them singly or in the drove. Then the walruses made their peace with him and admitted him to fellowship before his time; for your walrus cannot carry on a war and is only terrible in appearance.

Now, when the seal of silence was taken from Senator Hanway and he found himself consented to as a full-grown walrus possessed of every right of the Senate beaches, he became deferential to his fellow Senators. He curried their favor by pretending to consult with them, personally and privately, on every Senate question that arose. He could be a great courtier when he pleased and had a genius for flattery, and now that his right to go without a gag was no longer disputed he devoted himself to healing what wounds he had dealt the vanity of the oldsters. By this he grew both popular and powerful; as a finale no man oftener had his Senate way.

Senator Hanway, modestly and unobtrusively, did sundry Senate things that stamped him a leader of men. He bore the labor of a staggering filibuster, and more than any other prevented a measure that was meant for his party's destruction. In the lists of that filibuster he met the champion of the opposition—a Senator of pouter-pigeon characteristics, more formidable to look upon than to face—and, forensically speaking, beat him like a carpet.

On another day when one of his party associates was to be unseated by so close a vote that a single member of the Committee on Privileges and Elections would determine the business either way, it was Senator Hanway, no one knew how, who in manner secret captured that member from the enemy. The captured one voted sheepishly in committee and continued thus sheepish on the open Senate floor, although a beautiful woman smiled and beamed upon him from the gallery as women smile and beam when granted favors.

It was during Senator Hanway's second term, however, that he accomplished the work which placed him at his party's fore and confirmed him as its chief. The Senate, following a certain national election, fell to be a tie. The party of Senator Hanway still had control of the committees and generally of the Senate organization; but that election had sent to be the Senate's presiding officer a Vice-President who belonged with the opposition. On a tie, Senator Hanway's party would find defeat by the vote of that new Vice-President.

It was then the pouter-pigeon chieftain moved that the Senate organization be given over to him and his fellows. The motion would seem to settle it. The vote on the floor would be equal, and the sagacious pouter-pigeon reckoned on the new Vice-President to decide for him and his. The party colleagues of Senator Hanway, many of them four terms old in Senate mysteries, were eaten of despair; they saw no gateway of escape. The pouter-pigeon would take possession, remake the committees, and, practically speaking, thereby remake the legislation of that Congress.

At this crisis, Senator Hanway took down the Constitution and showed by that venerable document how the power of the Vice-President went no farther than deciding ties on legislative questions; that when the business at bay was a matter of Senate organization, he had no more to say than had the last appointed messenger on the gallery doors. The situation, in short, did not present a tie, for the settlement of which the Vice-Presidential decision was possible; therefore, Senate things must remain as they then were.

Senator Hanway's reading of Vice-Presidential powers was right, as even the opposition confessed; he saved the Senate and thereby the nation to his party, and his rule was established unchallenged over his people, his least opinion becoming their cloud and their pillar of fire to guide them day and night. He was made far and away the dominant figure of the Senate.

Finding himself thus loftily situated and his hands so clothed with power, Senator Hanway, looking over the plains of national politics, conceived the hour ripe for another and a last step upward. For twelve years a White House had been his dream; now he resolved to seek its realization. From the Senate he would move to a Presidency; a double term should close his career where Washington and Jefferson and Jackson and other great ones of the past closed theirs.

True, Senator Hanway must win his party's nomination; and it was here he took counsel with his Senate colleagues. Being consulted, the word of those grave ones proved the very climax of flattery. Senators Vice and Price and Dice and Ice, and Stuff and Bluff and Gruff and Muff, and Loot and Coot and Hoot and Toot, and Wink and Blink and Drink and Kink—statesmen all and of snow-capped eminence in the topography of party—endorsed Senator Hanway's ambition without a wrinkle of distrust to mar their brows or a moment lost in weighing the proposal. The Senate became a Hanway propaganda. Even the opposition, so far as slightly lay with them, were pleasantly willing to help the work along, and Senator Hanway blushed to find himself a Senate idol. By the encouragement which his colleagues gave him, and the generous light of it, Senator Hanway saw the way clear to become the choice of his party's national convention. But he must work.

It was in that prior day when Senator Hanway served his State in the legislature that he wedded Dorothy Harley. It is to be assumed that he loved her dearly; for twelve years later when she died his grief was like a storm, and for the rest of his days he would as soon think of a top hat without a crown as without a mourning band.

When Senator Hanway married Dorothy Harley, her brother, John Harley, married Barbara Hanway. Whether this exchange of sisters by the two was meant for retort or for compliment lived a point of dispute—without being settled—among the friends of the high contracting parties for many, many months.

Not that anyone suffered by these double nuptials; the families owned equal social standing, having none at all, and were evenly balanced in fortune, since neither had a dollar. Both Senator Hanway and John Harley had their fortunes to make when, each with the other's sister on his arm, they called in the preacher that day; and after the wedding they set about the accumulation of those fortunes.

In a half-sense the two became partners; for while a lawmaker can be highly useful to a man of energy outside the halls of legislation, the converse is every inch as true. They must be folk of course who know and trust one another; and, aside from marrying sisters—a fact calculated to quickly teach two gentlemen the worst and the best about each other—John Harley and Senator Hanway had been as Damon and Pythias for a decade. Not that either would have died for the other, but he would have lied and plotted and defrauded and stopped at nothing short of murder for him, which, considering the money appetites of the pair and those schemes they had for feeding them, should be vastly more important.

When Senator Hanway came to Washington, John Harley and his wife, Barbara Hanway-Harley as she preferred to style herself, came with him. Senator Hanway made his home with the Harleys, when now he was a widower; and the trio, with the daughter, Dorothy—named for the Senator's wife—who lost her boot heel when Richard lost his heart, made up a family of four, and took their place in Capital annals.

John Harley had a red and jovial face that promised conviviality. It was the custom with John Harley to slap a new acquaintance on the shoulder and hail him as "Old Man." He was long of body, short of leg, apoplectic as to neck—a girthy, thick, explosive, boisterous gentleman, who could order a good dinner and could eat one. He could find you a fair bottle of wine, and then assist in emptying it. He aimed at the open and frank and generous, and was willing you should think him of high temper, one who would on provocation deal a knock-down blow.

Senator Hanway was his opposite, being of no more color than a monk and of manners as precisely soft as a lady's. He never raised his voice, never lost his temper; he strove for an accurate gentility—to give the lie to noble foes at home—and far from owning any ferocities of fist, retorted to a heated person who charged him with flat falsehood by a mere shrug of the shoulders and a simple:

"I refuse to discuss it, sir!"

And all with a high air that left his opponent gasping and helpless and floundering with the feeling that he had been somehow most severely and completely, not to say most righteously, rebuked.

There you have vague charcoal sketches of Senator Hanway and John Harley; you may note as wide a difference between the two as lies between warclubs and poisons. And yet they fitted with each other like the halves of a shell. Also they were masters of intrigue; only John Harley intrigued like a Wolsey and Senator Hanway like a Richelieu.

John Harley played the business man, and was rough and plain and blunt— a man of no genius and with loads of common sense. He made a specialty of unpalatable truths and discarded sentiment. Indeed, he was so good a business man that he got possession of a rotund interest in a group of coal mines without the outlay of a dollar, and later became the owner of sundry sheaves of railway stocks on the same surprising terms.

Not that the coal and the railway companies lost by John Harley. When it was known that he possessed an interest in the mines, certain armor plate mills and shipbuilding concerns, as well as nineteen steamboat lines, came forward to buy the coal. As for the railway, whereas prior to John Harley's introduction as shareholder and director it could get no consideration in the way of freights from those giant corporations which have to do with beef and sugar and oil—it being both slow and crooked as a railroad—thereafter it was given all it could haul at rates even with the best, and its prosperity became such that fifty-five points were added to the quoted value of its stock.

It is possible that John Harley's nearness to Senator Hanway had something to do with founding for him a railway and a coal-mine popularity. The vote of a Senator may be important to armor plate and shipbuilding concerns; as much might be said of companies that deal in beef and sugar and oil. The action of a Senator may even become of moment to a steamship line. The last was evidenced on a day when those nineteen suddenly refused to purchase further coal from the Harley mines. They were buying five millions of tons a year, those five millions finding their way to the sea over the railway of which John Harley was a director and in which he owned those sheaves of stocks, and a fortune rose or fell by that refusal. The steamboats said they would have no more Harley coal; it was stones and slates, they said.

Senator Hanway at once introduced a bill, with every chance of its passage, which provided for a tariff reduction of ten per cent. *ad valorem* on goods brought to this country in American ships. Since the recalcitrant nineteen were, to the last rebellionist among them, foreign ships, flying alien flags, this threatened preference of American ships took away their breath. The owners of those lines went black with rage; however, their anger did not so obscure them but what they saw their penitent way to readopt the Harley coal, and with that the mining and carriage and sale of those annual five millions went forward as before. The Hanway bill, which promised such American advantages, perished in the pigeon holes of the committee; but not before the press of the country had time to ring with the patriotism of Senator Hanway, and praise that long-headed statesmanship which was about to build up a Yankee merchant marine without committing the crime of subsidy.

John Harley and Senator Hanway at the time when Dorothy suffered that momentous mishap of the heel, were both enrolled by popular opinion among the country's millionaires. Each had been the frequent subject of articles in the magazines, recounting his achievements and offering him to the youth of America as a "Self-Made Man," whose example it would be wise to steer by. In the Presidential plans of Senator Hanway, John Harley nourished a flaming interest. With his pale brother-in-law in the White House, what should better match the genius of John Harley than the rôle of Warwick. He would pose as a President-maker. When the President was made, and the world was saying "President Hanway," that man should be dull indeed who did not look upon John Harley as the power behind the curtain. He would control the backstairs; he would wear a White House pass-key as a watch-charm! John Harley as well as Senator Hanway had his dreams.

Both Dorothy and her mother were profound partisans of Senator Hanway. Dorothy loved her "Uncle Pat" as much as she loved her father. Dorothy, who could weigh a woman,—being of the sex,—might have felt occasional misgivings as to her mother. She might now and again observe an insufficiency that was almost the deficient. But of her father and "Uncle Pat" she never possessed a doubt; the one was the best and the other the greatest of men.

Dorothy was so far justified of her affection that to both John Harley and Senator Hanway she stood for the model of all that was good and beautiful in life. Hard and keen and never honest with the world at large, the love of those two for the girl Dorothy was gold itself. Neither said "No" to Dorothy; and neither made a dollar without thinking how one day it would go to her. She was the joint darling; they would divide her between them as the recipient of their loves while they lived and their fortunes when they died. And many thought Dorothy lucky with two such fathers to cherish her, two such men to conquer wealth wherewith to feather-line her future.

John Harley made no secret of Senator Hanway's Presidential prospects, and if he did not talk them over with his helpmeet, he listened while she talked them over with him. Mrs. Hanway-Harley, who insisted more vigorously than ever upon the hyphenation, would of necessity preside over the White House. She saw and said this herself. The Harley family would move to the White House. Anything short of that would be preposterous.

Under such conditions and facing such a future, the tremendous responsibilities of which already cast their shadow on her, Mrs. Hanway-Harley was driven to take an interest in her brother's canvass; and she took it. She gave her husband, John Harley, all sorts of advice, and however much it might fail in quality, no one would have said that in the matter of quantity Mrs. Hanway-Harley did not heap the measure high. Senator Hanway himself she was not so ready to approach. He never mentioned the question of his Presidential hopes and fears, holding to the position of one who is sought. Under the circumstances, Mrs. Hanway-Harley felt that it would be gross and forward to force the subject with her brother, although she was certain that her silence meant unmeasured loss to him. Mrs. Hanway-Harley was one of those excellent women whereof it is the good fortune of the world to have such store, who cherish the knowledge, not always shared by others, that whatever they touch they benefit and wherever they advise they improve.

"Barbara," said Senator Hanway, on the morning of that day when Richard meddled so crushingly with Storri's hand, "Barbara, there is a matter in which you might please me very much."

Mrs. Hanway-Harley looked across the table at her brother, for the four were at breakfast.

"I promise in advance," said she.

"There is a gentleman," went on Senator Hanway, "I met him for a moment—a Mr. Gwynn. You ladies know how to arrange these things. I want to have him—not too large a party, you know—have him meet Gruff and Stuff and two or three of my Senate friends. He is vastly rich, with tremendous railway connections. I need not explain; but conditions may arise that would make Mr. Gywnn prodigiously important—extremely so. I don't know how you'll manage; he is exceedingly conventional—one of your highbred English who must be approached just so or they take alarm. But I'm sure, Barbara, you'll bring the matter about; and I leave it to you with confidence."

CHAPTER III

HOW MR. GWYNN DINED WITH THE HARLEYS

Any man who says that he is a gentleman is not a gentleman. A gentleman no more tells you that he is a gentleman than a brave man tells you he is brave. Gentility is a quality which the possessor never seeks to establish as his own by word of mouth; he leaves it to inference and the rule has no exception. This brilliant speechlessness arises not through modesty, but ignorance. However clearly gentility reveals itself to others, he who possesses it has no more knowledge on that faultless point than have your hills of the yellow gold they hold within their breasts.

Storri was one who went far and frequently out of his conversational way to assure you that he was a gentleman. Though he did no more than just recount how he gave his seat to a woman in a car, or passed the salt at dinner, or made a morning call, somewhere in the narrative you were sure to hear that he was "a gentleman," or "a Russian gentleman," commonly the latter; and he always accompanied the news with a straightening of his heavy shoulders and a threatening pull at his mustache as though he expected to find his word disputed and planned a terrible return.

It could not be called Storri's fault that it was not three hundred years since his forebears wore sheepskins, carried clubs, and made a fire by judiciously rubbing one stick against another. None the less, this nearness to a stone age left him barbarous in his heart; and the layer of civilization that was upon him was not a layer, but a polish—a sheen, and neither so thick nor so tangible as moonshine on a lake. The savageries of Richard were quite as vivid as Storri's, perhaps; but at least they had been advantageously hidden beneath a top-dressing of eleven civilizing centuries instead of three; and those eight extra centuries made all the difference in life. They gave Richard steadiness and self-control; for the first separation between civilization and barbarism lies in this, that a civilized man is more readily quieted after a stampede than is your barbarous one. Also he is not so wide open to original surprise.

Wherefore, when Richard and Storri stood glaring at one another after the episode of the hands, Richard had vastly the better of Storri, who fell into a three-ply mood of amazement, fright, and rage. Finally, Storri seemed to mutter threats while he retreated; and at the last got himself out of the Harley front door in rather an incoherent way. It was understood that he mumbled "Good-afternoon!" to Dorothy; and that "he would talk with him again," to Richard; and all as he found his hat with his left hand, the right meanwhile wrapped in a handkerchief which was a smudge of blood. It could not be described as a graceful exit and had many of the features of a rout; but it was effective, and took Storri successfully into the street. Dorothy, still transfixed, turned with round eyes to Richard:

"What was it you did?" she asked again.

"It was nothing," replied Richard with a shrug. "Or if anything, then a piece of primitive sarcasm. Really, I'm sorry, since you were here; but I had no choice."

"Will there be a duel?" gurgled Dorothy, catching her breath.

Dorothy, among other valuable ideas derived from novels, had gained a middle-age impression that made flashing blades and gaping wounds a romantic probability.

"Storri is not so self-sacrificing," returned Richard with a grin, "and I am much too modern." Then in a bantering tone: "How much better was the old day when men might differ nobly foot to foot, with the fair lady to the victor and a funeral to the vanquished as the natural upshot. It is too bad! In the name of progress we have come too far and thrown away too much!"

It was among the marvels how Richard changed. As he talked with Dorothy those eyes, late flint, became tender and laughingly honest in a fashion good to see. He appeared younger by half, for anger is ancient and piles on the years.

"Really, Miss Harley," continued Richard, with a heroic determination to change the subject, "I haven't as yet paid my respects to you. Your mother said I might call. She was very kind!" And here Richard pressed the little hand in that one which had so discouraged Storri, while Mrs. Hanway-Harley suddenly swept into the room as if "Mother" were her cue.

"Mamma," cried Dorothy, presenting Richard, "this is Mr. Storms. You remember; he saved my—my nose."

Certainly Mrs. Hanway-Harley remembered. She recalled the event in a manner superbly amiable and condescending.

"And you told us then," said Mrs. Hanway-Harley, "that you would presently dwell in Washington. Is it your plan to make the town your permanent residence?"

"My plans depend on the plans of others, madam. I have become chained to their chariot and cannot call myself free." Here Richard looked audaciously sly at Dorothy, who interested herself with certain flowers that stood in the window.

"Ah! I see," returned Mrs. Hanway-Harley, who did not see at all. "You mean Mr. Gwynn." She had heard of Mr. Gwynn, so far as the town knew that personage, from her husband. "But you said 'others'?"

"Yes, madam; besides Mr. Gwynn, there are Matzai and Mr. Pickwick." Then, responding to Mrs. Hanway-Harley's inquiring brows, Richard went forward with explanations. "Matzai is my valet, while Mr. Pickwick is a terrier torn by an implacable hatred of rats; which latter is the more strange, madam, for I give you my word Mr. Pickwick never saw a rat in his life."

"What an extraordinary young man!" ruminated Mrs. Hanway-Harley, and she bestowed upon Richard a searching glance to see if by any miracle of impertinence he was poking fun at her.

That well-balanced gentleman realized the peril, and faced it with a countenance as blankly, not to say as blandly vacuous as the wrong side of a tombstone. He ran the less risk; for the lady could not conceive how anyone dare take so gross a liberty with a Hanway-Harley; one, too, whose future held tremendous chances of a White House. Being satisfied of Richard's seriousness, and concluding privily that he was only a dullard whom the honor of her notice had confused, she said:

"Umph! Matzai and Mr. Pickwick! Yes; certainly!"

Then Mrs. Hanway-Harley set herself to ask questions, the bald aggressiveness whereof gave the daughter a red brow. Richard answered readily, as though glad of the chance, and did not notice the crimson that painted Dorothy's face.

The latter young lady was as much puzzled by their caller as was her mother, without accounting for his oddities on any argument of dullness. Indeed, she could see how he played with them: that there flowed an undercurrent of irony in his replies. Moreover, while by his manner he had pedestaled and prayed to her as to a goddess, when they were alone and before her mother came, Dorothy now observed that Richard carried himself in a manner easy and masterful, and as one who knows much in the presence of ones who know little. This air of the ineffably invincible made Dorothy forget the adoration which had aforetime glowed in his eyes, and she longed to box his ears.

"Is Mr. Gwynn your relative?" asked the cool, though somewhat careless, Mrs. Hanway-Harley.

"No, madam; no relative." There drifted about the corners of Richard's mouth the shadow of a smile. "He is all English; I am all American."

"I'm sure I'm sorry," remarked the lady musingly. Then without saying upon what her sorrow was hinged, she proceeded. "Mr. Gwynn, I hear—I don't know him personally, but hope soon to have that pleasure—is a gentleman of highest breeding. My brother assures me that he has most delightful manners. I know I shall adore him. If there's anything I wholly admire it is an old-school English gentleman—they have so much refinement, so much elevation!"

"It might not become me," returned Richard, in what Mrs. Hanway-Harley took to be a spirit of diffidence, "to laud the deportment of Mr. Gwynn. But what should you expect in one who all his life has had about him the best society of England?"

"Ah! I can see you like him—venerate him!" This with ardor.

"I won't answer for the veneration," returned Richard. "I like him well enough—as Mr. Gwynn."

Mrs. Hanway-Harley stared in matronly reproof.

"You don't appear over grateful to your benefactor."

"No;" and Richard shook his head. "I'm quite the churl, I know; but I can't help it."

Richard found a chance to say to Dorothy,

"I see that you love flowers."

This was when Dorothy had taken refuge among those blossoms.

"I worship flowers," returned Dorothy.

"Now I don't wonder," exclaimed Richard. "You and they have so much in common."

Mrs. Hanway-Harley was for the moment preoccupied with thoughts of Mr. Gwynn, and plans for the small Senate dinner at which that austere gentleman would find himself in the place of honor. However, she caught some flash of Richard's remark. For the fraction of an instant it bred a doubt of his dullness. What if he should come philandering after Dorothy? Mrs. Hanway-Harley's feathers began to rise. No beggar fed by charity need hope for her daughter's hand; she was firm-set as to that. Perhaps Mr. Gwynn intended to make him rich by his will. At this Mrs. Hanway-Harley's feathers showed less excitement. Mr. Gwynn should be sounded on the subject of bequests. Why not put the question to Mr. Storms? It would at least lead to the development of that equivocal gentleman's expectations.

"Has Mr. Gwynn any family in England?" asked Mrs. Hanway-Harley.

"A nephew or two, I believe; possibly a brother."

"But he will make you his heir."

"Me?" Richard gave a negative shake of the head. "The old fellow wouldn't leave me a shilling. Why should he? Nor would I accept it if he did." Richard's sidelong look at Mrs. Hanway-Harley was full of amusement. "No, the old rogue hates me, if he would but tell the truth—which he won't—and if it were worth my while and compatible with my self-respect, I've no doubt I'd hate him."

This sentiment was delivered with the blasé air of weariness worn out, that should belong with him who has seen and heard and known a world's multitude; which manner is everywhere recognized as the very flower of good breeding.

Mrs. Hanway-Harley sat tongue-tied with astonishment. In the end she recalled herself. Mrs. Hanway-Harley scented nothing perilous in the situation. In any event, Dorothy would wed whomsoever she decreed; Mrs. Hanway-Harley was deservedly certain of that. While this came to her mind, Richard the enterprising went laying plans for the daily desolation of an entire greenhouse.

"Dorothy," observed Mrs. Hanway-Harley, after Richard had gone his way, "there you have a young man remarkable for two things: his dullness and his effrontery. Did you hear how he spoke of his benefactor? The wretch! After all that good, poor Mr. Gwynn has done for him!"

"How do you know what Mr. Gwynn has done for him?"

Dorothy, while she confessed the justice of her mother's strictures, felt uncommonly inclined to defend the absent one. Her memory of those tender glances was coming back.

"Why, it is all over town! Mr. Storms is dependent on Mr. Gwynn. By the way, I hope Count Storri did not meet him?" This was given in the rising inflection of a query.

"Only for a moment," returned Dorothy, breaking into a little crow of laughter. "The Count did not seem to like him." Dorothy thought of that combat of the hands, and how Storri was beaten to his knee, and how fiercely glorious Richard looked at that instant.

"What should you expect?" observed Mrs. Hanway-Harley. "The Count is a nobleman. And that reminds me: Dorothy, he appears a bit smitten. What if it were to prove serious?"

"You wouldn't have me marry him, mamma?"

"What! Not marry a Count!" Mrs. Hanway-Harley was shocked as only an American mother could have been shocked. She appealed to the ceiling with her horrified hands. "Oh! the callousness of children!" she cried. Following this outburst of despair, Mrs. Hanway-Harley composed herself. "We need not consider that now; it will be soon enough when the Count offers us his hand." Mrs. Hanway-Harley sank back in her chair with closed eyes and saw a vision of herself at the Court of the Czar. Then she continued her thoughts aloud. "It's more than likely, my dear, that the Czar would appoint Count Storri Ambassador to Washington."

"It would be extremely intelligent of the Czar, I'm sure," returned Dorothy with a twinkle.

The next morning a colored youth clad in the garish livery of an Avenue florist made his appearance on the Harley premises bearing aloft an armful of flowers as large as a sheaf of wheat. By the card they were for "Miss Harley." The morning following, and every morning, came the colored youth bearing an odorous armful. Who were they from? The card told nothing; it was the handwriting of the florist.

"Don't you think it might be Count Storri?" said Dorothy demurely, taking her pretty nose—the nose Richard saved—out of the flowers. "Those Russians are so extravagant, so eccentric!"

"Suppose I thank him for them," observed Mrs. Hanway-Harley; "that would bring him out!"

"No, no," exclaimed Dorothy hastily; "it might embarrass the Count."

"Pshaw! I'll ask the florist."

"No; that would offend the Count. You see, mamma, he thinks that we will know without asking. He would hardly regard our ignorance as a compliment," and Dorothy pouted. "You'd spoil everything."

Mrs. Hanway-Harley saw the force of this and yielded, though it cost her curiosity a pang.

Dorothy's dearest friend was with them—a tall, undulating blonde, who was sometimes like a willow and sometimes like a cat. When Mrs. Hanway-Harley had left the room, and Miss Marklin and Dorothy were alone, the former said firmly:

"Dorothy, who sent them?"

"Now, how should I know, Bess? You read the card."

"When a woman receives flowers, she always knows from whom," returned this wise virgin oracularly.

"Well, then," said Dorothy resignedly, drawing the golden head of the pythoness down until the small, pink ear was level with her lips, "if you must know, let me whisper."

There are people who hold that everybody they do not understand is a fool. There be others who hold that everybody who doesn't understand them is a fool. Mrs. Hanway-Harley belonged to the former class, and not making Richard out, she marked him "fool," and so informed Mr. Harley as she penned the dinner invitation to Mr. Gwynn.

"Of course, we shall not ask this Mr. Storms to the dinner. He would be misplaced by his years for one thing. Besides, I'm sure Mr. Gwynn wouldn't like it. I saw enough of Mr. Storms to doubt if, in their own house, he dines at the same table with Mr. Gwynn."

"At any rate," remarked the cautious Mr. Harley, "it's safe to leave him out this time. We'll establish his proper level, socially, by talking with Mr. Gwynn."

Mr. Gwynn came back from New York on Thursday afternoon. His traffic with Talon & Trehawke was successful, and he had bought the *Daily Tory*.

Richard was put in charge of the Washington correspondence. He was given a brace of assistants to protect, as he said, the subscribers; for be it known that Richard of the many blemishes knew no more of newspaper work than he did of navigation.

Mr. Gwynn found Mrs. Hanway-Harley's dinner invitation awaiting him; it was for the next evening. He brought it to Richard.

"You will go, Mr. Gwynn," said that gentleman. "I will consider; and tomorrow I will tell you what you are to say."

Richard has been referred to as a soul of many blemishes. The chief of these was his cynicism, although that cynicism had a cause if not a reason. With other traits, the same either virtues or vices according to the occasion and the way they were turned, Richard was sensitive. He was as thin-skinned as a woman and as greedy of approval. And yet his sensitiveness, with nerves all on the surface, worked to its own defeat. It rendered Richard fearful of jar and jolt; with that he turned brusque, repelled folk, and shrunk away from having them too near.

For a crowning disaster, throughout his years of manhood, Richard had had nothing to do. He had been idle with no work and no object to work for. You can suffer from brain famine and from hand famine. You may starve your brain and your hand with idleness as readily as you starve your stomach with no food. And Richard's nature, without his knowing, had pined for lack of work.

There had been other setbacks. Richard lost his mother before he could remember, and his father when he was twelve. He was an only child, and his father, as well as his mother, had been an only child. Richard stood as utterly without a family as did the first man. He grew up with schoolmasters and tutors, looked after by guardians who, infected of a fashion, held that the best place to rear an American was Europe. These maniacs kept Richard abroad for fairly the fifteen years next before he meets you in these pages. The guardians were honest men; they watched the dollars of their ward with all the jealous eyes of Argus. His mind they left to chance-blown influences, all alien; and to teachers, equally alien, and as equally the selection of chance. And so it came that Richard grew up and continued without an attachment or a friendship or a purpose; and with a distrust of men in the gross promoted to feather-edge. Altogether he should be called as loveless, not to say as, unlovable, a character as any you might encounter, and search throughout a summer's day.

Most of all, Richard had been spoiled by an admiration for Democritus, which Thracian's acquaintance he picked up at school. He saw, or thought he saw, much in the ease of the Abderite to remind him of his own; and to imitate him he traveled, professed a chuckling indifference to both the good and the ill in life, and, heedful to laugh at whatever turned up, humored himself with the notion that he was a philosopher. Democritus was Richard's affectation: being only an affectation Democritus did not carry him to the extreme of putting out his own eyes as a help to thought.

Richard, to reach his thirtieth year, had traveled far by many a twisting road. And for all the good his wanderings overtook, he would have come as well off standing still. But a change was risping at the door. In Dorothy Richard had found one to love. Now in his sudden rôle of working journalist, he had found work to do. Richard caught his bosom swelling with sensations never before known, as he loafed over a cigar in his rooms. Love and ambition both were busy at his heart's roots. He would win Dorothy; he would become a writer.

Richard, his cynicism touching the elbow of his dream, caught himself sourly smiling. He shook himself free, however, and was surprised to see how that ice of cynicism gave way before a little heat of hope. It was as if his nature were coming out of winter into spring; whereat Richard was cheered.

"Who knows?" quoth Richard, staring about the room in defiance of what cynic imps were present. "I may yet become a husband and an author before a twelvemonth."

Richard later took counsel with the gray Nestor of the press gallery—a past master at his craft of ink.

"Write new things in an old way," said this finished one whose name was known in two hemispheres; "write new things in an old way or old things in a new way or new things in a new way. Do not write old things in an old way; it will be as though you strove to build a fire with ashes."

"And is that all?" asked Richard.

"It is the whole of letters," said the finished one. With that Richard, nursing a stout heart, began his grind.

Every writer, not a mere bricklayer of words, has what for want of better epithet is called a style. There be writers whose style is broad and deep and lucid like a lake. It shimmers bravely as some ray of fancy touches it, or it tosses in billows with some stormy stress of feeling. And yet, you who read must spread some personal sail and bring some gale of favoring interest all your own, to carry you across. There be writers whose style is swift and flashing like a river, and has a current to whirl you along. The style seizes on you and takes you down the page, showing the right and the left of the subject as a river shows its banks. You are swept round some unexpected bend of incident, and given new impressions in new lights. Addison was the king of those who wrote like a lake; Macaulay of those who wrote like a river. The latter is the better style, giving more and carrying further and tiring less.

Richard belonged by native gift to the Macaulay school. He tasted the incense of his occupation when, having sent his first story, the night manager wired:

"Great! Keep it up."

Richard read and re-read the four words, and it must be confessed felt somewhat ashamed at the good they did him—being the first words of encomium that had ever come his way. They confirmed his ambition; he had found a pleasant, unexpected window from which to reconsider existence.

It was seven o'clock and Richard sat turning over a pile of papers which related to the purchase of the *Daily Tory*; they had been left by Mr. Gwynn. These he compared with a letter or two that had just come in.

"What a fool and old rogue it is!" cried Richard disgustedly. Then he pushed the button that summoned Mr. Gwynn.

That severe Briton appeared in flawless evening dress. It was the occasion of the Harley dinner, and Mr. Gwynn had ordered his carriage for half after seven.

"Mr. Gwynn," said Richard, "the Harley purpose is the Presidential hopes of Senator Hanway. You will offer aid in all of Senator Hanway's plans. Particularly, you are to let him know that the *Daily Tory* is at his service. Say that I, as its correspondent, shall make it my first duty to wait upon him."

"Very good, sir," said Mr. Gwynn.

"Another moment, Mr. Gwynn," said Richard, as the other was about to go. "Give me your personal check for eleven thousand six hundred and forty dollars."

Mr. Gywnn's face twitched; he hesitated, rocking a little on his feet. Richard had turned to scribble something; with that, repressing whatever had been upon his lips, Mr. Gwynn withdrew. He was instantly back with a strip of paper fluttering in his fingers. Richard placed it in his desk. Taking a similar strip from his writing pad he gave it to Mr. Gwynn.

"My own check for eleven thousand six hundred and forty dollars, Mr. Gwynn," said Richard. "I make you a present of it. That is to save your credit. Hereafter, when you see a chance to play the scoundrel, before you embrace it, please measure the probable pillage and let me know. I will then give you the amount. In that way you will have the profits of every act of villainy you might commit, while missing the mud and mire of its accomplishment. Remember, Mr. Gwynn; I will not tolerate a rascal."

"You are extremely good, sir," said the frozen Mr. Gwynn.

Mrs. Hanway-Harley placed Mr. Gwynn on her right hand, a distinction which that personage bore with a petrified grace most beautiful to look upon. Senator Hanway was on the other side of Mr. Gwynn. The party was not large—eight in all—and, besides the trio named and Mr. Harley, counted such partisans of Senator Hanway as Senators Gruff and Kink and Wink and Loot and Price. Mr. Gwynn was delighted to meet so much good company, and intimated it in a manner decorously conventional.

"Isn't he utterly English, and therefore utterly admirable?" whispered Mrs. Hanway-Harley to Senator Loot.

That statesman agreed to this as well as he could with a mouth at work on fish.

"Mr. Gwynn," said Mrs. Hanway-Harley affably, "I shall make the most of you while I may. You know I only intend to see you gentlemen safely launched, and then I shall retire."

Mr. Gwynn bowed gravely. Mr. Gwynn's strength lay in bowing. He was also remarkable for the unflagging attention which he paid to whatever was said to him. On such occasions his unblinking stare, wholly receptive like an underling taking orders, and never a glimmer of either contradiction or agreement or even intelligence to show therein, was almost disconcerting. Mrs. Hanway-Harley, however, declared that this receptive, inane stare was the hall-mark of exclusive English circles. Mr. Gwynn gave another proof of culture; he pitched upon the best wine and stuck to it, tasting and relishing with educated palate. This set him up with Mr. Harley.

"Yes, I shall make the most of you, Mr. Gwynn," said Mrs. Hanway-Harley.

By way of making the most of Mr. Gwynn, Mrs. Hanway-Harley spoke of meeting Mr. Storms. In her opinion that young man did not appreciate the goodness of Mr. Gwynn, and was far from grateful for those benefits which the latter showered upon him. At this intelligence, Mr. Gywnn was taken so aback that Mrs. Hanway-Harley stopped abruptly and shifted the conversation. Mrs. Hanway-Harley was one of those who have half-tact; they know enough to back out and not enough to keep out of a blunder.

The dinner was neither long nor formal. Mrs. Hanway-Harley at last removed the restraint of her presence, and thereupon Mr. Harley drank twice as much wine to help him bear her absence. Mr. Gwynn's health was proposed by Mr. Harley, and Mr. Gwynn bowed his thanks. It should be understood that Mr. Gwynn bowed like a Mandarin from beginning to end of the feast. There were no speeches; no man can make a speech to an audience of six. Cicero himself would have been dumb under such meager conditions.

When Mr. Harley drank Mr. Gwynn's health for the tenth time, and attempted, assisted by Senators Gruff and Price, to sing a song in his honor, Senator Hanway adroitly brought the dinner to a close. He was the more stirred to this as the plaster of Paris countenance of Mr. Gwynn, when Mr. Harley began to sing, betrayed manifest alarm.

After dinner Senator Hanway got Mr. Gwynn into a corner. Thereupon, in a manner creditable to himself, Mr. Gwynn gave Senator Hanway to know that he was his friend. The *Daily Tory* should be his; Richard should be his; Mr. Gwynn and all he called his own should be his; Senator Hanway was to make whatever use of Richard and the *Daily Tory* and Mr. Gwynn his experience and his interests might suggest. Indeed, Mr. Gwynn talked very well in private and in whispers; and Senator Hanway said later to Senator Kink that he was the deepest man he had ever met.

"And," said Senator Hanway, squeezing Mr. Gwynn's hand as that gentleman made ready for home, "tell your young man that I shall be glad to see him. There are certain contingencies touching the next Speakership of the House which should interest his paper. I shall see you to-morrow, Mr. Gwynn—with your permission. You can and should play a most important part in selecting that same Speaker. Your measureless interests in the great Anaconda Airline warrant me in the assertion."

CHAPTER IV

HOW A SPEAKERSHIP WAS FOUGHT FOR

Fate now and then turns jester in a bitter way, and stoops to ironies and grinning sarcasm. Often it gives with the right hand only to take with the left, and blinded ones are set to chop and saw and plane those trees which in the end make gallows for their hopes. The story of the world shows many an inadvertent Frankenstein and deeply justifies the grewsome Mrs. Shelley.

Something less than two years prior to that evening when Senator Hanway took the congealed Mr. Gwynn into a corner and told him how, with his great Anaconda Airline, he should cut a figure in the selection of a next Speaker for the House of Representatives, it had been that statesman's fortune to so reconstruct a tariff that it gave unusual riches and thereby unusual comfort to the dominant ones of a certain manufacturing Northeastern State. This commonwealth at the time was politically in the hands of the party opposed to Senator Hanway. Mollified by the friendly tariff and anxious to mark their gratitude, those dominant ones arose and in the following autumn elected to be Governor of said State a middle-aged individual, eminent for obstinacy and a kind of bovine integrity that nothing might corrupt or turn aside. The Obstinate One of course belonged with the party of Senator Hanway.

At this pinch a vile chance befell. No sooner was the Obstinate One given the Governorship of a State doubtful and accounted the enemy's country, than straightway he was looked upon as White House timber by sundry architects of politics, and thereafter his name went more or less linked with a possible Presidency. The situation stirred the spleen of Senator Hanway. It was discouraging to have those identical tariff triumphs, which had been intended as an argument favorable to himself, give birth to a rival; one also who, for his geography and the popularity which those personal obstinacies and thick-skulled integrities invoked, might work a grave disturbance in his plans. To make bad worse, the Obstinate One possessed a sinister luck of his own and with closed eyes backed into a fight on the right side and won it against a pack of lobby wolves who were yelping and snapping about the State Treasury. This, although the Obstinate One of all men least appreciated what he had done, confirmed him as a valuable asset of party; pending further honors the public to reward him gave him the title of Governor Obstinate.

In his white, still, rippleless way, Senator Hanway hated in his soul's soul the name of Governor Obstinate. Night and day he carried that dull, fortunate gentleman on his swell of thought and never ceased to consider how he might deal him a blow or withstand him in any Presidential stepping forward. And yet at no time had Senator Hanway—and himself the master of every art of cord and creese in politics—felt more helpless. If Governor Obstinate had been no more than just a finished politician, a mere Crillon of political fence, Senator Hanway might have flashed his ready point between his ribs. But the other's very crudities defended him. He was primitive to the verge of despair. Even his strength was primitive, inasmuch as it dwelt among the people rather than with the machinists of party. Senator Hanway's monkish brow went often puckered of a most uncanonical frown as he thought upon that sardonic Destiny which had thrust this Governor Obstinate forward to become a stumbling block in his way. In his angry contempt he could compare him to nothing save a grizzly bear.

Whatever the justice of this last shaggy simile, even Senator Hanway could not deny its formidable side. A grizzly, whether in fact or in hyperbole, is no one good to meet. There is a supremacy of the primitive; when the natural and the artificial have collided the latter has more than once come limping off. Our soldiers cannot make the Indians fight their fashion; the Indians make the soldiers fight *their* fashion. If the soldiers were dense enough to insist upon their formation, the Indians—fighting all over the field and each red warrior for himself—would fill them as full of holes as a colander. When, therefore, Senator Hanway called Governor Obstinate a grizzly, it was a name of respect. The usual methods would not prevail in his stubborn case. Most of all, money could not be employed to overthrow him; for his foundations, like the foundations of any other grizzly, were original and beyond the touch of money.

Now all this served to palsy the strength of Senator Hanway. In one shape or another, and whether by promise or actual present production, money was his one great tool; and where the tool has lost its power the artisan is also powerless. It is not to Senator Hanway's discredit that he would fail where money failed; Richelieu, wanting money, would have been a turtle on its back. Wherefore, let it be rewritten that Senator Hanway in the face of those clumsy, uncouth, half-seeing yet tremendous potentialities of his enemy was seized of a helplessness never before felt. To oppose the other with only those narrow means of money was like trying to put down a Sioux uprising with a resolution of the Board of Trade. Still, he must do his best; he must hold this Governor Obstinate as much as he might in check, trusting to the chapter of accidents, which in politics is a very lair of surprises, to suggest final ways and means to baffle his advance.

For the business of making him President, the complaisant Senate had become the workshop of Senator Hanway. Now, on the brink of a new Congress, one which would be in session when the nominating convention of his party was called to order and therefore might be supposed to own power over its action and the Presidential ticket it would put up, Senator Hanway resolved to add the House of Representatives to his machine. He would elect its Speaker, and make the House an annex to his workshop of a Senate. He would hook up House and Senate as a coachman hooks up his team, and driving them tandem or abreast as the exigencies of the hour suggested, see how far two such powerful agencies might take him on his White House road.

It was on the side of Senator Hanway a brilliant thought and a daring one, this plan to seize a Speakership and apply it to his personal fortunes; for your Speakership is that office second only to a Presidency, and comes often to be the latter's superior in practical force. Those wise ones who designed the government intended the House of Representatives to be a republic. Through its own groveling abjections, however, it long ago sunk to an autocracy with the Speaker in the rôle of autocrat. It sold its birthright for no one knows what mess of pottage to pass its slavish days beneath a tyranny of the gavel. The Speaker settles all things. No measure is proposed, no bill passes, no member speaks except by the Speaker's will. He constructs the committees and selects their chairmen and lays out their work. With a dozen members, every one of whom votes and acts beneath his thumb, the Speaker transacts the story of the House. So far as the other three hundred and forty odd members are concerned, the folk who sent them might as well have written a letter. They live as much without art or part or lot in planning and executing House affairs as do the caged menagerie animals in the planning and execution of the affairs of what show they happen to exist as the attractions. These caged ones of the House are never regarded and but seldom heard. The best that one of them may gain is "Leave to print"; which is a kind of consent to be fraudulent, and permits a member to pretend through the Congressional Record that he made a speech (which he never made) and was overwhelmed by applause (which he did not receive) which swept down in thunderous peals (during moments utterly silent) from crowded galleries (as empty as a church).

Senator Hanway, when he decided to pick out a House Speaker favorable to his hopes, had plenty of time wherein to lay his plans. The personnel of a coming House is known for over a year; the members are elected nearly thirteen months before they take their seats. These thirteen months of grace are granted the new member by the Constitution on a hopeful theory that he will devote them to a study of his country's needs. In this instance, as in many another, theory and practice wander wide apart; the new member gives those thirteen months to a profound study of his own needs, and concerns himself no more over the nation's than over wine-pressing in far-away Bordeaux. It is the glaring fault of every scheme of government, your own being no exception to the rule, that it seems meant for man as he should be rather than for man as he is.

Every member of the coming House, among matters of personal moment to himself, had given no little thought to what committees he would be placed upon; and this, in the nature of House things, likewise compelled him to a consideration of the Speakership and who should fill it. It was by remembering those committee hopes and fears of members, and adroitly fomenting them, that Senator Hanway expected to control the Speakership election.

But he must go warily to work. Coming from the Senate end of the Capitol, Senator Hanway, in his proposed interference in the organization of the House, must maintain himself discreetly in the dark. It was not a task to accomplish blowing a bugle. The House had surrendered its powers to the Speaker; but it had retained its vanity, and like all weak animals it was the more vain for being weak. The members, were it once known and parcel of the common gossip how they inclined to Senator Hanway's manipulation, would be compelled to rebel. They would be driven to oppose him as a method of preserving what they called their self-respect. Aware of this, Senator Hanway never came into the open, never appeared upon the surface. He secretly pitched upon a candidate among the older ones of the House and made his deal with him, working the wires of his diplomacy from below.

There was peculiar demand for effort on Senator Hanway's part. His man, when now he had selected him, would not find himself uninterrupted or unopposed in his march for that Speakership. There was another, and if native popularity were to count a stronger hand stretched forth to seize the gavel prize. Had it lain in the cards, Senator Hanway, who always sought his ends on lines of least resistance, would himself have pitched upon this stronger one. But such was beyond the question. The strong one claimed to be of that party clan which pushed the offensive Governor Obstinate for the Presidency; and this not only offered a perfect reason why Senator Hanway should make no alliance with him, but it multiplied the necessity for his defeat.

That member upon whom Senator Hanway settled for Speaker owned the biting name of Frost; it was an instance, however, when there was nothing in a name. Mr. Frost was a round, genial personage and only biting with occasional sarcasms; then, it is true, his sentences cut like a rawhide. He was big, breezy, careless, quick, and coming of an aquatic ancestry, oceanic in his sort; even his walk reminded one of a ground swell. And yet he was defective as a candidate. The House members liked him well, despite those verbal acridities which shaved the surface of debate as lawns are shaven by a scythe; but with the last word there existed no recognized House or party reason, whether of the past, the present or the future, why he should be made Speaker. In the lay of House topography he was on the wrong side of the river from the Speakership, and to land him within stretch of the gavel required that Senator Hanway either ferry or pontoon him across. This the latter gentleman set himself to accomplish by a series of intrigues and stratagems that would have brightened the fame of a Talleyrand.

The statesman opposed to Mr. Frost for the Speakership was a personage named Hawke. He stood possessed of honesty, intelligence, and energy; also he had been for long the leader of his party in the House, and given his name to a tariff measure. Without one gleam of humor, he was of a temper hot as that of any Hecla, and like his fellow volcano, being often in a state of eruption, he offered many reasons for being admired and none for being loved.

This should be a key to the man.

He had been a brave soldier during the Civil War, and when his men, most of whom were armed with shotguns—it being in the early hours of that strife and these men arming themselves—complained that their weapons were no match for the Enfields of the foe, rebuked them fiercely.

"General," said the spokesman of the soldiers; "these yere shotguns ain't no even break for them rifles the Yanks are shootin'!"

"They are a match for them," retorted the furious Mr. Hawke, "if you will only go close enough."

For all his soberness of humor and choleric upheavals, Mr. Hawke, because of his record as a House leader and a tariff maker—he had tinkered together that identical bill which, when Senator Hanway later revamped it in the Senate, produced the Obstinate One as a Governor—was the legitimate heir to the Speakership; and in the House, where tradition is something sacred and custom itself the strongest of arguments, his defeat for the place was thereby rendered well-nigh impossible. Senator Hanway had undertaken no child's task when he went about the gavel elevation of the popular, yet—by House usage—the illegitimate Mr. Frost.

Months before ever Senator Hanway was granted the honor of knowing Mr. Gwynn, he had been burrowingly busy about the Speakership. As a primary step he was obliged to suppress his ebullient brother-in-law. Mr. Harley, the moment a conquest of the House in the interests of Senator

Hanway was proposed, waxed threateningly exuberant. He was for issuing forth to vociferate and slap members upon their backs and jovially arrange committeeships on the giffgaff principle of give us the Speakership and you shall become a Chairman. The optimistic Mr. Harley, whose methods were somewhat coarse and who did most things with an ax, was precisely of that hopeful sort who would advertise an auction of the lion's hide while it was yet upon the beast. Senator Hanway, with instincts safer and more upon the order of the mole's, forbade such campaigns of noise.

"You must keep silent, John," said he, "and never let men know what we are about. You are inclined, apparently, to regard a Speakership as you might a swarm of bees; you think one has only to beat a tin pan long enough or blow a tin horn loud enough in order to hive it according to one's wish. The Speakership, however, so far from being a swarm of bees is more like a flock of blackbirds, and the system to which you incline would prove the readiest means of frightening away our every chance. In short, you must work by my orders and meet no one, say nothing, except as I direct."

Then Senator Hanway sent Mr. Harley, much modified of his vigor, with a secret invitation to Mr. Frost; when that personage was brought to the privacy of the Harley house, he laid open to his ambition those gavel prospects which he, Senator Hanway, had already constructed in his thoughts.

There was no conflict of argument with Mr. Frost; he rose to the suggestion like a bass to a fly. Knowing himself to be of a genius too openly bluff and frank, and no one to conquer those elements which his campaign would require, he put himself in the hollow of Senator Hanway's hand to be controlled by him with shut eyes. This voluntary prompt submission on the part of Mr. Frost had a further subduing effect upon Mr. Harley. In imitation thereof he, too, began to speak in whispers and step with care, and ask his eminent relative for orders in all he went about.

Now when Senator Hanway had trained his partner and his candidate to come to heel he began to unravel his diplomacy. By his suggestion, Mr. Frost took into confidence two of his party colleagues in the House. These would on every occasion act as his agents or lieutenants. Senator Hanway and Mr. Harley were not to appear too obviously.

Senator Hanway, lying back in the dark, looked over the field and sent those two lieutenants variously to a score of members. These were sounded on the engaging topic of committee chairmanships, and one by one such coigns of congressional, not to say personal, advantage as the heads of Ways and Means, the Appropriations, the Foreign Affairs, the Naval, the Military and a number of other great sub-bodies were disposed of—

bartered away on the contingency always of Mr. Frost's selection to be the Speaker. The entire House was laid off into lots like real estate and sold, the purchaser promising his vote and influence in the party caucus, taking therefor a verbal contract to give him the committee place he preferred.

This labor of an advance partition of the spoils and the linking of every possible faction with the campaign of Mr. Frost, was concluded about a fortnight prior to Mrs. Harley's dinner to Mr. Gwynn. As Senator Hanway ran his experienced eye over the list and counted the noses of Mr. Frost's array, he saw that it was not enough. The pontoon would not reach; there was still a wide expanse of water between his candidate and the coveted Speakership. As matters rested, and every morsel of House patronage disposed of to this hungry one or that, the enemy, Mr. Hawke—being doubly the enemy for that he was become an open supporter of Governor Obstinate and made no secret that his candidacy for the Speakership was meant to be a step towards making that gentleman President—would still rise victorious in caucus by full forty votes.

Senator Hanway's anxious wits were driven hard. He had drawn to Mr. Frost every splinter of power he could command by barter, and thrown in his own State delegation in the House by sheer stress of that machine which he had upreared for his own defense at home. It was not enough; even the subtraction of two State delegations from the standards of the foe, by the adroit scheme, applied to each delegation, of dragging one of its members forward to be a candidate for Speaker, was not enough. After ten months of labor, Senator Hanway went over the result and could read nothing therein save failure. And it was like an icicle through his heart; for aside from what advantage the control of the House might give his own ambitions, he knew beyond question that with the gavel in the fingers of a professed partisan of Governor Obstinate, the latter thick, yet fortunate, individual would occur as the next Presidential candidate of his party so surely as the sun came up on a convention morning.

Senator Hanway was in this valley of gloom when he heard of Mr. Gwynn. It was Mr. Harley, ever brisk in railway matters, who told him of that gentleman as the Colossus of the Anaconda Airline.

"He holds no offices in the management of the company," explained Mr. Harley, "but, being millions upon millions a majority shareholder his least word is Anaconda Airline law."

Senator Hanway did not have to be told of the influence of railways in the destinies of his country. He glanced up at a map on the wall; there he could see the nation caught like some great clumsy fish in a very seine of railways. He traced the black, thread-like flight, from seaboard to seaboard, of the Anaconda Airline. Then he made a calculation. The Anaconda Airline was the political backbone, first one State and then another, of forty House members, twenty-three of whom being of his own complexion of politics, would have a caucus vote. Of the twenty-three, luck upon good luck! twenty belonged to Mr. Hawke. If Senator Hanway might only get the Anaconda Airline to crack the thong of its authority over these recalcitrants, they could be whipped into the Frost traces. Not one would dare defy an Anaconda order; it would be political hari-kari. At this point our wily Senator Hanway began laying plans to bring Mr. Gwynn within his reach; it was in deference to those plans that our solemn capitalist found himself upon Mrs. Hanway-Harley's hospitable right hand on that evening of the dinner, with his severe legs outstretched beneath the Harley mahogany.

"I will see you to-morrow—with your permission," observed Senator Hanway, as he parted with Mr. Gwynn.

When Mr. Gwynn returned from Mrs. Hanway-Harley's he stood in the middle of the floor, and told Richard, word for word, all that had taken place. The latter young gentleman was in a prodigious good humor. For the first time in his life he had done a day's work, being the twenty-five hundred word story written and dispatched to the *Daily Tory*, and that was one reason for joy. Besides, there was the manager's wire of praise—and Richard thought it marked a weakness in him—that, too, had warmed the cockles of his heart. Being in good humor, he listened without interrupting comment to the rasping, parrot tones of Mr. Gwynn while that gentleman, without inflection or emphasis or slightest shade of personal interest, told the tale of the night's adventures, from Mrs. Hanway-Harley's flattery and Mr. Harley's song, to Senator Hanway's last handclasp and that parting promise of a call.

"And that is all, sir," said Mr. Gwynn, at the close, coughing apologetically behind his palm as though fearful of criticism.

"You did well," was Richard's response. "When Senator Hanway calls to-morrow, introduce me to him at once. After that, I shall talk and you will acquiesce. You may go."

"Thank you, sir. Very good, sir!" said Mr. Gwynn.

Mr. Gwynn received Senator Hanway in his library; Richard was present, considering the world at large from a window.

"And first of all," said Mr. Gwynn, after greeting Senator Hanway, "and first of all, let me introduce to your notice Mr. Storms. I may say to you, sir, I have confidence in Mr. Storms; I act much by his advice." And here Mr. Gwynn looked at Richard as though appealing for corroboration.

Senator Hanway, from whose nimble faculties nothing escaped, noted this appeal. He thought the less of it, since Mr. Harley had given him some glint of the measureless millions of Mr. Gwynn, and he deduced from this stiff turning towards Richard, this brittle deference, nothing save a theory that Mr. Gwynn, by virtue of his tremendous riches, had grown too great to do his own listening and thinking. It was as plain, as it was proper, that he should hire them done, precisely as he hired a groom for his horses or a valet to superintend his clothes. Senator Hanway, himself, was at bottom impressed by nothing so much as money, and was quite prepared to believe that one of the world's wealthiest men—for such he understood to be the case of Mr. Gwynn—would prove in word and deed and thought a being wholly different from everyone about him. Wherefore, his heaped millions accounted in Mr. Gwynn for what otherwise might have been considered by Senator Hanway as queernesses.

To add to this, Mr. Gwynn was of a certain select circle of English exclusives; Senator Hanway had learned that much from his sister, Mrs. Hanway-Harley. It was to be expected then that he would have someone about him to furnish brains for his deliberations, and to make up his mind as a laundress makes up shirts. Senator Hanway, knowing these things of Mr. Gwynn, was in no wise surprised that he possessed in his service one who was hearer, talker, and decider, just as ancient kings kept folk about whose business was to make witty retorts for them and conduct sparkling conversations in their stead, they themselves being too royal for anything so much beneath that level of exalted inanity, which as all men know is the only proper mark of princely minds. Something of this raced hit or miss through Senator Hanway's thoughts, as Mr. Gwynn presented Richard and then relapsed—hinge by hinge as though his joints were rusty with much aristocratic unbending—into a chair.

Richard gave him no space to dwell upon the phenomenon. He came forward with a little atmosphere of deference; for Richard had his own deep designs. Then, too, Senator Hanway was white of hair and twice his age, to say nothing of being a certain young lady's uncle.

"Mr. Gwynn has told me of you," said he. Then pushing straight for the point after methods of his own, he continued: "What is it the Anaconda Airline can do? Mr. Gwynn is quite convinced, from what he has been told of those positions you have from time to time assumed in the Senate, that his own interest with that of every railway owner lies in following your leadership. Indeed, I think he has decided to adopt whatever suggestion you may make." Richard glanced towards Mr. Gwynn, and that great man gave his mandarin bow.

Senator Hanway, while smitten of vague amazement at Mr. Gwynn's acquiescent spirit, accepted it without pause. However marvelous it might be, at least he himself ran no risk. More than that, on second thought it did not occur to him as so peculiarly unusual; a Senator in a measure becomes inured to the wondrous.

Senator Hanway did not reply directly to Richard's query. Direct replies were not the habit of this practiced one. He made a speech full of flattering generalities. He spoke of Richard's connection with the *Daily Tory*, and expanded upon the weight and influence of that journal. Also, with a beaming albeit delicate patronage which Richard stomached for reasons of his own, he intimated complimentary things of Richard himself and seemed to congratulate the *Daily Tory* on the services of one so keen, so sure, so graphic; which last was the more kind, since Senator Hanway could have known no single reason for assuming anything of the sort. He told Richard that he hoped to see him personally every day. Here Richard broke in on the Senatorial flow to ask if he might wait upon Senator Hanway every morning at eleven.

"For I am warned by Mr. Gwynn," explained Richard, with an alert mendacity which would have done honor, to Senator Hanway himself, "that he will hold anything short of calling upon you once a day as barefaced neglect of his interests."

"Certainly, sir; most barefaced!" creaked Mr. Gwynn, giving the mandarin bow.

Senator Hanway would be graciously pleased to see Richard every morning at eleven. Also, he would aid him, as far as was proper, with a recount of what gusts and windy currents of news were moving in the upper ethers of government.

Then, having been polite, Senator Hanway got down to business and stated that Mr. Frost, if Speaker, would favor a certain pooling bill, much desired by railways, and particularly dear to the Anaconda Airline. On the obdurate other hand, Mr. Hawke was an enemy to pooling bills and railways. Mr. Gwynn's interest was plainly with Mr. Frost.

"Not that I care personally for the success of Mr. Frost," remarked Senator Hanway, "but I know how the railways desire that pooling bill, and how that pooling bill is a darling measure with Mr. Frost."

"Which brings us back," observed Richard, who never took his eye off a question, once put, until he saw it mated with an answer, "to Mr. Gwynn's first interrogatory: What can the Anaconda Airline do?"

Senator Hanway explained. The Anaconda Airline could press down the weights of its influence upon those twenty-three members. The Anaconda influence might better be exerted through its President and General Attorney, and perhaps what special attorneys were local to the congressional districts of those twenty-three.

"Mr. Gwynn," observed Richard, "anticipated something of the kind, and I think is prepared to request those officers you name to come to Washington."

"They shall be requested, sir; certainly, sir," rasped Mr. Gwynn. Richard's words seemed ever to reverberate in Mr. Gwynn's noble interior as in a cavern, and thereafter to issue forth by way of his mouth in the manner of an echo. "Certainly, sir; they shall be requested," repeated the cavernous Mr. Gwynn.

"Now this is highly gratifying," said Senator Hanway. "And you will have them call upon me, too, I've no doubt. You should wire them at once; the caucus, you know, isn't ten days away; Congress convenes on the first Monday of next month."

Senator Hanway, being of a quick intelligence, had by this time found his rightful line. He divided himself fairly; for he gave his entire conversation to Richard while he conferred upon Mr. Gwynn his whole respect. In good truth, the less Mr. Gwynn said and the less he seemed to hear and understand, the more Senator Hanway did him honor in his heart. The rigid witlessness of Mr. Gwynn fairly came over him as the token and sign of an indubitable nobility, and it was with a feeling treading upon reverence for that wonderful man that Senator Hanway arose to go.

"I am much refreshed by this interview," said he, taking Mr. Gwynn's hand and shaking it pump-handlewise. "Your help should insure Mr. Frost's success. With Mr. Frost Speaker, railway interests will be safe-guarded. And," continued Senator Hanway, quoting from one of his Senate speeches, lifting his voice the while, and falling into a fine declamatory pose, "he who safeguards the railroads, safeguards his country. Patriotism cannot count the debt the nation owes the railroads. Had it not been for the knitting together of the country by the railroads, bringing into closer touch with one another the West and the East, the South and the North—the wiping out of sectionalism—the annihilation of special interests by making all interests general—all done by the railroads, sir!—this country, broken across the knee of mountain ranges and sawed into regions by great rivers, would ere this have been frittered into fragments; and where we have now the glorious United States—a free and unified people—Europe, who envies as well as fears us, would be gratified by the spectacle of four and perhaps a half dozen different and differing countries, each alien and, doubtless, each hostile to the others." Senator Hanway had reached the door. "And that this condition of disseverment does not exist," cried he, as he bowed with final grace to Mr. Gwynn, who approved stonily, "is due to you, sir; and to gentlemen like you; and to those railways which, like the Anaconda Airline, form the ties that bind us safe against such dismembering possibilities and give us, for war or for peace, absolute coherency as a commonwealth."

CHAPTER V

HOW RICHARD WAS TAUGHT MANY THINGS

Richard went every day at eleven for a brief conference with Senator Hanway. The latter was no wise backward in his use of the columns of the *Daily Tory*. There are so many things concerning both men and measures that statesmen want said, and which, because of their modesty, they themselves hesitate to say, that Senator Hanway, when now through Richard he might tell this story of politics or declare that proposal of state, and still keep his own name under cover, discovered in the *Daily Tory* a source of relief. So much, in truth, did Senator Hanway, by way of Richard and the *Daily Tory*, contribute to the gayety of the times, that the editor-in-chief was duly scandalized. He aroused himself on the third evening, killed Richard's dispatch, and rebuked that earnest journalist with the following:

"Send news; nothing but news. No one wants your notion of the motives of representatives in fight over Speakership."

This led to a word or two between Richard and Mr. Gwynn, the upcome being a wire from Mr. Gwynn to the editor desiring him on all occasions and without alteration or addition to print Richard's dispatches. The editor in retort reminded Mr. Gwynn that the *Daily Tory* had a reputation and a policy: also there were laws of libel. Mr. Gwynn declined to be moved by these high considerations, and reiterated his first command. After that Richard in each issue gave way to an unchecked column letter, which was run sullenly by the editor and never a word displaced.

This daily letter, signed "R. S.," brought Richard mighty comfort; he read it fresh and new each morning with mounting satisfaction. Richard, like other authors, found no literature so good to his palate as his own; and while his stories looked well enough when he wrote them, the types never failed in uncovering charms that had escaped his ken. These were complacent days for Richard the defective; ones to nourish his self-love.

Being his first work, and performed under his own tolerant mastery, with none to molest him or make him editorially afraid, it stood scant wonder that he went about the subject of his own sleepless self-congratulations. What Richard needed—and never knew it—was dismissal in rapid succession from at least four newspapers; such a course of journalistic sprouts would have set his feet in proper paths. Under the circumstances, however, this improving experience was impossible; missing the benefits thereof, Richard must struggle on as best he might without a bridle.

It was fortunate, when one remembers his blinded ignorance, a condition aggravated by his own acute approval of himself, that Richard had a no more radical guide than was the cautious Senator Hanway. While that designing gentleman—the *Daily Tory* turning the stone—grinded many a personal ax—*note bene*, never once without exciting the sophisticated wrath of the editor-in-chief—he was no such headlong temper of a man as to invite the paper into foolish extravagancies, whether of statement or of style. As the bug under the chip of the *Daily Tory's* Washington correspondence, Senator Hanway was neither a vindictive nor yet a reckless bug; and the paper, while it became the organ of his ambitions, made some reputational profit by the very melody of those guarded tunes he ground.

Richard, you are not to suppose, went unaware of those employments to which Senator Hanway put him in the vineyard of his policies. He realized the situation and walked therein with wide and willing eyes. It served his tender purpose; it would take him to the Harley house and throw him, perchance, into the society of Dorothy without that dulcet privilege being identified as the true purpose of his call.

One cannot but marvel that Richard should be at the trouble of so much difficult chicane. It is strange that he should so entangle what might have been the simplest of love stories; for you may as well know here as further on that, had Richard laid bare the truth of himself, Mrs. Hanway-Harley, far from fencing her daughter against him and his addresses, would have taken the door off its hinges to let him in. But Richard, as was heretofore suggested, had been most ignorantly brought up, or rather had been granted no bringing up at all. Moreover, in the sensitive cynicism of his nature, which made a laugh its armor and was harsh for fear of being hurt, our young Democritus had long ago bound himself with vows that he would accept no friendship, win no love, that did not come to him upon his mere and unsupported merits as a man. In his own fashion, so far from being the philosopher he thought, Richard was a knight errant—one as mad and as romantic as the most feather-headed Amadis that ever came out of Gaul; and so he is to make himself a deal of trouble and have himself much laughed at before ever he succeeds in slipping through the fingers of this history to seek obscurity with Dorothy by his side. For all that, it is Richard's due to say that his "R. S." letters attracted polite as well as political attention, and got him much respected and condemned. Also they lodged him high in the esteem of Senator Hanway, who discovered daily new excellencies in him; and this came somewhat to the rescue of Richard one day.

Senator Hanway had a room in a wing of the Harley house which Mrs. Hanway-Harley called his study. It was a sumptuous apartment, furnished in mahogany and leather, and a bookcase, filled with Congressional Records which nobody ever looked at, stood against the wall. Here it was that Senator Hanway held his conferences; it was here he laid his plans and brooded them. When Senator Hanway desired to meet a gentleman and preferred to keep the meeting dark, this study was the scene of that secrecy. In such event, the blinds were drawn to baffle what prying or casual eye might come marching up the street; for in Washington, to see two men conversing, is to know nine times in ten precisely what the conversation is about. Commonly, however, the blinds were thrown wide, as though the study's pure proprietor courted a world's scrutiny.

It was in this study that Richard was received by Senator Hanway. There was an outside door; a caller might be admitted from the veranda without troubling the main portals of the Harley house. To save the patience of that journalist, Senator Hanway called Richard's attention to the veranda door, and commissioned him to make use of it. Senator Hanway said that he did not wish to subject one whom he valued so highly, and who was on such near terms with his good friend, Mr. Gwynn, to the slow ceremony which attended a regular invasion of the premises.

Richard thanked Senator Hanway, although he could have liked it better had he been less thoughtfully polite. Richard would have preferred the main floor, with whatever delay and formal clatter such entrance made imperative. The more delay and the more clatter, the more chance of seeing Dorothy. It struck him with a dubious chill when Senator Hanway suddenly distinguished him with the freedom of that veranda door—a franchise upon which your statesman laid flattering emphasis, saying that not ten others had been granted it.

This episode of the veranda door befell upon the earliest visit which Richard made in his quality of correspondent of the *Daily Tory*. On that day, being admitted by way of the Harley front door, Richard had the felicity of coming in with the before-mentioned daily sheaf of roses. Richard and the blossom-bearing colored youth entered together, the door making the one opening to admit both; and by this fortunate chance—which Richard the wily had waited around the corner to secure—he was given the joy of seeing and hearing the beautiful Dorothy gurgle over the flowers.

"And to think," cried Dorothy, her nose in the bosom of a rose, "no one knows from whom they come! Mamma thinks Count Storri sends them. It's so good of him, if he does!"

Dorothy's head was bowed over the flowers. As she spoke, however, her blue eye, full of mischief, watched Richard through a silken lock of hair that had fallen forward.

"But you don't think it's Storri?" cried Richard dolorously.

"Oh, no!" returned Dorothy, shaking her head with wise decision, "I don't think it's Count Storri. But of course I wouldn't tell mamma so; she doesn't like to be contradicted. Still," and here Dorothy looked quite wistful, "I wish I knew who did send them."

Before Richard could take up the delicate question of the roses and their origin, there arrived the word of Senator Hanway that he be shown into the study.

"Now that I'm a working journalist, Miss Harley," said Richard, "I shall be obliged to see your uncle every day."

"Oh, dear!" exclaimed Dorothy, with a fine sympathy; "how hard they drive you poor newspaper people!"

"Still, we go not without our rewards," returned Richard.

Then observing that Senator Hanway's messenger—who had not those reasons for loitering which made slow the feet of Richard—was already halfway down the hall, Richard took Dorothy's small hand in his, and, before she knew her peril or might make an effort to avoid it, rapturously kissed the fingers, not once, not twice, but five times. The very fingers themselves burned with the scandal of it! Following this deed of rapine, Richard went his vandal way; Dorothy's face turned a twin red with the roses.

Dorothy said nothing in rebuke of Richard, and it is to be assumed that, so flagrant an outrage left her without breath to voice her condemnation. That she was disturbed to the heart is sure, for she went instantly to her friend, the sibyl of the golden locks, for conference, confidence, and consolation.

"Wasn't he wretchedly bold, Bess?" said Dorothy in an awe-stricken whisper.

"Absolutely abandoned!" said Bess.

Then the two sat in silence for ten impressive seconds.

"Bess," remarked Dorothy tentatively, "suppose mamma were to forbid me loving one whom I loved——" Here she broke down, aghast.

"My dear Dorothy," cried the other, surprised into deepest concern, "your mother didn't see him kissing your fingers, did she?"

"Oh, no, Bess," said Dorothy hurriedly, "we were quite alone."

"You foolish girl," returned Bess. "You alarmed me!"

"But really, Bess," persisted Dorothy, "to put it this way: if your mamma insisted, would you give way and marry a man you didn't love?"

"You mean Count Storri," replied Bess. "Now, Dorothy, listen to me. In the first place, you are an arrant hypocrite. You pretend to be soft and powerless and yielding, and to appeal to me for counsel. And all the time you are twice as obstinate as I am, and much less likely to accept a man you don't love, or give up one whom you love."

"Well, Bess," said Dorothy defensively, a bit stricken of these truths, "really, I want your opinions on marriage."

"Oh, that is it! Then snap your fingers in the teeth of command, and marry no man whom you do not love!"

"But the man you love might not want you!" sighed Dorothy.

"The man you love will always want you," declared Bess with firmness.

"How sweet you are!"

"And as for parents making matches for their daughters," continued Bess, unmoved of the tribute, and speaking as one who for long had made a study of the world's domestic affairs, "it is sure to lead to trouble and divorce."

"Is it?" asked Dorothy, appalled.

"It is!" returned Bess with a sepulchral air, as though pronouncing doom. Then, mocking Dorothy's serious face with a little tumult of laughter, she went on: "There; it's all decided now the way you wished. You are to refuse Count Storri and marry Mr. Storms without bestowing either care or thought on what Mamma Harley or Papa Harley or Uncle Pat may say or do about it."

"Really, Bess, how much better you have made me feel. After all, there's nobody like a wise, dear, true friend!"

"The value of such a friend is beyond conjecture," returned the mocking Bess, reassuming her tones of the oracle.

The memory of Richard's kisses on her fingers never left Dorothy all that day and all that night. Those fortunate little fingers seemed translated into something rosily better and apart from herself. And brow and ears and eyes and cheeks and lips went envying those lucky fingers; and in the end the lips crept upon them and kissed them for having been kissed; perhaps with vague thoughts of robbing them of some portion of the blissful wealth wherewith they had been invested. Richard, being male, for his part thought the less about it, and went simply meditating future sweet aggressions. And that shows the difference between a man and a maid.

Richard, feeding his love with thoughts of Dorothy and his vanity with ink, and thereby gaining two mighty reasons for living, began to keep earlier hours. He turned out at nine o'clock instead of eleven and twelve, hours which had formerly matched his languid fancy. These energetic doings bred alarm in both Matzai and Mr. Pickwick, evoking snappish protests from the latter, who, being of a nocturnal turn, held that the day was meant for sleep. On the morning after he had been honored with the privilege of the veranda door, Richard was borne upon by something akin to gloom. This feeling went with him from bed to bath, and from bath to breakfast, and finally walked with him all the way to the Harley house. He was willing to sacrifice the *Daily Tory* and yoke himself personally to the mills of Senator Hanway's designs; but he must see Dorothy. That brightness was the bribe, unspoken and unknown to all save himself, that had brought him into Washington and these sundry and divers plots and counterplots of state. And now to be cheated through the polite blunderings of a gentleman who was so engaged in considering himself that he had neither time nor eyes for any other! Richard swore roundly in mental fashion at his contrary fate. And yet he saw no way to better the situation; and perforce, for this morning at least, he was driven to push the bell of the veranda door. He might have gone about the ceremony with more cheer had he known how he was to gain an ally in his troubles; one, moreover, whose aid was sure to prove effective.

As Senator Hanway's black messenger ushered Richard into that statesman's study, the radiant Dorothy, perched at the end of Senator Hanway's table, was the picture that greeted his eyes. Our radiant one sought to stifle her effulgence beneath a look severe and practical. This expression of practical severity was a failure, and served to render her more dazzling.

"I have made up my mind," quoth Dorothy, the moment Richard was inside the door, and speaking in the loud, dead-level monotone which she conceived to be the voice for business conversations as against the giggling, gurgling ups and downs of conversations purely social, "I have made up my mind to come in every morning and help Uncle Pat. I'm tired of being a useless encumbrance."

Delivering which, Dorothy wore the resolved manner of a new Joan of Arc who had come seeking fields of politics rather than those of war.

"And I have been of use to you, haven't I, Uncle Pat?" demanded Dorothy.

"Of measureless use, dear," said Senator Hanway. Then, turning to his secretary, who had taken a score of letters shorthand and was about to seek his own quarters and run them off upon the typewriter: "Have those copied by three o'clock and bring them here for signature."

Senator Hanway had no more than given Richard good-morning when Senator Loot was announced.

"He won't stay long," said Senator Hanway; "but while he's here, dear, won't you take Mr. Storms into the library?" This request was preferred to Dorothy.

"Yes," began Dorothy, when she and Richard found themselves in the library, and nothing to interrupt them but the distant slumbrous rumble of Senator Loot. "Yes, I'm going to help Uncle Pat. And I'm going to learn how to be a newspaper woman, too. I think every girl should be capable of earning her own living. Not that I expect to be obliged to do so; but it is best to be prepared." Dorothy's face was funereal, as though disasters, clawed and fanged, were roaming the thickets of the future to spring upon her. "So I shall learn the newspaper trade; go in and be a writer as you are—only not so brilliant—and then, if it were necessary, I could earn my own way."

Now Richard knew these industrious resolutions to be the veriest webs of subterfuge. Their duplicity was apparent, and they were spun for him. Dorothy owned no thought of missing his morning calls, and had met Senator Hanway's courtesies of the veranda door with a move in flank. The news cocked up the spirits of Richard excessively, and gave to his Farnese shoulders an insolent swing as he strutted up and down the library. He had expected Dorothy to reproach him for the soft violence done her fingers; but she made no mention of it. Whereupon—in such manner do unchecked iniquities multiply upon themselves—Richard turned towards her with a purpose of again outraging those little fingers with the burden of a fresh caress. The little fingers, grown wary, however, were in discreet retirement behind Dorothy, as, with her back to the window, she stood facing him. Defeated in his campaign against the fingers before it had begun, Richard was driven to discuss Dorothy's work-a-day resolves.

"Newspaper work? Do society, I suppose?"

Richard had gotten hold of the idioms of the craft, and spoke of "doing society" as though reared among the types.

"No, not society," and Dorothy shook her head. "I'd pick 'em to pieces, the minxes; and the papers don't want that. No, I'm going to learn about politics with Uncle Pat. I shall write politics. You must teach me."

Richard said he would.

"Only you should know," said he, "that I need a deal of teaching myself."

"But you can write!" cried Dorothy, her hands emerging from their retreat to clasp each other in a glow of admiration. "I've read your letters. They remind me of Carlyle's 'French Revolution.'"

This staggered Richard; was his idol laughing at him? A glance into her eyes showed only a darkened enthusiasm; whereat Richard puffed and swelled. Perhaps his *Daily Tory* letters did have the rhetorical tread of the Scotchman's masterpiece. In any event it was pleasant to have Dorothy think so. Before he could frame his modesty to fit reply, the cumbrous retreat of Senator Loot was overheard.

"Now we must go back," said Dorothy.

"May I have a rose?" asked Richard, pointing to his blushing consignment of that day, where they luxuriated in a giant vase.

"Don't touch my hands!" cried Dorothy fiercely, whipping them behind her.

Richard gave his humble parole that he would not touch her hands. Being reassured, Dorothy pinned a bud in his lapel. The little fingers were so fondly confident of safety that they made no haste in these labors of the bud. Their confidence went unabused; Richard adhered to his parole and never touched them.

"I'm glad you can keep your promise!" said Dorothy, pouting from pure delight.

Later, the pair made love to one another with their eyes across the dignified desk of Senator Hanway, while that statesman told Richard matters to the detriment of Mr. Hawke's canvass for a Speakership and Governor Obstinate's claims upon a Presidency, of which, through the medium of the *Daily Tory*, he believed the public should be informed.

"My dear Dorothy," observed the sibyl of the golden locks, when the other related how faithfully Richard had kept his compact concerning her fingers, "you ought never to make a man promise the thing you do not want. They are such dullards; besides, they have a passion for keeping their word."

The President and General Attorney and thirty-two underling attorneys of the Anaconda Airline, in accord with Mr. Gwynn's request, descended upon Washington. The thirty-two underling attorneys, coming to town by twos and threes, were amazed when they found a gathering of the Anaconda Airline clans. They collected in groups and clots at the Shorcham, the Arlington, and Willard's to discuss their amazement.

The President and General Attorney, if they were smitten of wonder, concealed it, and within the hour after their arrival rang the doorbell of Mr.

Gwynn. They were ushered into a room the tamed splendors of which told the thorough taste that had conceived it. Then their cards went up to Mr. Gwynn.

Word came back that Mr. Gwynn was deeply engaged. Would the President and the General Attorney of the Anaconda Airline call again in an hour? The President and General Attorney had for long harbored a theory that Mr. Gwynn was the greatest man on earth. Now they knew it; the fact was displayed beyond dispute by his failure to instantly see them. The President and General Attorney withdrew, silent in their awe, and Mr. Gwynn dispatched Matzai to find Richard.

On the hour's even stroke, the President and General Attorney were again at Mr. Gwynn's. That personage was still unable to meet them; however, he sent Richard with written excuses for his absence and the suggestion that Richard, speaking in his place, would put them in possession of his wishes.

"Mr. Gwynn desired to say," observed Richard, "that Anaconda Airline interests deeply depend upon Mr. Frost for Speaker."

"What we've said from the beginning!" remarked the President to the General Attorney.

"Precisely what we've said!" observed the General Attorney.

They had said nothing on that point; but they were too well drilled in their own interests to fail of complete coincidence with a gentleman who could call a special shareholders' meeting, elect a new directory, and revise the entire official family of the Anaconda Airline within any given thirty days.

"Mr. Gwynn asks you, then," said Richard, "since you and he agree on the propriety of Mr. Frost for Speaker, to consult with Senator Hanway."

And now the Anaconda Airline was in the war for the House gavel. Under the supervision of Senator Hanway, it brought its whole smothering weight to bear upon the Hawke twenty of those twenty-three whose districts it dominated. The Hawke twenty wriggled and writhed, but in the end gave way—all save a rock-ribbed quartette. They must stay by the standards of Mr. Hawke.

"Our constituents will destroy us if we don't," said they.

"The Anaconda will destroy you if you do," was the blunt retort of the General Attorney.

The four stood firm, and were blacklisted for slaughter at the polls a year away, at which time they were faithfully knocked on the head. Sixteen of the twenty went over to Mr. Frost; the President of the Anaconda Airline came out in an interview in the *Daily Tory* and said that the shift of the excellent sixteen was a popular victory.

It was two days before the caucus. The line-up of forces, Frost against Hawke, Hanway against Obstinate, under able captains went vigorously forward. It pleased Senator Hanway to hear that the Frost fortunes were being unexpectedly served by the volcanic Mr. Hawke himself. That gentleman had fallen into a state of indignant eruption; his best friends could not approach him because of the smoke and flame and lava which his rage cast up.

"The most scoundrel thing I ever saw in Washington is that I am made to fight for the Speakership!" cried the eruptive Mr. Hawke; and this fashion of outburst does not help any man's cause.

To steal a simile from a dead gentleman who stole from others in his day, Mr. Hawke went into the final battle of the caucus much after the manner wherewith a horse approaches a drum, that is, with a deal of prance and but little progress, and, for the most part, wrong end foremost. Even then the count of Senator Hanway—a cold-blooded computation—gave that gavel to the violent Mr. Hawke. So much for being a House leader, a tariff monger, and a friend of Governor Obstinate.

On the afternoon before the caucus, Senator Hanway took a last look at the array. Besides Mr. Hawke and Mr. Frost, there were two other candidates, Mr. Patch and Mr. Swinger. These latter had been sent into the lists by the diplomacy of Senator Hanway to hold the delegations from their States, a majority whereof, if released, would fly to Mr. Hawke. With all four names before the caucus, Mr. Frost would lead Mr. Hawke by two, without having a majority. Eliminate Mr. Patch and Mr. Swinger, however, and Mr. Hawke would be chosen by a majority of seven. And, while the battle might be made to stagger on through forty ballots, in the end Mr. Patch and Mr. Swinger must perforce withdraw. They could give no excuse for holding on forever in a fight shown to be hopeless. Some method must be devised to break the Hawke alignment or in a last solution of the situation Mr. Frost would lose.

Senator Hanway made ready to play his last card—a card to which nothing short of the desperate turn of events would have caused him to resort. He made a list of eighteen of Mr. Hawke's supporters; he picked them out because they were nervous, hysterical souls whom one might hope to stampede. Senator Hanway then got the names, with the home addresses, of a score of the principal constituents of each of these aspen, hysterical gentlemen.

A telegraph operator, one close-mouthed and of a virtuous taciturnity, sat up all night with Senator Hanway in his study—the night before the caucus. There was none present but Senator Hanway and the wordless telegraphic one; the former, deeming the occasion one proper for that cautious rite, drew the blinds closely.

At Senator Hanway's dictation, the taciturn one who had been so forethoughtful as to bring with him envelopes and blanks, wrote messages to each of the hysterical eighteen, about twenty to a man, signing them with the names of those influential constituents. The messages were letter-perfect; in each instance, the message for signature bore the name of one upon whom the member who would receive it leaned in his destinies of politics. No two were worded alike, albeit each commanded and demanded the Speakership for Mr. Frost. When they were done, nearly four hundred of them, the taciturn one endowed them with those quirleyques and symbols and hieroglyphics which belong with genuine messages, and finished by sealing each in an envelope properly numbered and addressed. Then the taciturn one made a delivery book to match the messages.

"There!" exclaimed Senator Hanway, when at four in the morning the taciturn one tossed the last forged message upon the pile and said that all were done; "that's finished. Now at two o'clock put on a messenger's uniform and come to the Capitol. It's 4 a. m. now, and this is Saturday; the caucus convenes at two o'clock sharp. It will be held in the House chamber. There will be ten ballots; I have arranged for that, and Patch and Swinger will not withdraw before. The ten ballots will consume two hours and a half—fifteen minutes to a roll call. After they have gone through four roll calls, begin to send in these messages; the caucus officer on the door will sign for them. Send first one to each member; then two; then four; then five; then all you have. Give about fifteen minutes between consignments. Have you got my plan?"

The taciturn one nodded.

"Here is a one-hundred-dollar bill," observed Senator Hanway, "for your night's work. Four more wait for you when Mr. Frost is declared the caucus nominee."

Saturday afternoon; and the caucus met behind locked doors. It was a mighty struggle; now and then some waifword reached the outside world of what Titan deeds were being done. There were speeches, and roll calls; men lost their heads and then their reputations. The sixteen threatened of the Anaconda Airline, with the fear of political death upon them, voted for Mr. Frost. Messrs. Patch and Swinger held fast through ballot after ballot, keeping their delegations together, while the Hawke captains pleaded and begged and promised and threatened in their efforts to make them withdraw and release their followings to the main battle. Through roll call after roll call the tally never varied. With two hundred and ten members voting, the count stood: Frost, ninety-two; Hawke, ninety; Swinger, fifteen; Patch, thirteen. Of the twenty-eight who voted for Messrs. Patch and Swinger, it was understood that Mr. Hawke would take three-fourths upon a breakaway. For this reason the Hawke captains labored and moiled with Messrs. Patch and Swinger to withdraw and cast those twenty-eight votes into the general caldron.

AT THE DOOR OF THE CAUCUS ROOM

On the touch of three, and while the fourth roll-call was in progress, the first of Senator Hanway's prepared messages were received and signed for at the caucus door. Ten minutes later, and something like forty more were given entrance. During the sixth roll-call sixty messages came in, and a rickety little representative, with a beard like a goat and terror tugging at his heart, arose and changed his vote to Mr. Frost. The rickety little man had been for Mr. Hawke, and this sudden turning of his coat provoked a tempest of cheers from the Frosts and maledictions from the Hawkes. A dozen men of both factions crowded about the little rickety man, some to hold him for Mr. Frost and others to drag him back to Mr. Hawke. The rickety little man was well-nigh torn in two. Kingdoms and thrones were being gambled for and the players were in earnest.

In the height of the uproar over the rickety little man, two more of the flock of Hawke arose, and with faltering lip stated that, by the demands of constituents whom they were there to represent and whose wishes they dared not disregard, they would also change their votes to Mr. Frost. The cheers of the Frosts and the curses of the Hawkes were redoubled; but the Frosts drowned the Hawkes, since it is one of the admirable arrangements of Providence that men can cheer louder than they can curse.

And now a bevy of full one hundred of the Hanway messages came through the door. The stampede which started with the rickety, goat-bearded little man, to include the duo chronicled, upon a seventh roll call swept five more Hawkes from their perches and gave them over to Mr. Frost. More messages, more changes; and all to finish in a pandemonium in which Messrs. Patch and Swinger were withdrawn, and Mr. Frost was landed Speaker by the meager fringe of three. Speaker Frost it was; and everyone conceded that a staggering blow had been dealt the Presidential hopes of Governor Obstinate. Senator Hanway, waiting at the Senate end for news, sighed victoriously when word was brought him. It would be Speaker Frost; and now, with House and Senate his, he for the first time felt himself within sure and striking distance of a White House.

CHAPTER VI

HOW STORRI HAD A VIVID IMAGINATION

Storri had no more of moral nature than has a tiger or a kite. He was founded upon no integrity, would keep faith with no one save himself. Storri was not a moral lunatic, for that would suppose some original morality and its subversion to insane aims; rather he was the moral idiot. At that, his imbecility paused with his morals; in what a world calls business he was notably bright and forward.

Storri was of education, had traveled wide and far, as ones of his predatory stamp are prone to do, and with a Russian facility for tongues spoke English, German, French, and half the languages of Europe. The instinctive purpose of Storri's existence was to make money. To him, money was a prey, and stood as do deer to wolves; and yet, making a fine distinction, he was rapacious, not avaricious. Avarice includes some idea of a storekeeping commerce that amasses by buying for one dollar and selling for two. Storri would have failed at that. He was rapacious as the pirate is rapacious, and with a gambler's love for the uncertain, he balked at anything whereof the possible profits were cut and dried. He wanted to win, but he was willing to lose if he must; and above all he distasted the notion of a limit. Like every wild thing, Storri shied at a fence and loved the wilderness. While Storri knew nothing of honesty, he preferred his gold on legitimate lines. This leaning towards the lawful came not from any bias of probity; Storri simply wanted to be safe, having a horror of chains and bolts and cages and striped garments.

When Storri arrived in Washington, he came from Canada by way of New York. The year before he had been in Paris, and was something—not for long—of a figure on the Bourse. He had been in every capital of Asia and Europe, and all the while his restless eye sleepless in its search for money.

Gifted with an imagination, Storri evolved a scheme. Starting in moderation, it grew with his wanderings until, link upon link, it became endless and belted the earth. Storri's imagination was like a tar barrel; accident might set fire to it, but once in the least of flame it must burn on and on, with no power of self-extinguishment, until it burned itself out. Or it was like him who, given a halter, straightway takes a horse.

It is the theory of Europe that Americans are maniacs of money. European conservatism draws a money-line beyond which it will not pass. When any man of Europe has a proposal of business too big for the European mouth—wearing its self-imposed half-muzzle of conservatism—that promoter and his proposal head for America. It was this which gained Washington the advantage of a visit from Storri; his stop in Canada—being a six-months' stay in Ottawa—was only preliminary to his coming here.

While his own people of Russia drew back from those enterprises which Storri's agile imagination had in train, the government at St. Petersburg, in what was perhaps a natural hope that he might find Americans more reckless, endowed him as he came away with a guarded pat on the back. The St. Petersburg government advised its representatives in America to introduce without indorsing Storri.

Storri was by no means wise after the manner of a Franklin or a Humboldt or a Herschel; but he did possess the deep sapiency of the serpent or the fox. He owned inborn traits to steal and creep upon his prey of money. Being in Washington, and looking up and down, he was quick to note the strategic propriety of an alliance with Mr. Harley. Mr. Harley had connections with American millionaires; most of all, he was the *alter ego* of a powerful congressional figure. Storri could talk with Mr. Harley; Mr. Harley could talk with Senator Hanway. Since Congress would be required for the success of Storri's plans, this last was to be of prime importance.

Because Mr. Harley made it his affectation to be boisterously frank and friendly upon short acquaintance, Storri met no vexatious delays in coming to an understanding with him. You are not to assume that Mr. Harley was truthful because he was boisterous or his frankness went freighted of no guile. It is commonest error to believe your frankest talker, your greatest teller of truth; whereas, in a majority of instances, the delusive garrulity is a mask or a feint, meant only to cover facts and screen designs of which the victim's first notice is, snap! when they pin him like a steel-trap. Still, Storri entertained no risks when he broke into confidences with Mr. Harley. It was Mr. Harley who listened and Storri who talked; besides, Storri, in any conflicting tug of interest, could be as loquacious as Mr. Harley, and as false. It was diamond cutting diamond and Greek meeting Greek. Only, since Storri was a Count, and Mr. Harley one upon whom a title went not without blinding effect, Storri had a fractional advantage.

Storri and Mr. Harley enjoyed several casual talks; that is, Mr. Harley thought them casual, although every one was planned by Storri. In none did Storri unpack his enterprises; these talks were feelers, and he was studying Mr. Harley. Storri was gratified to find Mr. Harley, by native trend, as rapacious and as much the gambler as himself. Also, he observed the licking satisfaction wherewith Mr. Harley listened to every noble reference; with that, Storri contrived—for his conversation—a fashion of little personal Kingdom on the Caspian, tossed himself up a castle, and entertained therein from time to time about half the royal blood of Europe; all to the marvelous delight of Mr. Harley, whom Storri never failed to wish had been a guest on those purple occasions.

At this seductive rate, it was no more than a matter of ten days before Mr. Harley went quoting his friend Storri; he had that titled Slav to dinner, when the latter became as much the favorite with Mrs. Hanway-Harley as he was with her ruder spouse.

Storri saw Dorothy; and was set burning with a love for her that, if the flame were less pure, was as instant and as devouring as the love to sweep over Richard upon the boot-heel evening when he caught her in his arms. Storri forgot himself across table, and his onyx eyes were riveted upon Dorothy as though their owner were enthralled.

Dorothy felt at once flattered and repelled. She was interested, even while she shuddered; it was as though she had been made the object of the sudden, if venomous, admiration of a king-cobra.

"My friend," purred Storri, one afternoon when he and Mr. Harley were alone, "my good friend, I will no longer refrain from taking you into my confidence; and when I say that, you are to understand, also, into the confidence of my Czar."

Storri rested his head in his hand a moment, and seemed to ponder the propriety of what he was about. Mr. Harley said nothing, but sat a-fidget with curiosity. It is not given every American to be taken, via a Count with estates on the Caspian, into the confidence of a Czar.

"Yes, into the confidence of my Czar," repeated Storri. "See now, my friend, I will lay bare my soul to you. I am resolved you shall be with me in my vast adventure. With you—who are practical—who have business genius—my dreams will become realities. Without you, I—who am a mere poet of finance—an artist of commerce—would fail. I have genius to conceive; I cannot carry out. But you—you, my dear friend, are what you call executive."

Mr. Harley felt profoundly flattered, and showed it; Storri pushed on, watching the other with the tail of his eye. The slant survey was satisfactory; Mr. Harley showed half upon his guard and wholly interested.

"I have conceived projects so gigantic they will stagger belief. And yet they are feasible; you will make them so. You will take them and girdle the earth with them as Saturn is girdled by his rings. Observe now! These, my designs, have the good wishes of my Czar; and next to him you are that one to whom they are first told. Why do I come so far with my dreams? I will tell you; it was by command of my Czar.

"'Storri, you must go to America,' were his words. 'You would only stun Europe; you would not gain her aid. Go to America. There, and there only, will you find what you require. They, and they of all men, have the courage, the brains, the money, the enterprise, and—shall I say?—the honor!'"

Having quoted his Czar in these good opinions of Americans, Storri rapidly and in clearest sequence laid out his programmes. Before he was half finished, Mr. Harley went following every word with all his senses. Storri was lucid; Storri was hypnotic; Storri had his projects so faultlessly in hand that, as he piled up words, he piled up conviction in the breast of Mr. Harley.

Storri began with China. Being equipped for the conversation—which had not been so much the result of romantic chance as Mr. Harley might have supposed—he laid upon the table a square of yellow silk. It was written over with Chinese characters which, for all Mr. Harley knew, might have been inscriptions copied from a tea chest. As a matter of truth, they were genuine. The silk was the record of a concession by the Chinese Government. It gave Storri, or what company he might form, the privilege of building a railway across China from east to west. He might select his port on the Pacific, build his road, and break into Russia on the west and north at what point best matched the enterprise. Also, it granted a right to buy land wherever it became necessary, and to own what wharf and water rights were required. Incidentally, so Storri said, it permitted gold digging.

"You shall take it to the Chinese legation!" exclaimed Storri. "They shall translate for you. Yes; it gives gold rights. Gold? There is so much gold in China that your own California becomes laughable by comparison. See there," and Storri placed a little leathern pouch on the table. "There are three ounces. Do you know how they were obtained? I spread a blanket in the bed of a little stream, and weighted it with stones so that it lay flat. Then I took a stick, and tossed up the mud and the sand of that little stream, just above. The muddy water, thick as paint, flowed over the blanket. In thirty minutes I took my blanket ashore, and washed from the sediment it had caught and held this gold—three ounces! Bah! Gold? China is the home of gold! But China and these concessions are only the beginning."

Storri sketched a steamship line to connect his Chinese railway with Puget Sound. For this they ought to have a subsidy from the United States. From Puget they must have a railway to Duluth. On the Great Lakes, Storri would have a line of steamships.

"Only, we will improve upon those lakes!" cried Storri. "It was that to carry me to Ottawa."

Then Storri unrolled maps and reports from Canadian engineers which vouched the plausibility of a ship canal from a deep-water point on that eastern arm of Lake Huron called Georgian Bay to Toronto on Lake Ontario.

"It shall be two hundred feet wide," explained Storri, "and thirty feet deep. The distance is less than one hundred miles, and the fall less than one hundred feet. To dig it will be child's play; you may read the reports of the engineers; they show how advantage may be had of a Lake Simcoe, and of a little river. Here also are letters and guarantees from eminent men of Canada that their parliament will permit and protect the canal. Less than one hundred miles long; and yet that canal will cut off seven hundred."

Once in Lake Ontario at Toronto, Storri's boats, by way of the St. Lawrence—which might have to be dredged in places—were to make a straight wake for St. Petersburg, touching at English, French, and German ports. The ships were to clear in Duluth for St. Petersburg; and in St. Petersburg for Duluth. They were to fly the American flag; that, too, should mean a subsidy. Besides, there must be an American commission to confer with a Canadian commission touching the canal.

Once in St. Petersburg, Storri would have the aid of his own country in whatever might be necessary to carry him to the western terminus of his Chinese railway. He had writings in French from the Czar's government which set this forth. Only, the Russian assurances were made contingent upon a standing army of "Ifs." "If" Storri *should* throw a railway across China; and "if" he *should* launch a line of steamships across the Pacific—the same fostered by the Washington Government with a subsidy—and "if" all and singular the railway from Puget to Duluth, the Canadian Canal, and the line of steamships from Duluth to St. Petersburg—also with a subsidy—*were* once extant and in operation, then the Czar would step graciously in and see what might be done in forging those final Russian railway links required to unite the ends of this interesting chain.

"And you are to know," went on Storri, "that my government, the St. Petersburg Government, is paternal. It will give whatever, in the way of land rights and loans, is demanded by the exigencies of the project.

"And there," cried Storri in conclusion, as he shoved maps, papers, and concessions, Russian, Canadian, and Chinese, across to Mr. Harley, "is an idea the magnificence of which the ages cannot parallel! It is simple, it is great! We shall have three-score small companies—that is, small compared with the grand one I am to name. We shall have land and banking and lumber and mining and railway and steamship and canal companies. We shall have companies owning elevators and factories and stores and mills. Each will employ a capital of from two to two hundred millions of dollars.

Over all, and to own the stock of those smaller ones, we must throw a giant company. Do you know what it will require? Do you realize what its capital must be? It will call for the cost price of an empire, my friend; it will demand full thirty billions! Think of the president of such a company! He will have rank by himself; he will tower above kings. What shall we call it? Name it for that mighty Portuguese who was first to send his ship around the globe; name it Credit Magellan!"

Mr. Harley wiped the sweat from his forehead. It was a day in October, one reasonably cool, and yet, when Storri ended with his Credit Magellan and came to a full stop, Mr. Harley was in a perspiration. It was those thirty billions that did it. Mr. Harley was no stoic to sit unmoved in the presence of such wealth, and the graphic Storri made those billions real.

When Storri had done, Mr. Harley gulped and gasped a bit, and then asked if he might retain the armful of papers for further consideration. He would like to go over them carefully; particularly those Canadian reports and assurances that related to the canal.

"My dear, good friend," cried Storri, with a magnificent wave of the hand, "you may do what you will!"

There are men, reckoned shrewd in business, whose shrewdness can be overcome by ciphers. It is as though they were wise up to seven figures. Mr. Harley was of these; he had his boundaries. His instincts were solvent, his policies sound, his suspicions full of life and courage, so that you went no higher than nine millions. Burdened beyond that, his imagination would break down; and since his instincts, his policies, and his suspicions rested wholly upon his imagination, when the latter fell the others must of need go with it. There is a depth to money just as there is to a lake; when you led Mr. Harley in beyond the nine-million-dollar mark he began to drown. When Storri—Pelion upon Ossa—piled steamship on railway, and canal on steamship, and banking and lumber and mining and twenty other companies on top of these, Mr. Harley was dazed and benumbed. When Storri concluded and capped all with his Credit Magellan, capital thirty billions, it was, so far as Mr. Harley is to be considered, like taking a child to sea. In the haze and the blur of it, Mr. Harley could see nothing, say nothing; his impulse was to be alone and collect himself. He felt as might one who has been staring at the sun. Storri's picture of an enterprise so vast that it proposed to set out the world like a mighty pan of milk, and skim the cream from two hemispheres, dazzled him and caused his wits to lose their way.

At the end of three days Mr. Harley had begun to get his bearings; he was still fascinated, but the fog was lifting. Step by step he went over Storri's grand proposals; and, while he had now his eyes, each step seemed only to take him more deeply into a wilderness of admiration. That very admiration filled him with a sense of dull alarm. He resolved to have other counsel than his own. Were he and Storri to embark upon this world-girdling enterprise, they must have money-help. He would take the project to certain money-loving souls; he would get their opinions by asking their aid.

Mr. Harley went to New York and called about him a quintette of gentlemen, each of whom had been with him and Senator Hanway in more than one affair of shady profit. Mankind does not change, its methods change, and trade has still its Kidds and Blackbeards. Present commerce has its pirates and its piracies; only the buccaneers of now do not launch ships, but stock companies, while Wall and Broad Streets are their Spanish Main. They do not, like Francis Drake, lay off and on at the Isthmus to stop plate ships; they seek their galleons in the Stock Exchange. Those five to gather at the call of Mr. Harley were of our modern Drakes. He told them, under seal of secrecy, Storri's programme, and put before them the documents, Russian, Canadian, and Chinese.

Mr. Harley felt somewhat justified of his own enthusiasm when he observed the serious glow in the eyes of those five. They sent to Mott Street, and brought back a learned Oriental to translate the Chinese silk. The Mott Street one, himself a substantial merchant and a Mongol of high caste, appeared wrapped in rustling brocades and an odor of opium. When he beheld the yellow silk he bent himself, and smote the floor three times with his forehead. More than anything told by Mr. Harley did this profound obeisance of the Mott Street Oriental leave its impress upon the five. They, themselves, bowed to nothing save gold; the silken document must record a franchise of gravity and money-moment to thus set their visitor to beating the carpet with his head! Having done due honor to the Emperor's signature, the Mott Street one gave Mr. Harley and his friends the silken document's purport in English. It granted every right, railway, wharf, and gold, asserted by Storri. Then Mr. Harley wired that nobleman to join them in New York.

Storri had not been informed of Mr. Harley's New York visit. But he had counted on it, and the summons in no wise smote him with surprise. Once with Mr. Harley and the adventurous five, Storri again went over his project, beginning at the Chinese railway and closing with Credit Magellan, capital thirty billions. Not one who heard went unconvinced; not one but was willing to commence in practical fashion the carrying out of this high financial dream.

It was the romance—for money-making has its romances—and the adventurous uncertainty of the thing, the pushing into the unknown, which formed the lure. Have you ever considered that nine of ten among those who went with De Soto and Balboa and Coronado and Cortez and Pizarro, if asked by some quiet neighbor, would have refused him the loan of one hundred dollars unless secured by fivefold the value? And yet the last man jack would peril life and fortune blindly in a voyage to worlds unknown, for profits guessed at, against dangers neither to be counted nor foreseen. Be not too much stricken of amazement, therefore, when now these cold ones, who would not have bought an American railroad without counting the cross-ties and weighing every spike and fish-plate, were ready to send millions adrift on a sightless invasion of Asia ten thousand miles away. Besides, as the five with Mr. Harley laid out their campaign, any question of Oriental danger was for the present put aside.

"The way to commence," said one of the five—one grown gray in first looting companies and then scuttling them—"the way to commence is by getting possession of Northern Consolidated. Once in control of the railroad, we have linked the Pacific with the Great Lakes; after that we can turn to the matter of subsidies for the two steamship lines, and the appointment of those commissions to consider the Canadian Canal." Then, turning to Mr. Harley: "You, of course, speak for Senator Hanway?"

Mr. Harley gave assurance that Senator Hanway, for what might be demanded congressionally, would be with him. Then they laid their plotting heads together over a conquest of Northern Consolidated.

Under the experienced counsel of the old gray scuttler of innocent companies, this procedure was resolved upon. Northern Consolidated was selling at forty-three. At that figure, over forty millions of dollars would be required to buy the road. There was little or no chance of its reaching a higher quotation during the coming ninety days; and ninety days would bring them into February with Congress in session over two months.

No, it was not the purpose of the pool to buy Northern Consolidated at forty-three; those gifted stock ospreys knew a better plan. They would begin with a "bear" movement against the stock. It was their belief, if the market were properly undermined, that Northern Consolidated could be sold down below twenty, possibly as low as fifteen. When it had reached lowest levels they would make their swoop. The pool would have enough profit from the "bear" movement to pay for the road. If they succeeded in selling Northern Consolidated off twenty points—and they believed, by going cautiously and intelligently to work, the feat was easy—the profits would equal the purchase sum required.

In "bearing" the stock and breaking it down to a point where the pool might seize upon the road without risk or outlay on its own intriguing part, the potent Senator Hanway would come in. At the beginning of Congress he must offer a Senate resolution for a special committee of three to investigate certain claims and charges against Northern Consolidated. That corporation had long owed the government, no one knew how much. It had stolen timber and stripped mountain ranges with its larcenies; also it had laid rapacious paw upon vast stretches of the public domain. It was within the power of any committee, acting honestly, to report Northern Consolidated as in default to the government for what number of millions its indignant imagination might fix upon. Who was to measure the road's lumber robberies, or those thefts of land? Moreover, the vandal aggressions of Northern Consolidated made a reason for rescinding divers public grants—the present values whereof were almost too high for estimation, and without which the road could not exist—that, in its inception as a railroad, had been made it by Congress.

Senator Hanway, under Senate courtesies, would be named chairman of the special committees. He would conduct the investigation and write the report. It was reasonable to assume, under the public as well as the private conditions named, that Senator Hanway's findings, and the Senate action he must urge and bring about, would knock the bottom out of Northern Consolidated. It must fall to twenty by every rule of speculation. Facing collection by the government of those claims for lands ravished and pine trees swept away, to say naught of losing original grants which were as its life-blood to Northern Consolidated, the value of the stock—to speak most hopefully in its favor—would be diminished by one-half.

The conspirators grew in confidence as they talked, and at the end looked upon Northern Consolidated as already in their talons. They named the old gray buccaneer to manage for the pool. The amount to be paid in by each of the eight members—for they counted Senator Hanway—was settled at five hundred thousand dollars. Four millions would be required to start the ball rolling; the "bear" movement in the beginning would demand margins. Once under headway, it would take care of itself. It would succeed like a barrel downhill.

Storri did not protest the suggestion of the old gray buccaneer that four millions be contributed to form a working capital for the pool. His share of a half-million meant fifty thousand more dollars than Storri at the time possessed, but he did not propose to have the others discover the fact. Somehow he would scrape together those fifty thousand; his note might do. Being, like every savage, a congenital gambler, Storri went into the pool with zest as well as confidence, and rejoiced in speculation that offered chances wide enough to employ his last dollar in the stake. Moreover, those four millions would not be asked for before the first of January. Other speculations might intervene, and provide those lacking fifty thousand.

Mr. Harley laid the Storri project, and the plans of the pool to seize Northern Consolidated, before Senator Hanway. That candidate for a Presidency knitted his brows and pondered the business. As with Mr. Harley and the pirate five, the mad grandeur of the idea charmed him. One element seemed plain: there could come no loss from the raid on Northern Consolidated. He might go that far with safety, and a certainty of profit; for in the Senate committee of investigation he, himself, would play the controlling card.

"The proposal," said Senator Hanway, when he and Mr. Harley conferred, "while gigantic in its unfoldment, seems a reasonable one. After all, it is the amount involved that staggers rather than what obstacles must be overcome. Taken piecemeal, I do not say that the entire scheme, even Credit Magellan, with its thirty billions, may not work through. The resolution naming a committee to look into the claims and charges against Northern Securities ought to help my Presidential canvass. It cannot avoid telling in my favor with thoughtful men. They will see that I am one who is jealously guarding public interests."

"And the resolution," suggested Mr. Harley, "appointing a commission for the Canadian Canal, and inviting the Ottawa government to do the same, ought also to speak in your favor. Consider what an impetus such a waterway would give our Northwestern commerce."

"Yes," replied Senator Hanway, "I think you are right. It will knock a third off freight rates on much of the trade between the oceans, and save heavily in time. Those subsidies, however, must go over until next session. Subsidies are not popular, and these must be left until after next November's elections. Then, of course, they may be safely taken up."

The various conferences over Storri's enterprise, and the consequent coming together of Storri and Mr. Harley, took place a few weeks prior to Richard's appearance in this chronicle. Both Storri and Mr. Harley were fond of stocks in their ups and downs, and now, being much together, they were in and out as partners in a dozen different deals. Mr. Harley attended to most of these; and Storri learned certain peculiarities belonging to that gentleman. Mr. Harley, for one solvent matter, was penurious to the point of dimes; also, Mr. Harley took no risks. Mr. Harley was willing to book a joint deal in both Storri's name and his own; or in his own for the common good of Storri and himself. But Mr. Harley would not give a joint order solely in Storri's name. Evidently, Mr. Harley would not trust Storri to divide profits with him where the case rested only upon that Russian's honor. No more would he draw his own check for Storri's margins; and one day our nobleman lost money because of Mr. Harley's cautious delicacy in that behalf. The market went the wrong way, and Storri could not be found when additional margins were called for. Whereupon Mr. Harley closed out his friend at a loss of seven thousand dollars.

Storri knitted his brows when he knew, but offered no comment. In fact, he treated the affair so lightly that Mr. Harley felt relieved; that latter speculator had been somewhat disturbed in his mind concerning Storri's opinion of what, to give it a best description, evinced niggard distrust of Storri, and cast in negative fashion a slur upon that gentleman.

Mr. Harley was too ready with his belief in Storri's indifference; that the latter, for all his surface stoicism, took a serious, not to say a revengeful, view of the business, found indication on a later painful day. The experience taught Storri that he might expect neither favor nor generosity from Mr. Harley; and this, considering how in all they must adventure in Credit Magellan Mr. Harley would have him in his power, filled Storri with an angry uneasiness. He decided that for his own security, if nothing more, he might better bestir himself to gain a counter-grip upon Mr. Harley. And thereupon Storri began to lie in ambush for Mr. Harley; and at a lurking, sprawling warfare that sets gins and dead-falls, and bases itself on surprise, your savage makes a formidable soldier.

Storri, wisely and without price, had one day aided a sugar company in securing Russian foothold in Odessa. That aid was ground-bait meant to lure the sugar favor. This sugar company made more profit on its stocks than on its sugar. It was in the habit, with one device or another, of sending the quotations of its shares up and down like an elevator. In requital of that Odessa good, the president of the sugar company, the week after, gave Storri a private hint to sell sugar stock. Storri responded by placing an order selling ten thousand shares.

Storri took no one into his confidence touching sugar. Going the other way, he urged Mr. Harley to buy on their mutual account two thousand shares, assuring him that he had been given word, from sources absolutely sure, of a coming "bull" movement in the stock.

Mr. Harley, who knew of that Odessa favor, believed. Storri, as further evidence of faith, gave Mr. Harley a check covering what initial margins would be required for his half of the purchase; and then to make all secure, he placed in Mr. Harley's hands two hundred shares of a French company worth that day fifteen thousand dollars.

"I don't want any argument to exist," laughed Storri, as he gave Mr. Harley the French securities, "for closing me out should a squall strike the market. Now I shall go to the club."

Mr. Harley also laughed, and took the French stock; acceptance always came easy with Mr. Harley.

Mr. Harley bought those two thousand sugar shares at eleven o'clock. Two hours later an extra was being cried about the streets. The sugar company had ordered half its refineries closed; some alleged loose screw in sugar trade was given as the reason.

With the order closing down the refineries, the stock began to tumble. Within thirty minutes it had slumped off six points. There came a call for further margins, and Mr. Harley offered Storri's French stock.

The security was undeniable, but a technicality got in the way to trip Mr. Harley. The French securities were original shares, issued in Storri's name. On the back, however, there was no Storri signature making the usual assignment in blank. The shares, in their present shape, would not be received. Mr. Harley flew to a nearby telephone and called up Storri.

"There is not time for me to get there!" cried that designing gentleman excitedly. He was a half-mile away. "Don't hesitate; clap my name on the backs of the certificates yourself. They don't know my signature; and no one will think of questioning it, coming through your hands."

There was no other way; thereupon Mr. Harley, in a ferment with tumbling prices, picked up a pen, and, with the best intentions in life, forged Storri's name. Then he hurried to the broker's and got up the margins.

It was not a squall, it was a storm, and sugar was broken off at the roots, falling twenty points. Storri, on his private deal, made two hundred thousand, while Messrs. Harley and Storri, on their joint account, lost forty thousand dollars—twenty thousand for each. In the clean-up, Storri paid his losses and got back his French shares. He smiled an evil smile as he contemplated Mr. Harley's attempts to mock his signature.

"He loses twenty thousand," commented Storri, "and that should more than offset those seven thousand lost by me when he refused to protect my deals. As for these," and here Storri ran a dark, exultant glance over his imitated signatures, "every one of them makes a reason why my good friend, Mr. Harley, must now please me and obey me in everything he does. After all, is it a destiny beneath his jowlish fat deserts, that an American pig should become slave to a Russian noble?"

CHAPTER VII

HOW RICHARD GAINED IN KNOWLEDGE

Congress came together at noon upon the first Monday in December, and obedient to the mandate of the caucus Mr. Frost was made Speaker Frost. The eruptive Mr. Hawke wore an injured air, and when the drawing for seats took place, selected one in a far back row, as though retiring from public life. Mr. Hawke subsequently refused to serve as chairman of the triangular committee named to notify the President that the House had convened, and his declination was accepted by Speaker Frost, who calmly filled the place with a member whom Mr. Hawke despised. Then the House swung into the channel, and went plowing ahead upon the business of the session, and in forty-eight hours, Mr. Hawke, forgotten, had ceased to be important to any save himself. The whole of that first Monday night Speaker Frost put in with Senator Hanway, in the latter's study, revising committee lists and settling chairmanships with the purpose of advancing the White House chances of Senator Hanway and destroying those of Governor Obstinate.

Although Congress had begun its session, no change was made in those morning calls of Richard, who came religiously at eleven to listen to Senator Hanway and look at Dorothy. The latter young lady was never absent from these interviews; she had conceived a wonderful interest in politics, and gave her "Uncle Pat" no peace. Richard's call commonly lasted but a half-hour, for Senator Hanway must be in the Senate chamber at noon. Thirty heavenly minutes they were; Dorothy and Richard promised and again promised undying love to one another with their eyes. Senator Hanway never suspected this love-making, never intercepted one soft glance; for your politician is like a horse wearing blinders, seeing only the road before him, thinking of nothing but himself. One morning after Senator Hanway had departed, Dorothy took Richard across to meet the blonde pythoness. Dorothy said she wanted Richard to see Bess. This was fiction; she wanted Bess to see Richard, of whom she was privily proud.

The Marklins lived across the street from the Harley house. Mother Marklin was an invalid and seldom out of her own room. Father Marklin was dead, and had been these five years. When the situation promoted her to be the head of the Marklin household, Bess had taken on a quiet, grave atmosphere of authority that was ten years older than her age.

The Marklins were fair rich. Father Marklin had been a physician whose patients were women of fashion; and that makes a practice wherein your doctor may know less medicine and make more money than in any other walk of drugs. A woman likes big bills from a physician if the malady be her own; she draws importance from the size of the bills. When one reflects that there is nothing to some women except their aches and their ailments, it all seems rational enough. These be dangerous digressions; one might better return to the drug-dealing parent of Bess, who visited the fair sufferers in a Brewster brougham and measured out his calls by minutes, watch in hand. He heaped up a fortune for Bess and her mother, and then at one and the same moment quit both his practice and the world.

When Dorothy came in with Richard, they found Bess entertaining a caller. The caller was a helpless person named Mr. Fopling.

"Mr. Storms, permit me to make you acquainted with Mr. Fopling," observed Bess, after Dorothy had presented Richard.

When Bess named Richard to Mr. Fopling, she did so with a master-of-ceremony flourish that was protecting and mannish. Richard grinned in friendship upon Mr. Fopling, who shook hands flabbily and seemed uncertain of his mental direction. Richard said nothing through fear of overwhelming Mr. Fopling. Mr. Fopling was equally silent through fear of overwhelming himself. Released from Richard, Mr. Fopling found refuge in the chair he had quitted, and maintained himself without sound or motion, bolt upright, staring straight ahead. Mr. Fopling had a vacant expression, and his face was not an advantageous face. It was round, pudgy, weak, with shadows of petulance about the mouth, and the forehead sloped away at an angle which house-builders, speaking of roofs, call a quarter-pitch. His chin, acting on the hint offered by the forehead, was likewise in full retreat. Altogether, one might have said of Mr. Fopling that if he were not a delightful, at worst he would never become a dangerous companion. Richard surveyed him with a deal of curiosity; then he questioned Dorothy with a glance.

"Bess is to marry him," whispered Dorothy.

"What for?" whispered Richard, off his guard. Then, pulling himself together in confusion: "Of course, he loves her, I dare say. Your friend Bess is a beautiful girl!"

Richard brought forth the last with hurried unction. It was a cunning remark to make; it drew Dorothy's attention off Mr. Fopling, whom she was preparing to defend with spirit, and centered it upon herself. At Richard's observation, so flattering to Bess, she tossed her head.

"Is she?" said Dorothy, with a falling inflection, vastly severe.

The two were near a window and quite alone, for Bess had stepped into the hall to give directions to a servant. Mr. Fopling sat the length of the room away, wrapped in meditation. Richard looked tenderly apologetic, and Dorothy, after sparkling for a jealous moment, softened to be in sympathy with Richard.

And the strange thing was that neither had ever said one word of love to the other. They had begun to love at sight, taking each other for granted, worshiping frankly, sweetly, with the candid, innocent informality of barbarians to whom the conventional was the unknown. After all, why not? Isn't word of eye as sacred as word of mouth?

Bess returned to them from the hall.

"I say, Bess!" bleated Mr. Fopling anxiously.

"In a moment, child!" returned Bess, in maternal tones.

Mr. Fopling relapsed, while Richard was amused. Some corner of Richard's amusement must have stuck out to attract the notice of Bess. She met it finely, undisturbed.

"Some day, Mr. Storms," beamed Bess, as though replying to a question, "I shall talk to you on marriage and husbands."

"Why not on marriage and wives?"

"Because I would not speak of the philosopher and the experiment, but of the experiment and the result. Marriage is a cause; the husband an effect. Husbands are artificial and made by marriage. Wives, like poets, are born, not made. I shall talk to you on marriage and husbands; I have some original ideas, I assure you."

"Now I can well believe that!" declared Richard, much tumbled about in his mind. Bess's harangue left him wondering whether she might not be possessed of a mild mania on wedlock and husbands.

"You need have no misgivings," returned Bess, as though reading his thoughts; "you will find me sane to the verge of commonplace."

Richard's stare was the mate to Mr. Fopling's; he could not decide just how to lay hold on the sibyl of the golden locks. Perceiving him wandering in his wits, Dorothy took him up warmly.

"Can't you see Bess is laughing at you?" she cried.

"You know her so much better than I," argued Richard, in extenuation of his dullness. "Some day I hope to be so well acquainted with Miss Marklin as to know when she laughs."

"You are to know her as well as I do," returned Dorothy, with decision, "for Bess is my dearest friend."

"And that, I'm sure," observed Richard, craftily measuring forth a two-edged compliment, "is the highest possible word that could be spoken of either."

At this speech Dorothy was visibly disarmed; whereat Richard congratulated himself.

"To be earnest with you, Mr. Storms," said Bess, with just a flash of teasing wickedness towards Dorothy, "I go about, even now, carrying the impression of knowing you extremely well. Dorothy reads me your letters from the *Daily Tory*; she has elevated literary tastes, you know. No, it is not what you write, it is the way you write it, that charms her; and, that I may the better appreciate, she obligingly accompanies her readings with remarks descriptive of the author."

"Bess, do you think that fair?" and Dorothy's face put on a reproachful red.

"At least it's true," returned Bess composedly.

That morning Richard had been flattered with a letter from the editor of a magazine, asking for a five-thousand word article on a leading personality of the Cabinet. This helped him bear the raillery of Bess; and the raillery, per incident, told him how much and deeply he was in the thoughts of Dorothy, which information made the world extremely beautiful. Richard had waited until his thirtieth year to begin to live! He was brought back from a dream of Dorothy by the unexpected projection of Mr. Fopling into the conversation.

"The *Daily Tory*!" repeated Mr. Fopling, in feeble disgust. "I hate newspapahs; they inflame the mawsses."

"Inflame what?" asked Richard.

"Inflame the mawsses! the common fellahs!"

Mr. Fopling was emphatic; and when Mr. Fopling was emphatic he squeaked. Mr. Fopling's father had been a beef contractor. Likewise he had seen trouble with investigating committees, being convicted of bad beef. This may or may not have had to do with the younger Fopling's aversion to the press.

"Certainly," coincided Bess, again assuming the maternal, "the newspapers are exceedingly inflammatory."

"Your friend Bess," said Richard to Dorothy, later, "is a bit of a blue-stocking, isn't she?—one of those girls who give themselves to the dangerous practice of thinking?"

"I love her from my heart!" returned Dorothy, with a splendid irrelevance wholly feminine; "she is a girl of gold!"

"Mr. Fopling: he's of gold, too, I take it."

"Mr. Fopling is very wealthy."

"Well, I'm glad he's something," observed Richard.

"You hate him because he spoke ill of newspapers," said Dorothy teasingly.

"Naturally, when a giant hand is stretched forth against the tree by which one lives, one's alarm runs away into hate," laughed Richard.

Richard, now that the *Daily Tory* letters were winning praise, that is to say, were being greatly applauded and condemned, began to have in them a mightier pride than ever. Educated those years abroad, he felt the want of an American knowledge, and started in to study government at pointblank range. Nights he read history, mostly political, and days he went about like a Diogenes without the lamp. He put himself in the way of Cabinet men; and talked with Senators and Representatives concerning congressional movements of the day.

Being quick, he made discoveries; some of them personal to himself. As correspondent of a New York daily, those Cabinet folk and men of Congress encountered him affably; when he was not present they spoke ferociously of him and his craft, as convicts curse a guard behind his back, and for much a convict's reason.

It was the same at the club without the affability. Present or absent, there they turned unsparing back upon him. Richard's status as a newspaper man had been explained and fixed, and they of the club liked him less than before. The Fopling feeling towards the press predominated at the club, and although Richard was never openly snubbed—his shoulders were too wide for that—besides, some sigh of those hand-grips with Storri had gone about—the feeling was manifest. This cool distance pleased Richard rather than otherwise, and he went often to the club to enjoy it. It was parcel of his affected cynicism to like an enemy.

When Richard came to Washington it is more than a chance that he was a patriot. But as he went about he saw much to blunt the sentiment. A statesman is one who helps his country; a politician is one who helps himself. Richard found shoals of the latter and none of the other class. One day he asked Speaker Frost, whom he met in Senator Hanway's study, his definition of a statesman.

"A statesman," said that epigrammatist, "is a dead politician."

Richard frequented House and Senate galleries; it was interesting to watch the notables transacting their fame. The debates were a cross-fire of deceit. Not a member gave his true reasons for the votes he cast; he gave what he wanted the world to think were his reasons. Finance was on the carpet in that hour, and bimetallism and monometallism, silver versus gold, were in everyone's mouth. Richard saw that the goldbugs hailed from money—lending constituencies, while the silverbugs were invariably from either money-borrowing constituencies or constituencies that had silver to sell. And every man legislated for his district and never for the country; which Richard regarded as an extremely narrow course. Every man talked of the people's interest; every man was thinking of his own interest and striving only to locate the butter on his political bread.

There was a third class, made up of those who were neither goldbugs nor silverbugs; they were straddlebugs, and, like the two sides of the shield, would be gold when looked at by one contingent and silver when viewed by the other. Senator Hanway, whose monk's face seemed to mark him as private secretary of the Genius of Patriotism, was an eminent straddlebug. He was thinking on those delegations that would make up the convention and choose a candidate for the Presidency. The prudent Senator Hanway would be in line with all opinions, and occupied both sides of the money question without becoming the open champion of either.

Not alone did Richard, gazing from the galleries, lose faith in the patriotism of House and Senate men, but he began to doubt the verity of their partisanship. Considering what they did, rather than what they said, he discovered that the true difference between the two great political parties was the difference between cat owls and horned owls, and lay mainly in the noises they made. When it came to deeds, both killed chickens, and both appeared equally ready to pillage the hen roosts of government. As for government—that is to say, the thing controlling and not the thing controlled: it was made up of the President, the Speaker, and a dozen more in Cabinet and Congress; and that was government.

The picture nourished Richard's failing of cynicism, and served to dull that edge of native patriotism which it was assumed he owned when first he came. He got an impression of government that left him nothing to fight and bleed and die for should the thick mutter of the war-drums call folk to the field. Good politics, as the term is practiced, means bad patriotism, and Washington was a nest of politics and nothing else besides. It made decisively a situation, so Richard was driven to conclude, wherein that man should be the best patriot who knew least of his own government; he should fight harder and suffer more cheerfully and die more blithely in its defense in exact proportion to his ignorance of whom and what he was fighting and suffering and dying for. It was a sullen conclusion surely; but, forced home upon Richard, it taught him a vitriolic harshness that, getting into his letters to flavor all he wrote, gave him national vogue, and added to that mixture of hatred and admiration with which official Washington was already beginning to regard him.

Neither did he escape forming certain estimates of Senator Hanway, and the white purity of what motives underlay his public career. For all that, Richard was quite as sedulous as ever to advance our statesman's fortunes; loyalty is abstract, love concrete, and in a last analysis Richard was thinking on Dorothy and not upon the country. Richard, you may have observed, was no whit better, no less selfish, than were those about him; and it is as well to know our faulty young gentleman for what he really was.

Richard not only considered the politics of men, but he studied men themselves. The narrowest of these came from parts of the country where region was important, and where you would have been more thought of for the deeds of your grandfather than for anything that you yourself might do. This was peculiarly true of men from New England, whose intelligence as well as interest seemed continually walking a tight-rope. The New Englander was always and ever the sublimation of a blind, ineffable vanity that went about proposing him as an example to the race. And so consciously self-perfect was he that, while coming to opinions touching others, generally to their disadvantage, he never once bethought him that others might be forming opinions of him. Another New England weakness was to believe in the measure more than in the man, and there was not one from that section who did not think that if you but introduced among negroes or Indians the New England town meeting, those negroes or Indians, thus blessed, would all and instantly become Yankees.

Another sublime provincial whom Richard uncovered was the Southern man. He, like the New Englander, was so busy thinking on and revering a past that was dead, that he owned little space for anything else. There was, however, one characteristic, common to Southern men, which was wanting in folk from other corners of the country. Richard never met a Southern man who remembered, assuming such to be his official station, that he was in Cabinet or Congress, while he never met a Northern or a Western or a New England man who for a moment forgot it.

This amiable democracy on the Southern part, like other good things, has its explanation. Your Southern man, like a squab pigeon, is biggest when he is born. The one first great fact of his nativity is an honor beyond any other which the world can confer. It is as though he were cradled on a peak; and thereafter, wherever his wanderings may take him, and whether into Congress, Cabinet, or White House, he travels always downhill. It is this to account for that benignant urbanity, the inevitable mark of a Southern man, which teaches him faith in you as corollary of completest confidence in himself. It is a beautiful, even though an unreasonable trait, and as such the admiration of Richard recorded it.

Those others, not Southern, educated to a notion of office as a pedestal, were inclined to play the turkey cock and spread their tails a trifle. Since that sort of self-conceit never fails to transact itself at the expense of the spectator, Richard looked upon it with no favor, and it drew from him opinions, not of compliment, concerning those by whom it was exhibited. It set him to comparisons which ran much in Southern favor.

After Congressmen and Cabinet men, Richard studied Washington itself. The common condition—speaking now of residents, and not of those who were mere sojourners within the city's walls—he found to be one of idleness, the common trait an insatiable bent for gossip. Government was the sole product of the place, the one grist ground at those mills. No one was made to labor more than six hours of the twenty-four. And the term labor meant no more than one-tenth its definition in any other town. Wherefore, even those most engaged of the citizenry had leisure to settle the world's most perplexing concerns, and they generously devoted it to that purpose.

Nor were they abashed by any insignificance of their personal estate. Familiarity does not breed contempt, it breeds conceit. Those who dwell close to the hub of government, even though they build departmental fires, sweep departmental floors, and empty departmental waste baskets, from nearness of contact and a daily perusal of your truly great, come at last to look upon themselves as beings of tremendous importance—and all after the self-gratulatory example of the thoughtful fly on the chariot wheel in the fable. The least of them beholds a picture of the government in every looking-glass into which he peers.

Storri talked with Mr. Harley; Mr. Harley talked with Senator Hanway. These conferences were of Credit Magellan; in particular they had concern with the overthrow of Northern Consolidated. Congress had been in session ten days when Senator Hanway, one morning, asked Richard to call that evening at nine.

"There is something which your paper should print," said Senator Hanway.

Richard was with Senator Hanway in the latter's study sharp upon the hour set. Dorothy was not there; her mother had carried her and the yellow-haired sorceress, Bess, to the theater. It is to be doubted, even if she were free, whether Dorothy's interest in her political studies would have carried her through a night session. Besides, the preoccupied Senator Hanway had begun to observe that Richard looked at Dorothy more than he listened to him, and while he suffered no disturbance by virtue of this discovery, the present was an occasion when he wanted Richard's undivided attention. Once seated, Senator Hanway went to the heart of the affair; he made himself clear, for years of debate had educated him to lucidity. What he desired was a plain, sequential rehearsal in the *Daily Tory* of those claims and charges against Northern Consolidated.

"Nor will I," observed Senator Hanway, flatteringly confidential, "conceal my reasons. In the first place the charges have been made, and their effect is to injure Northern Consolidated. You will not state that you know these charges to be true; you will say—if you will be so good—that they are of common report. Once in print, I can make them the basis of an investigation. I've no doubt—though you will please say nothing on that point—but what an investigation will disclose how groundless the charges are."

"You are an owner in Northern Consolidated?" asked Richard.

Richard felt no interest beyond a willingness to be of service to Senator Hanway, and only put the question to show attention to his eminent friend.

"No, no owner," replied Senator Hanway; "but to be frank, since I know my confidence is safe, it will assist me in a certain political matter the name of which I think you can guess."

Senator Hanway's smooth face wore a smile which he intended should prove that he looked upon Richard as one possessing a rightful as well as an intimate knowledge of those White House plans which he cherished. Richard did not require the assurance; he was ready without it to come to the aid of Senator Hanway, whom he liked if he did not revere.

The next evening Richard's letter carried the story against Northern Consolidated. The afternoon of the day on which it was published, Senator Hanway arose in his place and requested that the article be read by the clerk. That done, he said he was pained and surprised by the publication of such a story, and asked for a committee of three to look into the truth of what was set forth.

"For," observed Senator Hanway, after paying a tribute to Richard and the *Daily Tory*, in which he extolled the honesty and intelligent conservatism of both the paper and its correspondent, "for it is only justice that the charges be sifted. The *Daily Tory* does not make them on its own behalf; it finds them in the mouths of others. They should be taken up and weighed. If there be aught due the government, we have a right to know and measure it. If the charges are without support—and I have reason to believe that such is the situation—then Northern Consolidated is entitled to the refutation of a calumny that, whispered in some quarters and talked aloud in others, has borne heavily upon its interests."

No one opposed, and Senator Hanway, with Senators Price and Loot, were selected to be a special committee. They were to send for men and papers, be open or secret in their sessions, and report to the Senate whenever they finished the inquiry. The affair excited no comment, and was forgotten within the hour by all except Storri and Mr. Harley and those others of the osprey pool.

After Richard left Senator Hanway upon the Northern Consolidated evening, he ran plump upon an incident that was to have a last profound effect upon this history. No one not a prophet would have guessed this from the incident's character, for on its ignoble face it was nothing better than just a drunken clash between a Caucasian, and an African triumvirate that had locked horns with him in the street. The Caucasian, moved of liquor and pride of skin, had demanded the entire sidewalk. He enforced his demands by shoving the obstructing Africans into the gutter. The latter, recalling amendments to the organic law of the land favorable to folk of color, objected. In the war that ensued, owing to an inequality of forces, the Caucasian—albeit a gallant soul—was given the bitter side of the argument. Richard came upon them as he rounded a corner; the quartette at the time made a struggling, scrambling, cursing tangle, rolling about the sidewalk.

Being one in whom the race instinct ran powerfully, and who was not untainted of antipathies to red men and yellow men and black men and all men not wholly white, Richard did not pause to inquire the rights and the wrongs of the altercation. He seized upon the topmost person of color and pitched him into the street. Then he pitched another after him. The third, getting some alarming notions of what was going on, arose and fled. None of the three came back; for discretion is not absent from the African, and those whom Richard personally disposed of felt as might ones who had escaped from some malignant providence which they did not think it wise or fitting to further tempt. As for number three, he was pleased to find himself a block away, and did all he might to add to it, like a miser to his hoard.

Negroes gone, Richard set the white man on his feet, and asked him how he fared. That gentleman shook himself and announced that he was uninjured. Then he said that he was drunk, which was an unnecessary confidence. It developed that he followed the trade of printer; also that he had just come to town. He had no money, he had no place to sleep; and, what was wonderful to Richard, he appeared in no whit cast down by his bankrupt and bedless state. He had had money; but like many pleasant optimistic members of his mystery of types, he had preferred to spend it in liquor, leaving humdrum questions, such as bed and board, to solve themselves.

"For," said the bedless one, "I'm a tramp printer!" And he flung forth the adjective as though it were a title of respect.

Having invested some little exertion in the affairs of the stranger, Richard thought he might as well go forward and invest a little money. With that he went out of his way to lead the drunken one to a cheap hotel, where the porter took him in charge under contract to put him to bed. The consideration for the latter attention was a quarter paid in hand to the porter; with the proprietor Richard left ten dollars, and orders to give the devious one the change in the morning after deducting for his entertainment.

The rescued printer, clothed and in his right mind, called upon Richard the next afternoon to thank him for his generosity and say that his name was Sands. Mr. Sands, being sober and shaven, with clothes brushed, was in no sense a spectacle of shame. Indeed, there were worse-looking people passing laws for the nation. Richard was pleased, and said so.

"If I had a job, I'd go to work," said Mr. Sands, having had, as he expressed it, "his drunk out."

The habit of charity grows upon one like the liquor habit; moreover, if once you help a man, you ever after feel compelled to help him to the end of time. Richard was no exception to these philanthropic laws, and when Mr. Sands declared an eagerness to go to work, brought him to Senator Hanway, who promptly berthed him upon the Government printing office, where he was given a "case," and commenced tossing up types after the manner of a master.

If Senator Hanway had been able to probe the future, instead of setting Mr. Sands to work that December afternoon, he would have paid his way to London, had a trans-Atlantic trip been made the price of being rid of him. But a Senator is not a soothsayer, and no impression of the kind once touched him. He got Mr. Sands his billet, and said it gave him pleasure to comply with the request of his young friend, Mr. Storms. To Richard, the hereafter was as opaque as it was to Senator Hanway, and, having seen his protégé installed, he walked away unconscious of a morn to dawn when Mr. Sands would recur as an instance of that bread upon the waters which returns after many days.

CHAPTER VIII

HOW STORRI WOOED MRS. HANWAY-HARLEY

Storri was a sensualist to his fingers' ends. Being a sensualist, he was perforce an egotist, and the smallest of his desires became the star by which he laid his course. Through stress of appetites, as powerful as they were gross, he had grown sharp to calculate, and quick to see. He was controlled and hurried down by currents of a turbid selfishness; nor would he have stopped at any cruelty, balked at any crime, when prompted of what brute hungers kept his soul awake. He might have wept over failure, never from remorse. And Storri had set his savage heart on Dorothy.

Dorothy felt an aversion to Storri, and she could not have told you why. The mystery of it, however, put no question to her; she yielded with folded hands, passive to its influence. She did not hate Storri, she shrunk from him; his nearness chilled her like the nearness of a reptile. Kipling, the matchless, tells how a Russian does not become alarming until he tucks in his shirt, and insists upon himself as the most Eastern of Western peoples instead of the most Western of Eastern peoples. There is truth to sit at the bottom of this. Dorothy would have met Storri with indifference had that nobleman seen fit to catalogue himself, socially, as a Kalmuck Tartar, not of her strain and tribe; she was set a-shudder when made to meet him under conditions which admitted the propriety of marriage between them, should she and he agree. As it stood, Dorothy was alive for flight the moment Storri stepped into her presence; she knew by intuition the foulness of his fiber, and shivered at any threat of contact therewith.

Storri was aware of Dorothy's dislike, since aversion is the one sentiment a woman cannot conceal. The discovery only made him laugh. He was too much the conqueror of women to look for failure here. Should he, Storri, who had been sighed for by the fairest of a dozen stately courts, receive defeat from a little American? Bah! he would have her at his ease, win her at his pleasure! Dorothy's efforts to avoid him gave pursuit a piquancy!

While Storri noted Dorothy's distaste of him, he did not get slightest slant of her tender preference for Richard. As far as he might, Storri had taught himself contempt for Richard. This was not the simplest task; it is hard to despise one whom your heart fears, and before whose glance your own eyes waver and give way. Still, Storri got on with his contempt beyond what one might have imagined. He considered all Americans beneath him, and Richard was an American. There he had an advantage at the start. Also, Richard was of the newspapers. Even those Americans about him, with their own sneers and shoulder-shrugs, showed him how such folk were unworthy genteel countenance. They looked down upon Richard, Storri looked down upon them; the greater included the less, and deductions were easy. Storri arrived at a most happy contempt of Richard as a mathematician gets to the solution of a problem, and, being mercurial, not thoughtful, arranged with himself that Richard was below consideration.

Richard and Storri made no sign of social recognition when their paths crossed by chance. At such times the latter held an attitude of staring superiority—the fellow, perhaps, to that which belonged with Captain Cook when first he saw the Sandwich Islanders. Had Storri been of reflective turn he might have remembered that, as a gustatory finale, those serene islanders roasted the mariner, and made their dinner off him.

Mr. Harley was a busy man, and yet he had no office rooms. This was not his fault; he had once set out to establish himself with such a theater of effort, but Senator Hanway put down his foot.

"No; no office, John!" said that statesman.

Then Senator Hanway, who was as furtive as a mink, called Mr. Harley's attention to the explanation which a narrow world would give. Those office rooms would be pointed to as the market-place where corporations might trade for his, Senator Hanway's, services.

"If you please, we'll have no such argument going about," observed Senator Hanway.

This want of a business headquarters, while it may have been an inconvenience to Mr. Harley, now arose to dovetail with the desires of Storri. It gave him a pretext for calling at the Harley house; with Mr. Harley as excuse, and making a pretense of having business with him, he could break in at all manner of queer hours.

Storri made a study of the Harley household. About four of the afternoon it was Mrs. Hanway-Harley's habit to retire and refresh herself with a nap, against the demands of dinner and what social gayeties might follow. Mr. Harley, himself, was apt to be hovering about the Senate corridors. Or he would be holding pow-wow with men of importance, that is to say, money, at one of the hotels. Dorothy, who was not interested in dark-lantern legislation, and required no restoring naps, would be alone. Wherefore, it became the practice of Storri to appear of an afternoon at the Harley house, and ask for Mr. Harley. Not finding that business man, Storri, who did not insist that his errand was desperate, would idle an hour with Dorothy.

Storri thought himself one to fascinate a woman, and had a fine confidence in his powers to charm. He had studied conquest as an art. When he beleaguered a girl's heart, his first approaches were modeled on the free and jovial. During these afternoon calls he talked much, laughed loudly, and by his manner would have it that Dorothy and he were on cheeriest terms. Storri made no headway; Dorothy met his laughter with a cool reserve that baffled while it left him furious.

Storri essayed the sentimental, and came worn with homesickness. He was near to tears as he related the imaginary sickness of a mother whom he had invented for the purpose. Dorothy's cool reserve continued. She sympathized, conversationally, and hoped that Storri would hurry to his expiring parent's side.

Storri, like Richard, craved a rose and got it; but he fastened it upon his lapel himself.

On Storri's fourth call Bess Marklin came in. Being there, Bess took Storri to herself. She betrayed a surprising interest in statistics—the populations of cities, crops, politics, and every other form of European what-not—and kept Storri answering questions like a school-boy. Thereafter, Storri was no sooner in the Harley house when, presto! from over the way our pythoness sweeps in. Bess was there before the servant had taken Storri's hat. This disturbing fortune depressed him; he attributed it to ill luck, never once observing that the instant he appeared, Dorothy's black maid skipped across to summon Bess.

"Really, Bess," pleaded Dorothy, following Storri's fourth call—she had gone to the Marklins' just after her admirer left—"really, Bess, if you love me, rescue me. There was never such a bore! Positively, the creature will send me to my grave! And, besides,"—with a little shiver,—"I have a horror of the man!"

And so the good Bess came each time, and faithfully refused to budge for the whole of Storri's visit. With that, the latter saw less and less reason to confer with Mr. Harley of an afternoon; also he resolved upon a change of tactics in his siege of Dorothy.

Thus far Storri had failed, and the failure set him on fire. The savage in him was stirred. His vanity found itself defied; and the onyx eyes would burn, and the mustaches twist like snakes, as he reflected on how he had been foiled and put aside. Had he known that Richard was in Dorothy's thought, that it was he to hold her heart against him, Storri would have choked. But he had gathered no such knowledge; nor was he posted as to those morning love trysts at which Senator Hanway unconsciously presided.

Storri still visited the Harley house, but his visits were now to Mrs. Hanway-Harley. And he would pour compliments for that shallow lady, which said compliments our shallow one drank in like water from the well. Mrs. Hanway-Harley had never known a more finished gentleman; and so she told her friends.

"It is a pity," cried Storri one day, "that Europe has none such as yourself to set examples of refinement! Now if your beautiful daughter would but make some nobleman happy as his wife! You would come to Europe, no?" and Storri spread his hands in rapture over so much possible good fortune. "Yes, if your lovely daughter would but condescend!" Storri paused, and sighed a sigh of power.

Mrs. Hanway-Harley thought this exceeding fine; the treacle of coarse compliment sweetened it to her lips. Some would have laughed at such fustian. Mrs. Hanway-Harley was none of these; the compliment she laughed at must emanate from someone not a Count. None the less, she could see that something was at the back of it all. There was Storri's sigh as though a heart had broken. Had Storri made some soft advance, and had Dorothy repulsed him? Mrs. Hanway-Harley could have shaken the girl!

Storri read all this in Mrs. Hanway-Harley's face as though it had been written upon paper. He saw that the mother would be his ally; Mrs. Hanway-Harley was ready to enlist upon his side. Thereupon, Storri drew himself together with dignity.

"In my own land, madam," said Storri, conveying the impression of a limitless deference for Mrs. Hanway-Harley, "it is not permitted that a gentleman pay his addresses to the daughter until he has her mother's consent. I adore your daughter—who could help!—but I cannot tell her unless you approve. And so, madam," with a deepest of bows, "I, who am a Russian gentleman, come to you."

Mrs. Hanway-Harley was not so sinuously adroit as her brother, Senator Hanway, but she was capable of every conventional art. If Storri's declaration stirred her pride, she never showed it; if her soul exulted at a title in her family and a probable presentation of herself to royalty, she concealed it. True, she was inclined to tilt her nose a vulgar bit; but she did not let Storri perceive it, reserving the nose-tilting for ladies of her acquaintance, when the betrothal of Dorothy and Storri should be announced. Indeed, her conduct, on the honorable occasion of Storri's request, could not have been more graceful nor more guarded. She said that she was honored by Storri's proposal, and touched by his delicacy in first coming to her. She could do no more, however, than grant him the permission craved, and secure to him her best wishes.

"For, much as I love my daughter," explained Mrs. Hanway-Harley, mounting a maternal pedestal and posing, "I could not think of coercing her choice. She will marry where she loves." A sigh at this period. "I can only say that, should she love where you desire, it cannot fail to engage my full approval."

Storri pressed his lips to Mrs. Hanway-Harley's hand as well as he could for the interfering crust of diamonds, and said she had made him happy.

"It will be bliss, madam, to call myself your daughter's husband," said Storri; "but it will be highest honor to find myself your son."

Storri did not tell Mrs. Hanway-Harley of those afternoon calls, and the blight of Bess to fall upon them with her eternal crops and politics and populations. Mrs. Hanway-Harley, while she grievously suspected from Storri's sigh—which little whisper of despair still sounded in her ears—that he had met reverses, would not voice her surmise. She would treat the affair as commencing with Storri's request. But she would watch Dorothy; and if she detected symptoms of failure to appreciate Storri as a nobleman possessing wealth and station,—in short, if Dorothy betrayed an intention to refuse his exalted hand,—then she, Mrs. Hanway-Harley, would interfere. She would take Dorothy in solemn charge, and compel that obtuse maiden to what redounded to her good. Mrs. Hanway-Harley doubted neither the propriety nor the feasibility of establishing a censorship over Dorothy's heart, should the young lady evince a blinded inability to see her own welfare.

"That is what a mother is for," she ruminated.

Mrs. Hanway-Harley had forcibly administered paregoric in Dorothy's babyhood; she was ready to forcibly administer a husband now Dorothy was grown up. The cases were in precise parallel, and never the ray of distrust entered Mrs. Hanway-Harley's mind. Dorothy was not to escape good fortune merely because, through some perversity of girlish ignorance, she might choose to waive it aside.

Mrs. Hanway-Harley had Mr. Harley ask Storri to dinner on an average twice a week; she made these slender banquets wholly informal, and quite as though Storri were an intimate family friend. Storri commended the absence of stilts, this abandonment of the conventional.

"It is what I like!" cried he; "it is the compliment I shall most speak of when I am back with my Czar."

Following dinner, Mrs. Hanway-Harley would have Storri to the library in engagingly familiar fashion.

Senator Hanway went always to his study after dinner, to receive visitors through that veranda door, and prune and train the vine of his Presidential hopes with confabs and new plans, into which he and those visitors—who were folk of power in their home States—unreservedly plunged. Mr. Harley, who was not domestic and feared nothing so much as an evening at home, would give an excuse more or less feeble and go abroad into the town. This left Mrs. Hanway-Harley, Dorothy, and Storri to themselves; and the maternal ally saw to it that the noble lover was granted a chance to press his suit. That is to say, Mrs. Hanway-Harley gave Storri a chance so far as lay in her accommodating power; for she developed an inexhaustible roll of reasons for leaving the room, and in her kind sagacity never failed to stay away at least five minutes. And a world and all of love may be made in five minutes, when both parties set their hearts and souls to the dulcet enterprise.

Storri was ardent, and Mrs. Hanway-Harley was discreet, and both displayed talents for intrigue and execution that, on other days, in other fields, might well have saved a state. And yet there was no blushing progress to the love-making! Dorothy's behavior was unaccountable. The first evening she sat in marble silence, like an image. The next, she would not come down to dinner, saying she was sick and could not eat. The invalid put in a most successful evening in her room, thinking of Richard, and gorging on miscellaneous dishes which her sable maid abstracted from below. She would have been ill the third time, but her mother set her face like flint against such excuse. Mrs. Hanway-Harley declared that Dorothy's desertion was disgraceful at a moment when she, her mother, needed her help to entertain their visitor. With that, Dorothy's indisposition yielded, and she so far recovered as to play her part at table with commendable spirit, eating quite as much as her mother, who was no one to dine like a bird. But Dorothy took her revenge; she talked of nothing but Richard, and the conversations on politics which he and "Uncle Pat" indulged in during those eleven-o'clock calls.

Storri glowered; more, he became aware of Richard as the daily comrade of Dorothy. Mrs. Hanway-Harley herself was struck by some shadow of the truth; but she got no more than what Scotchmen call a "glisk," and she gave the matter no sufficient weight. Later, she clothed it with more importance.

Mrs. Hanway-Harley, however, was moved to reprove Dorothy from out the wealth of her experiences.

"Child," said she, when Storri was gone, "you should never try to entertain one gentleman by telling him about another; it only makes him furious."

"I didn't, mamma," said Dorothy, her eyes innocently round.

"You did, only you failed to notice it," returned Mrs. Hanway-Harley. "After this, be more upon your guard."

"I will, mamma," replied Dorothy demurely; but she was too sly to say against what she should guard.

On the next Storri evening, Dorothy returned to the old ruse. She set a lamp in her chamber window, the effect of the beacon being that Bess came across from her house, as the clock scored eight and one-half, and joined the Harley party. It was nothing out of common for Bess to do this; she and Dorothy had been bosom friends since days when the two wore their hair in pigtails and their frocks to their knees. Bess came not only that evening, but every Storri evening; and whether or no she were a welcome, at least she was a pertinacious visitor, for she stayed unrelentingly until Storri, losing courage, went his way.

Storri bit his angry lip over Bess, for he now began to read the argument of her advent. It was Dorothy's defense against him, and in its kind an insult. Mrs. Hanway-Harley also became more and more instructed in this love-match so near her heart, and those difficulties which the capricious coldness of Dorothy arranged for its discouragement. The placidity of Mrs. Hanway-Harley was becoming ruffled; the hour was drawing on apace when she would make clear her position. She would issue those commands which were to fix the attitude of Dorothy towards the sighing Storri and his love.

Dorothy called Bess her guardian angel. The G. A. accepted the position and its duties with that admirable composure which you have already observed was among her characteristics. The fair Bess was one of those whom their friends, without intending offense, describe as mildly eccentric. That is to say, Bess had peculiarities which were in part native and in part the work of an environment. She was an only child, and that was bad; she was a doctor's child, and that was worse. Not that her father had been so recklessly dense as to try his drugs on her; he knew too much for that. But your doctor's children oft get an unusual bringing up, and the chances in favor of the extraordinary in that behalf are doubled where there is only one child.

Mother Marklin had been an invalid from the babyhood of Bess. Father Marklin, in those intervals when his brougham was not racing from one languid, dyspeptic, dance-tired, dinner-weary, rout-exhausted woman to another at ten dollars a drooping head, looked after Bess in that spirit of argus-eyed solicitude with which a government looks after its crown jewels. Bess was herded, not to say hived, and her childish days were days of captivity. She was prisoner to her father's loving apprehensions, he being afraid to have her out of sight.

Then came her father's death, and the Marklin household devolved upon Bess's hands when the hands were new and small and weak; and the load served to emphasize Bess in divers ways. When not waiting upon the invalid Mother Marklin, Bess broke into her father's bookshelves, and read the owlish authors such as Bacon and Dr. Johnson, with side-flights into Montaigne, Voltaire, Amiel, and others of hectic kidney. She discovered, moreover, a sympathy with those women of strong minds who have a quarrel with Providence for that they were not made men. Bess believed in the equality of the sexes, without pausing to ask in what they were unequal, and stood stoutly for the Rights of Woman, knowing not wherein She was wronged or in what manner and to what extent She had been given the worst of life's bargain. Bess was not a blue-stocking, as Richard would have had it, and made no literary pretenses; but she suffered from opinions concerning topics such as husband and wife, that so far had had nothing better than theory to rest upon. All the same, her friends were deeply satisfied with Bess; which helped that young lady to a sense of satisfaction with herself and with them.

As head of the Marklins, Bess was made to decide things for herself. At that, she decided in favor of nothing terrifying. She drank tea between three and six each afternoon; she kept a cat named Ajax; and she resolved to marry Mr. Fopling.

The latter young gentleman Bess called to her side when she pleased, dismissed when he wearied her, and in all respects controlled his conclusions, his conversations, and his whereabouts, as Heaven meant she should. Bess preferred that Mr. Fopling call during the afternoon; she required the morning for her household duties, and, when not screening Dorothy from Storri, saved the evening for her books.

Ajax was a grave and formal cat, and, in his way, a personage. He was decorous to a degree, unbended in no confidences with strangers, and hated Mr. Fopling, whom he regarded as either a graceless profligate or a domestic animal of unsettled species who, through no merit and by rank favoritism, had been granted a place in the household superior to his own. At sight of Mr. Fopling, Ajax would bottle-brush his tail, arch his back, and explode into that ejaculation peculiar to cats. Mr. Fopling feared Ajax, holding him to be rabid and not knowing when he would do those rending deeds of tooth and claw upon him, of which the ejaculation, the arched back, and the bottle-brush were signs and portents.

It was the afternoon of the day following one of those Harley dinners whereat Storri had been the sole and honored guest, and Bess was sipping her tea. Her two favorites, Ajax and Mr. Fopling, were sitting in their respective chairs, regarding each other with their usual suspicion and distrust. Mr. Fopling, by command of Bess and so far as he might control himself, was paying no attention to Ajax. Ajax, for his part, was surveying Mr. Fopling with a sour stare, as though he found much in that young gentleman's appearance to criticise. At intervals, he made growling comments upon Mr. Fopling.

"Unless you and Ajax can agree," observed Bess soberly, "one or the other might better go into the library."

Mr. Fopling made no demur; he was glad to go. When he was out of the room, Ajax came and rubbed about his mistress as though claiming credit for ousting Mr. Fopling, of whom he was certain Bess thought as badly as did he.

Bess was sitting where she commanded a prospect of the street. Who should come swinging up the way but Richard? It was the habit of that rising journalist to make one or two daily excursions past the Harley house. Richard was none of your moon-mad ones who would strum a midnight lute beneath a fair maid's window. Still, he liked to walk by the Harley house; the temporary nearness of Dorothy did his soul good. Besides, he now and then caught a glimpse of her through the window.

Richard was on the Marklin side of the street, and as he was for going by—back to Bess and eyes on the Harley house—Bess rapped on the pane and beckoned him.

Richard lifted his hat and obeyed directly. He had already met Bess several times when Dorothy and he, with a purpose to spin out their eleven-o'clock interview, had seized on Bess as a method. They could not remain staring at one another in Senator Hanway's study; even that preoccupied publicist would have been struck by the strangeness of such a maneuver. The best, because the only, thing was to make a pretext of Bess and transfer their love-glances to her premises. This was the earliest time, however, that Richard had been asked to visit Bess alone, and he confessed to a feeling of curiosity, as he climbed the steps, concerning the purpose of the summons.

Bess some time before had had that threatened talk with Richard concerning marriage and husbands.

"Wedlock," declared Bess, on that edifying occasion, while Richard grinned and Dorothy rebuked him with a frown, "wedlock results always in the owner and the owned—a slave and a despot. That is by the wife's decree. The husband is slave and she despot, or he the despot and she the slave, as best matches with her strength or weakness. Some women desire slavery; they would be unhappy without a tyrant to obey."

"And you—are you of those?" asked Richard, half mocking Bess.

"No; I prefer the rôle of despot. It is the reason why I shall marry Mr. Fopling."

"And yet Mr. Fopling might turn out a perfect Caligula," said Richard, with a vast pretense of warning. Mr. Fopling was not there to hear himself ill-used.

"Mr. Fopling," observed Bess, in tones of lofty conviction, "has no ambitions, no energies, no thoughts; and he has money. In brief, he is beset by none of those causes that excite and drive men into politics or literature or trade. He will have nothing to consider in his life but me."

"But," said Richard, "Mr. Fopling might turn out in the end a veritable Vesuvius. Mr. Fopling has often struck me as volcanic; who shall say that he will not some day erupt?"

Bess was not to be frightened.

"Mr. Fopling will do and say and think as I direct; and we shall be very, very happy."

Richard gave Dorothy a comical look of simulated dismay; and shook his head as though counseling against such heresies.

"Of course," Bess continued, "what I propose for Mr. Fopling would not do for you. Were you and I to marry"—Dorothy started—"it would result in civil war. I've no doubt that you will be given a wife worthy your tyrannical deserts. She will find her happiness in sitting at your feet, while her love will make you its trellis to climb and clamber on."

The conversation was not so foolishly serious as it sounds, and for the most part Bess and Richard were indulging in just no more than so much verbal sparring. Dorothy took no side; those questions of marriages and wives and husbands would ever find her tongue-tied if Richard were around.

"Will you have some tea?" asked Bess, when Richard, in response to the rapped window, made his way into her presence.

No, Richard would not have tea.

"Then you may smoke," said Bess. "That proves me your friend, doesn't it?" as Richard started a grateful cloud. "Now, to repay my friendship, I want to ask a question and a favor."

"You shall!" cried Richard magniloquently. Bess and he were on amiable terms, and he was secretly assured that the blonde pythoness approved him. "What am I to answer? What am I to do? Has the cherished Fopling gone astray? Say but the word, and I shall hale him to your feet."

"Mr. Fopling is in the library," replied Bess. "He and Ajax could not get along without quarreling, and I separated them. The question and the favor refer to Dorothy."

Richard colored.

"What is the question?" said he, his voice turning deep and soft.

"Do you love her?" This staggered Richard. Bess came to his aid. "I know you do," said she; "I'll answer the query for you. The real question I wanted to ask is, Have you told her? And that I'll answer: You have not."

"What does this lead to?" broke in Richard. A half-score of daunting surmises had come up to shake him.

"Don't you think you might better tell her?" continued Bess, not heeding the question.

"She knows," returned Richard, drawing a breath. "Dorothy knows. I've seen the knowledge in her eyes. And she loves me!"

"I've no doubt you've seen marvelous things in one another's eyes," retorted Bess in a matter-of-fact way; "but I say again: Wouldn't it be wise to tell her?"

"Frankly, yes," replied Richard, driven desperate. "I have been on the threshold of it, but somehow I couldn't lay hands on just the words. Dorothy knows I love her!" he repeated as though to himself. "It would be only a formality."

"There is the very point," observed Bess. "It is the formality that has become important. Do you think I would break in upon your dreams, else? A formality is a fence. If you owned a bed of flowers, would you build a fence about it? Then fence in your Dorothy with a formal offer of your love."

"I shall not rest until I've done so!" cried Richard, catching fire.

"And then you will have done the wise and safe and just and loving thing! Who taught you to ignore formalities? They are one's evidence of title. Build your fence. It will be like saying to Storri: So far shalt thou come and no farther."

Bess looked curiously at Richard. She had mentioned Storri in a mood of mischief, as one spurs a gamesome horse to stir its mettle. Richard's brow was a thundercloud.

"Why do you name Storri with Dorothy?—a serpent and a dove!" he said, in tones very slow and full.

"Dorothy will tell you," replied Bess. "She will turn marvelously loquacious, once she finds herself behind her fence."

"How shall I go to her?" exclaimed Richard. "My heart will be sick until I've told her."

"You will not have long to wait," said Bess laughingly. "She should have been here ten minutes ago. I can't see what detains her."

Richard looked bewildered and a little shocked. "Surely," he began, "Dorothy didn't——"

"No, no; you are not the victim of a plot, Sir Suspicious One!" cried Bess. "It is a wonder that you are not, for your dullness surpasses belief. Do you imagine Dorothy doesn't see you every time you walk this street? that she hasn't seen you to-day? that she didn't see you come in? that she won't invent some pretext for running over? Oh, foolish, foolish bridegroom! You may guess how foolish by peeping from the window, for here your Dorothy comes."

At this, the benignant Bess, having questioned, advised, admonished, and, in a measure, berated Richard, gave him her hand, as if she would give him courage; and Richard, with the praiseworthy purpose of getting all the courage he could, lifted it to his lips. That was the blasting tableau at the moment Dorothy stood in the door.

"Oh!" cried Dorothy. Then her brow crimsoned, and her eyes began to shine like angry stars.

CHAPTER IX

HOW STORRI MADE AN OFFER OF HIS LOVE

At the brow of red and those angry eyes like stars, Bess smiled superior, in beaming toleration and affection. Bess could afford these benevolences, being now engaged in that most delightful of all Christian tasks to a woman, viz., superintending the love-romance of another woman. She swept sweetly down on Dorothy; and even Richard, albeit full to blindness of his own great passion, could not help but see that she was as graceful as a goddess.

Bess placed a hand on each of Dorothy's shoulders, and kissed her brow where the angry red, already in doubt as to the propriety of its presence, was trying to steal away unnoticed.

"What have I done?" said Bess, as though repeating a query put by Dorothy. "Now I no more than found a wanderer, who loves you almost as dearly as you love him, and who would not see the way to go straight to you with his offer of a heart. He was for traveling miles and miles around, no one knows how many, by all kinds of hesitating roads. I stopped him and pointed cross-lots to you. That is my whole offense; and when you arrived, the wanderer, in a spirit of gratitude I entirely commend, was very properly mumbling over my hands."

Bess drew Dorothy into the room.

"There!" cried she, "I have done my utmost best for both. I shall now look after Mr. Fopling. Poor child, he has already been neglected too long!"

Bess, departing, left behind her two young people wondrously embarrassed. Richard had been plunged into a most craven condition; while Dorothy, head drooping like a flower gone to sleep, the flush creeping from her brow to her cheek, began to cry gently. Two large, round, woeful tears came slowly into the corners of her eyes, paused a moment as though to survey the world, and then ran timidly down, one on each side of her nose.

At this piteous sight, Richard became a hero. Being an extremist in all things, Richard, roused, caught Dorothy to his bosom—the first embrace since that blessed boot-heel evening in the Waldorf! He folded her in those Pict arms in most radical fashion, and kissed her—they were like unto glimpses of heaven, those kisses!—kissed her eyes, and her hair, and at last her lips, measuring one kiss from another with words of rapturous endearment, of which "heart's love" and "darling" were the most prudently cool. Richard refused to free Dorothy from out his arms, not that she struggled bitterly, and continued for full ten minutes in the utmost bliss and incoherency.

At these unexpected pictures of Paradise before the Fall, Ajax, sole spectator, felt profound dismay. He bottle-brushed and arched and exploded; and then, the wretched exhibition continuing, fled.

At last Richard listened to Dorothy, and released her to an armchair; he took another, fastened his eyes upon her like visual leeches, and drank her in.

"Who so blooming, who so lovely, who so glorious as Dorothy?" thought Richard, on whom her beauty grew with ever-increasing witchery, like a deep, clear night of stars.

And yet, the dough-like Fopling, at that moment in the library with Bess, would have fought Richard to the death on a simple issue that Bess was Dorothy's beauteous superior; which, so far from proving that love is blind, shows it to have the eyes of Argus.

Richard and Dorothy said a thousand loving things, and meant them; they made a thousand loving compacts, and kept them all.

Suddenly Richard burst forth as though a momentous and usual ceremony had been overlooked.

"Oh, ho!" cried he, "you haven't asked how I am to support a wife."

"And do you suppose I have been thinking of that?" returned Dorothy, beginning to bridle. "For that matter, I know you are poor."

"And how did you dig that up?"

"Dig!" This with the utmost resentment, as though repelling a slander. "Why, you told mamma and me yourself. It was the day she was rude and asked if Mr. Gwynn would make you his heir."

"Surely," said Richard, grinning cheerfully, as if a puzzle had been made plain, "so I did."

"Sweetheart, I loved you from that moment!" cried Dorothy; and with a half-sob to be company for the caress, she drifted about Richard's neck.

"Now I should call poverty worth while!" said Richard, manfully kissing Dorothy all over again, since she had come within his clutch. Then, replacing her in her chair, the more readily because he reflected that he might easily repossess himself of her, he continued: "And the prospect of being a poor man's wife does not alarm you, darling?"

"Oh, Richard!" Then, looking him squarely in the eyes: "No, dear, it does not alarm me."

Dorothy spoke truth. The prospect of being a poor man's wife alarms no woman—before marriage.

Richard was in a whirl when he left the Marklin door. Bess fairly drove him forth, or he might not have departed at all. The first shadows of night were falling, but the whole world seemed bright as noonday. He was stricken of vague surprise to observe a man running by him, torch in hand, lighting the street lamps. Controlling his astonishment, Richard greeted the man as though they were old friends. They were not old friends, and the effect of Richard's greeting was to lead the man of lamps to think him drunk.

"Got his load early!" quoth the one of lamps. He tippled himself, and was versed in cup proprieties, which forbade drunkenness prior to ten o'clock.

Richard continued down the street. It was as if he were translated, and had quitted earth to walk the clouds. And to think that not two hours before he had come swinging along this identical thoroughfare, never dreaming of the heaven of those loving arms into which he was walking! Blessed be Bess! He should never forget that sorceress, who to his weakness added her strength, and to his ignorance her wisdom. It was such an extraordinary thing, now that Richard had time to think of it, that Dorothy should love him! And more amazing that she should press her cheek to his and tell him of it! Oh, he could still feel that round, warm, velvet cheek against his own! It was such joy to remember, too, that it was merely the beginning of an eternity of those soft endearments! it remade the world; and all things, even those most week-a-day and commonplace, came upon him in colors so new and strange and rich and sweet—touched as they were with this transforming light of Dorothy's love! Richard plowed through the winter evening in a most ridiculous frame of mind, midway between transports and imbecility.

"You will see me to-morrow?" pleaded Dorothy, as he came away.

Whereat Richard averred doughtily that he should.

Neither of the two having the practical wit to settle hour or place, Bess, who the moment before had returned to them from Mr. Fopling with intelligence coolly unimpaired, said:

"Four o'clock, then; and, if I may make a suggestion, you might better meet here."

It was among the miracles how the high beatitude consequent upon that wonderful event of Dorothy's love put Richard in a vaguely belligerent mood. It was an amiable ferocity at that, and showed in nothing more dire than just an eye of overt challenge to all the world. Also, he dilated and swelled in sheer masculine pride of himself, and no longer walked the streets, but stalked. Naturalists will not be surprised by these revelations, having observed kindred phenomena in the males among other species of animals.

In this lofty spirit, and by a fashion of instinct, Richard headed for the club. At the club, by the best of fortune, as he would have said in his then temper, he located Storri; and thereupon he bent upon said patrician such an iron stare of confident insolence that the object of it was appreciably worried, turning white, then red, then white, and in the finish leaving the room, unable to sustain himself in the face of so much triumph and truculence.

In the midst of this splendor of the soul, and just as Richard had begun to feel a catholic pity for all mankind to think not one beyond himself was loved by Dorothy, a message was thrust between his fingers. It ran thus:

R. STORMS,

Washington, D. C.

What's the matter? Where is your letter to-night?

Daily Tory.

It was like a cupful of cold water, souse! in Richard's face; it brought him back to earth. In his successful bright estate of love he had forgotten about that letter. There was no help for it; Richard got pen and blank, and wired:

Daily Tory,

New York City.

Mr. Storms is ill; no letter to-night.

L. GWYNN.

When this was thirty minutes on its way, Richard had a further lucid interval. With the power of prophecy upon him, he dispatched the following:

Daily Tory,

New York City.

Mr. Storms will be ill a week.

L. GWYNN.

It gave Richard a pang to put aside those engaging letters, even for a week. Under the circumstances, however, and with a promise to see Dorothy the next day at four, and a purpose to see her every day at four if she permitted him, he deemed it prudent to send the second message. Besides, should his reason return before the week's end, he could recover from that illness and take up the letters again.

Being something sobered now, Richard lighted a cigar and strolled off through a fall of snow that had set in, thinking on Dorothy. Arriving at his home, he sat an hour in rose-colored reveries. He dived at last into the bronze casket, and brought out the little boot-heel which was the beginning of all First Causes.

"If I could but find the cheating bungler," thought Richard, "who slighted that little shoe in making, I'd pile fortune upon him for the balance of his life. And to think I owe my Dorothy to the cobbling scoundrel!"

At three o'clock, with the soft fingers of the snow drumming drowsily against the pane, Richard went to sleep and dreamed of angels, all of whom were blue-eyed replicas of Dorothy.

Richard, still in a glorified trance, was up betimes. Mr. Pickwick, who came to fawn upon him, the same being his doggish custom of a morning, found Richard tolerant but abstracted. Hurt by a lack of notice, Mr. Pickwick retired, and Matzai brought in breakfast. Richard could not avoid a feeling of distrustful contempt for himself when he discovered that he ate like a hod-carrier. It seemed treason to Dorothy to harbor so rude an appetite.

While Richard had laid aside those *Daily Tory* letters for a week, he would still call on Senator Hanway at eleven. He considered what an exquisite thrill would go over him as he sat gazing on Dorothy—that new and beautiful possession of his heart!

Rather to Richard's dismay, Dorothy was not with them that morning in Senator Hanway's study. Had her love of politics gone cooling? Senator Hanway was there, however, and uppermost in his mind was something that would again require countenance of the Anaconda Airline.

It was the subtile policy of Senator Hanway, in his move towards a Presidency, to seem to be standing still. His attitude was feminine; the nomination must abduct him; he must be dragged to the altar and wedded into the White House by force. In short, Senator Hanway was for giving the country a noble exhibition of the office seeking the man.

This attitude of holding delicately aloof did not prevent him in the privacy of his study—out of which no secrets escaped—from unbuckling confidentially with ones who, like Richard, were close about his counsel board. It was not that he required that young journalist's advice; but he needed his help, and so gave him his confidence because he couldn't avoid it.

Richard wore the honors of these confidences easily. Scores of times, Senator Hanway had gone into the detail of his arrangements to trap delegates, wherefore it bred no surprise in him when, upon this morning, that statesman took up the question of an Anaconda influence, and the extent to which it might be exercised. Senator Hanway showed Richard a list of fourteen States, all subject to the Anaconda's system of roads.

"In my opinion," said Senator Hanway, "the Anaconda could select the national delegations in these States. There is no doubt that the fourteen, acting together,—for the list includes three of the largest States in the country,—would decide the nomination. The query is, Would Mr. Gwynn be so amiably disposed as to move in the affair? I may say that I should not prove insensible to so great a favor."

"Mr. Gwynn," returned Richard, "has repeatedly instructed me that you were to regard the Anaconda as yours, and the *Daily Tory* as yours, for everything that either or both of them can do in your interest. It will not be necessary to see him unless you prefer an interview."

Senator Hanway never preferred an interview with anybody, where that formality was not demanded by the situation. He held to the doctrine that no one, not a fool, would talk beyond what was necessary to carry his projects to success. His present word to Richard, however, did not include this belief. He put it in this fashion:

"I do not feel at liberty," said he, "to disturb Mr. Gwynn with what are no more than just my personal concerns. He has much more weighty matters of his own to consider; and he ought not to be loaded down with those of other men. Besides, in this instance, his magnificent generosity has anticipated me. He tells you that I am to have the assistance of the Anaconda?"

"In what form and to what extent you choose," returned Richard. "He even said that, should you be set to head your party's ticket, the campaign might count upon the Anaconda for a contribution of no less than a half-million."

Senator Hanway's pale face flushed, not with gratitude, but exultation.

"I cannot tell you," said he, "which affects me most; Mr. Gwynn's immense kindness or his even greater condescension."

Then getting to things practical, Senator Hanway asked Richard if the President and General Attorney of the Anaconda might not again be brought to Washington.

"They shall come," replied Richard confidently. "You have only to fix the date."

"Any time between the second and tenth of January," suggested Senator Hanway. And that was settled.

Richard, not so much because of an interest,—if truth were told his thoughts went running away to Dorothy, and must be continually yanked back by the ear to topics common and earthly,—but for the sake of something to say, asked Senator Hanway about the committee of three selected to investigate Northern Consolidated.

"You know, the business came up because of my letters in the *Daily Tory*," observed Richard, by way of excuse for his curiosity.

The investigation was progressing slowly. It was secret; no part of the evidence could be given out. It would not join with senatorial propriety to let anything be known for publication.

"In a semi-judicial inquiry of this sort," explained Senator Hanway, in tones of patronizing dignity, "one of your discernment will recognize the impropriety, as well as the absolute injustice, of foreshadowing in any degree the finding of the committee. For yourself, however, I don't mind saying that the evidence, so far, is all in favor of Northern Consolidated. The company will emerge with a clean bill of health—clean as a whistle! The committee's finding," concluded Senator Hanway musingly, "will be like a new coat of paint to the road. It should help it immensely—help the stock; for these charges have hung over Northern Consolidated values like a shadow."

"And when should the committee report?" queried Richard.

"Those things come along very leisurely; the report ought to be public, I should think, about the middle of February. We may give it to the road for a valentine," and Senator Hanway smiled in congratulation of himself for something light and fluffy, something to mark in him a pliancy of sentiment.

Senator Hanway—such is the weakness of the really great—had his vanity as well as Richard, and would have been pleased had folk thought him of a fancy that, on occasion, could break away from those more sodden commodities of politics and law-building. Cæsar and Napoleon were both unhappy until they had written books, and Alexander cared more for Aristotle's good opinion than for conquest.

Just when Richard, who had been expecting with every moment his Dorothy to come rustling in, was beginning to despair, Dorothy's black maid appeared, and, under pretense of asking Senator Hanway on behalf of his devoted niece whether or no said niece might count on his escort to the White House reception New Year's Day, craftily slipped Richard a note.

"Why, she knows she may!"

Senator Hanway was somewhat astonished at Dorothy's forethoughtfulness; the more since the reception was a week and more away.

"Miss Dory wants to have Miss Bess, from 'cross d' street, go 'long," vouchsafed the maid.

"Oh, that's it!" said Senator Hanway, who mistook this for an explanation.

Richard was on nettles to get at Dorothy's note. Anxiety sharpened his faculties, and he took from his pocket a clipping, being indeed a *Daily Tory* editorial wherein was set forth what should be a proper tariff policy, and gravely besought Senator Hanway for his views thereon. While that statesman was donning glasses and running over the excerpt, Richard made furtive shift to read his note from Dorothy. It said:

DEAR:

I am with Bess. Something awful has happened. Don't wait a moment, but come. D.

Senator Hanway was not a little amazed when, just as he found himself midstream in those tariff studies to which Richard had invited him, that volatile individual arose in the utmost excitement and said that he must go.

"The truth is," said Richard, blundering about for the explanation which the questioning eye of Senator Hanway appeared to ask, "I forgot a matter of Mr. Gwynn's."

Senator Hanway waved his satisfied hand in a manner that meant "Say no more!" Senator Hanway did not doubt that the business was important. Any business of Mr. Gwynn's must be important. The sheer fact that it was Mr. Gwynn's business made it important. It bordered dangerously upon the criminal that Richard should have neglected it. The state of affairs described accounted most satisfactorily for Richard's breathless haste. Senator Hanway, when he recalled the assurance of Mr. Harley, made with bated breath but the evening before, that Mr. Gwynn's income was over twelve hundred thousand dollars a month, sympathized with Richard's zeal. Under similar circumstances, Senator Hanway's excitement would have mounted as high. It is such a privilege to serve the very rich!

Richard found Dorothy in that apartment which was but yesterday the theater of his great happiness. She was alone; for Bess must play the housewife, and was at that moment addressing a slattern maid upon the sin of dust in some far-off, lofty corridor of the premises. Richard swept Dorothy with a gray glance like a flashlight. Her face was troubled, but full of fortitude, and she was very white about the mouth. At sight of Richard, however, Dorothy's fortitude gave way, and went whirling down-stream in a tempest of tears and sobs. With her poor hands outstretched as if for protection, she felt her way blindly into the shelter of those arms; and Richard drew her close and closer, holding her to his heart as though she were a child. He asked no question, said no word, sure only as granite that, whatever the trouble, it should not take her from him. These rock-founded natures, self-reliant, world-defying, made all of love and iron, are a mighty comfort to weak ones; and so thought Dorothy as she lay crying in Richard's embrace.

And now, since you have seen Dorothy safe across the harbor-bar of her griefs, and she lies landlocked in the sure haven of the Pict arms, you might cross the way for a space, and learn what abode at the foot of all this disturbance of true lovers.

It was while Richard was closeted with Senator Hanway that the storm broke. Mrs. Hanway-Harley, after reflection, had decided to speak to her daughter upon the subject of Storri and that noble Russian's suit. To this end, Mrs. Hanway-Harley called Dorothy into a little parlor which opened off her bedchamber. It was that particular apartment where Mrs. Hanway-Harley took her naps, and afterward donned war-paint and feathers wherewith to burst upon society.

Dorothy came reluctantly, haunted with a forebode of impending griefs. The room was a fashion of torture chamber to Dorothy. Mrs. Hanway-Harley had summoned her to this room for admonition and reproach and punishment since ever she was ten years of age. Wherefore, there was little in her mother's call to engage Dorothy pleasantly; and she hung back, and answered slowly, with soles of lead.

When Dorothy at last came in, Mrs. Hanway-Harley lost no time in skirmishing, but at once opened the main battle.

"My child," said she, with a look that she meant should be ineffably affectionate, and which was not, "Count Storri has been talking of you."

"Yes?" queried Dorothy, with sinking heart, but making a gallant effort at childish innocence.

Mrs. Hanway-Harley lost patience. She observed and resented the childish innocence, rebuking it smartly.

"Rub that baby look out of your face, instantly! You are not a child!"

Dorothy stiffened like a grenadier. She remembered Richard; her mother was right; she was not a child, she was a woman, and so the world should find her. Dorothy's eyes began to gleam dangerously, and if Mrs. Hanway-Harley had owned any gift to read faces, she might have hesitated at this pinch.

"What would you have?" said Dorothy, and her tones were as brittle and as devoid of sentimental softness as Mrs. Hanway-Harley's.

"Marriage."

"Marriage with Storri?"

"Dorothy," said Mrs. Hanway-Harley with a sigh, softly returning to the lines she had originally laid out, "Count Storri, in the most delicate way, like the gentleman and nobleman he is, has asked for your hand."

Mrs. Hanway-Harley had read something like this in a magazine, and now reeled it off with tender majesty. When she spoke of Storri she had quite the empress air.

"For my hand!" said Dorothy, beginning to pant.

Mrs. Hanway-Harley looked up; there was a hardness in Dorothy's tone that was not only new, but unpleasant. Down deep in her nature, Dorothy hid those stubborn traits that distinguished her religious ancestor of the gate-post and the water-pan.

"For your hand," repeated Mrs. Hanway-Harley uneasily.

Dorothy making no return, Mrs. Hanway-Harley, after waiting a moment, gave herself to a recount of those glowing advantages promised by such a marriage. Was a nobleman, wealthy, young, handsome, on terms of comradeship with his Czar, to be refused? Half the women in Washington were wild for such an offer. It would place the Harleys on a footing by themselves.

"But I don't love him!" urged Dorothy, as though that had to do with the question.

At this foolishly unfortunate objection, Mrs. Hanway-Harley was rendered speechless. Then, as notice of Dorothy's white, cold obstinacy began to dawn upon her, she went suddenly into lamentations. To think her child, her only child, should deal her such a blow! Mrs. Hanway-Harley called herself the most ill-treated of parents. She said her best and dearest feelings had been trampled upon. In a shower of tears, and a cataract of complaint, she bemoaned her dark, ungrateful destiny. At this, Dorothy's tears began to flow, and the interview became hysterical.

Mrs. Hanway-Harley was the earlier to recover her balance. Drying her eyes, she said:

"Disobedient child!"—this was also from the magazine—"since you will not listen to the voice of love, since you will not listen to the voice of reason, you shall listen to the voice of command."

Then, striking a pose that was almost tragic, Mrs. Hanway-Harley told Dorothy she *must* marry Storri.

"As your mother, I command it!" said Mrs. Hanway-Harley, lifting her jeweled hand finely, as though the thing were settled and the conference at an end.

"And I tell you," said Dorothy, catching her breath and speaking with bitter slowness, "that I shall not marry him!"

"This to me!—your mother!—in my own house!"

"You shall not drive me!" cried Dorothy passionately, her eyes roving savagely, like the eyes of a badgered animal. "Am I to have no voice in disposal of myself? I tell you I shall marry whom I please! And since he makes his proffer through you, tell the creature Storri that I loathe him!"

"Have a care, child!"

This last was also from the magazine, and Mrs. Hanway-Harley got it off superbly. It missed fire, so far as Dorothy was concerned—Dorothy, strung like a bow, and now in full rebellion.

"It is you to have a care!" retorted Dorothy. "Papa and Uncle Pat shall hear of this!"

"They will say as I say!" observed Mrs. Hanway-Harley, who believed it.

"And if they should," cried Dorothy, "I have still a resource!"

"Flight?" said Mrs. Hanway-Harley, not without contempt.

"Marriage!" replied Dorothy, now as dry of eye as she was defiant. Bess Marklin was assuredly right in her estimate of formalities, and their saving and securing worth.

"Marriage!" repeated Dorothy, and her voice rang out in a composite note of love and triumph as she thought of Richard.

"Marriage!" Mrs. Hanway-Harley was staggered. Here was a pathway of escape she had not counted on. "Whom would you marry?"

"You shall not know," said Dorothy.

Mrs. Hanway-Harley saw truth in Dorothy's red cheek—she had been snow till now—saw it in her swimming eye and heaving bosom. Before she could phrase further question Dorothy had left the room, and Mrs. Hanway-Harley was beaten.

Somewhere in the unknown dark behind Dorothy's stubborn will stood a man; and that man loved Dorothy. She would draw on his love and his loyalty and his courage to make her war! Mrs. Hanway-Harley felt her defeat, and sighed to think how she had walked upon it blindfold. But she was not without military fairness; she must make her report.

Mrs. Hanway-Harley wrote Storri a note, saying that, for reasons not to be overcome, the honor of his hand must be denied her house. While Mrs. Hanway-Harley was writing Storri, Dorothy the baited was writing her note to Richard. And now you know why Dorothy sobbed her troubled, hunted, harassed way into Richard's arms.

After ten minutes of love and peace, Dorothy was so much renewed that, word for word, she gave Richard the entire story.

"What shall I do?" said Dorothy at the close. "Tell me, dear, what am I to do?"

"You are in no danger," said Richard, in a manner of grim tenderness, and folding her tight. "Before I'd see you marry Storri, I would kill him in the church—kill him at the altar rail!"

"You must not kill him!" whispered Dorothy, at once horrified and flattered.

"There's no chance," said Richard, with a quaver of comic regret. "Our civilization has so narrowed the times that murder is inexpressibly inconvenient. One thing I might do, however."

"What is that?"

"I might carry you off."

"Oh, that would never do!" said Dorothy, as, with a great sigh, she crept more and more into Richard's arms, thinking all the time it would do, and do nicely.

CHAPTER X

HOW STORRI PLOTTED A VENGEANCE

Richard asked Dorothy if she had told Bess. No, Dorothy had not told Bess.

"Do you think, dear heart, I would tell anyone before I had told you?"

As the most fitting reply to this question, Richard kissed Dorothy all over again as though for the first time, and with a fervor that told how his soul was in the work.

Bess was called in as a consulting engineer of hearts. That blonde tactician glanced over the situation with the eye of a field-marshal. This was the result of her survey. There must be no clandestine marriage, no elopement. Dorothy was in no peril; it was not a drawbridge day of moated castlewicks and donjon keeps. Damsels were no longer gagged and bound and carried to the altar, and there wedded perforce to dreadful ogres. Wherefore, a runaway match was not necessary. Moreover, it would be vulgar; and nothing could justify vulgarity. Dorothy and Richard should remain as they were. They must continue to love; they must learn to wait, and to take what advantage the flow of events provided.

"My wisdom," quoth Bess, pausing as if for congratulations, "my wisdom is, doubtless, so much beyond my years as to seem unearthly. It's due to the fact that, although young, I've been for long the responsible head of a family."

Bess mentioned this latter dignified condition with complacency. It left her exempt from those troubles, like a bramble patch, into which Dorothy was plunged.

Both Dorothy and Richard were inclined to agree with their monitress. Richard was too wholly of the battle-ax breed to favor stealth and creeping about. It was in his heart to marry Dorothy defiantly, and at noon. Dorothy's reasons were less robust; she was thinking on her father and "Uncle Pat," and all their kindnesses. She could not make up her loyal heart to any step that smacked of treachery to them.

"And yet," observed Richard, "here we are where we started." Then turning to Bess: "You have told us what we should not do, and told us extremely well. Now bend your sage brows to the question of what we ought to do. Or, to phrase it this fashion, What ought I to do?"

"Go to Mrs. Hanway-Harley and ask for her daughter."

Richard winced and made a wry face.

"I'd sooner go to Storri. The rascal might give me a reason for thrashing him."

"You are on no account to mention Dorothy's name to Storri."

"No?" somewhat ruefully.

"And you are to beat him only should he mention Dorothy's name to you."

"I shall;" and Richard brightened.

"Storri asked Mrs. Hanway-Harley for her daughter. I should think you might summon up an equal courage."

"But I haven't the advantage of being a Russian nobleman," returned Richard, with one of his cynical grins.

"Still you must ask Mrs. Hanway-Harley for Dorothy; and no later, mind you, than to-morrow night." Bess tossed her head as though a fiat had gone forth.

"Well," said Richard, drawing a deep breath, "if you have any such junk as a Joss about the house, I'd take it friendly if you would burn a handful of prayer-sticks in my interest." Then, with all love's softness, to Dorothy: "Your mother will say No; she will not entertain your views on poverty, little one."

Dorothy came behind Richard's chair and pressed her cheek to his.

"Whatever she may say, whatever anyone may say, you, and only you, dearest, shall have me," and Dorothy signed the promise after the fashion popular with lovers.

Storri came that evening to see Mrs. Hanway-Harley. Both parties were acting, Storri affecting melancholy while he was on fire with passionate rage, and Mrs. Hanway-Harley assuming the rôle of the mother who, although she regrets, is still tenderly unwilling to control those wrongly headstrong courses upon which her child is bent. There was a world of polite fencing between Mrs. Hanway-Harley and Storri, in which each bore testimony to the esteem in which the other was held. It was decided that Storri should continue those dinners with the Harleys; Dorothy might discover a final wisdom.

Storri told Mrs. Hanway-Harley that he feared Dorothy had given her heart to Richard. This admission was gall and wormwood to the self-love of Storri. He made it, however, and recalled Mrs. Hanway-Harley to Dorothy's chatter concerning the morning talks between Richard and Senator Hanway.

"That odious printer," said Storri, who called all newspaper people printers, "comes each day to get his budget of news from your illustrious brother, madam; and, believe me, your daughter makes some sly pretext for being with them—with him, the odious printer! Bah! I wish we were in Russia; I would blow out the rogue's life like a candle! Why, my Czar would laugh were so mean a being to succeed in obstructing the love of his Storri!"

Mrs. Hanway-Harley was struck by the suggestion that Richard was Dorothy's lover in the dark. She remembered Dorothy's teasing praises of Richard, and her talk of how sapiently he discoursed with "Uncle Pat." The praises occurred on that evening when, from her wisdom, she, Mrs. Hanway-Harley, had warned her innocent child against the error of entertaining one gentleman with the merits of another. Mrs. Hanway-Harley even brought to mind the replies made by her innocent child to those warnings; and her own wrath began to stir as the suspicion grew that her innocent child had been secretly laughing at her. Like all shallow folk, Mrs. Hanway-Harley prided herself upon being as deep as the sea, and it did her self-esteem no good to think that she had been sounded, not to say charted, by her own daughter, who had gone steering in and out, keeping always the channel of her credulity, and never once running aground. Little lamps of anger lighted their evil wicks in Mrs. Hanway-Harley's eyes as she thus reflected.

And that morning armful of roses? No, Storri was not the moving cause of their fragrant appearance upon the Harley premises. Storri regretted that he had not once bethought him of this delicate attention. Mrs. Hanway-Harley wrung her hands. It was Dorothy who first planted in her the belief that the flowers were from Storri. Oh, the artful jade! That was the cause of her timorous objections when Mrs. Hanway-Harley, with the fond yet honorable curiosity of a mother, spoke of mentioning those flowers to Storri. The perjured Dorothy was aware of their felon origin; doubtless, she even then encouraged the miserable Richard in his love.

As these lights burst one after the other upon Mrs. Hanway-Harley, she could have punished her own dullness by beating her head against the wall. However, she restrained herself, and closed by inviting Storri to dinner on the next day but one. Storri, still keeping up his tender melancholy, thanked Mrs. Hanway-Harley, accepted, and with many bows, and many sighs to impress upon Mrs. Hanway-Harley his stricken heart, backed himself out into the night.

When Storri was gone, Mrs. Hanway-Harley resolved on an instant talk with Dorothy—no more the innocent, but the artful one. She would make a last attempt to wring from her the name of that lover of the shadows.

Should it be Richard—and she was sure of it—that aspiring journalist must never again cross the Harley threshold.

Mrs. Hanway-Harley, who had the merit of expedition, repaired at once to Dorothy's room. That obdurate beauty was half undressed, and her maid had just finished arranging her hair in two raven braids—thick as a ship's cable, they were. As Mrs. Hanway-Harley entered, Dorothy glanced up with half-wistful eye. Poor child! she was hoping her mother might have softened from that granite attitude of the morning! But no, there was nothing tender in the selfish, austere gaze; at that, the spirit of the old astronomical ancestor who, with his water-pans and gate-posts, knew the earth was flat, began to chafe within Dorothy's girlish bosom.

Mrs. Hanway-Harley came to a dignified halt in the middle of the room.

"Cora, you may go," said Mrs. Hanway-Harley.

The black maid gave a parting touch to the braids, in which she contrived to mingle sympathy and affection, for with the wisdom of her caste she knew of Dorothy's love and gave it her approval.

"Dorothy," said Mrs. Hanway-Harley, when they were alone, and speaking in a high, superior vein, "I have come for the name of that man."

"Mr. Storms," returned Dorothy, in tones which for steadiness matched Mrs. Hanway-Harley's.

It was not the name so much as the relentless frankness that furnished it, which overcame Mrs. Hanway-Harley. She sat down with an emphasis so sudden that it was as though her knees were glass and the blow had broken them. Once in the chair, she waggled her head dolorously, and moaned out against upstart vulgarians who, without a name or a shilling, insinuated themselves like vipers into households of honor, and, coiling themselves upon the very hearthstones, dealt death to fondest hopes.

Dorothy, who, for all the selfish shallowness of that relative, loved her mother, tried to take her hand. At a shadow of sympathy she would have laid before Mrs. Hanway-Harley the last secret her bosom hid. There was no sympathy, nothing of mother's love; Mrs. Hanway-Harley, in the narrowness of her egotism, could consider no feelings not her own.

"Don't; don't touch me!" she cried. "Don't add hypocrisy to your ingratitude!" Then, in tones that seemed to pillory Dorothy as reprobate and lost, she cried: "You have disgraced me—disgraced your father, your uncle, and me!"

"Another word," cried Dorothy, moving with a resentful swoop towards the bell, "and I'll call Uncle Pat to judge between us! Yes; he is in his study. Uncle Pat shall hear you!"

Mrs. Hanway-Harley, glass knees and all, got between Dorothy and the bell. Dorothy's uncle and Dorothy's father should know; but not then. She had hoped that with reason she might rescue her daughter from a step so fatal as marriage with a hopeless beggar who could not live without the charity of his patron. These things and much more spake Mrs. Hanway-Harley; but she might as well have remonstrated with a storm. The gate-post grandsire had charge of Dorothy.

"And what is to be the end of this intrigue?" asked Mrs. Hanway-Harley.

"It is no more an intrigue," protested Dorothy, her eyes flashing, "than was your marriage to papa, or the marriage of Aunt Dorothy with Uncle Pat. Oh, mamma," she cried appealingly, "can't you see we love each other!"

Mrs. Hanway-Harley was a trifle touched, but it was her maternal duty to conceal it. She steadied herself to a severe sobriety, and, with the manner of one injured to the verge of martyrdom, said with a sigh:

"I shall see this person; I shall send for this Mr. Storms."

"It will be unnecessary," replied Dorothy, turning frigid; "Mr. Storms will call upon you to-morrow night."

"And does the puppy think that I'll give my consent?" demanded Mrs. Hanway-Harley, angrily aghast at the insolence of Richard.

"Now I don't know what the 'puppy' thinks," returned Dorothy, from whom the anger of her mother struck sympathetic sparks, "but I told him I would marry him without it."

In a whirl of indignation, Mrs. Hanway-Harley burst in upon Senator Hanway. That ambitious gentleman was employed in abstruse calculations as to tariff schedules, and how far they might be expected to bear upon his chances in the coming National Convention. Senator Hanway was somewhat impressed by Mrs. Hanway-Harley's visit; his study had never been that lady's favorite lounge. Moreover, her face proclaimed her errand no common one.

"Why, I thought you were all in bed, Barbara," said Senator Hanway, by way of opening conversation.

Mrs. Hanway-Harley, as calmly as she might, told of Dorothy's "mad infatuation." She held back nothing except what portions of the tangle referred to Storri. That nobleman's proposals she did not touch on. She spoke of Richard, and the disaster, not to say the disgrace, to the Harley name should he and Dorothy wed. Mrs. Hanway-Harley flowed on, sometimes eloquent, always severe, and closed in with a thunder-gust of tears.

Senator Hanway listened, first with wonder, then alarm; when she finished he sat with an air of helplessness. After rubbing his nose irresolutely with a pen-holder, he said:

"What can I do?"

"You can advise me."

"Well, then," observed Senator Hanway, looking right and left, being no one to face an angry woman, "why don't you let them marry?"

"Brother!"

Mrs. Hanway-Harley strove to bury Senator Hanway beneath a mountain of reproach with that one word.

"What can you do?" asked Senator Hanway defensively. "You say that Dorothy declares she will marry young Storms in the teeth of every opposition."

"Are we to permit the foolish girl to throw herself away?"

"But how will you restrain her?"

"One thing," exclaimed Mrs. Hanway-Harley, getting up to go; "that person, after to-morrow, shall never enter these doors! I shall have but one word; I shall warn him not to repeat his visits to this house."

The change that came over Senator Hanway struck Mrs. Hanway-Harley with dumb dismay. His eye, which had been prying about for an easiest way out of the dilemma, now filled with threatening interest.

"Barbara, sit down!" commanded Senator Hanway.

Mrs. Hanway-Harley sat down; she was, with the last word, in awe of her eminent brother. Senator Hanway arose and towered above her with forbidding brow. The threat to bar the Harley doors to Richard had set him agog with angry apprehensions. What! should his best agent of politics, one who was at once the correspondent of that powerful influence the *Daily Tory* and the authorized mouthpiece of the potential Mr. Gwynn who owned the Anaconda, nay, was the Anaconda, be insulted, and arrayed against him? And for what? Because of the baby heart of a girl scarce grown! Was a White House to be lost by such tawdry argument? Forbidding Richard the door might of itself appear a meager matter, but who was to say what results might not spring from it? Senator Hanway had seen the gravest catastrophies grow from reasons small as mustard seed! A city is burned, and the conflagration has its start in a cow and a candle! Mrs. Hanway-Harley shall not put his hopes to jeopardy in squabbles over Dorothy and her truant love. Senator Hanway felt the hot anxiety of one who, bearing a priceless vase through the streets, is jostled by the inconsiderate crowd. Domestic politics and national politics had come to a clash.

Senator Hanway stood staring at Mrs. Hanway-Harley. He required time to gather control of himself and lay out a verbal line of march. He decided for the lucid, icy style; it was his favorite manner in the Senate.

"Barbara," said he, "give careful ear to what I shall say. I do not request, I do not command, I tell you what *must* be done. I do not interfere between you and Dorothy; I interfere only between you and Mr. Storms. That young man is necessary to my plans. He is to come to this study, freely and without interference. Nor are you, on any occasion, or for any cause, to affront him or treat him otherwise than with respect."

"But, brother," urged Mrs. Hanway-Harley, "he has trapped Dorothy into a promise of marriage."

"Why do you object to him?"

"He has no fortune; the man's a beggar!"

"He has his money from the *Daily Tory*, say five thousand a year. That is as much as I am paid for being Senator."

"There is no parallel! Your salary may be five thousand; but you make twenty-fold that sum," which was quite true.

"Barbara," remarked Senator Hanway reprovingly, returning to the original bone of dispute, "why should you insist on this young man owning millions before he can think of Dorothy? You had nothing, John had nothing, when you married. You should remember these things."

Mrs. Hanway-Harley refused to remember. There was no reason why she should. Dorothy was the present issue; and Dorothy was—or would be—rich.

"I won't go into the business any further," retorted Senator Hanway at last, with a gesture of irritation and disgust. "I simply tell you that Mr. Storms is neither to be affronted nor driven away. Should you disregard my wishes, Barbara, I say to you plainly that I myself will bring the young people together, send for a preacher, and marry them in this very study. I am not to lose a Presidency because you choose to play the fool."

Mrs. Hanway-Harley, illustrious in all her diamonds, upon the next evening received Richard in vast state. She proposed to impress him with her splendors. Dorothy, in anticipation of the meeting between mother and lover, had gone across to Bess; her nervousness must have support.

Richard, whose diplomacy was barbaric and proceeded on straight lines, told Mrs. Hanway-Harley of his love for Dorothy. As his handsome face lighted up, even Mrs. Hanway-Harley was not unswept of admiration. She could look into Richard's eyes, and see for herself those gray beauties of tenderness and truth that had won Dorothy to his side. They might have won even Mrs. Hanway-Harley had she not been a mother. What if he were tender, what if he were true? He had no fortune, no place; even the Admirable Crichton, wanting social station and the riches whereon to base it, would have been impossible.

When Richard had ended his love-tale—which, considering that for all his outward fortitude he was inwardly quaking, he told full eloquently—Mrs. Hanway-Harley composed herself for reply. She hardly required those warnings of Senator Hanway; there was no wish now to insult or humble him. In truth, Mrs. Hanway-Harley was in the best possible temper to carry forward her side of the conference in manner most creditable to herself and most helpful for her purposes. More than ever, since she had heard him, she knew the perilous sway this man must own over her daughter. While he talked, the deep, true tones were like a spell; the great, tender, persistent will of a man in loving earnest seemed as with a thousand soft, resistless hands to draw her whither it would. Even she, Mrs. Hanway-Harley, selfish, guarded, worldly, cold, was shaken and all but conquered beneath the natural hypnotic power of the male when speaking, thinking, feeling, moving from the heart. Oh, she would warrant her daughter loved this wizard! She, herself, was driven to fence against his pleadings to keep from granting all he asked. But fence she did; Mrs. Hanway-Harley remembered that she was a mother, an American mother whose daughter had been asked in wedlock by a Count. She must protect that daughter from the wizard who would only love to blight.

Mrs. Hanway-Harley never spoke to more advantage. She did not doubt Mr. Storms's honesty, she did not distrust his love; but woman could not live by love alone, and she had her duty as a mother. Dorothy had been lapped in luxury; it was neither right nor safe that her daughter should marry downhill. Mrs. Hanway-Harley's voice was smoothly even. Mr. Storms must forgive a question. Something of the kind had been asked before, but changes might have intervened. Had Mr. Storms any expectations from Mr. Gwynn?

"Madam," replied Richard, while a queer smile played about his mouth, a smile whereof the reason was by no means clear to Mrs. Hanway-Harley, "madam, I shall be wholly honest. Living or dead, gift or will, I shall never have a shilling from Mr. Gwynn."

"Then, Mr. Storms," returned Mrs. Hanway-Harley, "I ask you whether I would be justified in wedding my daughter to poverty?"

"But is money, that is, much money, so important?" pleaded Richard. "I have education, health, brains—in moderation—and love to prompt all three. That should not mean beggary, even though it may not mean prodigious wealth."

"Every lover has talked the same," said Mrs. Hanway-Harley, not unkindly. "Believe me, Mr. Storms: no man should ask a woman in marriage unless he can care for her as she was cared for in her father's house."

"But the father's fortune is not sure," remonstrated Richard. "The father's riches, or the lover's poverty, may vanish in a night."

"We must deal with the present," said Mrs. Hanway-Harley.

Richard pondered the several perplexities of the case.

"If I had a fortune equal to Mr. Harley's, you would not object, madam?"

"It is the only bar I urge," said Mrs. Hanway-Harley suavely.

"Then I am to understand that, should a day come when I can measure wealth with Mr. Harley, I may claim Dorothy as my own?"

Mrs. Hanway-Harley bowed.

"My daughter, however, must not be bound by any promise."

"Your daughter, madam," returned Richard, with a color of pride, "shall never be bound by me. Though I held a score of promises, I would have no wife who did not come to me of her free choice. I do not look on love as a business proposition."

"Older people do," responded Mrs. Hanway-Harley dryly.

"Madam," said Richard, "I have only one more question to ask. What is to be my attitude towards your daughter, while I am searching for that fortune?"

It was here that Mrs. Hanway-Harley made her greatest stroke; she reached Richard where he had no defense.

"Your attitude, Mr. Storms, towards my daughter, I shall leave to you for adjustment as a man of honor."

Richard crossed the street to Dorothy and told her what had passed. Dorothy kissed him, and cried over him, and made a wail against their darkling fate.

"How I wish papa was poor!" cried Dorothy. "I wish he didn't have a dollar!" Then, conscience-stricken: "No, I don't! Poor pop; he doesn't hate money, if I do."

Richard took Dorothy's sweet face between his hands, and looked into her eyes.

"You will believe me, darling?"

"Yes!"

"Then don't weep, don't worry! I promise that within the year you shall be my wife. I'll find the way to find the money."

"And hear me promise," returned Dorothy. "Money or no money, I'll become your wife what day you will."

Of course, after such a speech, there befell a sweet world and all of foolish tenderness; but, since the scandalized Ajax would not stay to witness it, neither shall you.

Mrs. Hanway-Harley said nothing to Dorothy of her interview with Richard; she appeared to believe that Richard had saved her that labor. There was a kind of sneer in this. Feeling the sneer, Dorothy put no questions; she was willing, in her resentment, to have it understood that Richard had told her. Why should he not?—she who was to be his wife! Dorothy would have been proud to proclaim her troth from the house-tops.

Mrs. Hanway-Harley had Storri to dinner. Dorothy, when he was announced, sought her room. A moment later, Mrs. Hanway-Harley was at the door. She came in cool, collected, no trace of anger. Why did not Dorothy come down to dinner? Dorothy did not come down to dinner because Dorothy did not choose.

"You do not ask Mr. Storms to dinner," said Dorothy, her color coming and her eyes beginning to glow. "I will not meet your Storri."

"Mr. Storms is not in our set, dear," said Mrs. Hanway-Harley coldly.

"He is in my heart," returned Dorothy.

The self-willed one seated herself stoutly, and never another word could Mrs. Hanway-Harley draw from her.

Storri received the excuses for Dorothy's vacant place at table which Mrs. Hanway-Harley offered; for all that he read the reason of her absence, and his pride fretted under it as under a lash.

New Year's Day; and the diplomatic reception at the White House. The President stood in line with his Cabinet people, and the others filed by. Richard, being utterly the democrat, was, of course, utterly the aristocrat, since these be extremes that never fail to meet. Wherefore, Richard did not take his place in the procession and waver painfully forward, at a snail's pace, to shake the Presidential hand. It was a foolish ceremony at which Richard's self-respect rebelled. There was no hand, no masculine hand, at least, which Richard would wait in line to grasp.

Richard, while declining to become part of the pageant, looked on. It was worth while as a study in human nature. The President peculiarly claimed his notice; by every sign it was this man who would oppose Senator Hanway, if the latter gentleman achieved his ambition and was put forward to lead his party's ticket. Richard compared the present handshaking President with Senator Hanway, the latter being thereby advanced. The President was a smooth, smug personage, of an appetite rather than an ambition for office. Ambition is a captain, appetite a camp-follower; for which reason the President was one who would never lead, never oppose a movement. Essentially, he was of the candidate class. Indeed, he had, as an individual, the best characteristics of a canal. He was narrow, even, currentless, with a mental fall of two feet in the mile. He lived conservatively between his banks, and went never so foolishly lucid as to show you how shallow he was. Just a trifle thick, he seemed to the eye as deep as the skies were high; any six-foot question, however, would have sounded him.

And yet he was in his day much lauded as a safe executive. There may have been truth in that. Your man of timid, slim, and shallow mediocrities, comparable to a canal, is not to be despised. He will not be the Mississippi, truly; he will sweep away no bridges, overflow no regions roundabout; no navies will battle on his bosom; the world in its giant commerces will not make of him a thoroughfare. But he will mean safety and profit for a horde of little special selfish interests, and that is the sort of President a day dominated of Money demands. In the far Southwest the cattle barons knock the horns off cattle; a hornless steer comes to the slaughter pen more quietly and with less of threat to those who handle him. In a day when Money rules as King, its first care is to knock the horns off originality and brains. Money wants no great horned mental forces roaming the world; they might become a threat. Richard thought on these matters as he considered this conservative, careful White House one, whose pains had ever been to think nothing that hadn't been thought, say nothing that hadn't been said, do nothing that hadn't been done.

"He is like a bucket of spring water," thought Richard, as he turned away, "cool, pure, tasteless. But there isn't enough of him to put out a fire, or swim a boat, or turn the wheel of any mill of moment."

Richard went into the Green Drawing-room, where the younger, gayer spirits were "receiving behind the line." There he saw Dorothy and Bess. Before he could go to them, he caught the snarling accents of Storri. He turned; that Russ was almost at his elbow. Storri, as though for Richard's ear, was saying to a vapid young man whom Richard had seen at the club:

"Oh! that is Miss Harley;—the one with the blue eyes and black hair. Bad combination, believe me! I, who am a gentleman—a Russian gentleman—give you my word that blue eyes and black hair mean treason to a lover. No, I can't take you to her; she has shown a preference for me, and I do not care to distinguish her by too much notice until I have thought her over. On my soul, yes; I must think her over!"

Richard's hand fell heavy and rude on Storri's shoulder.

"Come with me," said he.

Storri had not counted on this; those sacred White House walls should have protected him. He looked appealingly at his friend.

"Your friend will pardon you," said Richard coolly, "and, for this time, you shall come back safe."

Richard drew Storri to a window, where they were by themselves.

"Pay heed to what I shall say," gritted Richard, and his eyes gave forth a gray glimmer, like a saber suddenly unsheathed: "You must never take Miss Harley's name upon your lips. Should you do so, I shall twist your neck as once I twisted your fingers."

Storri began a spluttering stammer of protest and reproach.

"Don't hector me!" whispered Richard, with a sharp fervor of ferocity that made Storri start, "or, when next we meet in the street, I'll take my cane and beat you like a dog!"

Storri turned and tried to hide the fear that fed upon him with a tinge of swagger. This in the White House—the palace of their President! Storri was more and more convinced that the Americans were a rabble and not a people!

"Remember!" said Richard, and the tones were like a threat of death.

That evening, early, Richard met Dorothy at Bess Marklin's. He made no revelations touching his colloquy with Storri. There was a thick down-come of snow, and the new flakes covered the street like feathers to a fluffy depth of two inches. As Dorothy and Richard reached the sidewalk on Dorothy's return to the Harley house, Richard, with the abrupt remark: "I'll save you from the snow, my dear!" caught Dorothy in those Pict arms and strode across.

Dorothy was so amazed by this gallant attention that she was over before she spoke a word. As Richard landed her, light as a leaf, within her father's portals, she said in remonstrance:

"What made you do it? Did you not see that odious Storri coming?"

"It was for Storri I did it. I wanted to emphasize some remarks I had the honor to make to him this afternoon."

Dorothy fluttered to her room to prepare for the seven-o'clock dinner, while her unconventional loved one turned with a hope of meeting Storri. The fierce truth was, Richard, who, as you have been told, was at bottom full as savage as the Russian, had gone hungering for hostilities with that nobleman. Storri's comments on Dorothy had exploded all the hateful powder in Richard's composition.

Storri may have had some glint of Richard's feeling; sure it was that, although bent upon dining at the Harley house when he was so unexpectedly treated by Richard and Dorothy to that picture of Paul and Virginia modernized, he wheeled upon his heel and disappeared. Richard, search as he might, met never the shadow nor the ghost of Storri.

Storri went direct to his rooms. All the wolves of anger and jealousy and hate were tearing at his soul. Richard's threats; and he too craven to make reply! Dorothy in Richard's arms; and he powerless to interfere! The day had been a day of fire for him! He must make a plan; he must have revenge.

Full of a black resolve, Storri tore open his desk. He took out those French shares and fluttered the little package of papers between his angry fingers as though the feel of them could give him consolation. He looked at those poor forgeries of his name by Mr. Harley. Then he wrote a note to that gentleman and urged him, by every name of business, to call without delay. Mr. Harley must come at once. The note in the hands of a messenger, Storri commenced to rove the floor like some rage-frenzied beast.

"We shall see!" he cried, tossing his hands. "I have the father in my fingers—aye! in these fingers! I can pull him to pieces like a toasted lark—yes, limb from pinion, I, Storri, shall tear him asunder! I can torture, I can crush! He is mine to destroy! My power over him shall be my power over her! The stubborn Dorothy shall come to me on her knees—to me, Storri, whom she has affronted! She shall beg my favor for her father! What should be the ransom? Who shall measure my demands when I have conquered? I, who am to have my neck twisted!—I, who am to be beaten like a dog!—I shall name to her the terms. They shall be ruin—ruin for her, ruin for him, ruin for all who have put their slights upon me! The proud Dorothy must give me herself to buy her father's safety! Her pride shall creep, her face lie in the dust! She shall be Storri's! When her beauty fades—in a year—in two years—I will cast her aside; I, Storri, whom these feeble people have defied!"

In the midst of the ravings of the hate-racked Storri, there came a tap. A card was thrust in. Storri's onyx eyes gloated as he read the name.

"Harley!" said Storri. Then to the one at the door: "Have him up!" His voice sunk to an exultant whisper as he heard Mr. Harley's step in the hall. "Now is my vengeance to begin the feast! They shall know, these feeble ones, what it is to brave a Russian!"

CHAPTER XI

HOW MR. HARLEY FOUND HIMSELF A FORGER

In the economy of the Harleys, the gray mare was the better horse, at least the gray mare thought so. Mrs. Hanway-Harley put no faith in Mr. Harley. He was an acquiescent if not an obedient husband, and, rather than bicker, would submit to be moderately henpecked. When the henpecking was carried to excess, Mr. Harley did not peck back; he clapped on his hat, bolted for the door, and escaped. These measures, while effective in so far that they carried Mr. Harley beyond the immediate range of Mrs. Hanway-Harley's guns, left that wife and mother with a depleted opinion of Mr. Harley. She could not respect one who failed to give her battle, being offered proper provocation; and in that Mrs. Hanway-Harley was one with all the world. To fight is now and then an obligation.

Thinking thus lightly of Mr. Harley, and remembering, too, that Dorothy could coil him round her finger, quell him with a tear, Mrs. Hanway-Harley did not take him into her confidence as to those love proffers of Storri, and Dorothy's rebellion. What would have been the good? Mr. Harley's advice was nothing, while his countenance, as far as it went, would be given to Dorothy the disobedient. Also, he would go to Senator Hanway with the tangle. Such a course might bring her brother actively upon the field; and Mrs. Hanway-Harley had gleaned enough from her talk with Senator Hanway to know that, should he assume a part, it would not be in support of her interest. These considerations came and went in Mrs. Hanway-Harley's mind, with the result that she decided to say nothing to Mr. Harley.

Dorothy, for argument of modesty and a girl's reserve, emulated her mother's example of silence. For one thing, she felt herself in no danger. As against the demands of Mrs. Hanway-Harley, Dorothy, thus far, had held the high ground. Moreover, she was confident of final victory. No one could compel her either to receive Storri's addresses or cease to think of Richard. Dorothy added to this the knowledge that, should she draw Mr. Harley into her troubles by even so much as a word of their existence, Mrs. Hanway-Harley might be relied upon from that moment to charge him with being the author of every disappointment she underwent. Thus it came to pass that, as Mr. Harley complacently sat down to dinner that particular New Year's evening, he had not been given a murmur of those loves and hates and commands and defiances and promises and intermediations which made busy the closing days of the recent year for Dorothy, Richard, Bess, Storri, and Mrs. Hanway-Harley. Mr. Harley possessed an excellent appetite that New Year's evening; it might have been diminished of edge had his ignorance been less.

Mrs. Hanway-Harley looked for Storri to drop in, but since the promise of his coming was known only to herself—she did not care to furnish the news of it to Dorothy the rebellious—the failure of that nobleman to appear bred no general dismay. The dinner went soberly forward, and Mr. Harley especially derived great benefit therefrom.

Mr. Harley had just finished his final glass of wine, and was saying something fictional about a gentleman at the Arlington upon whom he ought to call, and what a bore calling upon the fictional gentleman would be, when Storri's note came into his hands. He glanced it over, and then seized upon it as the very thing to furnish a look of integrity to his story of the mythical one. He gave the note a petulant slap with the back of his fingers, and remarked:

"I declare! Here he is writing me to come at once."

Mr. Harley got into his hat and coat, and then got into the street, observing as he did so that he feared the business in hand might keep him far into the morning.

The guilty truth was this: Mr. Harley concealed a private purpose to play cards with a select circle of statesmen who owned a taste to begin the year with draw poker at Chamberlin's. However, there existed in the destinies of Mr. Harley not the faintest call for all this elaboration of deceit. Mrs. Hanway-Harley would not have uttered a whisper of objection had he openly declared for an absence of a fortnight, with the design of playing poker, nothing but poker, every moment of the time. But it is the vain fancy of some men to believe themselves and their company those things most longed for at home, when the precise converse of such condition of longing is the one which exists, and this fancy was among the weaknesses of Mr. Harley. Besides, he revered the truth so much that, like his Sunday coat, he employed it only on rare occasions, and when advantage could be arrived at in no other way. Truth was a pearl, and Mr. Harley felt strongly against casting it before the swine of every common occurrence, when mendacity would do as well or better. Wherefore, and to keep his hand in, Mr. Harley invariably romanced in whatever he vouchsafed of himself or his habits to Mrs. Hanway-Harley. Nor was this so unjust as at a first blink it might seem. If Mr. Harley misled Mrs. Hanway-Harley as to his personal movements, she in return told him nothing at all of her own, the result, to wit, total darkness, being the same for both. However, they were perfectly satisfied, rightly esteeming the situation one wherein, if ignorance were not bliss, at least it was folly to be wise.

The winter evening, still, not cold, was clear and crisp, with the snow squeaking cheerfully under foot, and Mr. Harley waddled on his way towards Storri's door in that blandness of mood which comes to one whose wine and dinner and stomach are in comfortable accord. Waddled is the word; for with his short legs, and that profundity of belt proper to gentlemen who have reached the thither side of middle age, and given years to good eating and drinking, Mr. Harley had long since ceased to walk.

Mr. Harley was not surprised by the urgent character of Storri's summons. Doubtless, the business related to Credit Magellan, and what steps in Wall Street and the Senate were being taken for a conquest of Northern Consolidated. Affairs in those theaters of commercial effort were as they should be. Things were moving slowly, they must of necessity move slowly, and Storri had grown impatient. The Russian's warmth was expected; Mr. Harley had read him long since like a primer book. Storri was excitable, volatile, full of fever and impulse, prone to go off at tangents. In some stress of nerves he had sent for Mr. Harley to urge expedition or ask for explanations. The thing had chanced before. Mr. Harley would cool him into calmness with a dozen words. Storri's poise restored, Mr. Harley would seek those speculative statesmen, lusting for draw-poker. He should be with them by ten o'clock—a ripe hour for cards. Mr. Harley would oppose poker in its usual form and argue for table-stakes—five thousand dollars a corner. Two of the speculative statesmen were not worth five thousand dollars. So much the better; in case he were fortunate, Mr. Harley would accept their paper. The last was to be preferred to money. Mr. Harley had many irons of legislation in the congressional fires; a statesman's note of hand should operate to pave the way when his influence and his vote were to be asked for. Should Mr. Harley lose at poker, his losses would be charged against that railroad and those coal companies whose interests about Congress it was Mr. Harley's mission to conserve. There was no doubt of the propriety of such charges; they belonged in any account which was intended to register the cost of legislation. If you but stop and think, you must see the truth of the above. Thus cantered the cogitations of Mr. Harley until, fetching up at his journey's end, he sent in his card to Storri.

At Mr. Harley's appearance, Storri's arm-tossing and raving ended abruptly. He became oily and purringly suave, and bid Mr. Harley light a cigar which he tendered. A cat will play with a mouse before coming to the final kill; and there was a broad streak of the feline in Storri. Now that his victim was within spring, he would play with him as preliminary to the supreme joy of that last lethal crunch.

Following the usual salutations, Mr. Harley sat in peace and favor with himself, waiting for Storri to begin. He would let Storri vent his excitement, blow off steam, as Mr. Harley expressed it; and then he would go about those calmative steps of explanation and assurance suggested of the case.

Storri strode up and down, eying Mr. Harley with a mixed expression of cruelty and triumph which, had Mr. Harley caught the picture of it, might have made him feel uneasy. However, Mr. Harley was not looking at Storri. He was thinking on ending the interview as quickly and conveniently as he might, and hurrying posthaste to those speculative ones.

"Why did I bring you here to-night?" asked Storri at last.

"Northern Consolidated, I suppose," said Mr. Harley, looking up.

Storri laughed, and a white flash of his teeth showed in a tigerish way.

"Come!" cried Storri, smiting his hands in a kind of rapture of cruelty; "I will not, what you call it, beat about the bush. It is not Credit Magellan; it is not Northern Consolidated; no, it is not business at all. What! shall Storri be forever at some grind of business? Shall he never pause for love? My Czar would tell you another tale. Listen, my friend. I have done you the honor—I, Storri, a Russian nobleman, have done you the honor to adore your daughter."

Mr. Harley gaped and stared; he could not have been more impressed had the statue of Liberty which topped the Capitol dome stepped down for a stroll in the Capitol grounds. And yet he was not shocked; if Dorothy had decided on Storri for her husband, well and good; he was too indulgent a father to quarrel with her.

"I have spoken to Mrs. Hanway-Harley of my passion," continued Storri, still pacing to and fro. "She is so charming as to encourage it."

"Why, then," broke in Mr. Harley, in evident relief, "you have gone the right way about the matter. If my wife favors you, assuredly you may count upon my consent."

"Bah!" returned Storri, snapping his fingers. "Mrs. Hanway-Harley consents; you consent; I am flattered! The fastidious Miss Dorothy, however, refuses my love—puts it aside! Storri is not the man! On my soul! Storri is declined by a little American who draws her blood from peasants!" and Storri threw his hands palm upward, expressing self-contempt in view of the insult thus put upon him.

"Does my daughter decline your love?"

"It is not that." Storri could not for his vanity's sake, even after he himself had used them, accept those terms. "Her heart has—what shall we say?—a tenant. Your daughter has gone among her own kind with her love. It is that fellow Storms—it is he whom your daughter's taste prefers."

"Dorothy loves Mr. Storms," said Mr. Harley, speaking slowly, as men will on the receipt of surprising news. "And she does not love you." After a thoughtful pause, Mr. Harley concluded: "It is a subject about which I should hesitate to counsel my daughter."

"I do not ask you to counsel her; you shall compel her."

"Why, sir!" exclaimed Mr. Harley, starting up and growing apoplectic with anger, "do you imagine that I'll force my child into your arms? If you were that Czar whom you are so fond of quoting, I would not do it!"

This came off in a great burst, and Mr. Harley in his turn began to pace the floor. The two passed and repassed each other as they walked up and down, Mr. Harley puffing and swelling, Storri surveying him with leering superiority.

"Sit down!" cried Storri suddenly, after a minute spent in marching and countermarching. "I will show you that you are in my hand."

Storri had become calm and business-like; his new manner mystified Mr. Harley and worked upon him. He dropped into the chair to which Storri motioned him. From his pocket, Storri took out those French shares.

"Do you see where you forged my name?" said he. "Can you tell me the punishment for forgery?"

"Forgery!" panted Mr. Harley, in a whirl of rage and wonder. "Did you not tell me to write your name? Was it not to sustain your deal in sugar?"

"Come—you Harley—you John Harley," returned Storri, his cruelty beginning to bubble into exultation, "how small a thing you are when opposed to Storri! See, now; it begins when you sacrifice for me those seven thousand dollars. It was then I set a trap for you—you, the cunning Mr. Harley! It was so simple; I need only give you a chance to forge my name and you forge it. From that moment you have had but the one alternative. You must follow my commands, or you must take the common course of criminals, and go to prison. And now—you Harley—you John Harley—you, who pride yourself for your respectability, for your place in the world, for your illustrious relative Senator Hanway—hear me: You are to be my slave—my dog to fetch and carry. You are to do my will; or I swear by my Czar and by the heart in the breast of my Czar that I'll drag you before the world as a felon."

Storri delivered this menace with a ruthless energy that sent it home like a javelin. It struck the color from the ruddy countenance of Mr. Harley, and left him white as linen three times bleached.

"Yes," went on the vindictive Storri in an exultant crow, "did you little people believe you were to laugh at Storri and pass unpunished? Did you think to insult him and escape his vengeance? Bah! the super-fine Dorothy is to spurn Storri for a varlet like this Storms! She is to laugh at Storri's love, and tell how she refused a nobleman! Excellent; we shall see her laugh when her father—Mr. Harley—Mr. John Harley—the great Mr. John Harley—brother-by-law of the still greater Senator Hanway—stands in the dock as a forger. Will not our Dorothy laugh? John Harley, forger; why not!"

Mr. Harley sat ghastly and still, while Storri rambled on for the mere pleasure of torture. He did not leave Mr. Harley a hope wherewith to prop himself. The deal in sugar had been in Mr. Harley's sole name—an individual deal. There was not the flourish of a pen to prove Storri's interest. Storri would even show how, for that very sugar stock, in that very market, he was dealing the other way, selling ten thousand shares.

"But you paid your half of the losses in the deal in my name." Mr. Harley's voice, commonly rich and full, was huskily dry. "That, when I show it, will prove your interest."

"And how are you to show it?" cried Storri. "I paid in money; I did not give you a check. There's not an exculpatory scrap at bank or broker's in your defense. You make a deal; you are crowded for margins; you have my French shares in your pocket as my agent in another transaction; you offer them; the broker will not accept, they do not have my signature; you are back in five minutes with a forgery, and obtain the money you require. The thing is complete; I tell you, Harley—Mr. John Harley—you are trapped. There is no escape; I have my knee on your neck."

Mr. Harley, still white, was beginning to regain his mental feet. He saw the apparent hold that Storri had upon him. It was enough. To be merely charged as a forger—to be apprehended as a criminal, would be ruin, utter ruin, even if the affair were there to end. It would mean the downfall of Senator Hanway's hopes of a White House. The simple arrest—it would go like wildfire throughout the press—meant destruction for Senator Hanway, for Dorothy, for Mrs. Hanway-Harley, for all.

White and stricken, Mr. Harley pondered these questions, while Storri watched him. Storri himself did not care to push for extremes. In his vain egotism, which was like a madness, he would not have scrupled to brand Mr. Harley as a forger had he been defied. But such a step was not what Storri aimed at. It was his own possession of Dorothy rather than a vengeance upon Mr. Harley that he sought to compass. Therefore, as Storri made plain his power and threatened its exercise, he considered Mr. Harley with the narrow intentness of a lynx. He was striving to measure the other's resistance. He noted the horror of Mr. Harley at the term forger; he observed Mr. Harley's growing sense of helplessness as he, Storri, set forth how Mr. Harley lay in the toils. Now, when Mr. Harley was prostrate beneath the harrow of every alarm, Storri, sure of success, went off on an easier tack—that is, easier for Mr. Harley.

"But why do we lose our self-control?" cried Storri, voice and manner changed from black to white, clouds to sunshine; "we are men, not angry children! See, now, I want nothing a gentleman of honor might not grant. I love your daughter—good! a Russian nobleman loves your daughter! Is that disgrace? You approve; your wife approves! The daughter is young; she must be wooed before she is won. What then: Is Storri to despair? The lady would put Storri's love to the test. She says: 'You must court me before you shall wed me. You are not to have me without a struggle, lest you think me of small worth.' The lady has pride; the lady has discretion; the lady sets a value upon herself. Why should she not? It compels me, Storri, to appreciate her charms still more and more. There; I have painted the state of affairs. I have now but two requests; I will not call those requests commands," and Storri rustled the French shares suggestively. "No, I am to call them requests. Can you not exercise a paternal authority to have your daughter receive my respectful visits? Also, can you not exercise it to put an end, absolutely an end, to her interviews with this Mr. Storms?"

"How can I compel her?"

"You must do it!" roared Storri, his anger taking renewed edge. "You must, you shall! What! am I to be thwarted, affronted, undone by a girl? Two things I demand: she is to see me; and she is not to see that Storms. Do I ask much? It is little for a child to pay for a father's safety; little for a man to pay for his own. What forger or what forger's daughter has made such terms? Bah!"

The insult scarcely roused Mr. Harley; he was stunned, his face was clammy with sweat. It was like a dream of horror! Look where he would, there showed but the one door of escape. Storri was to see Dorothy; Dorothy was not to see Richard!

After all, it did not present unbearable conditions. Moreover, time would bring about its shifts. In a week, in a month, in six months, Mr. Harley might have Storri helpless as Storri now had him. It was a case for delay; Mr. Harley must have breathing space.

"That is all you require?" said Mr. Harley, his voice the same dry, husky croak. "You are to see my daughter? and Mr. Storms is not to see her?"

"Do that, and I will answer for the balance!" cried Storri. "Do that, and she will love me—she will be my wife!"

"And no more talk of—of forgeries?"

"My dear Mr. Harley!" exclaimed Storri, "I am a gentleman—a Russian gentleman. I ask you, in candor, does a gentleman arrest his wife's father on a charge of forgery? Come; let us have confidence in one another. We are friends, are we not?—we, who are to be in closer alliance when your daughter becomes my Countess wife. Bah! who shall talk of forgeries then?"

The evening was still young—nine o'clock—when Mr. Harley found himself again in the street, bending his slow step homeward. He was wholly adrift now from any thought of those speculative ones at Chamberlin's. What Storri had said engrossed him miserably. He entertained no doubt but what Storri would carry into execution those threats of arrest, should his desires concerning Dorothy meet with opposition. The fear of his own disgrace appalled Mr. Harley. He did not lack for courage, but his interview with Storri had buried him beneath a spell of terror.

It was peculiarly a condition to frighten Mr. Harley to the core. He was proud in a coarse way of the fortune he had gathered. He had based himself on his position as a business, not to say a legislative, force, and used it to patronize, not always delicately, those among his fellows who had not climbed so high. In exacting what was a money due, he had ever proceeded with but little scruple. He had measured his right by measuring his strength, and had not failed to take his pound of flesh. In brief, Mr. Harley, possessing, like many another fat gentleman, those numerous porcine traits of brutal selfishness and a lack of sentiment or sympathy, had considered always his own interests, following them though they took him roughshod over another's dearest hopes. For which good reasons Mr. Harley had foes, and knew it; there would be no absence of rejoicing over his downfall.

But what could Mr. Harley offer for defense? What, beyond mere compliance with Storri's wishes, might avert those calamities that seemed swinging in the air above him? He considered everything, and devised nothing; he was like a man without eyes or as one shut in by night. In his desperation, a flighty thought of taking Storri's life appealed to him for one murderous moment. It was only for a moment, and then he thrust it aside with a shudder; not from any morality, but his instant common sense showed how insane it would be as a method of escape, and with that he shrunk back from it as from a precipice. And yet there was to be no standing still; he must push on in some direction.

Mr. Harley, being himself a business soul, did not omit to consider how far Storri might be held at bay by showing him the certain destruction of Credit Magellan, should he persist to the bitter length of forgery charges and open war. Mr. Harley might be disgraced, destroyed; but what then?

Storri's plans would assuredly be trampled flat; millions, about to come into his hands, would be swept away.

These, as arguments to be addressed to Storri, no sooner entered the mind of Mr. Harley than he dismissed them as offering no solution of his perils. He had felt, rather than seen, the barbarism of Storri beneath the tissue of what that nobleman would have styled his elegant refinement. Storri was a coward, and therefore Storri was malignant; he had shown, as he went promising disgrace to Mr. Harley, that petulance of evil which is remarked in savages and cruel children. Storri was dominated of a passion for revenge; under sway of that passion no chance of money-loss would stay him; he would sacrifice all and begin his schemes anew before he would deny himself those vainglorious triumphs upon which he had set his heart. He hated Richard; he hungered for Dorothy; and Mr. Harley knew how he would go to every extravagant extent in feeding those two sentiments.

Mr. Harley sighed dismally as he reviewed these conclusions; he could do nothing, and must serve, or seem to serve, the villain humor of Storri. What were those two demands? Storri must meet Dorothy; and Richard must not. There was no help; Mr. Harley, in his present stress, would see Dorothy and beg her co-operation. He could not tell the whole story; but he would say that he was borne upon by trouble, and ask her to acquiesce in Storri's conditions. He would promise that those conditions were not to live forever.

Deciding thus, Mr. Harley went forward on his homeward course; he must see Dorothy without delay, for he would be upon the rack until the painful conference was over. The night was chill as New Year's nights have a right to be, and yet Mr. Harley was fain to mop his forehead as though it were the Dog days. As he neared his own door, his reluctant pace became as slow as sick men find the flight of time.

There had come no one to the Harley house this New Year's evening to engage the polite attentions of Mrs. Hanway-Harley, and that lady, being armored to the teeth, in the name of comfort had retired to her own apartments with a purpose to unloose what buttons and remove what pins and untie what strings stood between her and a great bodily relief. Dorothy was of neither the size nor the years at which women torture themselves, and, having no quarrel with her buttons and pins and strings, sat alone in the library. She was deep in a novel that reeled with ardent love, and had fallen to despising the lover because he did not resemble Richard.

It was in the library that Mr. Harley came seeking Dorothy. When he found her, he stood stock-still, unable to speak one word of all that tide of talk which would be necessary to bring before her his dangerous perplexities and the one manner of their possible relief.

Dorothy at his step looked up, pleased to have him home so early. She was about to say as much, but at sight of him the words perished on her tongue. It was as though her heart were touched with ice. Mr. Harley's countenance had been of that quasi claret hue called rubicund. It was now turned gray and pasty, and his cheeks, as firmly round as those of a trumpeter, were pouched and fallen as with the palsy of age. He looked ten years worse than when he went forth two hours before.

Dorothy sprang up in alarm; she feared that he was ill.

"Let me call mamma!" she cried; "let me call Uncle Pat! You are sick."

"No; call nobody!" said Mr. Harley feebly, and speaking with difficulty. "I'm not ill; I'll be right in a moment." Then he had Dorothy back into her chair, gazing upon her the while in a stricken way, as though she were hangman or headsman, and he before her for execution. Mr. Harley was held between terror of Storri and shame for what he must say to Dorothy. Wondering what fearful blow had fallen upon them, Dorothy sat facing her father the color of death.

"Tell me, papa," she whispered, with a terror in her tones, "tell me what has happened."

Despair brought a sickly calmness to Mr. Harley; he cleared his mind with a struggle and controlled himself to speak. He would say all at once, and leave the rest with Dorothy.

"Dorothy," he began, the iron effort he was making being plainly apparent, "Dorothy, I have had a talk with that scoundrel without a conscience, Count Storri. I do not pretend that I come willingly to you from him. I tell you, however, that I am fearfully within that villain's power, and cannot help myself. No, I've done no crime; but none the less he has it in his hands to cover me with disgrace—destroy me, and every sign of me, from the midst of respectable men. It would avail nothing should I show you how he spread a snare for my feet, and how blindly I walked into it. I can only say again that he has me helpless, hand and foot; I am his to make or break in all that a man of honor or station holds dearest. He can cover me with infamy at will; he can unloose upon me an avalanche of disgrace, and with the one blow crush us all. I keep back nothing, exaggerate nothing, I merely lay bare to you what is. Once the stroke falls, I shall never again hold up my head. Indeed, I shall not live to see it fall, for when I know it is inevitable I shall take my own life."

Mr. Harley paused a moment to recall his coolness, while Dorothy, her little hands crushed between her knees, sat panting like a spent hare.

"I have given you my precise position," continued Mr. Harley, with a sort of hopelessness. "I shall now tell you the conditions upon which my safety depends. They rest with you; I stand or fall as you decide." Dorothy tried to speak, but her voice died on her lips. "If you receive Count Storri, not as a lover, but as an acquaintance, or, if you will, a friend; and if you have no further meeting—that is, for a month—or perhaps two—or at the most three—have no further interviews, I say"—Mr. Harley blundered a trifle as he saw Dorothy's face whitening with the sorrows he was laying upon her—"have no further interviews with Mr. Storms, I am saved. Forgive me—forgive your father who has so failed of his duty that, instead of protecting you, he comes to you for protection. There is no more: You have my fortune, my good repute, my life in your charge. If you meet Count Storri in friendship, if you refuse Mr. Storms, I am secure. Should you fail of either, then, by heart and soul! I think it is my end!"

CHAPTER XII

HOW MR. FOPLING WAS INSPIRED

Next to Richard, Dorothy worshiped her father. Women never weigh men closely; with them it is the kindness of men that counts, and all her life no one could have been more generously affectionate than was Mr. Harley to Dorothy. And now her estimate of him became her memory of his unflagging goodness; and this kept her from harsh judgment as he told what heartbreaking sacrifices she must make. Nor did she distrust a syllable; nor would she ask for explanation. The latter she would avoid; it was enough that Storri held her father at his horrid mercy. As against the setting forth in detail of Storri's cruel power she instinctively closed her ears as she would have shut her eyes against a fearsome sight. Dorothy had never a question; and when Mr. Harley was done she seemed simply to bow to the will of events too strong for her to cope with.

"But you must never ask me to marry that man!" cried Dorothy. There went a tremor through her words that marked how deep of root was the feeling that prompted them. "I couldn't, wouldn't marry him! Before that, I would die—yes, and die again! You must not ask it!" and she lifted up her face, all wrung with pain and anxious terror.

"I shall never ask it!" declared Mr. Harley; and he spoke stoutly, for the worst was over and his heart was coming back. This gave Dorothy a better confidence, and she began to hope that things in the end might come fairer than they threatened. "No," repeated Mr. Harley with even greater courage, and smoothing her black, thick hair in a fatherly way, "you shall never be asked to marry the scoundrel. That I promise; and let him do his worst."

And now, when both were measurably recovered from the shame and the shock of it, Mr. Harley began to elaborate. He went no further, however, than just to point out how nothing was really required of Dorothy beyond those common courtesies good women exhibit to what men the respectable chances of existence bring into their society. He said nothing, asked nothing concerning her love for Richard: he appeared to consider that love admitted, and found no fault with it. What he impressed upon Dorothy was the present danger of her love's display, and how his safety rested upon her not meeting with Richard for a space. Surely that might be borne; it would not be for long. Given room wherein to work, he, Mr. Harley, would find some pathway out. Also, it would be unwise to say aught of what had taken place to Dorothy's mother. Mr. Harley and Dorothy would keep it secret from both Mrs. Hanway-Harley and Senator Hanway. Storri would not broach the subject to Mrs. Hanway-Harley; he could not without revealing more than he desired known.

"Nor will the rascal do more," observed Mr. Harley, with the hope of adding to the fortitude of Dorothy, "than come here now and then to dine or sit an hour. That is all he will count upon; and before he seeks anything nearer I'll have him under my foot as now he has me under his. When that hour comes," concluded Mr. Harley, rapping out a sudden great oath that made Dorothy start in her frock, "there will be no saving limits in his favor. I'll apply the torch, and burn him like so much refuse off the earth."

When Mrs. Hanway-Harley endeavored to break Dorothy to the yoke of her ambitions concerning Storri, Dorothy sparkled and blazed and wept and did those divers warlike things that ladies do when engaged in conflict with each other. Dorothy, down in her heart, attached no more than a surface importance to the efforts of Mrs. Hanway-Harley; and that was the reason why on those fierce occasions she only sparkled and blazed and wept. Now, be it known, what Mr. Harley told her seared like hot iron; what he asked of kindness to Storri and cruelty to Richard cut like a knife; and yet there was never tear nor spark to show throughout. She waited cold and white and steady. Dorothy was convinced of her father's danger without knowing its cause or what form it might take; and she filled up with a resolution to do whatever she could, saving only the acceptance of Storri and his love, to buckler him against it. Nor was this difference which Dorothy made between Mrs. Hanway-Harley and Mr. Harley to be marveled at; for just as a mother exerts more influence over a son than would his father, so will a father have weight with a daughter beyond any that her mother might possess.

While Dorothy remained firm and brave as Mr. Harley revealed his troubles and their remedy, she broke down later when she found herself in her own room. She did not call her maid; she must be alone. What had transpired began to come over her in such slow fashion that she was given time to fully feel the ignoble position into which she had fallen. She must not see the man whom she adored; she must meet—with politeness even if she could not with grace—the man whom she loathed. To one of Dorothy's spirit and fineness there dwelt in this an infamy, a baseness, of which Mr. Harley with his lucky coarseness of fiber escaped all notice.

Throwing herself on the bed, Dorothy burrowed her face in the pillow and gave her tears their way. It was the happiest impulse she could have had; when the tears were dried, and in the calm of that relief which was their afterglow, she considered what she had to do. Oh! if only she might have sought her mother with her sorrow! Dorothy shivered; her mother was the ally of her enemy. How Dorothy hated and feared that black and savage man! What fiend's power must he possess to thus gain a fearful mastery over her father! What could be his secret tipped with terror? Dorothy again buried her face as though she would hide herself from any blasting chance of its discovery.

When Dorothy was with Mr. Harley she had been in a maze, a whirl. Wrapped in a cloud of fear, she had reached out blindly through the awful fog of it and seized upon the dear fact of Richard. By Richard she held on; by Richard she sustained herself. She entertained no quaking doubts as to his loyalty; loyal herself, as ever was flower to sun, to distrust Richard was to doubt the ground beneath her little feet. In her innocence, she felt that sublime confidence which is the fruit, the sweet purpose, of a young girl's earliest love. Dorothy must write Richard a letter; she must tell him of the sad gap in their happiness. Yes; she would put him in possession of the entire story so far as it was known to her. He owned a right to hear it. Must his heart be broken, and he not learn the secret or know the author of the blow?

When Dorothy was again mistress of herself, between sobs and tender showers she blotted down those words which were to warn Richard from her side. His love, like her own, would go on; there was to be no final breaking away. It was faith in a dear day that should find them reunited which upheld Dorothy through the ordeal of her letter; her prayer was that the day might be close at hand.

Her letter finished, Dorothy, late as was the hour, sent for Bess; she must have someone's love, someone's sympathy to lean upon. Bess came; and, saying no more than she was driven to reveal of her father's helplessness and Storri's baleful strength, Dorothy told Bess what dolorous fate had overtaken her.

"I've written Richard to go to you, Bess," whispered Dorothy at the woeful close. "Have him write me a letter every day; I shall write one to him. I didn't promise not to write, you know, only not to see him. But you must not let Richard go to Storri, that above all. Poor Richard! he is very fierce; and if he were to arouse Storri's anger it would provoke him to some awful step."

There was a man of robust curiosity who once suggested that it would prove entertaining if one were to lift the roofs off a city as one might the upper crust off a pie, and then, looking down into the very bowels of life, observe what plots and counterplots, defeats and triumphs, loves and hates, pains and pleasures, losses and gains, hopes and despairs, honors and disgraces belonged with the struggles of everyday humanity. It is by no means sure the survey would repay the cost of making it, and the chances run heavily that the student would gather more of grief than good from the lesson. Proceeding, however, by the hint of contradiction furnished above, had one, at the moment when Storri was binding Mr. Harley by fetters wrought from the metal of Mr. Harley's own fearful apprehensions, glanced in upon Richard, he would have found that worthy young gentleman seated by his fireside, soothing himself with tobacco smoke, and reveling in thoughts of Dorothy. And the cogitations of Richard, if written down in words, would have read like this:

"Why should I defer a dénouement that will rejoice them all? Dorothy loves me—loves me for myself, and for nothing but myself. Who could have offered deeper proof of it? She has come to me in the face of her mother, in the face of poverty; she is willing to abandon everything to become my wife. And if her mother objects—as she does object—why not cure the objection with a trifle of truth? I am not seeking to make a conquest of Mrs. Hanway-Harley; that tremendous ambition does not claim me. I am not to marry her. What she thinks, or why she thinks it, should not be so important. It is Dorothy whom I love, Dorothy who is to be my wife—none but Dorothy. No, I'll end a farce which no longer can defend its own existence. To-morrow I'll seek out my intended mother-in-law, and make her happy in the only way I may. I trust the good news may not kill her!" and Richard put on one of those grins of cynicism.

In this frame, Richard retired to bed and dreamed of Dorothy. His heart was enjoying a prodigious calm; he would no longer play at Democritus; he would fill Mrs. Hanway-Harley's soul with radiance, restrain to what extent he might his contempt for that radiance and the reason of it, and with Dorothy on his arm march away to bliss forever after. No, he would not have Dorothy to the altar within the moment following the enthronement of Mrs. Hanway-Harley in the midst of that splendid happiness he plotted for her. He was not so precipitate. Dorothy should have a voice and a will in fixing her marriage day; most young women had. But he would advise expedition—nay, he would pray for speed in the matter of that wedlock; for every hour that barred him from his loved one's arms would seem an age.

Thus dreamed Richard. And in the irony of fate, even while Richard was coming to these sage, not to say delicious, decisions and giving himself to these dreams, Storri was raving, Mr. Harley was cowering, and Dorothy was weeping and writing that they must not meet.

When Richard arose in the morning, the first object his fond eye caught was that dear hand-write sprawling all across the envelope: "Mr. Richard Storms." He tore it open, and this is what he read:

DEAR ONE:

As I write, my heart is breaking for us both. If I knew how, I would soften what I must say. Storri has gained some fearful ascendency over papa. Never have I seen papa look so gray and worn and old as when he came to me. He tells me that his safety, his life, depend on me. I am not to see you for a while. He says that if we meet it will mean his disgrace—his destruction. I can't explain; I have only my love for you, sweetheart, and you must not fail me now. It will all come right, I feel sure of that; only you must write me every day how dear I am to you, so that I shall have something to help my courage with. Go to Bess, and believe me yours with all my heart's love.

D.

Richard read and re-read Dorothy's note. He did not ramp off into a temper; the first effects of it were to drive the color out of his face and steal away his appetite. His eye grew moody, and in the end angry. Some flame of wrath was kindled against poor Dorothy, who was so ready—that is the way he put it to himself—to sacrifice him in defense of her father. But the flame went out, and never attained either height or intensity as a flame of repute and standing among flames. Richard was too normal, too healthy, too much in love. Besides, Dorothy's note was warped and polka-dotted with small round scars where her poor tears had fallen as she wrote; and with that the flame of anger was quenched by the mere sight of those tear-scars; and Richard kissed them one by one—the tear-scars—and found, when he had kissed the last one and then kissed it again for love and for luck, that he worshiped Dorothy the more for being in trouble. And now Richard felt a vast yearning over her as though she were a child. Had she not fought a gallant war with her mother for love of him? Richard was all but swept away on a very tide of tenderness. He would comply with Dorothy's requests; he would not press to see her; he would write her every day; he would love her more passionately than before. Incidentally, he would go questing Bess.

Richard did not permit himself to dwell upon Storri. He knew him for the source of all this poison in his cup. In his then temper, he put Storri out of his thought. He feared that if he considered that Russian too long he would be drawn into some indiscretion that, while curing nothing, might pull down upon Mr. Harley, and in that way upon Dorothy, the catastrophe that hung over their heads. There could be no doubt of the black measure of that catastrophe, whatever it might be. Richard, while no mighty admirer of Mr. Harley, had been enough in that gentleman's company to realize that it was more than a common apprehension which had sent him, limp and fear-shaken, to Dorothy begging for defense. The longer Richard pondered, the clearer the truth grew that some deadly chance was pending against Mr. Harley, and that Storri held the key which might unlock that chance against him. Until he understood the trend of affairs, a hostile collision with Storri would be the likeliest method by which disaster might be invoked. He must avoid Storri. This prudence on Richard's part went tremendously against the grain, for he was full of stalwart, primitive impulses that moved him to find Storri by every shortest cut and beat him to rags. He must keep away from Storri. Also, he would defer those revelations to Mrs. Hanway-Harley which were to have filled her soul with that radiance and made her as ready for Dorothy's marriage with Richard as was Richard himself. Those confidences could not aid now when it was Storri, not Mrs. Hanway-Harley, who stood in the way. And they might even work a harm. Richard went on his road to Bess, while these thoughts came flying thick as twilight bats.

Richard found the blonde sorceress bending above a flower, and doing something to the flower's advantage with a pair of scissors. As Bess hung over the leafy object of her solicitude, with her yellow wealth of hair coiled round and round, she herself looked not unlike a graceful, gaudy chrysanthemum. This poetic reflection, which would have been creditable to Mr. Fopling, never occurred to Richard; he was too full of Dorothy to have room for Bess. However, the good Bess found no fault with his loving preoccupation; she, too, was pensively thinking on poor Dorothy, and at once abandoned the invalid flower to console and counsel Richard.

"For you see," quoth Bess, as though a call had been made for the reason of her interest in another's love troubles, "I feel responsible for Dorothy. It was I who told you to love her."

This was not quite true, and gave too much blame or credit—whichever you will—to Bess; but Richard made no objections, and permitted Bess to define her position as best pleased her.

Bess laid out Richard's programme as though she were his mother or his guardian; she told him what his conduct should be. He must write Dorothy a daily letter; there ought to be a world of love in it, Bess thought, in view of those conditions of present distress which surrounded Dorothy.

"Her lot," observed Bess, "is much harder than yours, you know!"

Richard, being selfish, did not know; but he was for no dispute with Bess and kept his want of knowledge to himself. Yes; Richard was to write Dorothy every day; and she, for her sweet part, was likewise to write Richard every day. The good Bess, like an angel turned postman, would manage the exchange of tender missives.

Bess said nothing about Storri's coming visits to the Harley house or that he would insist on seeing Dorothy. She and Dorothy had been of one mind on that point of ticklish diplomacy. The bare notion of Storri meeting

Dorothy would send the fiery lover into a fury whereof the end could be only feared, not guessed. Richard was to be told nothing beyond the present impossibility of meeting Dorothy.

"And most of all," said Bess to Richard warningly, "you are not to involve yourself with Storri. Remember, should you and he have differences upon which the gossips can take hold, there will be a perfect scandal, and Dorothy the central figure."

Richard was horrified at Bess's picture.

"And so," concluded Bess, "you must do exactly as Dorothy requests. Have a little patience and a deal of love, and the cloud, be sure, will pass away."

"While I am having patience and love, I would give my left hand if I might bring that cobra Storri to account," said Richard.

What was written concerning the mouths of babes and sucklings? Mr. Fopling sat with Bess and Richard while they considered those above-related ways and means of interrupted love. Mr. Fopling was experiencing an uncommon elevation of spirits; for he had stared Ajax out of countenance—a notable feat—and sent the rival favorite growling and bristling from the room. Usually Mr. Fopling took no part in what conversations raged around him; it was the reason of some surprise, therefore, to both Bess and Richard when, at the mention of Storri's name, Mr. Fopling's ears pricked up a flicker of interest and he betrayed symptoms of being about to speak.

"Stow-wy!" exclaimed Mr. Fopling thoughtfully, as though identifying that nobleman, while Bess and Richard looked on as do folk who behold a miracle, "Stow-wy! I say, Stawms, why don't you go into Wall Stweet and bweak the beggah? He's always gambling, don't y' know! Bweak him; that's the way to punish such a fellah."

"Why! what a malicious soul you have grown!" cried Bess in astonishment. "Really, Algy,"—Mr. Fopling's name was Algernon,—"if you burst on us in this guise often, I for one shall stand in terror of you!"

"But, weally," protested Mr. Fopling, "if you want to get even with a fellah, Bess, just bweak him! It's simply awful, they say, for a chap to be bwoke. As for this Stow-wy, if Stawms hasn't got the money to go aftah him, I'll let him have some of mine. You see, Bess," concluded Mr. Fopling, with a broad candor that proved his love, "I hate this cweature Stow-wy."

"Why?" asked Richard, somewhat interested in his unexpected ally.

"He spoke dewisively of me," and with that Mr. Fopling lapsed.

Richard went slowly homeward, his chin on his chest, not in discouragement, but thought. The counsel of the vacuous Mr. Fopling followed him to ring in his ears like words of guidance.

"Bweak him!" squeaked Mr. Fopling, feebly vicious.

Since Mr. Fopling had never been known to think anything or say anything anterior to this singular outburst, the conclusion forced itself upon Richard that Mr. Fopling was inspired. Nor could Richard put Mr. Fopling and his violent advice out of his head.

"Money is the villain's heart's-blood!" thought Richard. "I'm inclined to conclude that Fopling is right. If I take his money from him, he is helpless—a viper without its fangs, a bear with its back broken!"

Richard put in that evening in his own apartments. Had you been there to watch his face, you would have been struck by the capacity for hate and love and thought displayed in the lowering brow and brooding eye. Richard smoked and considered; at eight o'clock he rang for Mr. Gwynn.

That precise gentleman of stiffness and English immobility appeared, clothed in extreme evening dress, and established himself, ramrod-like, in a customary spot in the center of the floor. There was a figure on the Persian rug whereon Mr. Gwynn never failed to take position. Once in place, eye as expressionless as the eye of a fish, Mr. Gwynn would wait in dead silence for Richard to speak.

Mr. Gwynn had occupied his wonted spot on the rug two minutes before Richard came out of his reverie. Turning to Mr. Gwynn, he addressed him through murky wreaths.

"I shall go to New York to-morrow."

"Very good, sir," said Mr. Gwynn, and his back creaked in just the specter of a bow.

"When are the President and General Attorney of the Anaconda to be here?"

"Tuesday, sir; the eighth of the month."

"I shall return before that time."

"Very good, sir!" and Mr. Gwynn again approved the utterances of Richard with a creaky mandarin inclination of the head and shoulders.

"They will arrive on the eighth. Say to them that they must remain until the fifteenth, one week. On Thursday—the tenth—you will give a dinner in honor of Senator Hanway; it is to be fifty covers. The Anaconda people will come. I'll furnish you the completed list of guests when I get back."

"Very good, sir."

"You may go."

"Yes, sir; you are very kind, sir;" and the austere Mr. Gwynn creaked himself out.

Richard was left with his thoughts, while the silent Matzai, who had heard the word New York, began packing what trunks were needed for the journey.

Storri was ruthlessly eager to get some taste of his great triumph, and came that same evening to the Harley house. Senator Hanway had been detained by a night session, and the quartette—Dorothy, Mr. Harley, Mrs. Hanway-Harley, and Storri—sat together at dinner. Dorothy, pale and still and chill, was like a girlish image made of snow. There was a queer look of fright and shame and horror all in one about her virgin eyes. How she got through the dinner she could not have told, and only her love for her father held her up.

Mr. Harley was in no livelier case; and, albeit he drank much more than usual, the wine put no color in his muddy cheek nor did it cure its flabbiness. To sit at his own table and tremble before his own guest might have wasted the spirits of even a hardier man than Mr. Harley.

Dorothy was in agony—a kind of despair of shame, eating nothing, saying less, and this attracted the shallow attention of Mrs. Hanway-Harley.

"What makes you so gloomy, Dorothy?" she asked. Mrs. Hanway-Harley was in most cheerful feather. A nobleman at her table, and though for the fortieth time, was ever fresh and delightful to Mrs. Hanway-Harley. "You are not ill?" Then, with arch politeness to Storri: "She has been out of sorts all day, Count, and given us all the blues. I was delighted when you came in to cheer us up."

"It is to my great honor, madam," responded Storri, smiling and fixing Dorothy with that beady glance which serpents keep for what linnets they mean to fascinate and swallow, "it is to my great honor, madam, that you say so. I shall tell my Czar of your charming goodness to his Storri. If I might only think that the bewitching Miss Dorothy was also glad, I should be in heaven! Truly, it would make a paradise; ah, yes, why not!"

As Storri threw off this languishing speech, Dorothy could feel his eyes like points of hateful fire piercing her satirically. It taught her vaguely, even through the torture her soul was undergoing, that composite sentiment of passion and cruelty felt for her by this Tartar in evening dress who mixed sneer with compliment in all he said. Dorothy could have shrieked out in the mere torment of it, and only the sight of Mr. Harley, broken and hopeless and helpless and old, gave her strength and courage to refrain.

Storri departed on the heels of dinner to the profound regret of Mrs. Hanway-Harley, who pressed him to remain. The Russian was wise; he must not attempt too much. Dorothy should have respite for a week. In seven days he would again take dinner with the Harleys. Dorothy would have employed those seven days in thinking on the perils to her father which he, Storri, could launch; she would have considered how he, Storri, must be courted and flattered and finally loved to insure her father's safety. It was victory as it stood. Was he not compelling the proud Dorothy to receive his compliments, his glances, his sighs, his love? Was not Richard, the detestable, excluded, and the Harley door closed fast in his face? Ah! Storri would impress upon these little people the terrors of him whom they had affronted! He would cause them to mourn in bitterness the day they heard first his name!

Storri, in midswing of all these comforting ruminations, felt a light hand on his arm. He was sauntering leisurely along the street at the time, and had not journeyed a block from the Harley house.

Storri started at the touch, and wheeled.

"What!" he exclaimed, "is it you, my San Reve? And what fetched you out so cold an evening?"

Storri attempted a manner of light and confident assurance. Somehow, he did not altogether attain it; a sharp ear would have caught the false note in his tones which told of an uneasiness he was trying to conceal.

That one whom Storri addressed as San Reve and who, following the touch that startled Storri, had taken his arm, was a woman. In the dark of the winter evening, nothing could be known of her save that she was above a middle height.

"Yes; it is I, Sara," said the woman, in a pure contralto. "Come with me to-night, Storri; I have not seen you for four days."

"We are pleasantly met!" cried Storri, still affecting an acquiescent gayety. "And is it not strange? I was on my way to your fond, sweet presence, my San Reve. Yes, your Storri was flying to you even now!"

All of which were lies, being leaf and stalk of that uneasiness which rang so falsely in his voice and manner. Still, if Mademoiselle San Reve took notice of his insincerity, she kept the fact to herself. Storri drew her hand further within his arm, and the two walked slowly onward, while the street lamps as they passed merged and separated and again merged and separated their shadows as though the pair were agreeing and disagreeing in endless alternation.

Richard, the next day, departed for New York as he had planned. Sending Matzai and his luggage to the hotel, Richard on his arrival drove straight from the station to Thirty, Broad. He glanced at a card as he entered the elevator.

"Tenth floor!" was his word to the resplendent functionary in gold and blue who presided in the elevator.

"Tenth floor!" cried the resplendent functionary in the sing-song of a seaman taking soundings and calling the marks, and the elevator came to a kind of bouncing stop.

"Mr. Bayard?" inquired Richard.

"Second floor to th' left," sang the blue and golden one; then the iron door clashed and the cage flew on.

Richard entered a reception room, and from this outer harbor, like a newly arrived ship sending up a signal, he dispatched his card to Mr. Bayard. Under "Mr. Richard Storms" he wrote the words, "son of the late Mr. Dudley Storms."

The stealthy, whispering individual, who spoke with a hiss and scrutinized Richard as he took his card with a jealous intensity which might have distinguished a hawk in a state of half alarm and whole suspicion, presently returned. His air was altered to one of confidence.

"You are to come in, please!" he hissed like a respectful snake.

It was two hours later, five o'clock, when Richard emerged from that private room of Mr. Bayard's. Taking the carriage which had waited, he returned to the station and caught a train for Washington. A message went to Matzai notifying that Mongol of what changes had been determined on in the destinies of himself and the luggage.

It was the following morning at the hour of eight. Richard called for Mr. Gwynn. When that severe personage had taken his proper station on the rug, he rolled his piscatorial eye on Richard as though inviting notice. The latter young gentleman was improving himself with coffee, now and then pausing to thoughtfully glance over a roll of names.

"What were the last quotations on Anaconda stock?" demanded Richard, still contemplating the names.

"Common, two hundred and eleven; preferred, two hundred and seventeen, sir," and Mr. Gwynn creaked by way of ending the sentence.

"Here are the keys to my boxes in the Colonial Trust. Here also are the names of fifty New York banks. Please establish a credit of two millions in each of them—one hundred millions of dollars in all. Use Anaconda stock. Bring me certified checks for the one hundred millions, with a statement from each bank showing what Anaconda shares it holds as security. I think you understand. I want one hundred millions instantly available. You will go to New York at once and make the arrangements. Day after to-morrow meet me in Mr. Bayard's rooms, Thirty, Broad, at three o'clock P. M., with everything as I have outlined."

"Very good, sir; you are very kind, sir," creaked Mr. Gwynn.

CHAPTER XIII

HOW THE SAN REVE GAVE STORRI WARNING

Had you, at the time Richard visited that gentleman, written Mr. Bayard a letter, you would have addressed it to Mr. Robert Lance Bayard, and anyone who saw you do it would have gazed in wonder and respect to think you were upon terms of personal correspondence with that blinding meteor of speculation. Mr. Bayard sat in his rooms at Thirty, Broad, like an astrologer in his tower cell; he considered the stars and cast the horoscopes of companies. That done, he took profitable advantage of his prescience.

In the kingdom of stocks Mr. Bayard's position was unique. He, like Napoleon, was without a model and without a shadow. He constructed no corporations, shoved no companies from shore; he stood at the ticker and took his money off the tape. Whenever he won a dollar he had risked a dollar.

In person Mr. Bayard was slim, elegant, thoroughbred, with blood as red and pure of strain as the blood of a racing horse. To see him was to realize the silk and steel whereof he was compounded. There was a vanity about him, too; but it was a regal vanity, as though a king were vain. His brow was full and grave, his face dignified, his eye thoughtful, and he knew men in the dark by feel of bark, as woodmen know a tree. He stepped about with a high carriage of the head, as might one who has prides well founded. His health was even, his nerves were true; he owned a military courage that remained cool with victory, steady with defeat. It was these which rendered Mr. Bayard the Bourse-force men accounted him, and compelled consideration even from folk most powerful whenever they would float an enterprise or foray a field of stocks. Did Oil or Sugar or Steel come into the Street with purpose of revenge or profit, its first care was a peace-treaty with Mr. Bayard. That was not because Oil or Steel or Sugar loved, but because it feared him. The King might not hunt in Sherwood without permission of Robin Hood, nor Montrose walk in Glenfruin wanting the MacGregor's consent.

In his youth—that is to say, almost a third of a century away—Mr. Bayard had been of open, frank, and generous impulse. He believed in humanity and relied upon his friends. Mr. Bayard at sixty was changed from that pose of thirty years before. He was cold and distant and serene in a cloud-capped way of ice. He trusted no one but himself, took no man's word save his own, was self-reliant to the point of bitterness, and rife of proud suspicions. Also, he had carried concealment to the plane of Art, and those who knew him best were most in the dark concerning him. And yet Mr. Bayard made a specialty of verbal truth, and his word was a word of gold.

It was not that Mr. Bayard deceived men, he allowed them to deceive themselves. They watched and they listened; and in the last they learned, commonly at the cost of a gaping wound in their bank balances, that what they thought they saw they did not see, and what they were sure they heard they did not hear; that from the beginning they had been the victims of self-constructed delusions, and were cast away by errors all their own. Once burned, twice wise; and the paradox crept upon Wall and Broad Streets, as mosses creep upon stones, that the more one knew of Mr. Bayard the less one was aware of. The feeling was expressed by a gentleman rich in Exchange experiences when he said:

"If I were to meet him in Broadway, I wouldn't believe it."

And that experienced one spoke well. For as the tiger, striped black and gold, is made to match and blend with the sun-slashed shadows of the jungle through which he hunts his prey, so was Mr. Bayard invisible in that speculation whereof he crouched a most formidable factor, with this to add to the long-toothed peril of it, that, although always in sight, he was never more unseen than at the moment of his spring.

The change from faith and friendship and a genial warmth that had taken place in Mr. Bayard and left him their rock-bound opposites, had its origin in the treachery of a friend. Mr. Bayard those years before was, in his stock sailing, beaten upon by a sudden squall of treason and lying ingratitude; his nature was capsized, and those softer and more generous graces were spilled out. They went to the bottom, as things golden will; and they never came up. Mr. Bayard was betrayed by one who had taken his hand in friendship not the hour before—one who was his partner in business and had risen through his favor. Struck in the dark, Mr. Bayard stood at the ticker and watched his fortune of eight millions bleed away; when he dropped the tape he was two millions worse than bankrupt. It was that case-hardening experience which had worked the callous metamorphosis.

"It has taught me caution," was all he said as the quotations chattered off the loss of his last dollar.

From that hour of night and wormwood, Mr. Bayard was another individual. He gave men his acquaintance, but not his faith; he listened and never believed; he had allies, not friends, and the limits of his confidence in a man were the limits of that man's interest.

And yet in this arctic hardness there remained one generous spot. There was one name to retain a sweetness and a perfume for Mr. Bayard that one finds in flowers, and the perishing years had not withered it on the hillsides of his regard. When Mr. Bayard went down on that day of storm and the dark waters of defeat and bankruptcy closed above him, there had been stretched one hand to save. Dudley Storms was hardly known to Mr. Bayard, for the former was of your silent, retiring men whom no one discovers until the time of need. His sort was evidenced on this occasion. He did not send to Mr. Bayard, he came. He told him by shortest possible sentences that his fortune was at his, Mr. Bayard's, disposal to put him again upon his feet. And Mr. Bayard availed himself of the aid thus proffered; he regained his feet; he paid off his bankruptcy of two millions; he repaid Dudley Storms; and then he went on—and no more slips or treason-founded setbacks—to pile up new millions for himself.

Following that one visit of succor from Dudley Storms, he and Mr. Bayard were no oftener in one another's company than before. The former retreated into his native reticence and the fastnesses of his own multitudinous affairs, coming no more to Mr. Bayard, who did not require help. Dudley Storms was a lake of fire in a rim of ice, as somebody somewhere once said of someone else, and labored under peculiarities of temperament and trait-contradictions which you may have observed in Richard. For his side, Mr. Bayard, proudly sensitive, while he never forgot, never failed to feel in the edge of that saving favor done him by Dudley Storms the edge of a sword; and this served to hold him aloof from one who any hour might have had his life and fortune, without a question, to do with as he would.

Richard had never met Mr. Bayard, nor did he know aught of that gentleman's long-ago disasters, for they occurred in the year of Richard's birth. But he had heard his father speak of Mr. Bayard in terms of glowing praise; wherefore, when it became Richard's turn to know somewhat the ins and outs of Wall Street, a dark interior trade-region of which his ignorance for depth was like unto the depth of the ocean, and as wide, our young gentleman went instantly in search of him. Had he beheld the softened eye of Mr. Bayard when that war-lord of the Street first read his card, had he heard his voice as he repeated the line "son of the late Mr. Dudley Storms," he might have been encouraged in a notion that he had not rapped at the wrong door. But Richard, in the anteroom awaiting the return of that person of the serpent hiss, did not witness these phenomena. When he was shown into the presence of Mr. Bayard, he saw only one who for dignity and courteous poise seemed the superior brother of the best-finished gentleman he had ever met.

"So you are the son of Dudley Storms," said Mr. Bayard, running his eye over the visitor as though looking for a confirmatory resemblance. Then, having concluded his scrutiny: "You are like him. Have a chair; tell me what I can do to serve you."

Richard was taken with Mr. Bayard's words, for that gentleman managed to put into them a reassuring emphasis that was from nowhere save the heart. Thus led, Richard began by asking Mr. Bayard if he knew aught of Storri.

"Storri? He is the Russian who helped the sugar people get their hold in Odessa. The oil interests have some thought of employing him in their affairs. What of Storri?"

Richard explained the propriety of destroying Storri; this he did with an ingenuous ferocity that caused Mr. Bayard to smile.

"The man," observed Richard in conclusion, "is no more than so much vermin. He is a menace to my friends; he has intrigued villainously against me. I have no option; I must destroy him out of my path as I would any footpad or any brigand."

Being primal in his instincts, as every great man is, Mr. Bayard, at this hostile declaration, could not avoid a quick side-glance at Richard's door-wide shoulders, Pict arms, and panther build. Richard caught the look.

"Oh, if it might have been settled in that way," cried he, "I should have had his head wrung round ere this!"

"You will readily conceive," observed Mr. Bayard, after musing a bit, "that I keep myself posted concerning the least movement of the least man who comes speculating into stocks. You may take it for granted that I know a trifle or so of your Count Storri. To be frank, he and Mr. Harley, with Senator Hanway and five others, are preparing for some movement in Northern Consolidated. I don't know whether it is to be a 'bull' or a 'bear' movement, or when they will begin. Those are matters which rest heavily on the finding of that special committee of which Senator Hanway is the chief. Do you know when the finding may be looked for? Can you tell me what the committee will report?"

Richard could not bring himself to speak of Senator Hanway's confidential assurances of a white report for Northern Consolidated. From those assurances he was sure that the pool meditated a "bull" campaign, but he did not say so since he could not give his reasons.

Mr. Bayard came to the protection of his anxieties.

"Senator Hanway," went on Mr. Bayard, "has privately told a number of people that the report will favor the road."

Richard was struck by the cool fullness of Mr. Bayard's information. It was likewise impressive to learn that he was not the only one in Senator Hanway's confidence. On top of Richard's wonder Mr. Bayard piled another marvel. He declared that he did not believe the word of Senator Hanway.

"He is a fox for caution," quoth Mr. Bayard, "and I cannot think he told the truth. Believe me, the committee's report will tear Northern Consolidated to pieces. The market has been exceedingly strong since the beginning of the year. He will watch, and plump in that adverse report the moment general prices show a weakness."

Richard, while taken by the reasoning of Mr. Bayard, was not convinced. However, he asked Mr. Bayard what might be done.

"Remembering always," said Richard, "that the one purpose I have in view is the overthrow of Storri."

"Every member of that pool," returned Mr. Bayard, "has made himself fair game. A pool is like a declaration of war against the world; the pool itself would tell you so. And speaking of the pool, you understand that the eight are bound together like a fagot. You can't break one without breaking all; if Storri fall, Mr. Harley, Senator Hanway, and the others fall."

Richard could not forbear a smile as he recalled how Mrs. Hanway-Harley had said that her only objection to him was his lack of riches, and how, should his fortune one day mend and measure up with Mr. Harley's, Dorothy and he might wed. The peculiar humor of those possibilities which the situation offered began to address itself to Richard. Was not here a chance to remove Mrs. Hanway-Harley's objection?

"Since they are open game," said Richard, "I see no reason why the whole octagonal combination should not be wiped out. Indeed, there might be a distinct advantage in it," he concluded, thinking on Dorothy.

"There would be a distinct advantage of several millions in it," returned Mr. Bayard, who was thinking on dollars and cents. Then, as might one who, having decided, takes the first step in a great enterprise: "Where, by the way, are those millions that were left by Dudley Storms?"

"They are where you may put your hand upon them," returned Richard, "in any hunting of this vermin Storri."

The eyes of Mr. Bayard began to glitter and light up like the windows of a palace on the evening of a ball.

"I fancy," said he, "that I shall go with you for this Storri's destruction."

"I shall put the matter wholly into your hands. It is a game of which I know nothing but the name."

"The game is not difficult; it is mere purse-matching."

"How much of a fund will you require?"

"At the least, fifty millions. We must lie concealed until the pool develop its purpose. It will make but little difference, once it be developed; 'bull' or 'bear,' we meet them either way. Fifty millions should do. If that sum crowd you, we must recollect that I, myself, am not without a handful of millions that can never have better employment than fighting the battles of a son of Dudley Storms."

"Fifty millions would be no strain," replied Richard quickly. "To be safe, let us call those fifty millions one hundred. Still, I am deeply obliged for your proffer."

"One hundred millions be it," quoth Mr. Bayard. "We'll organize ourselves, and we'll wait and watch. When they move, we meet them. Should they sell, we buy; should they buy,—which they won't,—we sell; in either event we buy or sell them to a standstill. Should they connive a 'bear' raid, they'll sell their way into as formidable a corner as ever 'bear' was squeezed in."

This befell upon that first visit of Richard to Mr. Bayard. Two days later, Richard returned. Mr. Gwynn met him, brisk upon the hour, in one of the numerous private rooms of Mr. Bayard, and turned over one hundred millions in certified checks upon those fifty banks. Richard dismissed Mr. Gwynn and went in to Mr. Bayard.

"I shall deposit these," said Mr. Bayard, "in ten banks, twenty millions in the City Bank and the balance scattered among the other nine. You may leave the details of our enterprise to me; I have been through many of similar color. I need not suggest the value of silence. Meanwhile, and I can't emphasize this too much, if you would busy yourself to advantage make what discoveries you may touching the pending report on Northern Consolidated."

On that evening when they came together outside the Harley house, Storri and the San Reve continued slowly on their way, turning now east, now south, until after ten minutes of walking they entered a narrow thoroughfare to which the street lamp on the corner gave the name of Grant Place. The houses were sober and reputable. Up the steps of one of the soberest went Storri and the San Reve; the latter let them in with a latch-key. Storri consigned his overcoat and hat to the rack in the hall as though his surroundings were familiar, and he with the San Reve passed into what in the original plan of the house had been meant for a drawing-room.

The house was occupied by a stirring lady named Warmdollar, who served her country as head scrubwoman in one of the big departments—a place of fatter salary than its menial name implies. There was a Mr. Warmdollar, who in an earlier hour had held through two terms a seat in Congress. This was years before. Failing of a second re-election, and having become fixed in the habit of officeholding, which habit seizes upon certain natures like a taste for opium, Mr. Warmdollar urged his claims for some appointive place. The Senators from his home-State felt compelled to moderately bestir themselves, the result of their joint efforts being that Mr. Warmdollar was tendered a position as guard about the congressional cemetery, said last resting-place of greatness-gone-to-sleep being a wild, weird tract in a semi-farmerish region on the fringe of town. Mr. Warmdollar objected to the place, and the gloomy kind of its duties; but since this was before Mrs. Warmdollar had begun to earn a salary as scrubwoman, he was driven to accept.

"Take it until something better turns up," urged one of the Senators, who had grown tired of having Mr. Warmdollar on his hands.

It was a blustering night of rain when Mr. Warmdollar entered upon his initial vigil as a guardian of the dead. Wet, weary, disgusted, Mr. Warmdollar sought refuge in a coop of a sentry-box, which stood upon the crest of a hill through which the road that bounded one side of the burying ground had been cut. The sentry-box was waterproof and to that extent a comfort, being designed for deluges of the sort then soaking Mr. Warmdollar.

Had there been nothing but a downpour, Mr. Warmdollar might have borne it until his watch was relieved; he might have even continued to perform the duties and draw the emoluments of his place indefinitely. But the winds rose; and they blew down Mr. Warmdollar's sentry-box. Toppling into the road, it rolled merrily down a steep and then lay upon its front, door downward, in the mud. Mr. Warmdollar could not get out; being discouraged by what he had undergone, he broke into yells and cries like a soul weltering in torment.

The yells and cries engaged the heated admiration of a farmer's dog that dwelt hard by, and the dog descended upon the sentry-box and Mr. Warmdollar, attacking both with an impartiality which showed him no one to split hairs. Then the farmer came to his door, arrayed in a shirt and a shotgun, and emptied both barrels of the latter at Mr. Warmdollar and his sentry-box—the agriculturist not understanding the case, as sometimes happens to agriculturists, notably in politics.

Following his baptism of dog and fire, Mr. Warmdollar crawled back to town and worked no more. Mrs. Warmdollar was named scrubwoman, while her disheartened spouse devoted himself to strong drink, as though to color one's nose and fuddle one's wits were the great purposes of existence. Being eager of gain, Mrs. Warmdollar had sub-rented her parlor floor to the San Reve; and since Mrs. Warmdollar was a lady in whom curiosity had had its day and died, she asked no questions the answers to which might prove embarrassing.

The San Reve, like Mrs. Warmdollar, worked in a department, being a draughtswoman in the Treasury Building, and attached to the staff of the supervising architect. The place had been granted the San Reve at the request of Senator Hanway, who was urged thereunto by Mr. Harley, to whom Storri explained the San Reve's skill in plates and plans and the propriety of work.

The San Reve's apartments were comfortable with chairs, lounges, and ottomans; a piano occupied one corner, while two or three good pictures hung upon the walls. In the bow-window was a window-seat piled high with cushions, from which by daylight one might have surveyed the passing show—dull enough in Grant Place.

"Have you no kiss for your Storri, my San Reve?" cried Storri plaintively, but still sticking to the lightly confident.

The San Reve accepted Storri's gallant attention as though thinking on other things than kisses. Then she threw aside her hat and wraps, and glanced at herself in the glass.

She was a striking figure, the San Reve, with brick-colored hair and eyes more green than gray. Her skin showed white as ivory; her nose and mouth and chin, heavy for a woman, told of a dangerous energy when aroused. The eyebrows, too, had a lowering falcon trick that touched the face with fierceness. The forehead gave proof of brains, and yet the San Reve was one more apt to act than think, particularly if she felt herself aggrieved. If you must pry into a matter so delicate, the San Reve was twenty-eight; standing straight as a spear, with small hands and feet, she displayed that ripeness of outline which sculptors give their Phrynes.

"Storri," said the San Reve, with a chill bluntness that promised the disagreeable while it lost no time, "why do you visit that house—the Harley house?"

Storri was in an easy-chair, puffing a cigar as though at home. The San Reve, half lying, half sitting, reclined upon a sofa. They looked at each other; Storri trying to seem brave, the San Reve with staring courage, open and more real.

"You know, my San Reve, I have business with Mr. Harley. Let me tell you: Mr. Harley, through his relative, Senator Hanway——"

"You go to see the girl," interrupted the San Reve, and the sullen contralto was vibrant of danger. "You go to see Miss Harley, not her father."

"And if I do?"

Storri put his query blusteringly.

"You will marry her," went on the San Reve, who appeared to care as little for Storri's bluster as his kiss.

"I never promised to marry you."

"I do not ask you to marry me. I want neither your name nor your title. But you promised me your love; I want that." The San Reve's tones were unruffled. They did not lift or mount, and told only of passionate resolution. "Storri, why did you bring me from Ottawa?"

"If it come to that," retorted Storri spitefully, "why did you leave Ottawa?"

"I left Ottawa for love," the San Reve replied, as though considering with herself. "I left Ottawa for love of you, just as four years before I came to Ottawa for love of another."

"You have had adventures," remarked Storri sarcastically. "I have never heard your story, my San Reve; go on, I beseech you!"

"I will tell you one thing," said the San Reve, "from which you may wring a warning. My father was a showman—a tamer of lions and leopards. When I was twelve, I went into the den with him to hold a hoop while he lashed those big cats through it. Yes, Storri," cried the San Reve, a sudden flame to burst forth in her voice like an oral brightness, and as apparent as a fire in a forest, "when to fear was to die, I have held aloft my little hoop to the lions and the leopards! And for all their snarls they jumped tamely; for all their threats they did nothing. I, as a child, was not afraid of a lion under the lash; am I now to fear a bear, a Russian bear, I, who am a woman?"

"Why, my San Reve," protested Storri, "and what has stirred your anger?"

Storri was startled by the San Reve's fury rather than her revelations. Having a politic mind to soothe her, he sought to take her hand.

"Keep your attentions to yourself!" cried the San Reve; "I am in no temper for tenderness."

"Ah, as to that," said Storri, turning proud, "I, who am a Russian gentleman, yes, a Russian nobleman, shall not offend. Yes," yawning and giving himself an air, "I am relieved by your cold attitude. That is the folly of being noble! One cannot be attentive to those beneath one save at a loss of self-respect. Bah! my Czar, could he but see, would call his Storri disgraced by the mere nearness of such as you."

"And you name your Czar to me!" returned the San Reve, now sneering calm, her cool contralto restored; "to me, a French woman! And your nobility, too—that thing of Caspian mud! Storri, the San Reves were soldiers with Napoleon; your noble kind ran from them like hares. The San Reves stabled their horses in the audience chambers of your Czars."

The San Reve rippled off these periods in quiet, invincible scorn. Storri, beaten, frightened, began to whine. His bluster, his bombast, his nobility, his affected elevations, were alike broken down. He professed love; he said that he had wronged his San Reve. His San Reve was a goddess, a flower, a star! Would she make her Storri desolate?—her Storri who would die for love of her!

The San Reve became sensibly composed; her falcon brow relaxed, her spirit took on a tranquil frame, her anger was cooled by the cooing contrition of Storri. The San Reve permitted herself to be soothed.

"Let us go no more in that direction," said the San Reve. "Such tauntings are but a childish barter of words."

The San Reve delivered this sentiment in a serene, high way that brought her honor. Then she lighted a cigarette and blew peaceful rings. Storri, encouraged in his soul by the return of his San Reve to reason, solaced himself with a fresh cigar. The two smoked in silent truce.

"It was a love quarrel, my San Reve!" said Storri.

"Only a love quarrel!" assented San Reve.

Silence and smoke; with Storri timid, shrinking from fresh offense and further outbreak.

Storri, fearing all who had no fear of him, feared the San Reve. Nor were his apprehensions void of warrant; the San Reve was of that hot and blinded strain which loves and slays.

"Your father dead," said Storri, pretending a perking interest, "your father dead, my San Reve, what then became of you?"

"I fell into the hands of a doting old architect of Paris. He was good to me; it was with him I learned my trade. No, I did not love him; but I was grateful. He died, and I came to Ottawa as a draughtswoman for the young engineer, Balue. I did not love Balue; he was tame. And then Ottawa, with those sodden Canadians, their Scotch whiskey, and narrow lives framed in with snow—how I loathed them! What a weariness of the heart they were, those frozen people! Then came you—Storri!"

The San Reve's gray-green eyes burned with white fire. She got up from the couch where she had lain curled like a tawny lioness.

"Yes; you came!" purred the San Reve, and she stooped and kissed Storri with her fierce lips. "Then for the first time I loved."

The San Reve recurled herself on the couch. Storri, who had met her kiss valorously, considered whether he might not please her by solicitude in a new direction.

"There is one thing, my San Reve," he observed, a show of feeling in his words. "Why do you tie yourself to that draughting? It grieves your Storri! Am I a pauper that my San Reve should work? Is Storri so miserly that the idol of his heart must be a slave?"

The San Reve shook her head.

"I must have something to do," she explained, a half-smile parting her rose-red lips. "I am like those poor rats of which my father told me who must gnaw and gnaw and forever gnaw to wear away their teeth, which otherwise would grow and kill them. No, I like my work; let me alone with it."

Storri tossed his hand and shrugged his shoulders in mute resignation and reproof. His San Reve would work; he consented, while he deprecated her so mad resolve.

"Let us return to our first concern," said the San Reve.

Storri quaked; he could follow her trail of thought by mental smell as the hound follows the fox.

"Storri, tell me; do you love this Miss Harley?"

"My San Reve, how can you ask? Look in the mirror! No, I do not love Miss Harley."

The San Reve toyed with her cigarette. Storri, thinking on escape, arose to go. He stepped into the hallway for his coat and hat. Then he returned, and, giving his hand to the reclining San Reve, drew her to her feet. Storri, about to go, was beaming; the kiss he printed lightly on the San Reve's lips spoke of a heart relieved. The San Reve herself was amiably placid; her anger apparently had died with her doubts.

"And you do not love Miss Harley?"

"No; I swear by my mother's grave!"

"By your mother's grave!" Then, voice deep as the mellow pipe of an organ: "Storri, you lie!"

Storri, aghast, was surprised into his usual defense of bluster. He started to bully; the San Reve raised her shapely hand.

"Storri, let me show you." The San Reve took from the drawer of a cabinet a beautiful pistol. She partly raised the hammer and buzzed the liberated cylinder. It gave forth clear, musical clicks. "Do you see?" said the San Reve half wistfully. "I have this!"

"You would not kill Miss Harley!" exclaimed Storri nervously.

"No! Storri, no!"

"Whom then?" and Storri moistened his dry lips. His San Reve was such a heathen! The thought parched him. "Whom would you kill, my San Reve?" This came off pleadingly.

"Whom would I kill?" the San Reve repeated tenderly, stretching for a kiss. "I would kill you! No, not now, my Storri; but some time. My resolution is only born; it is not yet grown. Storri, you must beware! I come of the race that kill! I have now only the tiny root of that blood resolution. Do not let us nourish it! We must destroy it—blight it with much love! I speak for you, for me!" The San Reve began to cry convulsively. "I speak against a dark day! I feel, I know it! It is you, you whom I shall kill! And then myself—oh, yes, my Storri, you cannot go alone!"

The San Reve threw herself weeping upon the couch; her gusty nature seemed torn by whirlwinds of passion and jealous love. Storri hung in the door, and the white of his cravat was not so white as his face. He could neither go nor stay, neither speak nor do; craven to the heart, he quailed before the stormy San Reve. An artist might have painted him as the Genius of Cowardice.

"Good-night, my Storri," said the San Reve, her voice mournfully sweet.

CHAPTER XIV

HOW THEY TALKED POLITICS AT MR. GWYNN's

In accord with the requests of Mr. Gwynn, which with them had those graver aspects the requests of royalty possess for London shopkeepers, the President and General Attorney of the Anaconda Airline came to Washington. The Anaconda president was a short, corpulent man, with dark skin, eyes black as beads, round, alert face, and a nose like the ace of clubs. The General Attorney was no taller than his superior officer, but differed from him in a figure so spare and starved that it snapped its fingers at description. As though to make amends for a niggardliness of the physical, Providence had conferred upon our legal one a prodigious head. A facetious opponent once said that he had a seven and a half hat and a six and a half belt, being, as steamboat folk would put it, over-engined for his beam. Both the President and the General Attorney were devoted to their company, and neither would have scrupled to loot an orphanage or burn a church had such drastic measure been demanded by Anaconda interests. Once in town, these excellent officers lost no time in presenting themselves at Mr. Gwynn's. To their joy that unbending personage was so good as to grant them a personal audience. Richard was present—such, as you have discovered, being the invariable usage with Mr. Gwynn. After the latter had shaken each visitor by the hand, a shake of mighty formality, he sat in state while Richard did the talking.

Mr. Gwynn was a spectacle of gravity when posed in a chair. He established himself on the edge of that piece of furniture, and for all the employment he gave its back it might as well have been a stool. Mr. Gwynn maintained himself bolt-upright, chin pointed high, with a general rigidity of attitude that made one fear he had swallowed the poker as a preliminary to the interview, and was bearing himself in accordance with the unyielding fact. The result was highly effective, and gave Mr. Gwynn a kingly air not likely to be wasted on impressionable ones such as the President and General Attorney. When the four were seated, Richard, using the potential name of Mr. Gwynn, proceeded to speak, while Mr. Gwynn at measured intervals creaked concurrence.

It had been decided by Mr. Gwynn, so Richard laid bare, that the future of the Anaconda would be advanced by the nomination of Senator Hanway for the Presidency. It would pleasure Mr. Gwynn were he to hear that the President and General Attorney shared this conclusion. If such were the flattering case, Mr. Gwynn would be delighted to have the President and

General Attorney call upon Senator Hanway, and consider what might be done towards the practical furtherance of his hopes. In short, the situation, word and argument, was precisely the same as when the visitors came on in the affair of Speaker Frost. Incidentally, Mr. Gwynn was to give a dinner in honor of Senator Hanway. It was understood that certain of that statesman's friends would take advantage of the occasion to announce his candidacy. The President and General Attorney were to be invited to the dinner. Mr. Gwynn would esteem it an honor if they found it convenient to be present and lend countenance to the movement in Senator Hanway's favor.

Throughout this setting forth, the President and General Attorney took advantage of pauses and periods to bow and murmur agreement with Mr. Gwynn's opinions and desires as Richard reeled them off; the murmurs and nods were as "Amens," and must have been gratifying to Mr. Gwynn. Nothing could give the President and General Attorney so much satisfaction as the elevation of Senator Hanway to the White House. They were a unit with Mr. Gwynn; they believed that not alone the future of the Anaconda but the prosperity of the nation, not to say the round advantage of the world at large, would be subserved thereby. They would confer with Senator Hanway as Mr. Gwynn suggested.

So hot were they that the President and General Attorney, with Richard, at once sought Senator Hanway; since it was no later than eleven in the morning they caught that great statesman before he started for the Senate. He greeted them with dignified warmth, and, aided by Richard, who conversationally went ahead to break the ice, the trio quickly came to an understanding.

Senator Hanway talked with a freedom that was of itself a compliment, when one remembers how it had ever been his common strategy in this business of President-catching to appear both ignorant and indifferent. Senator Hanway explained that the thing just then was the nomination. It would be necessary to control the coming National Convention. Governor Obstinate was a formidable figure; he was popular with the people; and, although Governor Obstinate was a man who would prove most perilous if armed with those thunderbolts of veto and patronage wherewith the position of chief executive would clothe his hand, Senator Hanway was sorry to say there were many among the leading spirits of party who cared so little for the public welfare and so much for their own that they would push Governor Obstinate's fortunes as a method of making personal capital in their home regions with the ignorant herd. Senator Hanway would not go into the details of what in his opinion might be accomplished by the President and General Attorney and the great railway system they controlled. It would be wiser, and perhaps in better taste,—here Senator

Hanway smiled with becoming modesty,—if others were permitted to do that. If his good friends of the Anaconda who had come so far in his honor—a mark of regard which he, Senator Hanway, could never forget nor underestimate—gave him their company to the Capitol, he would be proud to make them acquainted with Senators Gruff and Loot and Toot and Drink and Dice and others of his friends, and those gentlemen would go more deeply into the affair. The President and General Attorney, he was sure, could so exert the Anaconda influence that the delegations from those States through which it ran might be selected and controlled.

Senator Hanway and the President and General Attorney departed in high good feeling to meet with those statesmen named, while Richard sought Bess to hear word of his Dorothy and receive that letter which was already the particular ray of sunshine in days which were cloudy and dark.

It would do mankind no service to break in at this place with wideflung descriptions of Mr. Gwynn's dinner. It is among things strange that the world in the matter of proposing a candidate for public favor or celebrating a victory has made little or no advance from earliest ages. It has been immemorial custom when one had a candidate on his hands and desired to obtain for him the countenance of men, to give a dinner for those who were reckoned leaders of sentiment and, first filling them with meat and wine, make them stirring speeches to bring them to the candidate's support. From the initial dinner sub-dinners would radiate, and others be born of these, until a whole population might be considered fed and filled with food and speeches, and the candidate dined, not to say dinned, into the popular heart, or, what is the same thing, the popular stomach—in either case the popular regard. In celebrations the procedure was equally archaic. Did some admiral win a sea fight or some general a land fight or some candidate a ballot fight, instantly one-half the population marched in the middle of the street while the other half banked the curbs in screaming, kerchief-waving lines of admiration. And thus has it ever been since that far-distant morning of Eternity, when Time with his scythe let down the bars and went upon his mowing of the meadows of men's existences. Mr. Gwynn, you may be sure, has nothing novel to propose; wherefore at this crisis he gives a dinner, as doubtless did Nero and Moses and Noah and Adam and others of the mighty dead on similar occasions in their day.

Mr. Gwynn's dinner began with Senator Gruff. This wise man, with the sanction of Senator Hanway, intimated to Richard the uses of such a festival. Mr. Gwynn was not in politics; his dinner table would be neutral ground. When therefore some fiery orator, carefully primed and cocked, suddenly exploded into eloquent demands that Senator Hanway offer himself for the White House, subject of course, as the phrase is, to the action of his party's convention thereafter to assemble, it would have a look of spontaneity that was of prime importance. No other could do this so well as Mr. Gwynn; no other table would so escape that charge of personal interest which the friends of Governor Obstinate might be expected to make. The very fact of Mr. Gwynn being an Englishman would defend it. Mr. Gwynn, at the word of Richard, was willing to serve the views of Senator Gruff, and the dinner was arranged.

There were full sixty present, including Speaker Frost and those high officials of the Anaconda. Mr. Gwynn had also dispatched an invitation to Mr. Bayard, and Richard inclosed therewith a personal note which had for its result the bringing of that astrologer of stocks, albeit dinners political were not precisely his habit.

"Who is your friend Gwynn?" asked Mr. Bayard, the afternoon before the dinner.

"I'll explain Mr. Gwynn later," replied Richard. "He is quite devoted to my interests, I assure you, and to nothing else."

"I can well believe so," returned Mr. Bayard, who had already half solved the enigma of Mr. Gwynn. "I begin to fear that you are a quixotic, not to say an eccentric, not to add a most egotistical young man. At that I'm not prepared to say you are wrong. One is justified in extreme concealments to avoid those animals the snobs."

Mr. Gwynn, the picture of all that was imperial, sat at the table's head, with Senator Hanway on his right. At the foot was Senator Gruff, who, if not the founder, might be called the architect of the feast, since, with the exception of Mr. Bayard, he had pricked off the list of guests. Mr. Harley, sad and worn with thoughts of Storri, sat next to Senator Gruff, while Mr. Bayard and Richard occupied inconspicuous places midway of the board.

When in the procession of courses the dinner attained to birds, a famous editor of the Middle West, who had been consuming wine with diligence to the end that he be fluent, addressed the table's head. He recited the public interests; then, paying a tribute to their party as the guardian of those interests, he wound up in words of fire with the declaration that Senator Hanway must be the next standard-bearer of that party. The cheering was tremendous, considering the small numbers to furnish it.

When the joyful sounds subsided, Senator Hanway, in a few placid, gentle sentences, explained his flattered amazement, and how helplessly he was in the hands of his friends, who would do with him as they deemed best for party welfare and for public good. He had not sought this honor, he did not look for the nomination; his own small estimate of his powers and importance, an estimate which gentlemen who heard him must be aware of, was proof of it. But no man might set his inclinations against a popular demand. Private preferences must yield, private plans must be abandoned. The country was entitled to the services of every citizen, the party was at liberty to command the name of every member. Believing these things, and owing what he did to both public and party, Senator Hanway must acquiesce. He thanked his friends for thus distinguishing him; he gave himself passively to their will. There was a second tempest of approbation when Senator Hanway was through.

Senator Gruff proposed the health of the President of the Anaconda. That potentate of railways made a short, jerky oration. He gave his hearty concurrence to the proposal of Senator Hanway to be President. He did this as a patriot and not as the head of a great railway. The Anaconda would take no part in politics; it never did. The Anaconda was a business, not a political, concern; it would do nothing unbecoming a corporation of discretion and repute. However, he, the President, was more or less acquainted with sentiment in those regions threaded by the Anaconda. He made no doubt, nay, he could squarely promise, that the delegations from those States, as he knew and read their people's feeling, would go to the next convention instructed for Senator Hanway. More applause, and a buzz of congratulatory whispers. The powerful Anaconda, that political dictator of a region so vast that it was washed by two oceans, was to champion Senator Hanway.

Senator Coot, whose home-State was shaky beneath his Senate feet, and who was therefore anxiously afraid lest he himself be committed to a position on the perilous subject of finance that might provoke his destruction, now addressed the table. He yielded to no one in his admiration for Senator Hanway. In view of what had been proposed, however, he, Senator Coot, would like to ask Senator Hanway to define his position in that controversy of Silver versus Gold.

No one was looking for this, no such baleful curiosity had been anticipated. It was Senator Gruff that came to the rescue, and Richard, to whom the scene was new and full of interest, could not admire too deeply the dexterity wherewith he held the shield of his humor between Senator Hanway and the shaft of that interrogatory.

Senator Gruff thought the question premature. The convention was months away; sentiment had been known to shift in a day like the bed of a river and seek new channels with its currents. Senator Gruff distrusted the wisdom of binding anybody at that time to a hard and fast declaration whether for silver or gold or both. He was sure that on soberer thought his friend Senator Coot would see the impropriety of his question.

Senator Coot declined to see the impropriety to which Senator Gruff had adverted. To commit himself to any gentleman's canvass was to commit himself to that gentleman's opinions. Those opinions might not be consistent with ones held by his, Senator Coot's, constituents, to whom he must in all things adhere. He, Senator Coot, was no one to buy pigs in pokes—if Senator Hanway would forgive a homely expression which was not intended as personal to himself. Senator Coot must insist upon his question.

Senator Gruff still came forward in defense. He said he had heard that Senator Coot's native State of Indiana was originally settled by people who had started for the West but lost their nerve. In view of the timidity and weak irresolution of his Senate brother, he, Senator Gruff, was inclined to credit the tradition. He must protest against question-asking at this time. Senator Gruff must even warn his friend Senator Coot that to ask a question now might result in later disaster to himself.

On that point of question-putting, might he, Senator Gruff, impart a word of counsel? A question was often a trap to catch the questioner. One should step warily with a question. A man who puts a question should never fail to know the answer in advance. When he pulls the trigger of a question, as when he pulls the trigger of a gun, he must look out for the kick. Many a perfect situation had been destroyed by the wrong question asked in the dark. Senator Gruff begged permission to tell a story.

"Once a good and optimistic dominie," said Senator Gruff, "was being shown through Sing Sing Prison. In his company went a pessimist who took darkling views of humanity in the lump, and particularly what fractions of the lump had gotten themselves locked up. The pessimist could see no good in them.

"'But you are wrong,' argued the dominie. 'There's good in the worst among them all. Stay; I'll prove it.' Then, turning to the guard: 'Sir, please bring us to the very worst character who is prisoner here.' On their way to the abandoned one, the dominie observed to the pessimist: 'I'll guarantee, by a few adroit questions, to so develop the good side of this fallen creature that you will be driven to confess its existence.'

"They traveled the corridors, and finally the guard threw open a cell wherein was a man whose face was so utterly brutal that its softest expression was a breach of the peace. The man, who was in for life, had committed an atrocious murder.

"The only thing in the cell besides the man was a rat, which—wheel within wheel—was confined in a little cage. This rat was the prisoner's darling; the guard said that he would draw blood from his arm to feed it. The good dominie—who knew his business—instantly seized upon the rat for his cue.

"'And you love the rat?' he said to the prisoner.

"'I love it better than my life!' cried the prisoner. 'There isn't anything I wouldn't sacrifice for that rat.'

"'There,' said the good dominie, wheeling on the pessimist, who was visibly subdued by the poor prisoner's love for his humble pet, 'there, you see! Here is a captive wretch whose estate is hopeless. He wears the brand of a felon and is doomed to stone-caged solitude throughout his life. And yet, without friends or light or liberty, with everything to sour and harden and promote the worst that's in him, he finds it in his heart to love! From those white seed which were planted by Providence in the beginning that beautiful love springs up to blossom in a dreary prison, and, for want of a nobler object, waste its tender fragrance on a rat. It touches me to the heart!' and the good dominie watered the floor of the cell with his tears.

"The pessimist had no more to say; he murmured his contrition and declared that he had received a lesson. He would never again distrust or contradict the existence of that spark of divine goodness which, at the bottom of every nature like a diamond at the bottom of a pit, would live quenchless through the ages to save the soul at last.

"The good dominie and the reformed pessimist were retiring, when the dominie paused, like Senator Coot, to ask one question—the only one he couldn't have answered in advance.

"'Why, my poor man, do you love that rat?'

"The prisoner's face became more brutal with the light of a diabolical joy.

"'Why do I love him?' he cried. Then, with a chuckle of fiendish exultation: 'Because he bit the warden.'"

The adroit Senator Gruff might have found it hard to show the application of his story. That, however, was not going to worry the sagacious Senator Gruff. He reckoned only upon raising a laugh at the anxious Senator Coot's expense which would silence that question-asking personage, who was more afraid of present ridicule, being sensitive, than of future condemnation by his constituents. The yarn succeeded in winning peals of laughter, and without giving Senator Coot a chance to reply or repeat his poking about to discover the position of Senator Hanway upon the issue of finance, Senator Gruff proposed the health of Mr. Bayard.

"And perhaps," remarked Senator Gruff, "that eminent authority on markets, and therefore upon finance, will favor us with his views on money. I do not hesitate," concluded Senator Gruff, turning to Mr. Bayard, "to cast you into the breach, because, of all who are here, you are the one best qualified and, I might add, least afraid to be heard. You have no constituents to be either shocked at your opinions or to punish their expression."

Senator Coot's curiosity touching Senator Hanway's money position, a fatal curiosity that had it not been smothered might have spread, was overwhelmed in a general desire to hear Mr. Bayard. The great speculator was known to every statesman about the table, and the whisper of conversation became hushed.

"As said the gentleman who has so honored me,"—here Mr. Bayard bowed to Senator Gruff, who complimented him by lifting his glass,—"there are no reasons why I should not give you my beliefs of money. I will tell you what I would and would not do for a currency, if I were business manager of a country. I would not coin silver money, because the low intrinsic value of such currency would make it a cumbrous one. I would not coin both silver and gold, because of the impossibility of maintaining an equality of values between the two coins. I would coin gold and nothing but gold, because it offers those qualities, important above others in a money metal, of high value and high durability."

"But is there gold enough to furnish all the money required?" asked Senator Coot, who was nervously interested.

"For centuries," replied Mr. Bayard, who began to feel a warmer interest than he had in any situation or any topic for over thirty years, "for centuries production has been filling the annual lap of the world with millions upon millions of gold. No part of it has been lost, none destroyed. For every possible appropriation there exists a plenty, even a plethora, of gold. And let me say this: there is a deal of claptrap talked and written and printed and practiced concerning this business of a currency, a subject which when given a right survey presents no difficulty. Mankind has been taught that in the essence of things fiscal your question of currency is as intricate and involved as was the labyrinth of Minos. And then, to add ill-doing to ill-teaching, our own crazy-patch system of finance has been in every one of its patches cut and basted and stitched with an interest of politics or of private gain to guide the shears and needle of what money-tailor was at work. A country, if it would, could have a circulating medium, and all coined yellow gold, of two hundred dollars, or five hundred dollars, or one thousand dollars per capita for population, and, beyond the expense of the mint, without costing that country a shilling. One, being business manager of the nation, as fast as the mints would work could pour forth an unbroken stream of gold money, half-eagles, eagles, and double eagles, to what breadth and depth for a whole circulation one would, and never spend a shilling beyond the working of the mints.

"Observe, now; as a nation we have a business manager. He holds in his fingers five twenty-dollar gold pieces. He buys one hundred dollars' worth of gold bullion with them. The public, if it would, might buy gold as freely as does any private individual. Our business manager gets the bullion, while the other, a gold miner perhaps, takes the gold coin. Then our business manager stamps the bullion he has bought—one hundred dollars' worth—into five new twenty-dollar gold pieces.

"With these in his palm he is ready for another bargain with the gold miner. Again the miner gets the gold pieces, and again our business manager gets one hundred dollars' worth of yellow bullion. This he coins; and being thereby re-equipped with five more new twenty-dollar pieces he returns to the experiment.

"This barter and this coinage might go on while a grain of the world's gold remained uncoined. At the finish, our business manager would have only one hundred yellow dollars in his fist; but there would be billions coined and stamped and in circulation. And the country would be neither in nor out a dollar. I am talking of coinage, not taxation, remember.

"Once in circulation the law would protect the money from being clipped or mutilated or melted down. Once money, always money, and he who alters its money status we lock up as a felon. There is no legal reason and no moral reason and no market reason to militate against what I have outlined as a policy. Finance as a science is simpler than the science of soap-boiling, although the money-changers in the temple for their own selfish advantage prefer you to think otherwise."

"Your wholesale consumption of gold," interrupted Senator Coot, "would raise the price of gold beyond measure."

"Wherein would lie the harm? So that it did not disturb the comparative prices of soap and pork and sugar and flour and lumber and on through the list of a world's commodities—and it would not—no one would experience either jolt or squeeze. With wheat at a dollar a bushel, a reduction to ten cents a bushel would work no injury if at the same time every other commodity in its price fell ninety per cent. To merely multiply the 'price' of gold, a metal which when it isn't money is jewelry, would cut no more important figure in the economy of life than would the making of one thousand marks upon a thermometer where now we make one hundred. Suppose, instead of one hundred degrees, we scratched off one thousand degrees on a thermometer in the same space: would it make the weather any hotter? I grant you a cautious business manager would not walk in among the gold-sellers and purchase ten billion dollars' worth of gold in a day; and for the same reason that a cautious cowboy wouldn't ride in among a bunch of cattle and flap a blanket. Not because there lurks inherent peril in so doing, but for that in the timid ignorance of the herd it would produce a stampede."

"But don't you see," objected Senator Coot, who was learned in the cant of currency and believed it, "don't you see that what you propose, by putting up the price of gold and putting down the price of everything else, would multiply riches in the hands of the creditor class? Wouldn't it work injustice to the debtors of the land?"

"Without pausing to guess," said Mr. Bayard, "for that is all one might do, whether the extravagant coinage of gold would promote its 'price,' I will submit that such contention should be disregarded. It is too general, and too incessant. If such were permitted the rank of argument, it would trip up every tariff, every appropriation, every governmental thing.

"Also, one must not put a too narrow limit upon the term 'creditor class.' Every man with a dollar in his pocket, or who owns a farm or a horse or a bolt of cloth or one hundred bushels of wheat, belongs to the extent of that dollar or farm or horse or bolt of cloth or one hundred bushels of wheat to the creditor class. The world is his debtor, and he has it in pawn and pledge to him for the value of that dollar or farm or horse or cloth or wheat. Now, a tariff law can be and frequently is framed so as to lift or lower the 'prices' of all or any of these. If your argument be good it should be just as potent to prevent a tariff law that augments riches in one hand or detracts from riches in another, as to prevent a coinage law that does the same.

"Properly speaking, there can be no separation of mankind into creditor and debtor classes, since, as we have seen, every man with a dollar's worth of property is in the creditor class to the extent of that dollar, while the world is in the debtor class and owes him therefor. There can be but two classes: those who own something, and those who don't. There lies the sole natural division; and not a law is framed, whether it be for a tariff or an appropriation or an army or a navy or a coinage or a bond issue or what you will, that does not, in lesser or greater degree, add to or take from the riches of some man or men. No government can go its clumsy necessary way without stepping on somebody's toes, and if one cannot have a currency because to have it will help this individual or hurt that one, by the same token one cannot have a government at all.

"However," concluded Mr. Bayard, "I think your talked-of advance in a gold 'price' born of coined billions might prove in the test to be imaginary rather than real. There has been ever a gold-ghost to frighten folk. There was once a time when men talked of resuming specie payment, and the public hung away from it, fearful and trembling, like an elephant about to cross a bridge. Horace Greeley cried, 'The way to resume is to resume!' and every dollar-dullard called him crazy. And yet, as the simple sequel demonstrated, the elephant need not have shivered, the bridge was wholly safe, and Horace Greeley was right."

Senator Gruff, whom Mr. Gwynn had privately requested to assume control so far as speeches and toasts and sentiments to be expressed were involved, now held forth in terms of flowery compliment concerning Mr. Bayard. He thanked that able gentleman for his theory of finance. Senator Gruff would not discuss its soundness; this was not the time nor yet the place. He would say, however, that it was unique and interesting.

Referring to what Mr. Bayard had called our "crazy-patch" system of currency, he, Senator Gruff, was willing to make this statement. The greenbacks, as all knew, were exempt from taxation. To discover how far greenbacks and their exemption had been made to affect the whole taxes of the several States, he, Senator Gruff, the year before had addressed a letter to every county tax-gatherer in the country. He had asked each to state the amount of greenbacks returned that year for his particular county as exempt.

"I received a reply," said Senator Gruff, "from every county auditor between Eastport and San Diego, Vancouver's and the Florida Keys. The aggregate of greenbacks returned exempt for that one year was over thirteen billions of dollars, while, as we know, the entire amount of greenbacks extant in the country is but a shadow above two hundred and forty millions. I shall make no comment on the miracle, and cite it only as an incidental expression of one element of our money system."

Senator Gruff, continuing, recurred to the pushing forward of Senator Hanway as a Presidential candidate. It was, while unexpected by him, a movement so full of righteous politics that he confessed heartfelt gratification thereat. Senator Gruff would suggest that one and only one gentleman among those present be selected to furnish the story to the press.

"In that way," explained Senator Gruff, "we will escape the confusion sure to be the consequence should a half-dozen of us answer inquiries."

Senator Gruff, by common acclaim, was pitched upon as the one to deal with the papers.

"Why, then," returned Senator Gruff, with a quizzical eye, "I foresaw this honorable occasion and prepared for it. I shall give what we have done to the *Daily Tory*, whose intelligent representative is with us as a guest." And thereupon Senator Gruff, while a smile went round at this evidence of fullest preparation for the unexpected, a smile which he met with a merry face, drew from his pocket a document and passed it over to Richard. In another moment a messenger was called; the story went on the wire, and the candidacy of Senator Hanway was formally declared.

Senator Hanway, as the dinner neared its close, proposed the health of Mr. Gwynn. In response, that remarkable man filled a goblet to the brim, arose, and bowed with gravity and condescension to Senator Hanway. Everybody stood up, and Mr. Gwynn's health was drunk with proper solemnity.

The highbred conduct of Mr. Gwynn from the beginning had been worthy of him as an old-school English gentleman. He said nothing; but he took wine with a decorous persistency that was almost pious and seemed like a religious rite. It should be observed that while he drank twice as much as did any other gentleman, not excepting Mr. Harley himself, it in no whit altered the stony propriety of his visage. There came no color to his cheek; nor did the piscatorial eye blaze up, but abode as pikelike as before. Also, with every bumper Mr. Gwynn became more rigid, and more rigid still, as though instead of wine he quaffed libations of starch. Of those who experienced Mr. Gwynn's kingly hospitality that night there departed none who failed to carry with him a multiplied respect for his host—a respect which with the President and General Attorney of the Anaconda fair mounted to veneration. Altogether, from the standpoint of everyone except the alarmed Senator Coot, the affair was not a dinner, but a victory.

It was ten o'clock the morning after, and Richard had just reached the street. From across the way came a gentleman who apparently had been waiting for him to appear. It was none other than Mr. Sands, that warlike printer whom Richard rescued from the Africans and set to work. Richard had not had the pleasure of meeting Mr. Sands since bestowing those benefits upon him.

"There was nothing to come for," explained Mr. Sands when Richard mentioned that deprivation. "I wouldn't bother you now, only, being in the business, I've naturally a nose for news. I thought I might put you onto a scoop for the *Daily Tory*. Would a complete copy, verbatim, of the coming report of Senator Hanway's committee on Northern Consolidated be of any service to you?"

CHAPTER XV

HOW RICHARD MET INSPECTOR VAL

When, prior to the hour of Mr. Gwynn's dinner, Richard talked with Mr. Bayard, the burden of their conversation was Northern Consolidated, and what manner of report might be expected from Senator Hanway's committee. Mr. Bayard was sure the members of the osprey pool designed a "bear" campaign. For all that, he could not overstate the importance of getting possession of the Hanway report the moment it was prepared. Mr. Bayard's belief in a "bear" movement to occur was only a deduction; it was not information—he did not know. There was no such thing as being positive until the written report was in Mr. Bayard's hands. He would then have absolute knowledge of the pool's intentions. Once clear in that behalf, he would be able to meet and defeat them.

"Our start," quoth Mr. Bayard, "will be the Hanway report. Nor can we come by that report too soon. It may lie buried for weeks before Senator Hanway produces it in open Senate. Its production will take place the day before the pool's activities begin. It will be deferred until the market in its strength or weakness favors their aims. Wherefore, my young friend," concluded Mr. Bayard, clapping a slim hand on Richard's shoulder, "to work! That report is the key. Every day we have it in our hands before it is read in the Senate means a million dollars."

Mr. Bayard forced upon Richard the mighty propriety of getting hold of Senator Hanway's report; and Richard—to whom the report meant Dorothy the peerless, not paltry millions—was carried to the impolite length of bringing up the topic of Northern Consolidated at Mr. Gwynn's dinner. Richard asked Senator Hanway the plump question of the committee's labors, and what time its report would appear.

"The sessions," said Senator Hanway, who, being about his departure, was getting into his Inverness at the time, "are still in progress. It will be several weeks before the close of the hearings. Then there must be time for deliberation; and finally a day or more for writing the report. You may be sure, however," concluded Senator Hanway, "that the *Daily Tory* shall have it before the other papers. It shall be an exclusive story; I promise you that."

And the next day comes the veracious Mr. Sands asking whether a verbatim copy of that report would be of service to him!

No marvel Richard stared.

"Because," observed Mr. Sands, puffing an extremely repulsive cigar, "I've got it here."

"Do you mean the report of Senator Hanway's committee that is investigating Northern Consolidated?" cried Richard.

Mr. Sands tilted his derby over a confident left eye, blew a devastating cloud, and said he did.

"It was only last night," observed Richard, still bitten of doubt, "that Senator Hanway told me the committee had not ended its hearings."

Mr. Sands of the malignant cigar was not discouraged. Senator Hanway had lied. All Senators lied, according to Mr. Sands. No man could be a Senator unless he were a liar any more than a man could be a runner without first being able to walk. The committee was through with the inquiry; the report had come into the Government printing office the day before in the handwriting of the truthless Senator Hanway himself. It was now set up in types, and the forethoughtful Mr. Sands had abstracted a copy.

"As I said," explained that enterprising printer, "I've got a nose for news. I thought it might do for a scoop, d'ye see, so I swiped it for you."

"Let me look at it," said Richard, whose pulses were beginning to beat a quickstep. He was remembering the value of the report as explained by Mr. Bayard. "Let me see it, please."

Mr. Sands took from his pocket two strips of paper. Richard looked at one and then the other; they were white as snow, guiltless of mark or sign of ink.

"There's nothing here," said Richard, the thing beginning to be mysterious.

For a moment Richard feared that Mr. Sands might be again immersed in his cups. That follower of Franklin reassured him.

"The report is there all right," he observed, "only we can't read it out here in the light. Now if we could find a dark room, one with a window, I'd show you what I mean."

Richard returned to Mr. Gwynn's. Before they entered he gave Mr. Sands a perfecto. The latter, who knew a good cigar from smoking many bad ones, threw away the devastator and lighted Richard's. He rolled it from one corner of his mouth to the other, sucked it tentatively, then passed the fire end beneath his nose after the manner of a connoisseur. His experiments exhausted, he pronounced it a "corker."

Richard conveyed Mr. Sands to his own apartments. The front window was what Mr. Sands required. He pinned the slips to the top of the lower sash.

As the depended slips were brought with their backs to the light, Mr. Sands showed Richard how they were in the nature of stencils, the white light showing through in printed words. Richard was dumb; it was a kind of prodigy. He read the stencils, beginning at the top of the one which Mr. Sands said was the "lead."

It was a Kind of Prodigy

IT WAS A KIND OF PRODIGY

"The report is set in minion," explained Mr. Sands, "and with this light you can read it plain as ink."

Richard discovered the truth of what Mr. Sands averred; here indeed was Senator Hanway's Northern Consolidated report, and as readily made out as though printed in a book.

"This is the idea," vouchsafed Mr. Sands, who saw that Richard was warm for explanations. "The boss gave out the report in little 'takes' of about fifty words each. That was because it must be kept secret. Fifty printers set it up; then the boss locked the galleys in the strong room. No one except the boss himself had had a glimpse of it. Of course, that made me the more eager to nail it; anything a fellow wants to hide is bound to be big news, d'ye see. Now I'm the man who takes the proofs, and this morning the boss tells me that Senator Hanway wants a copy—one proof, no more. The boss goes to the strong room and brings the galleys to the proof-press. I'm ready for him; I've dampened two sheets of proof-paper and pasted them together. I spread both of them on the types. After I've sent the roller over them, I peel the sheets apart and throw the white one, the one that was on top, on the floor. The bottom one that has the ink-impression on it I pass to the boss. He sees me peel the top sheet off, and it rouses his suspicions.

"'What's that for?' he asks.

"I'm filling my pipe as calm as duck-ponds, and explain that the proof-press in which the galley lies is too deep. It takes two thicknesses to force the sheet down on the face of the types and get a good impression. The boss is only a politician, not a printer, so this explanation does him. While he's locking up the galleys again, I get away with these. You see, with two thicknesses of paper, the types cut through; it makes a stencil of it. With a little light behind, the stencil shows up as well as a regular proof. After I'd got organized, I took a day off, clapped a 'sub' on my stool, and headed for you. As I've said, it struck me like a big piece of news."

"It's bigger than you know, Mr. Sands," observed Richard, giving that worthy's hand a squeeze that made him flinch. "If you don't mind, I'll not use it as news. You will not mention the fact, but there's a deal on in Wall Street; I can do better with it there. I cannot thank you too much for what you've done."

Mr. Sands was pleased, and departed for the nearest rum counter, his face expressing complacency. He had partly evened up, he said, for what Richard did the night that he, Mr. Sands, became entangled with the Hottentots. He, Mr. Sands, would lie in ambush for further scoops; he could promise Richard everything in the Government printing office which any statesman was trying to conceal.

Richard drew his desk before the window and, reading the stencils line by line, made a perfect copy. As his pen swept across the paper he reflected on the deceitfulness of Senator Hanway, who, with the report written out in full, was for having him think that the committee would not conclude its labors for weeks.

"What a mendacious ingrate it is!" thought Richard.

Mr. Bayard had taken the ten-o'clock limited for New York that identical morning. Richard caught a train a trifle after one, wiring Mr. Bayard to meet him at the hotel. They would have dinner together. To make sure of Mr. Bayard, Richard's message read:

"I have that report. You were right."

Mr. Bayard pored over the Hanway findings, and the further he read the more his satisfaction stood on tiptoe. Conceive a gallery hung round with paintings that would baffle a Rubens and set a Murillo to biting the nail of envy! Have an orchestra polished to the last touch of execution, discoursing the divinest work of some highest priest of music. Sentinel the scene with marbles that would have doubled the fame of a Praxiteles. Now, with your stage set, invite to its sumptuous midst some amateur of all the arts whose senses were born for the beautiful. Do what you will to endow your artist with contentment in perfection. Fill his pockets with gold, give him wine of his fancy, have the woman he loves by his side, so surround him that the eye, the ear, the stomach, the heart, the pocket, or whatever is the soul of his soul may be appealed to and enthralled—this artist, with whom love is a religion, wine a cult, music a passion, and pictures are as dreams! When you have him thus fortunately established, this artist of yours—for you are not to forget he is none of mine—peruse his face. You should find it expressing ecstasy in sublimation—you should discover it wearing the twin to that look which mounted the brow of Mr. Bayard as he devoured the Hanway report.

"Beautiful!" he whispered when he had finished.

Then he fell silent, prisoner to himself, walled in with his own thoughts. A moment passed and the clouds rolled away; the delight faded, and this artist among gamblers for whom speculation possessed harmony and color and form, and whose life had been an Odyssey of Stocks, recovered the practical.

"It is as I surmised," he said, with a sigh of content. "They will fall upon Northern Consolidated bear-fashion—all claw and tooth. This report finds the road to be a thief for millions; and a debtor for millions upon that. The Attorney General must collect. The road must be taken by a receiver until the public is repaid—the public indeed! Then those priceless grants are to be repealed. Northern Consolidated is to be stabbed with a score of knives at once. Beautiful! What a trap they have set for themselves!"

Richard, not knowing what reply might be expected, smiled to fetch his countenance into sympathy with Mr. Bayard's, and retreated to his usual refuge of a cigar.

"Now," went on Mr. Bayard briskly, "I can give you the rougher outlines of what will occur. This report, as I told you, may be weeks in finding its way into the Senate. Stocks opened the year very strong; the markets are upon an upgrade. While the boom continues, the pool will do nothing. The moment prices show a weakness our friends will act. Given three days of falling prices, this report will come out. The Senate will be invoked to an attack upon Northern Consolidated. The pool will spring upon the market, right and left, selling thousands upon thousands of shares. They will try for a stampede. They look to drop Northern Consolidated twenty-five points, as woodmen fell a tree."

"And what is to be our course?" asked Richard.

"We shall buy every share of Northern Consolidated as fast as it is offered; go with them to the end. They will find themselves in their own net.

"Since our first talk," Mr. Bayard continued, "I have been gathering information. Of the one million shares which form the stock of Northern Consolidated, over six hundred thousand are held in England, France, Belgium, Holland, Germany, Denmark, and even a bundle or two in Sweden. I shall keep the cables warm to-morrow. The day following, our agents will be quietly buying those European shares at private sale in London, Paris, Brussels, Berlin, Copenhagen, Hamburg, Stockholm, wherever they are to be found. Should they give us a week, we shall have so narrowed the field of operations for our 'bears' that their first day's sales will land them in a corner. Once we have them penned, we may take our time. They will be as helpless as so many caged animals."

When Storri on that jealous evening left the San Reve, his nerves were somewhat tossed and shaken. It was not over-late; he would stroll to the club by roundabout paths, the walk and cold night air might steady him.

That roundabout route led Storri past the Treasury Building, and, as he slowly paced the pavement bordering one side of the massive structure, he was brought to sudden stop by a heavy timber platform six feet square and lifted a foot and a half from the ground, which cumbered the sidewalk nearest the curb. Storri surveyed the platform in a lack-luster way. It had, from its appearance, been there years; it was strange he had never noticed it before.

An old man, one of the night guards of the Treasury, buttoned to the chin, was standing in a narrowish basement door-way of the great building not fifteen feet away. The old man took his pipe out of his mouth, and seeing Storri survey the obstructing platform, observed:

"If I had a sack or two of the billions of gold that's been dumped on that platform, I wouldn't be smokin' my pipe 'round here to-night."

Gold as a term never failed to attract the Storri ear. He opened converse with the old man of the pipe. It was to this heavy platform the treasure-wagons backed up when they brought bullion to the Treasury. Storri learned another thing that gave him the sort of thrill that setters feel when in the near vicinity of a covey of grouse. The vault that held the gold reserve was within sixty feet of him as he stood in the street. Just inside those thick, hopeless walls they lay—millions of piled-up yellow treasure. Storri stared hard at the impassive granite and licked his lips. The nearness of those millions pleased him like music.

"Sixty feet!" exclaimed Storri unctuously. "That doesn't sound far, but before a robber pierced such a wall as that he would fancy it far enough."

"Oh, a robber wouldn't try the wall," said the old man, turning to look at it. "I've often wondered though that no one ever thought of the sewer out there;" and the old man marked a line in the air with his pipe-stem as though tracing the direction of the great street drain that ran beneath the pavement.

Storri kept on his journey to the club, but the notion of those millions, almost within hand's touch of the open street, continued to haunt him pleasantly. The sewer, too! Would a tunnel reach this treasure? The question used to come back upon Storri. Also he got into the habit, as he went about the streets, of walking by the Treasury. This was not offspring of any purpose; Storri had none. It was only that he took an instinctive satisfaction in the nearness of that heaped-up gold. He could feel its close neighborhood, and the feeling was as wine to his imagination.

Storri was not permitted respite by the San Reve concerning the Harleys. The jealous one of the green-gray eyes insisted upon seeing Storri often; and he, putting on a best face, pretended that he loved the San Reve the better for her jealousy. To keep the peace, he was wont to drop round to Grant Place three or four times a week.

These concessions to the San Reve and her rather too fervid love would not get in the way of Storri's dinners at the Harleys'. For a time he should go there but once a week. When despair had chilled Dorothy to tameness he would go oftener. Just then he must give her terrors opportunity to do their freezing work.

Storri could not have told whether he loved or hated Dorothy; he was only conscious of a fire-fed passion that consumed him. He must possess her; or, if not that, then he must grind her into the earth. He would torture her as he was tortured; he would blacken her by blackening Mr. Harley; with her pride in the dirt, with disgrace upon her, where then was that man who would wed her? The daughter of a forger—she would stain the name of wife! Richard might have her then; Storri would give her to him for a revenge! These were the mutterings of Storri as he went preyed upon by love and hate at once.

"If you do not love Miss Harley," said the flushed but logical San Reve, "why do you go there? You say, 'Once a week!' Why once a week? Why once a month? Why at any time? Storri, you do love her! And you come to me with lies!" This was on the evening following the scene that gave Storri such disquiet.

Storri, being spurred, and resolute to silence the San Reve, took that pertinacious beauty into his confidence, lying wherever it was inconvenient to tell the truth, and bragging always like a Cheyenne. Storri strode about the San Reve's rooms and told his tale grandly. His San Reve must listen; he would show her how a Russian gentleman avenged himself. He, Storri, hated the Harleys. Mr. Harley had cheated him; Dorothy had laughed at him; her lover, that Richard, bah! he had even threatened Storri. Chastise him? Could a nobleman chastise a toad—a reptile? No; there was a debt due his caste.

Mrs. Hanway-Harley?—a vapid fool! Storri despised her. He despised them all and hated them all. They had affronted him. And for those injuries done his pride he would punish and spare not. He, Storri, would bring sorrow and shame to them; he would mark their lives with black.

Being launched, Storri drew great joy from the rehearsal of what griefs he had devised against the Harleys. To prove his own superior cleverness, Storri told the San Reve how he trapped Mr. Harley into forging his name to the French shares.

"There is my weapon!" cried the triumphant Storri. "With that I may smite them when I choose! To-morrow, within the hour, I could have this scoundrel Harley in a criminal's cell! Some day I shall do that. Meanwhile, he knows; the proud girl knows. It is for vengeance I go to the Harleys', my San Reve, not love. I sit at their table, I eat their food, I drink their wine; and I laugh and I gloat over them—these little people! Yes, my San Reve, the hand of the coward Harley shakes as he lifts his glass; the fair, proud Dorothy shows me my triumph in her whitened cheek and frightened eye. And best of all, the empty chatter of the magpie Mrs. Hanway-Harley—who knows nothing, being a fool! It is that magpie chatter to be poison in the ears of the others! Oh, you should behold them, my San Reve! You should witness how they writhe and how they tremble in the presence of your Storri!"

The San Reve listened, but the gloom hung low on her brow. She did not believe her Storri who said he ate a weekly dinner for revenge. Yes, he had obtained a mastery over Mr. Harley; he had forced his way into the company of Dorothy and shut the door on Richard! The San Reve shook her jealous head; that was not vengeance, that was love.

And Storri would succeed, too! This Dorothy would come to love him as she, the San Reve, loved. Dorothy was a woman; and what woman could resist Storri? This Dorothy loved him even now; her coldness was an attitude, a fiction. It was meant to be a lure to Storri and whet his eagerness!

These were the thoughts like living coals which the San Reve hid in her heart. But while her head whirled, and her sight was blurred, and her pulses set a-throb with the jealous storms that swept her, it was wonderful to note how the San Reve's office-trained mind seized upon and registered those French shares. It was those shares that constituted Storri's hold upon the Harleys. Could she break the hold? Those shares were the locks of her Samson. Oh, if she might but shear the locks! Then she would have her Storri again—in his weakness she would have him. The San Reve knitted her brows.

These days of separation were more easily borne by Richard than by Dorothy. Richard was rich in a dogged fortitude common enough with men. Moreover, he had his work, and he went into it more deeply than before. Eleven o'clock still found him in the study with Senator Hanway, albeit Dorothy was no longer there to make a lovely third. Perhaps for that reason more politics and news of legislation were discussed by Richard and Senator Hanway.

The latter gentleman, these days, was in the best of tempers. Nothing could be more smoothly hopeful than the outlook for that nomination. Senator Gruff, who was indefatigable for Senator Hanway, told him that Speaker Frost reported his own State delegation as already in line. Also the President of the Anaconda, from whom Senator Gruff had letters every week, described the Hanway sentiment in Anaconda regions as invincible. The National Convention, in the interests of Senator Hanway and over the objection of the friends of Governor Obstinate, had been fixed for the last of May. This was a help; Senator Hanway's forces were organized and Governor Obstinate's were not. The less space permitted that candidate and his henchmen, the better for Senator Hanway. As Senator Gruff and Richard sat together in Senator Hanway's study one morning, the Senator pointed out on the map a sufficient number of States, and each certain to send a Hanway delegation, to carry the nomination.

"If the convention were held to-morrow," observed Senator Gruff, "we would win. The effort now must be to head off encroachments by Governor Obstinate."

The above came on an occasion when Senator Gruff was in a confidential mood. Commonly, as a chief Hanway manager, he lay as blandly close and noncommittal as a clam.

There was the issue of finance, Senator Gruff explained, and that was a growing source of trouble to Senator Hanway. The latter gentleman's endeavor had always been to say nothing upon finance, but silence was becoming difficult. Governor Obstinate was openly and offensively for gold in a sod-pawing, horn-lowering, threatening way, and just as a buffalo bull might have been for gold. This settled the standing of Governor Obstinate in silver communities; they would have none of him. Those same silver people, however, demanded all the more that Senator Hanway define his position in the money war. They gave tongue to those pig-and-poke objections voiced by Senator Coot. It was clamors such as these, so Senator Gruff told Richard, that made silence a work of weariness.

"Now I thought," observed Richard, "that Mr. Bayard talked wisely upon silver and gold the evening of the dinner. Why wouldn't it be well to talk to the people in the same manner even if one did not adopt the theories expressed? Let Senator Hanway clearly announce his views and give his reasons. The latter should defend him with thinking men."

"Thinking men," retorted Senator Gruff with an experienced smile, "are in a hopeless minority. Talk reason to the public? One might as well talk reason to the winds. Politics, as a science, is not addressed to the intelligence but to the ignorance of men."

Senator Hanway, after sundry conferences with Senator Gruff and others, offered the resolution asking for a committee to meet with the Ottawa government on the matter of that Georgian Bay-Ontario Canal. The majority opinion of those consulted was that the resolution ought to strengthen Senator Hanway. Certain railways might object; there were influences infinitely larger, however, that would applaud. Besides, the resolution had a big look and sounded like statesmanship. It could not do otherwise than dignify Senator Hanway in public estimation. Senator Hanway gave Richard for the *Daily Tory* an interview of depth and power in which he urged the international value of such a waterway America and Canada should dig and own it together; it would be a bond to unite them. It would promote friendship, and what was better than friendship between countries? Senator Hanway said nothing about Credit Magellan, nor did he intimate any relationship between his Georgian Bay-Ontario Canal and the investigation of Northern Consolidated.

Storri had become very fond of the company of Mr. Harley. He would find him in the Marble Room in the rear of the Senate Chamber, or he might cross his path at Chamberlin's. Washington is a small town; there it is not difficult to keep a man in sight. Storri kept Mr. Harley excessively in sight; and it wore visibly on Mr. Harley, whose health was breaking down. Storri liked the pain his presence gave Mr. Harley; and besides, he argued that to see him frequently strengthened his hold upon that unhappy man. When they were together, Storri's manner was hideously cheerful; he would talk Credit Magellan and consider Northern Consolidated as though nothing were awry. This was the refinement of cruelty, as when a cat pretends to let the mouse escape.

One day, when Storri and Mr. Harley were together, the former's face was purposely dark. Mr. Harley grew uneasy; his courage had all slipped from him by now, and he waited in terror upon the looks of Storri.

"Harley," cried Storri, having sufficiently enjoyed the effect of his scowls, "you John Harley, I have ever your credit at heart. Yes, Harley, I have kept a guard, what you call a spy, about your house to see if the vile Storms would enter when you were not there to repel him. He goes each day, I find, to see the honorable Senator Hanway. It does not please me, who am a Russian gentleman and a nobleman, that so low a being, although he does not personally meet her, should yet come beneath the same roof with your lovely daughter who is to become my Countess wife. You will correct this; eh, you Harley—you John Harley?"

Mr. Harley had not named Storri to Dorothy since that awful New Year's night. However, so worn to abject thinness was now his spirit on the constant wheel of fear that he carried Storri's latest word to her without apology. Richard must not visit Senator Hanway in his study. Mr. Harley could not go to Senator Hanway, he could not go to Richard; he could come only to her.

Dorothy, whose trembling concern was her father, and who felt ever more and more like some fly caught fast in a spider's web, made no reply. There was nothing to say—nothing save obedience. She wrote Richard that Storri had set a spy upon the house, and asked him to forego his calls upon Senator Hanway. The close of the letter was a hysteria of love and grief.

Richard sought Bess; he saw much of the pythoness now. Dorothy, for her part, never crossed the street lest she meet him, and bring down Storri's wrath upon her father. Richard knew what Bess would say, but he must have someone to converse with. Bess took the course anticipated: he must obey Dorothy in this as in the rest.

"It comes to little either way, the calling upon Senator Hanway," was Bess's comment.

"It comes to this," cried Richard, "that we are the slaves of Storri! I'd give ten years off my life if he and I might settle this together."

"The real settlement would be made by Mr. Harley—by Dorothy. You must not go near Storri. But isn't there a hint in this?" Bess considered. "Would it not be wise to imitate the gentleman and set a spy to dogging him? Perhaps something worth while might be discovered."

The thought found favor with Richard, who, under usual circumstances, would have been against the proposal. Yes, he would have Storri shadowed day and night. It would be a retort for that spy about the Harley house.

Richard sent a message to Mr. Bayard, reciting his determination and asking advice. He desired to do nothing that might work an interference in Mr. Bayard's arrangements concerning Northern Consolidated.

Mr. Bayard replied that he thought a better knowledge of Storri could do no harm; news of the enemy was ever a good thing. Mr. Bayard went a step beyond, and said that he would send a man to Richard whom he could trust for the work.

The morning following the receipt of Mr. Bayard's message, a foppish, slender young gentleman accosted Richard.

"Mr. Storms, I believe?" remarked the foppish stranger, lifting his hat.

"Yes, sir; Mr. Storms," said Richard.

"Mr. Bayard asked me to say that I am Inspector Val of the Central Office, New York, with two months' leave of absence at your service."

CHAPTER XVI

HOW RICHARD RECEIVED A LETTER

Inspector Val did not resemble the detective officer of literature. His foppishness arose from an over-elegance of costume rather than any violence of color. The famous thief-taker might have stood for what was latest in fashionable dress, with every detail of hat and glove and cravat and boot worked out. There befell no touch of vulgarity; the effect was as retiringly genteel as though the taste providing it belonged to a Howard or a Vere de Vere and based itself upon ten unstained centuries of patricianism. When he lifted his hat, one might see that the dark hair, speciously waved, was as accurately parted in the middle as though the line had been run by an engineer. The voice of Inspector Val, low and lazy, fell on the ear as plausibly soft as the ripple of a brook. His eyes wore a sleepy, intolerant expression, as if tired with much seeing and inclined to resent the infliction of further spectacles. The nose was thin and high, and jaw and cheek bones were thin and high to be in sympathy.

There were two impressions furnished the student of faces by Inspector Val. Glanced at carelessly, one would have called him not more than twenty-five; a second and a sharper survey showed him fifteen years older. Also, there came now and then a look, quiet at once and quick, which was calculated to arrest the trained attention. What one thought following that second sharp canvass was in exact opposition to what one thought after the glance earlier and more upon the casual.

Inspector Val baffled Richard's conception of the man concerning whom all who read papers had heard so much. Was this indolent individual that inveterate man-hunter who, with courage of berserk and strength of steel, had pulled down his quarry in the midst of desperate criminals, and then, victim in clutch, cleared his path through? Something of this may have glimmered in Richard's eye; if so, Inspector Val assumed to have no hint of it, and busied himself in a more precise adjustment of his boutonnière, which floral adornment had become disarranged. The longer Richard contemplated Inspector Val the more he felt his whalebone sort. The slim form and sleepy eyes began to suggest that activity and ferocious genius for pursuit which are the first qualities of a ferret.

"If we could be more private," suggested Inspector Val, casting a tired glance about the big public room at Willard's where the two had met.

"We will go to my house," replied Richard.

"And if you don't mind, we'll ride." This with the rising inflection of a request. "There are carriages at the door."

"My own," said Richard, "should be across the way. I seldom require it; but I might, and so it follows me about."

Richard and Inspector Val stepped to the Fourteenth Street door. At Richard's lifted hand an olive-tinted brougham, coachman and footman liveried to match, drawn by a pair of restless bay horses, came plunging to the curb. The footman swung down in three motions, like a soldier about some point of drill.

"Home!" said Richard.

The footman in three motions regained his perch; the whip cracked and the brougham went plunging off for Mr. Gwynn's.

Richard came to the common-sense conclusion to lay the complete story of his perplexities before Inspector Val. A detective was so much like a doctor that frankness would be worth while. One was called to cure the health, the other to cure a situation; the more one told either scientist the faster and better he could work. Acting on this thought, Richard related all there was to tell of himself, Dorothy, Mr. Harley, and Storri, being full as to his exclusion from the Harley house and the manner in which it was brought about. When he had finished, he waited for Inspector Val.

That Artist of Pursuit

THAT ARTIST OF PURSUIT

That artist of pursuit did not speak at once, and asked permission to smoke a cigarette. Richard offered no objection, although he privily condemned cigarettes as implying the effeminate. Inspector Val lighted one, and blew the smoke thoughtfully through the thin, high nose. Suddenly he threw the cigarette away half smoked; it had served the purpose of its appearance. Inspector Val had smoked himself into a conclusion.

"This is the way the thing strikes me," began Inspector Val. "Storri, as you say, has a hold on Mr. Harley—has him frightened. There are three ways to frighten a man; you can threaten him physically, or with disgrace, or with the loss of money. Storri, by your report, is a coward with not half the courage of Mr. Harley; besides, in this case, a physical threat is out of the question. So is a threat of money loss; it is preposterous to suppose that this half-baked Russian has got the upper hand in a business way of a shrewd one like Mr. Harley, or that the latter would permit him to drive him about like a dog if he had. No, Storri has caught Mr. Harley in some wrong-doing, or, what is as bad, the appearance of it—something that looks like crime. Doubtless it refers to money, as from Mr. Harley's sort it isn't likely to include a woman."

Inspector Val was here interrupted by Matzai, who said in excuse that the note he bore was marked "important."

"Open it," observed Inspector Val. "Once in one thousand times a letter marked 'important' is important."

Richard cut the envelope with a paper knife and, after silently running the missive up and down, remarked:

"This note works into our conversation as though timed to find us together. I'll read it to you. It's in French, and if you aren't familiar with that language I'll translate."

Inspector Val said that he preferred a translation, and Richard gave him the following. The address and the entire note were in typewriting:

MR. STORMS:

Count Storri's hold on Mr. Harley consists in this: Mr. Harley wrote Count Storri's name on five stock certificates aggregating two hundred shares of the Company Provence of Paris, France. It was done to borrow money, but with honest intentions and at Count Storri's request. Now Count Storri, who has the shares in his possession, threatens Mr. Harley with a charge of forgery. In that way he compels him to do his bidding. The man who writes you this does not do it for your interest, but for

HIS OWN.

"This did not come through the mails," said Inspector Val. "Ask your man who handed it in."

Matzai said that the note was not handed in, but thrust beneath the door. The bell had been rung; when the door was opened no one appeared. The note was lying in the entry.

"Will you mind," said Inspector Val, "if I call a man from across the street?"

"Certainly not," replied Richard, somewhat astonished.

Inspector Val stepped to the window. Over the way a man was sauntering, for all the world like a sightseer from out of town. He was admiring the stately residences, and seemed interested particularly in Mr. Gwynn's. Inspector Val made a slight signal, and the sightseer came over and rang Mr. Gwynn's bell.

"Have him up," said Inspector Val to Richard. Then, as the sightseer was marshaled into the room by Matzai: "Mr. Storms, this is Mr. England."

Mr. England's eye was bright and quick like a bird's; with that exception he was commonplace. Inspector Val, without wasting time, began to ask questions:

"Who shoved this note under the door?"

"A colored man, sir. He sneaked up and tucked it beneath the door as though trying not to be caught at it. Then he pushed the bell and skipped. The thing looked queer, and Mr. Duff thought he'd follow him. He'll be back, Mr. Duff will, presently."

"That will do," said Inspector Val. "When Mr. Duff returns, tell him to come in."

Mr. England withdrew, and recommenced his sightseeing on the opposite side of the street.

"Mr. England and Mr. Duff," explained Inspector Val, "came down with me. I shall use them to shadow Storri, as that kind of work is their specialty. It is difficult work, too, and demands a man who has talents for seeing without being seen. Also, he must be sharp to think and act, and full of enterprise. To keep at the heels of a gentleman who may take a cab, or a street-car, or enter a building by one door for the purpose of leaving it by another, is no simple task; so I brought with me the best in the business."

"How did your men come to be outside the door?" asked Richard, whose curiosity concerning metropolitan detective methods had been sensibly aroused.

"To save delay," returned Inspector Val, "which is the great rule in detective work. They were within ten feet of us when I met you; they saw us drive away, called a coupé, and followed. I should have given them a jacketing if they hadn't."

Inspector Val asked Richard to slowly translate the note, while he made a copy in English. This Richard did; at the close, being interested in the workings of the man-hunting mind, he asked Inspector Val for his theory of its truth and origin.

"Why, then," observed Inspector Val, pausing over Richard's translation as he had written it down, "this would be my surmise. The note tells the truth. It was written by a Frenchwoman who probably came from Ottawa. She is in love with Storri, and jealous of Miss Harley, whom she thinks Storri aims to marry. You said nothing about Storri seeing Miss Harley, but he does. Miss Marklin was afraid to tell you and Miss Harley was afraid to write you that feature of the situation, fearing you would pitch in rough. It shows they have sense."

This was the first time Richard had heard how Storri enjoyed the privilege of Dorothy's society while he was warned from the door. The thought was fire. He sprang to his feet, growling an oath under his breath.

"Take it easy," said Inspector Val, with a manner full of warning. "Don't spoil a game just as the cards begin to run your way. After we get our hands upon those French shares you may raise what row you like. But take it easy now; try another cigar."

The prudent sagacity of Inspector Val was not thrown away, and Richard saw the force of that gentleman's arguments.

"Tell me how you arrive at those beliefs about the note," said Richard.

"That's not so simple," returned Inspector Val. "It's like asking a pointer to tell you how he scents a partridge. My argument takes somewhat this route: I think the note tells the truth, as there's no reason why it should lie. Moreover, it is a reasonable explanation of Storri's command over Mr. Harley. I know a woman wrote it because she's at such pains to call herself a man. Another thing, a man wouldn't have marked this note 'Important!' It's important, but it gains no advantage from being labeled. A woman, who acts from feeling, marks it 'important' because she feels its importance. Now a man might feel its importance, but he acts from reason rather than feeling, and in that respect is the antithesis of a woman. It would never occur to a man to mark the note 'important,' because it would never occur to him that by so doing anything would be gained. Then a man would have sent this through the post office. A man is more cunning than a woman. The mails would have served as well, and a messenger might be recognized and followed. To send messengers is essentially a trick of the feminine. Your District Messenger Service will tell you that nine-tenths of its calls are from women."

"You have read Edgar Allan Poe, I take it," observed Richard, smiling over the processes of Inspector Val.

"I've read Poe, Gaboriau, and Conan Doyle," returned Inspector Val; "all detectives have. They are amusing if not instructive. But to resume: There is another reason why I'm certain a woman wrote this note. All the writer knows the writer got from Storri. It's a long yarn; it must cover in its transaction a dozen interviews between Storri and Mr. Harley. And they were not interviews at which a third party was present. You will see the truth of that the instant I mention it. No; Storri told the whole tale to the writer of the note. Mr. Harley wouldn't tell it for obvious reasons. Neither would he write it to you or anybody else; it is the publication of it that he fears. Storri was the only one besides Mr. Harley who knew of those French shares; or of Mr. Harley's imitation of Storri's signature and the threats of arrest for forgery which Storri made. It's as plain as the stars at night that Storri furnished the information upon which this letter is based. Now whom would he tell? Not a man; there would be nothing to gain and much to risk in that. A woman, then? Sure; this fellow has been strutting and bragging to a woman. It is the commonest weakness of the congenital criminal. It is his way of swaggering and seeming powerful. But mark you: he never takes a woman into dangerous confidences unless he thinks she loves him. Do you follow? Storri has told this to a woman in whose love he believes."

"You reason well, at any rate," observed Richard.

"Yes, sir, I reason well," returned Inspector Val. "I have reasoned like this a thousand times, and a thousand times I was right. To go on: I agree with Storri; the woman does love him. Why does she write this letter? Because she wants to break Storri's grip on Mr. Harley. On Mr. Harley's account? No, she cares nothing for Mr. Harley. In a clash between the two her sympathies would be with Storri, whom she loves. Now the woman in telling a lie—the only one in the letter—has also told an important truth. It is in her last sentence. She was thinking to throw you off as to her sex, and went out of her way to do it. She was hunting a chance to write 'man' and 'his' and at the same time not advise you of her purpose. The 'man' and the 'his' were to be by way of incident. With her mind on fooling you as to her sex, she was so wholly engaged that she told an unwitting truth; she did write this letter in her own service. One step further: The object of the lady, as I've said, is to break Storri's hold on Mr. Harley. Now how could the lady who writes you benefit by that? What could there be about Storri's ascendency over Mr. Harley to which a woman who loves Storri would object? I will tell you. That ascendency gives him not only a hold on Mr. Harley, but a hold through him on some woman whom the writer fears as a rival. And there you are; I've brought the argument to Miss Harley. Storri threatens Mr. Harley. What does he demand? That you be excluded from the Harley house. Why? Because you see Miss Harley. Why should Storri object to that? Because he desires to court the lady himself, and would do away with dangerous competition. His simple hatred of you, and nothing more, would not set Storri to talking forgery charges to Mr. Harley; that would sound too much like burning a barn to boil an egg."

Richard growled an acquiescence.

"Very well; the woman who wrote the note would have you get possession of those French shares. Storri has described you to her as Miss Harley's lover; that sets her to writing you—you who have an interest as strong as her own. Storri has never told her that he loves Miss Harley. She has guessed it and accused him of it, being jealous; and he in reply and denial has laid especial emphasis upon you as Miss Harley's lover. It's more than a chance he told her the whole story as part of a jealous row. As to the woman being French, I infer that from the note. She couldn't trust her English or she would not have written in French. That note, being in French, would narrow any search for its author; and that, too, whether the author were English or French. Certainly there are fewer people in Washington who can write French than English. You see the point?"

"But you said a Frenchwoman from Ottawa."

"The note is on paper that was made and sold in Ottawa, as you see by the raised mark in the corner. We've no trade with Canada for note-paper; besides, our stores wouldn't handle such as this. It's not of fashionable shape and size as Americans understand fashions in note-paper. It's scented, too; and that's vulgar from American standpoints. Also, it's feminine. No, my word for it, the woman who wrote that note bought the paper in Ottawa and brought it here. She did the typewriting herself, which was but natural; and she is not an adept, as anyone may tell by the clumsy, irregular way in which she begins her lines. Now take——"

Matzai came in and announced Mr. Duff.

"Bring him up," said Inspector Val, and then, turning apologetically to Richard, he added: "Pardon the liberty of giving commands in your house. I'm so eager to hear whether Mr. Duff's investigation corroborates my theory that for a moment I thought I was back in Mulberry Street. Well, Mr. Duff," as that worthy was ushered in, "what did you learn? This gentleman is Mr. Storms."

Mr. Duff seemed to know all about Richard; probably his partner sightseeing over the way had told him. He nodded blandly as Inspector Val gave his name, and then proceeded to answer that superior officer.

"The man is a laborer in the Treasury Department. He went to the Treasury Building from here, and made a straight wake for a woman who works at drawing plans and that sort of thing in the office of the Supervising Architect. He whispered something to her, and she nodded. When he got about ten feet away, he turned like a man who has overlooked a point, and said: 'I rang the bell; they'll get it right off.' Then he went away. The woman's name is San Reve—Sara San Reve. She's a Frenchwoman, and came from Ottawa. She has had her place only a short time, and was appointed on the recommendation of a member of the Senate—Senator Hanway."

"Senator Hanway!" repeated Inspector Val, looking dubiously at Richard. "He's a brother-in-law, you say, of Mr. Harley?"

"Your deductions were none the less right," returned Richard, who saw the doubts which the name of Hanway bred in the other's mind. "I'd wager my life on it. I never heard of this Miss San Reve, but she is from Ottawa, Mr. Duff says. I ought to have told you that Storri came to Washington from Ottawa."

"Oh, I see!" exclaimed Inspector Val, his brow clearing. "Storri came from Ottawa, and brought his sweetheart. Storri worked Senator Hanway through our friend Mr. Harley, and Senator Hanway found her a place."

"Yes," returned Richard, "I think you've hit it off. The next thing is to get hold of those French shares."

"Right there," said Inspector Val, "let me say a word. I'll first go and put my people on the track of Storri; they'll run him, turn and turn about, until further orders, and report each morning. That done, you and I will take the Limited, and run over and talk with Mr. Bayard. It will require his help to get those French shares. I'll meet you at the station then at four."

"I shall be there," responded Richard. "Before you go, let me give you this by way of anticipated expense," and Richard tendered Inspector Val a check for one thousand dollars.

"That wasn't necessary," said Inspector Val, as he calmly pocketed the check.

When Richard arrived at the station he found Inspector Val already there. "I've taken a drawing-room," said the latter. "It may be a weakness, but my inclination runs heavily towards concealment. I have a horror of being seen."

"I have horrors of much the same color," returned Richard.

Richard showed Mr. Bayard the note he had received, and told of its appearance, and the construction of the note as given by Inspector Val.

"And the question is," concluded Richard, "can we by any chance get hold of those French shares?"

"Can we get those French shares?" repeated Mr. Bayard, as though revolving the question in his thoughts. "I should say we might; yes, I'm quite sure. I think it will offer no more of difficulty than just finding out where this Storri negotiates his loans. I know where to go for the information and, if I ask it in person, it will be forthcoming." While Mr. Bayard spoke, his wits were working like a flashlight, displaying for his consideration every possibility presented by the situation. His confidence must have been strengthened by the survey, for he closed with emphasis, saying: "I am a false prophet if I do not place those French shares in your hands, your own property and bought with your own money, within a fortnight."

"Within a fortnight!" exclaimed Richard, his face brightening with the satisfaction the promise gave him.

There was that in Mr. Bayard's manner which invested his utterance with all the credit granted his signature at the banks. Richard felt as though the French certificates, which meant so much to Dorothy and to him, were as good as in his hands.

"When I say a fortnight," observed Mr. Bayard, "I ought to add my reasons. The source of my news is unimportant, but you may accept it as settled that Tuesday next has been secretly pitched upon by our worthy President for divers warlike declarations, founded on the Monroe Doctrine, and pointed at Germany, whose cruisers are just now nosing about on a debt-collecting errand against one of the South American states. The President will resent the nosing, call German attention to our Monroe Doctrine as the line fence between the hemispheres, and then mount guard over the sacred rails of that venerated barrier with a gun. All of which might excite but little interest were it not, as a demonstration, sure to send the market tumbling like a shot pigeon. I'm not certain that the whole affair hasn't some such commercial purpose. Be that as it may, the day following that valorous manifesto will be a time of panic, and the bottom will fall out of stocks. You remember what I told you as to the plans of our friends to 'bear' Northern Consolidated? This will bring their opportunity. When the markets begin to toss and heave and fall with those White House antics touching Germany and the Monroe Doctrine, Senator Hanway's report will be sprung in the Senate. He will give it to the press the night before, so that the morning papers may ring an alarm to the 'bulls.' This will be the procession of affairs: The President will threaten Germany on Tuesday;

Senator Hanway's report will be in the papers and the Senate on Wednesday; by Wednesday night our 'bear' pool will have been clamorously selling Northern Consolidated all day. Per incident, we will have been buying Northern Consolidated all day. By Friday evening—I give them three selling days in which to work their ruin—I shall wire you that they are caught in the trap by all their feet at once. It is then I shall mail you those French shares."

"No letter will ever mean so much to me, be sure," said Richard.

"You shall receive it," returned Mr. Bayard. "By the way, we are prepared to the last detail for that raid. I've bought more than five hundred thousand shares of Northern Consolidated in Europe at an average of forty-two. In order that our raiders may have what rope they require to thoroughly hang themselves, I've brought more than two hundred thousand of those shares to this country. It is placed where they may reach it for the purpose of borrowing stock for delivery. In fact, our arrangements are perfect; they make as complete a deadfall as ever waited for its prey."

Richard and Inspector Val returned to Washington, Richard to write Dorothy a letter freighted of promise and hope and love. In it he told her that soon he would have canceled the last element of Storri's power, removed the last fear of Mr. Harley, and, in loving brief, destroyed the last bar which separated them and kept them apart.

Dorothy read the letter again and again, and then kissed it pending the advent of something more kissable. Richard's promise was like the smell of flowers to refresh her jaded, fear-wearied heart. The one regret was, since Richard had forbidden it, that she could not share the blessed promise with her father.

Richard wrote nothing of the note of warning; nor did he speak of Inspector Val and his deductions as to Storri's visits to the Harley house. His only thought had been to cheer the drooping soul of Dorothy with the glad nearness of happier days. The word of comfort came in good time, for the shameful weight of the situation was crushing Dorothy.

Mr. Harley these days walked in troubles as deep as those of Dorothy, but not the same. Mr. Harley was not borne upon by the shame of the thing; that did not depress him any more than the knowledge that he was guiltless of wrong upheld him. A man of finer nature would have been strengthened by his innocence. To such a man his self-respect would have been important; while he retained that support he could have summoned up a fortitude to bear the worst that lay in Storri's hands. But Mr. Harley was no such one of fineness, upon whom he would have looked down as a visionary and a sentimentalist. There arose the less cause why he should be, perhaps, since Mr. Harley was sure of being popular with himself in spite of any conduct that could be his. His ideals were not lofty, his moral senses not keen, and what original decent point the latter might have once possessed had long been dulled away. True, Mr. Harley was shaken of an ague of fear; but his tremblings were born of the practical. He was agitated by thoughts of what havoc, in his own and in Senator Hanway's affairs of politics and business, naming him formally as a forger would work. Such a disaster would be tangible; he could appreciate, and, appreciating, shrink from it.

One thing to feather the wing of his apprehensions and set them soaring was his uncertainty concerning Storri. He could not gauge Storri; he would have felt safer had that nobleman been an American or an Englishman. Storri was so loaded of alarming contradictions; he could so snarl and purr, threaten and promise, beam and glower, smile and frown, and all in the one moment of time! Mr. Harley could not read a spirit so perverse and in such perpetual head-on collision with itself! Nor could he, being fear-blind, see that in most, if not all of these, Storri was acting. If Mr. Harley had realized what a joy it was to Storri to frighten him, the knowledge might have made for his peace of mind. As it was, he looked upon Storri as at the best half mad, and capable, in some beckoning moment of caprice, of any lunatic move that should level the worst against him.

Mr. Harley had one hope, and that rested with Northern Consolidated. If he could stand off disaster until the raid on Northern Consolidated had been made, and the profits, namely the road, were in their hands, he might then arrange a permanent truce. In this he reckoned on Storri's rapacity, to which a million of dollars was as a mouthful. Given a foretaste of what riches should dwell therein, Storri would desire with triple intensity to push forward in his earth-girdling dream of Credit Magellan. The conquest of Northern Consolidated would teach him to look upon the rest as sure. Being in this frame, Mr. Harley argued that Storri, feeling his inability to go forward without him, might be softened to the touch of reason. Under these pleasant new conditions, with Credit Magellan hopefully launched, Storri could be treated with. Mr. Harley would then feel his way to some safe compromise; he would invent an offer for those French shares which should present both peril and profit. He would threaten to go no further with Credit Magellan unless Storri put those French shares in his hands; and he would give him twenty-fold their value if he did. Mr. Harley harbored the thought that Storri would yield; and yield all the more readily since his passion for Dorothy and his appetite for revenge against Mr. Harley would have had time to cool. Thus reasoning, and thus hoping, and, one had almost said, thus fearing, Mr. Harley gave himself to the task in two parts of keeping Storri in paths of peace, and praying for a break in the market so that the attack on Northern Consolidated might begin.

You are not to suppose those changes in Mr. Harley and Dorothy went uncounted by Mrs. Hanway-Harley; that would be claiming too much against the lady's vigilance. In her double rôle of wife and mother, it was her duty to observe the haggard face of Mr. Harley and the woe that settled about Dorothy's young eyes; and Mrs. Hanway-Harley, as wife and mother, observed them. And this is how that perspicacious matron read those signs. She translated Mr. Harley's haggard looks at a glance; he was losing money. Legislation, or stocks, or both, were going the wrong way; but in legislation, or stocks, or both, or the way they went, Mrs. Hanway-Harley refused to have an interest. If Mr. Harley had lost money, Mr. Harley must make some more; that was all.

In divining Dorothy's griefs, Mrs. Hanway-Harley showed even greater ingenuity. Dorothy and Richard had quarreled; Mrs. Hanway-Harley was sharp to note that now she neither saw nor heard of Richard. Also, Dorothy came to the dinner table when Storri was there, and neither fled to her room nor called Bess to her shoulder on hearing that nobleman's name announced. Mrs. Hanway-Harley saw how the land lay; Dorothy took a more lenient view of Storri when now her fancy for Richard was wearing dim. After all, it had been only a fancy; it asked just a trifle of care, and the happy dénouement would be as Mrs. Hanway-Harley wished.

Mrs. Hanway-Harley began now to play her game exceeding deep. She would say nothing of Richard; to name him would serve to keep him in Dorothy's memory. She would say nothing of Storri; to speak of him would heat Dorothy's obstinacy, and Mrs. Hanway-Harley had learned not to desire that. No, she would be wisely, forbearingly diplomatic; the present arrangement was perfect for the ends in view. Storri came to the house; Richard stayed away; the conclusion was natural and solitary, and Dorothy would marry Storri. Mrs. Hanway-Harley, fully understanding the currents of events and the flowing thereof, became serenely joyful, and the charm of her manner gained accent from those clouds so visibly resting upon Mr. Harley and Dorothy. Yes, indeed; it must not be written that the sun did not shine for Mrs. Hanway-Harley, whose conversation the satirical Storri told the San Reve was as the conversation of a magpie.

Tuesday came, and the President of this republic shook a pugnacious fist beneath the German nose. Some impression of the weird suddenness of the maneuver might have been gathered from the comment of Senator Gruff. Speaking for the Senate, that sagacious man remarked:

"It came down upon us like a pan of milk from a top shelf!"

In Wall Street the effect was all that Mr. Bayard foretold. Prices began to melt and dwindle like ice in August. Panic prevailed; three brokerage firms fell, a dozen more were rocking on their foundations.

In the midst of the hubbub, Senator Hanway sent for Richard. Our statesman's smile was bland, his brow untroubled.

"You see I do not forget," said Senator Hanway sweetly. "I promised that I'd give you an exclusive story when the committee on Northern Consolidated was ready to report. Here is the report, it was finished last evening; I have added a brief interview to explain it."

Richard's impulse was to ask a dozen questions; he restrained himself and asked none. Richard was not so fond of fiction as to invite it. He sent the report and interview to the *Daily Tory*, and dispatched a private message to Mr. Bayard, giving him the news and congratulating him on his unerring gifts as a seer.

CHAPTER XVII

HOW NORTHERN CONSOLIDATED WAS SOLD

When the President of these United States so dauntlessly flourished the Monroe Doctrine in the German face, and shook the Presidential fist beneath the German nose, the flourishing and fist-shaking were accomplished through the medium of a special message to Congress which—a clap of thunder from a cloudless sky—made its appearance in House and Senate upon a certain Tuesday afternoon at four of the congressional clock. The hour of four had been settled upon to diminish as much as might be, so the President said, the chances of an earthquake in the New York stock market, which closed at three. In San Francisco, which is three hours younger than New York, the winds of disastrous speculation blew a hurricane that afternoon; but no one east of the Mississippi cares what happens in San Francisco. Besides, the New York hurricane was only deferred.

Tuesday afternoon, after word of that Presidential fist-shaking had soaked into the souls of men, speculative New York went nervous to the frontiers of hysteria. Tuesday night, speculative New York couldn't sleep; it sat up till morning, for, like cattle, it could smell in the breeze the coming storm. Wednesday heard the crash; and the crashing continued unabated throughout Thursday and Friday. The papers of that hour in attempting to describe stock conditions drew exhaustively on such terms as "tornado," "blizzard," "simoon," "maelstrom," "cyclone," "landslide," "avalanche," and whatever else in the English language means death and devastation. No one found fault of those similes, which were justified of the hopeless truth. Values were beaten as flat as a field of turnips. The best feature was that no banks failed; two or three of the weaker sisters wavered, but the big, burly concerns gave them the arm of their aid and led them through.

Days before the smash, that osprey pool had perfected the last fragment of its arrangements. The old gray buccaneer, who had charge of the pool's interests, was as ready for action as was Mr. Bayard. The latter stock-King was perhaps the only one in the Street who possessed a foreknowledge of what daring deeds our White House meditated. To Mr. Bayard the secrets of Courts and Cabinets were told, for he had an agent at the elbow of every possibility. The old gray buccaneer was not so well provided; none the less, with decks cleared, guns shotted, cutlasses ground to razor-edge, he was prompt on the instant to put forth against Northern Consolidated now when the tempest which lashed the market favored his pirate purposes.

Those four millions which had been decided upon as the fund of the osprey pool were banked ready to the hand of the old gray buccaneer. Storri, who had been losing money, exhausted himself in providing the five hundred thousand which made up his one-eighth of the four millions. By squeezing out his last drop of credit, he succeeded in gathering those thousands; once gathered, he tossed them into the pool's fund as carelessly as though they had been nothing more than the common furniture of his pocket, without which he would not think of beginning the day. Storri at least was a magnificent actor.

In collecting those five hundred thousand dollars, Storri, among other securities, put up the French shares. He thought nothing of that, since following victory over Northern Consolidated they would be back in his hands again. Incidentally, a gratifying thing happened, something in the nature of a compliment or a concession, which he attributed to the snobbish eagerness of Americans to pay homage to his nobility. Fatuous Storri; he should never have looked for compliment or concession or snobbish adulation in a plain lend-and-borrow traffic of dollars and cents! Men will buy a coat of arms; but they will not take a coat of arms in pawn. No; Storri, instead of feeling flattered, should have grown suspicious when the gentleman from whom he borrowed those five hundred thousand proposed to let him have the full value of his securities if in return he were given the right to confiscate should the loans not be repaid on the nail. Why not? The new arrangement meant no real risk; the security might always be sold in case of default. And under the arrangement offered, Storri's credit would be enlarged by twenty per cent. He agreed, and had immediate advantage of the fact. Drawing to the last dollar, he made his share of the pool's four millions good.

When the storm descended Wednesday morning, the old gray buccaneer was instantly in the middle of it doing all he might to encourage the storm. As the stock world went to its sleepless bed on Tuesday night, it knew about the Presidential defiance of Germany. That news was enough to keep the stock world shivering till morning. When it arose and read the *Daily Tory*, its chills were multiplied by two. As if trouble with Germany were not sufficient invitation to general ruin, here came the Hanway report driving a knife to the heart of Northern Consolidated! At sight of that, the stock world's last hope abandoned it, and the work of slaughter commenced. The old gray buccaneer grinned with happiness that awful morning as he looked across the field of coming war.

Andrew Jackson, being half Scotch and half Irish, was wont before a battle to think and plan with the prudent sagacity of a Bailey Jarvie. Once the battle began, he ceased to be Scotch and became wholly Irish; he quit thinking and devoted himself desperately to execution. The old gray buccaneer of stocks was like Andrew Jackson. His plan, thoroughly cautious and Scotch, had been laid to sell and sell and sell Northern Consolidated until the stock was beaten down to twenty. He would sell savagely, relentlessly, sell with his eyes shut, until the twenty point was reached. And if necessary, he would sell four hundred thousand shares.

The old gray buccaneer, under the conditions existing, did not think it would require a sale of four hundred thousand shares before the market broke to the figure he had fixed his heart upon. The general conflagration raging must of necessity smoke out thousands and thousands of innocent Northern Consolidated shares. These, blind and frenzied, would rush plungingly into the flames like horses at a fire. The old gray buccaneer felt sure that while he was selling four hundred thousand shares, full two hundred thousand, mayhap three hundred thousand, shares in addition would be offered. What stock could support itself against such a flood as that? When the bottom was reached, and the time was ripe, the pool would gather in the harvest. It was a beautiful plan; the more beautiful because of its simplicity!

Instantly on the morning of that black Wednesday the sale of Northern Consolidated began. Thousands of shares in two thousand, five thousand, and even ten thousand lots were thrown upon the market by the old gray buccaneer. In the roar and tumult of that disastrous day, what would have been in calmer moments a spectacle of astonishment passed much unnoticed. The stock world was busy saving itself out of the teeth of destruction, and the smashing and slugging in Northern Consolidated attracted the less attention.

Northern Consolidated merited admiring attention; against that desperate hammering, it stood like a wall of granite. Ten, twenty, forty, eighty, over one hundred thousand shares were sold that Wednesday; and yet, marvel of marvels, Northern Consolidated at the day's close had fallen off no more than six points. It retreated sullenly, slowly, step by step and eighth by eighth; ever and anon it would make a stand and hold a price an hour. Other stocks lost twice and threefold the ground; the stubbornness of Northern Consolidated began to engage the notice of men. More than one poor "bull" when sore beset that day took fresh heart from the obstinacy of Northern Consolidated; his own foothold was steadied and made the stronger for it.

But the old gray buccaneer refused to be denied; he had quit thinking and begun to act; he would break the back of Northern Consolidated if it took the last share of those four hundred thousand! His courage never wavered; he would charge and keep charging; in the end his cavalry work must tell and the lines of Northern Consolidated crumple up like paper. All it required was dash and confidence, with an underlying grim determination to win or die, and Northern Consolidated must yield.

The war was renewed upon Thursday, and staggered fiercely on throughout the day. Then Friday followed, a roaring, tottering, crashing, smashing fellow of the two days gone before. Millionaires became beggars and beggars millionaires between breakfast and lunch.

As on Wednesday, so also on Thursday and Friday the stock which best sustained itself was Northern Consolidated. And yet no other stock was so bitterly sold! As against this it should be added that no other was so bitterly bought! Every offer to sell was closed with at the very moment of its birth.

At last the end came; the old gray buccaneer could go no further. He had already oversold his self-fixed limit, having parted with four hundred and eleven thousand shares. The sales were made in the names of the various members of the pool, each selling one-eighth of the whole. Senator Hanway's interest, as well as that of Mr. Harley, being fifty-one thousand three hundred and fifty shares for each, for reasons that do not require exhibition, was handled in the name of an agent. Full one hundred and fifty thousand innocent shares, smoked into the open market as the old gray buccaneer had anticipated, were also sold, making the round total of five hundred and sixty-one thousand shares of Northern Consolidated offered and snapped up during those three days of fire. It was the greatest "bear" raid in the annals of the Stock Exchange, so graybeards said; and what peculiarly marked it for the admiration of mankind was that it had had the least success. In three days, with five hundred and sixty-one thousand shares sold, the stock had fallen only eleven points. The raid was over and the "bears" had growlingly retreated thirty minutes before the close on Friday. Within ten minutes after the last offer to sell, and when it was plain the "bears" had quit the field, under a cross-fire of bids that fell as briskly thick as hail, Northern Consolidated was bid up thirteen points. It had stood forty-one at Tuesday's close; it was forty-three when, "bears" routed, the market was over Friday afternoon. And thus disastrously fared the osprey pool.

"We're ruined, gentlemen," coolly remarked the old gray buccaneer when, with the exception of Senator Hanway, the members of the pool gathered themselves together Friday evening. "We're in a corner; we're gone—hook, line, and sinker!"

"What can we do?" asked Mr. Harley, his face the hue of putty.

"Nothing!" said the old gray buccaneer, lighting a Spartan cigar. "We're penned up; whoever has us cornered may now come round and knock us on the head whenever he finds it convenient."

"The market is still weak," observed one, "for all it lived through the panic. Suppose we creep in to-morrow and cover our shorts. The shares are forty-three; I for one think it might be wise to close the deal and take our losses, even if we go as high as fifty."

"For myself," remarked the old gray buccaneer, with a half-sneer at what he regarded as a most childish suggestion, "I'd be pleased to settle at sixty-five or even seventy." Then, turning to him who was for softly buying his way out: "Do you imagine that what has happened was accident? I tell you there's a shark swimming in these waters—a shark so big that by comparison Port Royal Tom would seem like a dolphin. And, gentlemen, that shark is after us. He's been after us from the beginning; he's got between us and the shore, and he'll pull us under when the spirit moves him. If you think differently, go into the market to-morrow and try to buy Northern Consolidated. An attempt to buy five hundred shares will put it up ten points."

The next day, Saturday, the pool sent quietly into the Exchange to buy one thousand shares; that, by way of feeler. The old gray buccaneer was right; Northern Consolidated climbed fifteen points with the vivacity of a squirrel, and rested mockingly at fifty-eight. Following this disheartening experiment, which resulted in nothing more hopeful than a demand for further margins from the pool's brokers, there were no more efforts to "buy." The pool was marked for death; but that, while discouraging, offered no argument in favor of self-destruction.

When the markets opened upon that storm-swept Wednesday, there were forty brokers on the floor of the Exchange to execute the orders of Mr. Bayard. Not one of the forty knew of the other thirty-nine; not one was aware of Mr. Bayard in the business of the day. Thirty as a maximum had been commissioned to buy—each man twenty thousand shares—six hundred thousand shares of Northern Consolidated. The orders had come through banks in the city, and from banks and brokerages in London, Paris, Berlin, and a dozen points in Europe. They ran from five hundred to as high as twelve thousand shares the order. Each broker was given a certain limit below which he might buy, and the orders of no two were in conflict. Each for his orders would have the unobstructed market to himself.

Mr. Bayard arranged for that fall of eleven points; the "bear" raid must seem to have effect to encourage the pool. To thus foster the pool in its hopes, ten of the forty were to "sell" Northern Consolidated in limited lots; these sales should augment "bear" enthusiasm.

In each instance the stock thus offered was taken by one of Mr. Bayard's brokers, who little imagined that both he and the broker selling drew their inspirations from the same source. As demonstrating the finesse of Mr.

Bayard, if one had collected from the forty those orders which they brought upon the floor that Wednesday morning, and spread them on a table, they would have exhibited a perfect picture of speculation. One would have fitted with another, and each in its proper place, until the whole was like a mosaic of defense. The "bear" pool was met on the threshold; it was permitted to press forward eighth by eighth according to a plan; one Bayard broker having made his purchases, another took his place; it was like clockwork. The whole five hundred and sixty-one thousand shares were bought and sold; and from first to last there came never a glimpse of Mr. Bayard.

It had been Mr. Bayard's earlier thought to let Northern Consolidated fall as low as twenty-five. For the sake of poor men in peril from that defiance of all things German, Mr. Bayard in the last hours of his preparations decided to support the market. To hold Northern Consolidated above thirty against the double pressure of a falling market and a "bear" raid would be to the general stock list as a prop to a leaning wall. It would save hundreds from annihilation, and Mr. Bayard resolved for their rescue. It would cost him nothing, lose him nothing; once cornered, the question whether that osprey pool were cornered at twenty or at thirty or at forty was unimportant. The corner complete, Mr. Bayard with a breath could put Northern Consolidated to fifty, to one hundred, to five hundred, to one thousand! The measure of his triumph would be the measure of the mercy of Mr. Bayard. *Væ Victis!* Our Brennus of the Stocks might demand from the members of the vanquished pool their final shilling. He might strip them as he was stripped those thirty years before, and turn them forth naked. For thus read the iron statutes of the Stock Exchange where quarter is unknown.

It was Mr. Bayard who caused Northern Consolidated to climb, squirrel-wise, to forty-three as the market closed on Friday, and later to fifty-eight. It had the effect desired; there came the call for margins. Storri, who had put his last dollar to the hazard, went down, exhausted, destroyed, and under foot, and, as parcel of the spoils of that Russian's overthrow, those French shares were sent to Mr. Bayard. Within ten minutes after he received them they were on their way to Richard, with a letter telling how complete had been the osprey pool's defeat. For all his dignity and his gray crown of sixty years, Mr. Bayard's eyes were shining like the eyes of a child with a new toy. What battle was to that Scriptural hero's warhorse so was the strife of stocks as breath in the nostrils of Mr. Bayard. Richard's eyes were as bright as those of Mr. Bayard when he received the French shares, but it was a softer brightness born of thoughts of Dorothy, and in no wise to be confounded with that battle-glitter which shone in the eyes of the other. Thus ran the note of Mr. Bayard:

Dear Mr. Storms:

Our bears are safely in the pit which we digged for them. The New York five are taking it in a temper of stolid philosophy, being bruins of experience. We may keep them in the pit what time you will before we begin the butchery—one week, one month, one year. They cannot escape, since my agents on the floor of the Exchange will be always on the watch to see that they don't climb out. The first time an offer to buy or sell a share of Northern Consolidated is made, I shall put the price to three hundred. Our bears, however, know this, and will make no attempt to get away, realizing its hopelessness. The Storri bear is already dead; that first call for margins killed him, and I send you a specimen of his pelt, to wit, the French shares, with this. As for the others, whenever you are ready we will call on them for their fur and their grease and what else is valuable about a bear. Believe me your friend, as was your father the friend of

Robert Lance Bayard.

Richard, now he had possession of those fateful securities, was somewhat put about as to the best manner of getting them into the hands of Mr. Harley. He, Richard, could not personally appear in the transaction. He thought of using the excellent Mr. Gwynn; but that course offered objections, since it would be assumed hereafter by Mr. Harley that Richard, because of his confidential relations with Mr. Gwynn, must know the history of those shares. Richard did not care to have such a thought take hold on Mr. Harley; it might later embarrass both Mr. Harley and Richard when the latter called at the Harley house, as he meant shortly to do. Finally he hit upon an idea; he would employ the worthy name of Mr. Fopling. The secret would be safe with one who, like Mr. Fopling, could never be brought to understand it.

Being decided as to a path, Richard inclosed those dangerous shares with a typewritten note to Mr. Harley. The note, speaking in the third person, presented Mr. Fopling's compliments, explained that Mr. Fopling was given to understand that Mr. Harley would purchase those particular shares, stated their value as fifteen thousand dollars, and said that Mr. Harley might send his check to Mr. Fopling.

This missive and those shares being safely on their road to Mr. Harley, Richard made speed to hunt up Mr. Fopling. He found the sinless one at the house of his beloved. Fortune favored Richard; Bess was not there, being across with Dorothy, and, save for the company of Ajax, Mr. Fopling was alone. Mr. Fopling was in the Marklin library, glaring ferociously at Ajax, who was blinking disdainful yellow eyes at Mr. Fopling by way of retort.

Richard explained to Mr. Fopling that through certain deals in stocks he had become possessed of two hundred shares of one of Mr. Harley's pet stocks. Mr. Harley would give anything to regain them. Richard desired to return them to Mr. Harley without being known in the business. Would Mr. Fopling permit him the favor of his name? He would employ Mr. Fopling's name most guardedly. Richard did not tell Mr. Fopling that his sacred name was already in the harness of the affair.

The benumbed Mr. Fopling, by listening attentively, succeeded in getting an impression that Richard through lucky dexterity and sleight had obtained some strange hold in stocks on Mr. Harley, and now in a foolish leniency was about to let him go. This excited Mr. Fopling hugely; he put in a most vigorous protest.

"Weally, Stawms," he squeaked, "if you've twapped the old curmudgeon you must stwip him for his last dime, don't y' know! I wemembah a song my governor used to sing; he said it was his motto. The song wan like this:

"'When you catch a black cat, skin it, skin it!When you catch a black cat, skin it to the tail!'

"Yes, Stawms, use my name as fweely as you please; but I pwotest against letting up on this old cweature Harley."

"But, my dear boy," observed Richard, "you must consider! Mr. Harley is to be my father-in-law, he's Dorothy's father."

Mr. Fopling declined to consider what he called a "technicality." Mr. Harley must be squeezed.

"Weally, Stawms," said Mr. Fopling, "it's the wules of the game, don't y' know."

After no little argument, Mr. Fopling yielded his point. Mr. Fopling, however, bethought him of troubles of his own, and made condition that Richard stand his friend with Bess as against his enemy, Ajax.

"Bees always sides with Ajax," explained Mr. Fopling plaintively, "and it ain't wight!"

Richard gave Mr. Fopling a fraternal grip with his mighty hand. He would be to Mr. Fopling as was Jonathan to David. It should be back to back and heel to heel with them against Ajax, Bess, and all the world! The violent loyalty of Richard alarmed Mr. Fopling; he threw in a word of caution.

"You mustn't be weckless, Stawms."

Bess came back from the Harley house, and found Richard with Mr. Fopling. Bess reported Dorothy's spirits as improved; those rays of comfort emanating from Richard's promises had put a color in her cheek.

"The promises have been redeemed," observed Richard, "and I came to tell you first of all—you who have been our truest friend," and here, to the utter outrage of Mr. Fopling's sensibilities, Richard kissed Bess's yellow hair.

"Oh, I say, Stawms!" squeaked Mr. Fopling reproachfully.

"Mistake, I assure you!" said Richard, again giving Mr. Fopling his hand.

"Well, please don't wepeat it!" returned Mr. Fopling a bit sulkily. "It gives me a most beastly sensation, don't y' know, to see a chap cawessing Bess; it does, weally!"

"Hush, child!" said Bess; "you excite yourself about nothing."

Bess was for having Dorothy over on the strength of the good news, but Richard was against it, proudly.

"No," said he. "With Storri's hold upon him, Mr. Harley asked me to stay away from his house. Now Storri's hold is broken, I shall give him a chance to ask me to return."

"Oh, I see," replied Bess teasingly. "Sir Launcelot having done a knightly deed and rescued a fair damsel, and the fair damsel's family, from a dragon, will give his vanity an outing."

"Only till to-morrow evening!" protested Richard, humbled from the high horse. "If Mr. Harley doesn't invite me by that time, I'll invite myself."

"If Mr. Harley doesn't invite you by that time," returned Bess, "I will interfere. Those who can't see their duty must be shown their duty, Mr. Harley among the rest. On the whole, I think you take a very proper stand."

Storri, without a dollar, lay in his rooms like a wounded wolf. He did not go to the San Reve; he would see no one until he had worn down his anguish and regained control of himself. Hurt to the death, Storri was too cunning to furnish word of it to mankind. No one must know; it was the instinct of self-preservation. The wounded wolf, while his wounds are fresh, avoids the pack lest the pack destroy him. And so with Storri; he would hide until he could command that old-time manner of unclouded ease. He would stifle every surmise, deny every rumor if rumor blew about, of the blow he had received. A few days, and Storri would be himself again. As for immediate money, Storri would extort that from Mr. Harley, who, in his dull-head ignorance or worse, had been the author of his losses. Who first spoke of Northern Consolidated? Who suggested the "bear" raid? Was it not Mr. Harley? The affair had been his; the loss should be his; Mr. Harley must repay, or face the wrath of Storri.

"Face the wrath of Storri!" exclaimed that furious nobleman with an oath. "He would face nobody—nothing! Bah! that Harley; he is a dog and the coward son of a dog! Yes, he shall come here; he shall crawl and crouch! I, Storri, will give him the treatment due a dog!"

Storri wrote a blunt word to Mr. Harley and dispatched it to that shattered capitalist.

"Come to-night at nine, you Harley," said the note, "and do not presume to fail, or my next communication will be through one of your officers of police."

Storri was aware that the French shares were gone from him, but he counted on easily tracking them and buying them back. He would force Mr. Harley to give him the very money that was to buy them. The thought lighted up his cruel face like a red ray from the pit; it would be such a joke—such a triumph over the pig American! Meanwhile he would bully Mr. Harley, who did not know but what the shares were in his pocket.

If Storri had been informed of how, through the deep arrangements of that strategist of stocks, he had borrowed every dollar of those five hundred thousand from Mr. Bayard, as well as every share of Northern Consolidated delivered to perfect those sales that had brought him down in ruin—in short, if he had been told the whole romance, from Mr. Fopling's exhortation to "Bweak him!" to the close of the market on that crashing Friday afternoon, he might have been less sure of recapturing those French shares. But he was ignorant of those truths; and, with confidence bred of ignorance, he summoned Mr. Harley. He, Storri, would browbeat and bleed him; he would teach the caitiff Harley to be more careful of the favor, not to say the fortune, of a Russian nobleman.

Mr. Harley, with the defeat of the "bear" attack on Northern Consolidated, was left in forlornest case. He was aware that it spelled money-ruin for both him and Senator Hanway; but the picture of the rage of Storri, and what that savage might do in his bitterness, so filled up his thoughts that he scarcely heeded anything beyond. Mr. Harley was stricken sick by his own fears, and, after returning from New York on the evening of that fearful Friday, never moved from his room. To the anxious tap of Dorothy, he sent word that he was not ill, but very busy; he must not be disturbed. Like Storri, only more a-droop, Mr. Harley owned no wish for company.

Mr. Harley was thus broken to the ground when Storri's message found him. The threat at the tail, like the sting at the tail of a scorpion, stunned Mr. Harley past thinking. He could neither do nor plan; he could only utter his despair in groans.

Two hours later, and while he lay writhing, Richard's inclosure of the French shares arrived by post. Mr. Harley at sight of them came as near fainting as any gentleman coarsely grained and hearty ever comes. Ten minutes went by in stupid gazing, and in handling and feeling those certificates that were to him as is the reprieve that comes to one who else would die within the hour.

There is such a thing as compensation, and the very coarseness of which you have now and again complained made most for the rescue of Mr. Harley at this crisis. By dint of that valuable coarseness, Mr. Harley, discovering that he could trust his eyes,—he at one time doubted those visual organs,—recovered such strength, not to say composure, that he ordered up a quart of burgundy and drank it by the goblet. Under this wise treatment, and with the reassuring shares in his clutch, Mr. Harley became a new man.

The first evidence of this newness given to the world was when at eight o'clock Mr. Harley, faultlessly caparisoned and in full evening dress, descended upon Mrs. Hanway-Harley and Dorothy. The ladies were together in the back drawing-room as the restored Mr. Harley, with brow of Jove and warlike eye, strode into their startled midst. Establishing himself in mighty state before the fireplace, rear to the blaze, he gazed with fondness, but as though from towering altitudes, on Dorothy.

"Come and kiss me, child!" said Mr. Harley.

Dorothy obeyed without daring to guess the cause of this abrupt affection.

"You act strangely, Mr. Harley!" commented Mrs. Hanway-Harley, with a tinge of severity. "I hope you will compose yourself. It is quite possible that Count Storri will drop in!"

"Madam," shouted Mr. Harley explosively, "I shall shoot that scoundrel Storri if he puts hand to my front gate!"

"John!" screamed Mrs. Hanway-Harley.

"Madam, I shall shoot him like a rat!"

Mr. Harley got this off with such fury that it struck Mrs. Hanway-Harley speechless. She was the more amazed, since she knew nothing of either Mr. Harley's wrongs or his burgundy. After surveying her with the utmost majesty for a moment, Mr. Harley came back to Dorothy.

"There's a gentleman named Mr. Storms?"

"Yes, papa!" (timidly).

"You love him?"

"Yes, papa!" (feebly).

"You shall marry him!"

"Yes, papa!" (blushingly).

"John!" (with horror).

"Invite him to dinner to-morrow."

"Yes, papa!" (rapturously).

"And every other evening you choose!"

"Yes, papa!" (more rapturously).

"John!" (with a gasp).

"And now, madam," observed Mr. Harley, wheeling on Mrs. Hanway-Harley with politeness sudden and vast, "I am ready to attend to you. Let me commence by mentioning that I am master of this house, and shall give dinners when I will to whomsoever I please."

"But you said marriage, John, and Mr. Storms is a pauper! Think what you do!"

"It may entertain you, madam," returned Mr. Harley, in a manner of grim triumph, "to hear that you also are a pauper. Yes, madam, you, I, Pat Hanway—we are all paupers. Now I shall go to your scoundrel Storri and tell him what I have told you. Oh! I shall not murder the villain, madam; though I give you my word, if there were no one to think of but Jack Harley, I'd return to you blood to my elbows; yes, madam, to my elbows!" and Mr. Harley pulled up his coatsleeves very high to give force to his words.

Lighting a cigar, which he set between his teeth so that it projected outward and upward at an angle of defiance, Mr. Harley got into his hat and greatcoat, and made for the door. As he threw it open preparatory to issuing forth, there floated back with a puff of cigar smoke these words, delivered presumably for the good of Mrs. Hanway-Harley:

"Yes, madam; blood to my elbows!"

"Your father is insane!" groaned Mrs. Hanway-Harley to Dorothy, when the door had slammed and Mr. Harley was on his way to Storri, "absolutely insane!"

Then Mrs. Hanway-Harley, with many an ejaculation of self-pity over a fate that had made her helpmeet to a lunatic, called her maid to aid her in creeping to her room. As for Dorothy, she danced about as light as air; in the finale she danced across the way to Bess to tell that sorceress what wonders had befallen.

"Eh! you Harley—you John Harley, is it you?" jeered Storri, as Mr. Harley was shown in.

"Yes, you black villain and thief, it is I!" roared Mr. Harley, planting himself in front of Storri, who had not taken the polite trouble to get up from the sofa where he reclined. "Yes, you world's scoundrel, who but I!"

"Scoundrel?" repeated Storri with a screech, springing to his feet.

"Sit down!" thundered Mr. Harley, a pistol coming from his pocket like a flash.

"Sit Down!" Thundered Mr. Harley

Mr. Harley was from a region where pistols were regarded in the light of arguments, and gentlemen gravely debating therewith at ten paces had the approving countenance of the public. This may explain the ready grace with which Mr. Harley produced a specimen of that species of artillery when Storri seemed to threaten violence.

"Sit down!" thundered Mr. Harley, and Storri, with terror twitching at his lips, obeyed. Mr. Harley replaced the pistol in his pocket, and surveyed

Storri with a look so sinister it alarmed that nobleman to the heart. "I have come," continued Mr. Harley, taking a chair and maintaining the while a dangerous eye on Storri, "I have come to return your insults, you blackmailing rogue, in the room where I received them."

CHAPTER XVIII

HOW STORRI EXPLORED FOR GOLD

Should it ever be your fancy to witness on the part of any gentleman an exhibition of ferocity unrestrained, that you may have him at his best for your experiment, it would be wise to commence by subjecting him to a tremendous fright. Being first frightened and then relieved from his terror, and particularly if his nature be a trifle rough, he will if brought suddenly into the presence of one who has injured him furnish all you could desire in a picture of the sort adverted to. And thus was it with Mr. Harley that evening when he called on Storri—now no longer terrible.

The offensive utmost that one gentleman might say to another, Mr. Harley said to his aforetime noble friend. He crushed Storri beneath fourfold what bulk of insolence and contumelious remark he himself had received, for at that fashion of conversation Mr. Harley was Storri's superior. Mr. Harley rendered Storri such shameful accounts of himself that the latter was well-nigh consumed with what inward fires were ignited. Storri burned the more because his own cowardly alarms tied his hands and gagged retort upon his tongue. Mr. Harley, who had been frightened to the brink of collapse in the only manner that Storri might have frightened him, now refreshed himself unchecked and fed retaliation to the full.

Storri, craven to the roots, must fain submit. The murderous facility wherewith Mr. Harley in the beginning invested the conversation with that pistol had not been lost upon Storri, and he shivered lest the interview conclude with his own murder. Mr. Harley, having exhausted expletive and opprobrious term, might empty the six chambers of his dreadful weapon into Storri. Thus spake Storri's fears, and he cowered while Mr. Harley raged. Indeed, the tables had been turned, and Mr. Harley was taking virulent advantage of the reversal. Among other matters, he taunted Storri with his, Mr. Harley's, possession of those French shares, and gave him to know that the happy transfer had been the fruit of his, Mr. Harley's, own superior wit.

"For," said Mr. Harley, with no more noble purpose than to augment Storri's pangs, "did you think that one of my depth was for long to be held at the mercy of such a dolt as yourself?"

"Then it was you," moaned Storri, who made the mistake of believing what Mr. Harley said, "then it was you who bought Northern Consolidated—you, and your confederates to whom you betrayed us?"

Mr. Harley smiled loftily, and was silent as though disdaining reply. He was willing to have Storri think his overthrow due to him and him alone. It would please him should Storri believe that he, Mr. Harley, had conquered not only the possession of those shares, but of the five hundred thousand dollars which were so painfully collected as Storri's contribution to the pool's four millions. It would promote Mr. Harley's satisfaction to the superlative; it would make Storri's humiliation complete. By all means teach Storri that he, Mr. Harley, constructed the ambush into which the pool had sold its blindfold way. Wherefore, Mr. Harley with shrug and sneer consented to Storri's charges of betrayal, and intimated his own profitable joy of that treason. After thirty minutes of triumph, Mr. Harley, mightily restored in his own graces, arose to depart.

"And for a last word, you scoundrel," quoth the loud Mr. Harley, "I told Mrs. Hanway-Harley I would shoot you if you so much as laid hand to my front gate. You might do well to remember that promise; I have been known on occasion to tell Mrs. Hanway-Harley the truth."

After the last gloomy notice Mr. Harley went his defiant way, while Storri sank back a more deeply wounded wolf than ever.

Mr. Harley drew his check and dispatched it to Mr. Fopling, and Richard in due course received a check from the latter. Mr. Harley did not allude to the transaction on those few and distant occasions when he and Mr. Fopling met; and Mr. Fopling, burdened of his feuds with Ajax, soon forgot the affair in matters more important.

Mr. Harley, when emancipated from the thraldom of Storri, was as dollarless so far as immediate cash was concerned as was the stripped Storri himself. But in the rebound of spirit which followed, Mr. Harley's genius regained its old-time elasticity. A member of the House with whom he was in touch, being one of that speculative party who opened the New Year at Chamberlin's with cards, was so conveniently good-natured as to offer a measure putting coal on the free list. This, if passed, would be a woundy blow to the Harley mines; also to that railway whereof Mr. Harley was a director, since it hauled the Harley coal to the seaboard. With coal on the free list, Nova Scotia could undersell the Harley mines in every Atlantic port; likewise the Harley road would lose two millions in annual freight. Under these threatening conditions, Mr. Harley was instantly given one hundred thousand dollars by the mines and the railroad to kill the iniquitous bill, and convert to a right opinion any and all who talked of coal and free lists in one and the same breath. Those one hundred thousand dollars relieved the pressing needs of Mr. Harley, and the bill that threatened coal and railroads was heard of no more.

When, following Mr. Harley's gracious words concerning Richard and Mrs. Hanway-Harley's disconsolate departure for her own room, Dorothy danced across to Bess, the yellow-haired sorceress rose grandly to the opportunity. She sent Mr. Fopling to find Richard; and since Mr. Fopling's weakness was not of the legs—he being a very Mercury, with feet as fleet as his wits were slow—Dorothy and Bess had no more than finished giving and receiving congratulations, *i. e.*, kisses, when Richard appeared and took Bess's labor of congratulation off her hands—or should one say her lips? Bess was of those excellent folk whose fine friendships know when to go as well as when to stay, and, Richard arriving, she conveyed Mr. Fopling and Ajax from the room, leaving the restored lovers to themselves.

Of what worth now to tell you those sweetheart things that Richard and his angel said and did? How would it advantage a world to hear that he took her in his arms and held her close? You, who have loved and have been loved, who were lost and have been found again, well know the blissful routine. Richard said that no woman was ever loved as he loved Dorothy. Dorothy the beloved replied that no man was ever loved as she loved Richard. Both believed both statements as they did the Word. And yet Adam said the same thing when, wandering in Eden, he first met lovely Eve, and every lover has said the same thing ever since. Every fire boasts itself the hottest, every lover does the same. It is the virtue of love that this is so, and none will object while Dorothy and Richard work out their tinted destiny on lines of paradise. They had been held apart; they were now together; rely upon it they said and looked those softly tender, foolish, happy, precedental things which have been best among the best lessons of the ages.

HE HELD HER CLOSE

Mr. Harley was pompous and patronizing the next evening when he met Richard at dinner; but Mr. Harley was no less kind. Richard submitted himself to Mr. Harley's patronage, for in it he recognized the inalienable right of a father-in-law. Mrs. Hanway-Harley on that dinner occasion did not pretend to the rugged, high good humor of her spouse, and cultivated a manner at once blighted and resigned. But she was civil even as she sighed, and he would have been a carper who complained. Dorothy was beset of many shynesses now that she was brought with her beloved into the presence of ones who were aware of her secret without possessing sympathy therewith. Bess was there; but Bess did not weigh upon her, since Bess applauded her love. Senator Hanway was there; but "Uncle Pat" did not confuse her, since he cared nothing about her love. It was Mr. Harley who permitted, and Mrs. Hanway-Harley who tolerated, her heart's choice that set her cheeks aflame. Still it was good to see Richard sitting across in the serpent stead of Storri—to see one whom she worshiped where one whom she feared and loathed had been before! It was twice good to think the present was immortal while the past was dead. As Dorothy thought these things and sweetly blushed to think them, you would have been reminded of a rose, if her blue eyes had not made you remember violets, or by their clear, true, tranquil depths led you away to muse on summer skies.

Richard bore the ordeal of that dinner manfully; ordeal it was, for he felt himself on exhibition. He was rigorous to seem unruffled, and defended his calmness by talking general politics with Senator Hanway. Nor did he fall into the error of speaking of tempests in the stock market; and as for the recreant Storri, no one named him. Bess might have brought Mr. Fopling, for he was asked, could she have trusted that young gentleman on this point of Storri. But Mr. Fopling was prone to bring up the one subject which others were trying to forget; and, realizing his tenacious aptitude for crime of that character, Bess sent him home and came alone.

Richard, like Storri before him, only with a better conscience, did not crowd good fortune to the wall; he left early. As he made ready to go, Mr. Harley invited him not only to another dinner, but to a multitude of such refections. Mr. Harley, having been thus hospitable, swept Mrs. Hanway-Harley with arrogant eye as who should say:

"There lies my glove, madam! We shall see who lifts it!"

Altogether, Richard's coming to the Harley house in the rôle of suitor for Dorothy's small hand went off well; and Dorothy was thinking that life seemed very beautiful and very bright when four hours later she fell asleep, and rosy dreams relieved her thoughts from further duty about her pillow for that night.

Senator Hanway and Mr. Harley, being veterans of the tape, were not ignorant of the hopeless state into which the failure of that "bear" raid on Northern Consolidated had plunged them. They could not name him who had worked the "corner" against them and the other members of the osprey pool, the hand that defeated them had been played from behind a curtain. Time, however, would develop the identity of their conqueror; nor was his identity of first importance, since the great thing was that they were caught. The best they might do was quietly await destruction in its coming. It would surely come; "corners" were not made in vain, and a day would dawn when he who held them captive would disclose himself. That disclosure would mean for them, financially, the beginning of the end.

Mr. Harley and Senator Hanway might have repudiated the deal, and so saved their fortunes at the sacrifice of their names. Indeed they thought of it; and then they shook their heads. Such a step would ruin Senator Hanway's hopes of a Presidency; those hard years of political labor would be canceled; his chances, now the fairest, would be swept away not only for the present but for time. The discovery of Senator Hanway—he who wrote the report against Northern Consolidated—as a partner in that "bear" raid, would strike his name forever from the roll of Presidential possibilities. It might even result in his expulsion from the Senate, for conspiracy is no good charge to face when true. Of those who were "bears" against Northern Consolidated, from Storri to the old gray buccaneer, the ones who must submit without a cry to being flayed were Mr. Harley and Senator Hanway, for with them to be discovered was to be destroyed.

After fullest conference, Mr. Harley went again to New York. It was settled that the old gray buccaneer should continue in command. When he who had beaten them unmasked himself, the old gray buccaneer was to treat for generous terms. With the bankrupt Storri out, there remained but seven to consider; the old gray buccaneer was to offer a round ransom of seven millions of dollars, or one million for each. In similar fashion beaten knights compounded in the dusty lists of Ashby eight hundred years ago; the amount of ransom that Ashby day was less, but the principle throughout the centuries has remained unshaken and unchanged.

After four days of wound-nursing, Storri went to the San Reve. He found that lady of the gray-green eyes sitting sullen and silent, wrapped in resentful anger like a witch's cloak. One thing in his favor; the San Reve had not heard of his return, and supposed him just back from New York.

Storri did his best to be on cheerful terms with the San Reve; he said his business was now accomplished and he would see her every day. Storri strove all he knew to soften the San Reve and turn her frowns to smiles. He failed; nothing would unlock that flinty, hard reserve.

"About the Harleys," said the jealous San Reve at last. "How do you stand with the Harleys? You still go there?"

The San Reve shot a sharp, inquiring glance at Storri from her sea-green, sea-gray eyes.

Storri, being feline, was as has been written no one hard to rout, and could be readily driven from an enterprise. With the loss of those French shares, his designs on Mr. Harley and his power over Dorothy had fallen to the ground. He was left with nothing more potent than his naked hatred. He was more hungry than before for harm against the Harleys, but the new conditions baffled him as might some bridgeless gulf. He could see no open way through which he might find his enemies and overcome them.

But Storri had his miserable prides, and would perish where he stood rather than tell the San Reve this. With her he must pretend to power; he must swagger and boast more loudly than before. This was the vanity and the strategy of the man. He would have thrust his hand into the fire sooner than confess himself beaten by Mr. Harley to the San Reve. She must continue to wonder at and worship him; it was the incense demanded by the nostrils of his self-love.

"How do I stand with those Harleys, my San Reve?" Storri's tone was supercilious and tired, as though he had been forced to remember ones who wearied him by vulgarest dint of their inconsequence. "I do not stand with the Harleys, I stand upon them. Where should such crawling, footless creatures be?" and Storri pointed to his own somewhat ample foundations as indicating the groveling whereabouts of the Harleys.

"But you go there?" remarked the San Reve, flintily suspicious.

"No, my San Reve," yawned Storri. "Pardon my grossness;—a yawn in the presence of a lady, and I a Russian gentleman! I took the habit from these pig Americans! You should know, my dear San Reve, that the very name of Harley bores me. No, I shall no more go to those Harleys. They send, they beg; I do not go. Why should I so honor them? Bah! let them come to me! Is a Russian—is a nobleman to be at the beck of such vile little people? No, they must come to me, your Storri, my San Reve; and when they arrive, bah! I shall not see them. I shall tell them they must come again!" And Storri lifted his hand grandly, as though the Harleys were now disposed of and their trivial status fixed.

Storri threw this off with a lazy insolence that, all things considered, did him credit. And yet he was not wise. He might not have told the San Reve that he had ended his visits to the Harleys, but her bold brow and thoughtful face misled him. He regarded her as deeper than she was; he considered that she would soon discover how he no longer was a guest at the Harley table, and thought to save himself from an inference by a proclamation. He would take the initiative and seem to cast the Harleys into the outer darkness of his disregard. It would make for his standing with the San Reve; more, it would soothe her jealousies.

Storri might have been justified of his reasonings had there existed no flaw in his premises. The San Reve was far from being gifted with that cold, incisive wisdom which he ascribed to her. Given a situation wherein the San Reve had no concern, and she would be sound enough; her speculations would defend themselves, her advice be worth a following. Endow the San Reve with a personal interest, the more if that interest were one mixed of love and jealousy, and her reason, if that be its name, would go blind and deaf and lapse into the merest frenzy of insanity. She would hasten to believe the worst and disbelieve the best. Under spell of jealousy, the San Reve would accept nothing that told in her own favor; and just now, despite an outward serenity—for, though sullen, she was serene—the San Reve was afire with jealousy like a torch.

The San Reve listened to Storri and said nothing; she could see how matters stood. Storri still dominated the Harleys; he went there; he saw Miss Harley; his suit was advancing; that was what had sent him to her, the San Reve, with a lie on his lips about having quit his calls at the Harleys'; he was seeking to blind her to what was passing. But she, the San Reve, would be cunning; she would fathom the traitor Storri. Even then she could foretell the end. In a week, or mayhap a month, the news would reach her of the wedding of Storri and Miss Harley. What else could come? Storri was a Count. Were not Americans mad after Counts? And such a nobleman! Wealthy, handsome, brilliant, bold—who could refuse his love? Not the Harleys—not Miss Harley! No, the transparent sureness of it set sneeringly a-curl the San Reve's mouth. Soon or late, Storri would lead Miss Harley to the altar. The bells would ring, the organ swell, the people gape and comment. And then Storri and his bride would ride away; while she, the San Reve—she, the disgraced—she, the daughter of a man who tamed lions—she would be left alone with her despised heart!

All this wild driftwood of conjecture came riding down on the swift, tumbling currents of the San Reve's thoughts, and to her these mad conclusions were as prophecy. What should she do—she and her poor love? She must not lose her idol—her Storri! What should she do? She had written this Mr. Storms of the French shares and nothing had come of that! Should she disclose herself to Miss Harley? Of what avail? What woman was ever withheld from wedding a man by the word of that man's mistress? The San Reve could have scorned herself for a fool! She was handless to interfere; the San Reve clenched her white, strong teeth to find herself so much at bay.

Stop; there was one chance of defeating fate—a sure chance; the thought had come before! And now the San Reve looked strangely at Storri; her teeth showed pearl against the coral of her parted lips while her nostrils dilated like the nostrils of an animal.

The little world you have been considering through the medium of this veracious chronicle began now to adjust itself to the changes that have been recorded. Mr. Harley and Senator Hanway, for their parts, gave themselves wholly to that winning of a White House; their ardor, if it were possible, had been promoted by the reverse in Northern Consolidated, and Senator Hanway's anxiety to be President appeared to brighten as his money-fortunes dimmed. And, as though Fate meditated amends for those disasters of stocks, from every angle of politics there came flattering reports. Senator Hanway was sure, so said the reports, to write himself "President Hanway"; politicians were shouldering one another to secure seats in the bandwagon of that statesman's prospects. True, for all their preoccupation, Mr. Harley and Senator Hanway would now and then glance up from those details of practical politics over which they were employed, to wonder why the hidden one of that "corner" did not close the transaction by peeling off their fiscal pelts. So far there had come neither word nor sign of him.

The old gray buccaneer exhorted them in no wise to be uneasy.

"You needn't fret," said the old gray buccaneer; "he's got us as fast as two and two make four. For us to be wondering why he doesn't come around is as though a coop full of turkeys went wondering why the poulterer didn't come around. No; I can't tell you why he—whoever he is—so leaves us in protracted peace. Perhaps he's fattening us," and the old gray buccaneer cheered the conversation with a laugh as strident as saw-filing.

Richard and Dorothy, following the selfish fashion of lovers, thought on nothing but themselves. Our young journalist's contributions to the *Daily Tory* fell away in both quantity and quality, and the editor commented thereon sarcastically, saying they were becoming "baggy at the knee." Richard did not resent the criticism; he cheered himself with the theory that when he had recovered from his happiness he would do better. Meanwhile, he and Dorothy privily appointed their nuptials for the first of June, taking Bess into the secret.

Dorothy asked Richard how he had rescued her father from beneath the hand of Storri; which natural inquisition Richard avoided in right man-fashion by kissing the questioning lips and saying that Dorothy wouldn't understand.

Mrs. Hanway-Harley was different from Dorothy. With a wifely experience of many years to guide her, she did not ask Mr. Harley why he had gone to furious war with Storri. Mrs. Hanway-Harley would not put the query for two reasons: Mr. Harley would prevaricate; besides, Mrs. Hanway-Harley knew. It was as obvious as a pikestaff to that sagacious gentlewoman; Mr. Harley and Storri had quarreled over stocks. Mr. Harley had been detected in some effort to swindle Storri; or he had detected Storri in some effort to swindle him; men were always swindling and quarreling, according to Mrs. Hanway-Harley. She put no question to Mr. Harley, and only marveled at a thickness that would sacrifice the family's chance of possessing a Count over a low, trifling matter of dollars and cents.

Inspector Val, when the capture of the French shares had removed the reason of his appearance in Storri's destinies, told Richard that he would, with his permission, still continue on the trail of that nobleman.

"Unless my judgment be at fault," explained Inspector Val, "there's something coming off that I wouldn't miss for anything you can name."

Richard, held fast with sweeter problems, cared not at all for Storri nor Inspector Val's pursuit of him. If it jumped with the humor of that scientist of stealth, Inspector Val might follow Storri to the grave. Richard would be pleased to have him do so, and to pay the costs thereof as rapidly as they accrued.

Inspector Val, whose trade it was to read men, smiled upon Richard at this and went his satisfied way. He would stick to Storri; and he would notify Richard should aught unusual either promise or occur. Inspector Val saw that in Richard's present mood of beatific imbecility a conference with him would mean no more than would a conference with the Monument.

Storri, while easily beaten from any specific enterprise, was ever ready with a fresh one. During those days when, like a convalescing wolf, he lay hiding with his wounds from the sight and search of men, his disorderly and, one might say, his criminal, imagination busied itself in sketching a giant scheme. It was as unique as had been the fallen Credit Magellan without owning to a shadow of Credit Magellan's legitimacy. This time Storri would have no partners; there would be no Mr. Harleys and no osprey pools to sell him out. Before all was done he might require men; but of the sort one controls like slaves.

There was one need that must be supplied, however; Storri must have money. Stimulated with the necessities that pricked him, Storri bethought himself of the Chinese Concession. That precious document was in his possession; the osprey pool had not been granted its custody. Storri carried the saffron silk to a rich and avaricious man; he asked the loan of fifty thousand dollars, and offered interest steeple-high. The man of wealth and avarice was deeply affected; he, like the others, sent for the brocaded, poppy-scented Mongol. The poppy Mongol came, salaamed, translated, and went his way. Then the one of gold and avarice counted down the fifty thousand, and locked up the yellow silk with Storri's note for ninety days in his safe.

Being strengthened with those fifty thousand dollars, Storri sought an ancient surveyor. Did the ancient one possess an accurate map of Washington?—a map that showed every public building and park and street-railway and water-main and sewer, all done to the final fraction of an inch? Storri's Czar has asked for such;—his Czar who so admired the Americans and their beautiful Capital!

The ancient one of chains and levels had such a map. Being a man to whom a unit was like a human being and every fraction as a child, the map was accurate in its measurements to the thickness of a hair. Storri bought the map; it showed the line of that drain which ran so temptingly close to the Treasury gold, and Storri's eye glistened as he followed it to the river's edge.

Storri collected photographs of the Capitol, the White House, and other public structures as a blind to conceal his purpose and lend luster of truth to those tales of his Czar's interest in things American. One evening Storri related to the San Reve his Czar's desires touching maps and plans and pictures, and showed her, among others, a picture of the Treasury.

Ah, that reminded Storri! His San Reve worked in the office of the supervising architect! Could his San Reve procure him a ground-plan of the Treasury Building? His Czar had laid especial stress upon such a drawing!

Yes, Storri's San Reve could get the desired ground-plan without difficulty. It would show everything foundational, with a cross-section displaying the depth of the walls below street grades.

The San Reve accepted as genuine Storri's eagerness to serve his Czar. Nor did she doubt Storri's description of the Czar's American curiosity; from what she had heard of that potentate, the San Reve believed him to be as crazy as a woman's watch. Certainly, if Storri wished to send the imperial lunatic a cartload of plans, the San Reve would contribute what lay in her power.

The next day Storri received from the San Reve a ground-plan of the Treasury Building. It exhibited in red ink the vault that held the gold reserve. Storri gazed upon that oblong smudge of red and studied its location with the devotion of a poet.

And now what was to be more expected than that the curious Czar would ask questions of Storri, when that illustrious Russian returned to St. Petersburg, concerning those many superiorities which the American buildings possessed? The thought set the indefatigable Storri to visiting the public buildings. He made a tour of the State War and Navy Building, the Corcoran Gallery, the Capitol, and finally the Treasury Building. Who should escort him through that latter grim, gray edifice but an Assistant Secretary? The affable A. S. had met Storri at the club; certainly he could do no less than give him the polite credit of his countenance for his instructive rambles. Under such distinguished patronage Storri went from roof to basement; even the vault that guarded the nation's gold was thrown open for his regard.

This gold vault was of particular moment to Storri; his Czar had laid weight upon that vault. Yes; he, Storri, could see how it was constructed—thick walls of masonry—an inner lining of chilled steel that would laugh at drills and almost break the teeth of nitric acid—the steel ceiling and sides bolted to the masonry—the floor, steel slabs two feet in width, laid side by side but not bolted, and bedded upon masonry that rested on the ground! Surely, nothing could be more solid or more secure! The door and the complicated machinery that locked it were wonders, marvels! Nowhere had he, Storri, beheld such a door or such a lock, and he had peeped into the strong rooms of a dozen kings. The gold, too, one hundred and ninety-three millions in all, packed five thousand dollars to a sack in little canvas sacks like bags of birdshot, and each sack weighing twenty pounds—Storri saw it all!

"And yet," quoth Storri, giving the polite Assistant Secretary a kind of leer, "do not that door and lock remind you of the chains and locks upon your leathern letterbags?—a leathern bag which the most ignorant of men would slash wide open with a penknife in an instant and never worry chains and locks?"

Storri traced that drain in its course to the river. It ran south past the corner of the Treasury Building for the matter of a hundred yards or more, and then broke south and west across the White Lot between the White House and the Monument. In the end it abandoned this diagonal flight and soberly took to the center of a street that lay to the west of the White House, and followed it to the Potomac.

Storri, hands in pocket and puffing an easy cigar, sauntered to the water front and took a look at the drain where it finished. The inspection gratified him; the drain was like a great tunnel; one might have driven a horse and wagon into it. Storri was especially struck by the fact that a considerable stream of water gushed from the drain's mouth; the stream had a fair current, four miles an hour at least, and showed a depth of full six inches. This was a discovery that set Storri's wits in motion; the drain boxed in a living brook.

It was eleven o'clock that night when Storri returned to the mouth of the drain; he was wrapped in a greatcoat and wore high boots. There were no houses about; as for loiterers, the region was deserted after dark. Storri looked out on the broad bosom of the river; he noticed that even at low tide a boat drawing no more than eighteen inches might push within a dozen feet of the drain.

Satisfied that no one observed him, Storri stepped to the mouth of the drain and disappeared. He splashed along in the running water with his heavy boots for something like a rod; then he stopped and lighted a bicycle lantern which he took from his greatcoat pocket. The lantern threw a bright flare after the manner of the headlight of a locomotive, and Storri could hear the scurrying splash of the rats as it sent an alarming ray ahead like a little searchlight. Being lighted on his way, Storri kept steadily forward until, turning the corner where the drain broke to the right across the White Lot, he was lost to sight.

As Storri disappeared, two men far behind him at the mouth of the drain stood watching. They had thus far followed Storri dimly with their eyes by the light he carried.

"What's become of him, Inspector?" whispered Mr. Duff, the shorter of the men. "He hasn't doused his glim, has he?"

"No," replied Inspector Val, "there's a bend at that point."

"What's next?" asked Mr. Duff; "do we follow him in and collar him? or do we just wait here?"

"Collar him!" repeated Inspector Val disgustedly. "I'd like to catch you collaring him! Is this a time to talk of collaring, and we no further than the threshold of the job? Let him alone; he's only laying out the work to-night."

CHAPTER XIX

HOW LONDON BILL TOOK A PAL

Perhaps the golden rule of all detective work is, Never let the detected one detect. Inspector Val was alive to this ordinance of his craft, and an hour later, when Storri cautiously emerged from the drain, he met neither sign nor sound of Inspector Val and Mr. Duff. Feeling sure that his exploration had not been observed, Storri wended homeward to his rooms, his chin sunk in meditation.

Storri the next day went to New York, and immediately on arrival at that hotel which he designed to honor with his custom he sprang into a hansom, and within ten minutes was at a private-detective agency, being the one whereat he aforetime procured those spies to set about the Harley house—spies long since withdrawn. The head of this detective bureau was a coarse-visaged, brandy-blotched man named Slater.

"And so," observed Mr. Slater, following a statement of Storri's errand, "you want to be put next to a 'peter-man, what we call a box-worker?"

"I would like to meet the best in the business," said Storri; "one also who is acquainted with others in his line, and who can be relied upon to the death."

"You want something desperate, eh?" said Mr. Slater, in a tone of suspicion. "Might I ask whether you have a safe to blow or a crib to crack on your own private account? I'm a cautious man, myself," he concluded, with a harsh chuckle, "and like to know what I'm getting mixed up with."

"Your caution is to be commended," returned Storri, "and I'll answer freely. No, I've no one to rob, no safe to break open. The truth is, I want to prosecute a search for a certain criminal, and I think a man of the stamp I wish to meet could help me more than a regular detective whose person is known and who would be instantly suspected. I'm not looking to arrest, but only to find a certain man. I shall pay him to whom you send me for his trouble, and you for putting me in touch with him."

"It's an irregular thing to do," remarked Mr. Slater, "but I see no harm."

Mr. Slater rang a bell and asked for Mr. Norris.

"Norris," said Mr. Slater, "this party wants to be put next to London Bill—wants to be made solid with Bill. That's as far as you go."

"All right," said Mr. Norris. Then addressing Storri: "If you come now, I think I can locate your man in fifteen minutes."

Storri and Mr. Norris drove to a doggery near the East River, in the vicinity of James Slip. It was called the Albion House. The lower floor was a barroom, and two or three sinister-looking characters lounged about the room. Mr. Norris ordered beer; then he leaned across to the barman and whispered a question.

"Why, yes," returned the barman, looking hard at Mr. Norris as though to read his errand, "Bill's been here. But it's on the square; he ain't doin' nothin'. I don't think he's seein' company neither."

"This is on the level, Dan," said Mr. Norris, who appeared to be on terms of acquaintance with the barman. "Let me make you known to Mr. Brown," he continued, introducing Storri. "Now here's all there is to it. Mr. Brown thinks Bill can put him wise to a party he's got business with. There's no pinch goes with it, and Mr. Brown's willing to do the handsome."

"Well," replied the barman doubtfully, "if Bill's about, I'll see what he thinks himself." With this, the barman, who was a brutal specimen with lumpy shoulders and a nose that had seen better days, called one of the loungers to preside in his stead, and retired through a door to the rear. He returned in a moment saying that Bill would see the caller, and jerked his stubby thumb in the direction of a back room.

"This is a boozing ken for hold-up people," explained Mr. Norris in a whisper, as he and Storri obeyed the hint tendered by the barman's thumb. "That bar-keep, Dan, used to be a strong-arm man himself; but since he's got this joint, he doesn't do any work, and has turned fall-guy for a fleet that operates along the Bowery."

Storri knew nothing of "strong-arm men," and "fall-guys," and "fleets," but he put no questions, and only seemed intent on meeting London Bill.

In the rear room that formidable outlaw was discovered seated at a table. He was alone, and evidently had just come from upstairs, as a door leading to the stairway was ajar. Mr. Norris presented Storri to London Bill, and, this social ceremony over, made few words of it before withdrawing altogether, leaving Storri and his new friend to themselves.

"Suppose we drink something," said London Bill, in noncommittal tones.

Storri ordered beer in a bottle, cork untouched; Storri had heard of knockout mixtures, and did not care to make his advent into upper criminal circles in the rôle of victim. London Bill grinned in a wise way, but made no comment, calling for gin himself.

"What is it?" said London Bill, after the gin had appeared and disappeared; "what's the argument you want to hand me?"

"I don't care to talk here," observed Storri, glancing suspiciously at the walls within touch of his hand. "Let us go outside."

"That's it," observed London Bill; "now if we was to go plantin' ourselves in Union Square, or any little open-air place like that, it's ten to one some Bull from the Central Office would come along an' spot us. They're onto my mug; got it in the gallery in fact."

"We can't talk here," said Storri decidedly.

"Wait a minute," suggested London Bill, who it was clear had grown curious as to Storri's errand, "I think I can fix the thing." He stepped into the bar and returned with a key. "Come on," said he; "there's an empty hall upstairs that ought to do us. It's as big as a rink."

London Bill led the way up the foul, creaking stairs, and opened a door on the top floor. It was a room the bigness of the building, and had been used for dancing. Drawing a couple of wooden chairs to a front window, Storri's guide motioned him to a seat.

"Here we be," he said; "now what's it all about?"

Storri, nothing backward when assured that no one was playing eavesdropper, began to talk, carefully avoiding his usual jerky Russian mannerisms. You have been told of Storri's graphic clearness of statement, once he had fully perfected the outlines of some enterprise. In fifteen minutes, but only in vaguest way, he laid his proposal before London Bill; the proposal was so framed that the 'peter-man understood no more than that a bank of unusual richness was to be broken into, and his aid was sought.

"Your share alone," whispered Storri, "will foot up for a million."

London Bill's little black eyes twinkled like those of a rat. He didn't make reply at once, but looked out of the grimy, cobwebby pane at the sky. The face of London Bill was rough, but not unpleasant, and, though he had killed his man and was a desperate individual if cornered, the only trait expressed was a patient capacity for enterprises that might require days or even weeks in their carrying out.

"Don't you think now you're a bit of a come-on?" observed London Bill, swinging around to Storri from his survey of the distant heavens.

"Why?" asked Storri, as cool as the other.

"This is why," returned London Bill. "Here you butt in, a dead stranger, and make a proposition. Suppose I was to rap?"

"I'd declare that you lied," replied Storri cheerfully, "and no one with sense would believe you. They would say that if I intended to ask your help in such work as I have described, I wouldn't seek an introduction through a detective agency."

"Something in that," said London Bill, a gleam of admiration in his beady gimlet eye. "Well, I never squeal, an' only put the question to try you out. Go on, an' tell me what it is an' where it is; whether I go into the job or not, at least you've nothin' to be leary of in me."

Storri, who had been studying London Bill as hard as ever that cracksman was studying him, re-began in earnest. He now laid bare the proposal in its every corner, and showed London Bill the plans and maps, including the valuable cross-section drawing that displayed the relation of the Treasury Building to street levels. London Bill, who appeared to have gifts as an engineer, bent over the maps and drawings, considering and measuring distances.

"What sort of ground is this?" said London Bill, laying a finger on the cross-section drawing, where it was painted dove-color as showing the earth beneath the street; "is it clay or sand?"

"Gray clay," returned Storri, "and fairly hard and dry."

"Good," remarked London Bill; "no fear of caving." Recurring to the drawings, London Bill proceeded: "It'll take two months to dig that tunnel. I'll have to dip as I go in, in order to creep beneath the footstones of the sidewall; then I'll bring the tunnel up on a long slant. The tunnel should be four feet high and about three wide; the earth I'd throw into the sewer, the water would wash it away. There's no risk in digging the tunnel, as no one would get an inkling of what's afoot until the last shove, when we made direct for the money. On that point let me ask: How long can we count on being undisturbed after we've got to the gold? Now if it was a bank, we'd time the play for Saturday afternoon after closing hours; that would give us until Monday morning at nine before they'd tumble."

"IT'LL TAKE TWO MONTHS TO DIG THAT TUNNEL."

"We can do better than that," returned Storri. "Saturday, May twenty-eighth, is the anniversary of the death of a former Secretary of the Treasury, and a special holiday has been already declared for that day. Monday, May thirtieth, is Decoration Day, a general holiday. We should have, you see, from Friday at four o'clock until Tuesday at ten; time enough to carry out several fortunes in twenty-pound packages worth five thousand dollars each."

"How do you expect to get away with the swag?" asked London Bill.

"Steam yacht," replied Storri sententiously. "I shall carry it from the mouth of the drain to the yacht with a launch. It's as silent as a bird flying, is that launch. Oh, I've thought everything out in full; I can get the yacht and the launch. The latter will freight an even ton every trip. Do you know how much gold money it takes to make a ton?"

"Half a million dollars," said London Bill, with his professional grin. "You see, partner, I've had to do a deal of studyin' along the same line as yourself."

"Precisely," returned Storri, disregarding the compliment implied by the epithet partner; "five hundred thousand dollars. We shall have seven hours a night for three nights, in which to freight the gold from the mouth of the drain to the yacht."

"Four nights," said London Bill correctively; "Friday, Saturday, Sunday, and Monday nights. I can carry that tunnel to a place within two hours of the stuff, with the Treasury full of people; no one would catch on. Take my word for it, you can begin getting out the gold the moment it turns dark on Friday night. Let's pray for a storm for those four nights."

"Your argument is right," observed Storri, "but there's a point you overlook. We shall have but three nights; Monday and Monday night will be required to take the yacht down the river, and into the open ocean. The instant the loss is discovered, they'll know the business was managed with the yacht; they will recall her as having been in the river the three or four days before. I mean to repaint her from black to white, the moment we're out of sight from the shore. I shall change her name, and have papers ready to match the change. Oh, my friend, you will see that I"—here Storri, who had studiously refrained from his usual bragging, exultant, staccato style of speech, and aped the plain and commonplace, almost forget himself; he was on the brink of giving his name, which thus far had been withheld. He checked himself in time, and ended soberly by saying: "You will see that I have left nothing unconsidered."

"Seven hours a night," ruminated London Bill, "and three nights: In considering everything, as you say, have you figured on how many trips your launch, bearing five hundred thousand dollars a trip, can make between shore an' ship?"

"The launch can make as many as twenty-one trips a night. In three nights she ought to put more than thirty millions of dollars aboard the yacht. That region around the drain's mouth is wholly deserted. By working without lights there isn't a chance of being detected."

"Thirty millions!" repeated London Bill, grinning cynically, "and all in five-thousand-dollar sacks! Did it ever occur to you that it will take some time to carry the gold down to the drain's mouth? It's close by three-quarters of a mile, that trip is."

"My friend," retorted Storri, with just a tinge of patronage, "leave that to me. I'll find a way to send the gold to the drain's mouth without breeding any backaches. All you are to do is dig the tunnel, and dig it so we can reach the gold."

"That's simple," observed London Bill. "I shall dig so as to undermine an end of one of those steel slabs that make the vault's floor, running my tunnel for the rear end of the vault. The weight of the gold will force down the slab when undermined. I'll open that vault like lifting the cover of a chest, only the cover will drop from the bottom instead of lifting from the top. The minute that slab of steel drops six inches, the sacks of gold will begin sliding into our tunnel of their own accord. You needn't worry about my part of the job; I can take thirty millions out of the vault if you can get them to the mouth of the drain."

"I can get them to the mouth of the drain," responded Storri confidently, "and another thirty with them. The real limit to our operations is the yacht itself. The one I have in mind will only carry one hundred tons, and thirty millions in gold makes sixty tons, to say nothing of ship's stores and coal."

"What place will you head the boat for when the job's done?"

"That," said Storri, "I shall leave to be settled in the open Atlantic. The question now is: Are you going with me? I've told you that your share is to be a million."

"One thirtieth?" said London Bill, with the ring of complaint in his voice.

"One thirtieth," returned Storri with emphasis. "Where else can you get one million for ten weeks' digging and a six-months' cruise in a yacht? Besides, there will be a dozen others to share; to say nothing of the yacht, and what it costs to coal her and buy her stores. Come now; do you go with me?"

London Bill put out a small, hairy hand, and gave Storri a squeeze of acquiescence that was almost a mate for the grip bestowed upon our nobleman by Richard that snow-freighted day in November.

"I'm with you, live or die," said London Bill; "an' I never weaken, an' never split on a pal."

Storri and London Bill put in an hour discussing plans. There were to be no more men brought into the affair until late in May. London Bill would come to Washington and commence his tunnel work at once. It would be a slow employment and require care; it was best to have plenty of time.

"Because," explained London Bill, "if these maps an' drawings ain't accurate to the splinter of an inch, it may throw me abroad in my digging. In that case I'd need an extra week or so to find myself."

Storri coincided with the view, but added that the yacht would have to be manned as early as the middle of May.

"The men needn't know the purpose," said Storri, "till the last moment. When it comes to selecting them, I shall ask your advice."

"I can give you that to-day," said London Bill, "better than in May. I'll be busy in my tunnel in May, and won't have time to come out. Here's what I'll do: I'll call up Dan right now. Dan's an old sailor, as well as a first-class gun and hold-up man—the gang calls him Steamboat Dan. I'll call Dan, an' put him into the play. Then when the time comes, Dan will get you the men, an' of the right proper sort. There won't be one of 'em who hasn't done a stretch."

"But," remonstrated Storri uneasily, "are you sure of this Steamboat Dan?"

"I wouldn't be lushin' gin in his crib else," responded London Bill. "No, Dan's as sure as death. Besides, I'm not goin' to put him wise; I shall only tell him to do whatever you ask, whenever you show up."

London Bill called Dan, and the trio broadened their confidence in each other with further gin and beer. Dan gave his word for whatever was required; Storri had but to appear and issue his orders.

"You'll be in at the finish, Dan," said London Bill; "an' for the others, pick out a dozen of the flossiest coves you can find. You'll be bringin' them to where I'm workin', d'ye see; an' the job will be ripe."

"Will it be much of a play?" asked Dan.

"Biggest ever," said London Bill; "an' yet, no harder than prickin' a blister."

Storri jumped into the cab, which had waited for him at the door, and rattled swiftly away. Within five minutes thereafter, a ragged gamin strutted into the Albion bar.

"Be you Steamboat Dan?" chirped the gamin, fixing the eye of a sparrow upon that tapster.

"Well, s'ppose I be?" said Dan, not too well pleased with the sparrow-eyed.

"Then this is for you," quoth the gamin, thrusting a note across the bar.

Dan glanced at the note; next he smote the bar, accompanying the smiting with soft curses.

"What's the row?" asked one of the loungers.

"Nothin'," said Dan, his face clearing into a look of easy craft. "Here's a pal of mine gets himself run over an' fractured by the cable cars, an' is took to the hospital. You hold down the bar, Jimmy, while I go look him over."

The person addressed as Jimmy had no objection to an arrangement that meant free drinks, and once he was installed Dan put on his hat and moved rapidly up the street. A turn or two and a brisk walk of ten minutes found him in Mulberry Bend. Dan walked more slowly, and was rewarded by the sight of Inspector Val sauntering along half a block ahead. The great thief-taker rounded a corner, and albeit Dan made no effort to overtake him, he was scrupulous to make the same turn. As he came into the cross-street he glanced about for Inspector Val; that personage was nowhere to be seen. Dan kept on his way, and before he had journeyed another block Inspector Val caught up with him from the rear, and passed him. Two doors further and Inspector Val entered an Italian restaurant; Dan, after going fifty yards beyond and returning, stepped into the same place. As he laid his hand on the restaurant's door, he shot a swift look up and down the street. There was no one in view whom he knew, and Dan brought a breath of relief.

"This bein' a stool ain't no hit with me," sighed Dan, "but will any sport show me how to sidestep it?"

As no sport was there to hear the plaint of Dan, the latter must have despaired of a reply before he put the question. Once more he cheerfully greeted Inspector Val, and the two withdrew to a private room.

"Dan," said Inspector Val, when they were seated at a table with a flask of chianti between them, "I needn't tell you that you're still wanted for that trick you turned in Chicago, or remind you of the many little things I've overlooked in your case in New York."

"No, Inspector," replied Dan, sorrowfully tasting his chianti, "I'm dead onto 'em all. What is it? Give it a name."

"Do you know what that black-bearded man wanted in your place?"

"No," said Dan, "I don't."

"He came to meet London Bill, and you floor-managed the play."

"But I don't know what he wanted of Bill," said Dan, a bit staggered.

"Well, I know what he wanted of Bill. And I know what he will want of you. I'll tell you what you are to do; and if you cross me, or fall down, it will mean several spaces in Joliet, so have a care. I'll put you easy on one point. Neither you, nor London Bill, nor any of the pals you'll put into this game about the middle of May, will get the collar. You have my word for that."

"Your word goes with me, Inspector," interjected Dan, plainly relieved, and bending to his chianti as though after all it might not be red poison.

"Good; my word goes with you—which is fortunate for you. These are your orders: You're to say never a word; and you're to proceed with this as though nothing queer was in the wind. As fast as you know anything, you will find that I'll call for it. Do whatever this black-bearded party asks; go with him as far as he wants to go, and go with your eyes shut. I'll step in and get him when the time comes; he's the one I'm after. Now you understand: say nothing, do whatever the black-beard desires; and when I want to see you I'll send. And be careful about London Bill; he's foxy. That was why I let you go by me a moment ago; I didn't know but Bill was fly enough to tail you here. He'll be gone, however, in a day, or at the most two, and then you'll have no more risk with Bill."

"How did you know Bill was goin' to-morrow? It wasn't settled thirty minutes ago."

"I know it just as I know that you, about May fifteenth, will pick up a dozen or more pals who are whole crooks and half sailors; that you will then leave on a boat, probably a steam yacht, May twenty-sixth, bound for Washington; and that the job of bin-cracking you will engage in is to be pulled off May twenty-seventh to twenty-ninth inclusive."

"You know more'n me, Inspector," observed Dan, with wonder undisguised.

"If I didn't I wouldn't be telling you what to do. That's all, Dan; have you got your orders straight?"

"Straight as a gun," declared Dan, wiping the last drops of the chianti from his mouth.

"Screw out then," commanded Inspector Val, "and come only when I send for you."

Two days later, a laborer, clean-shaven and of rather superior exterior, fastened a tape measure to the iron cover of a manhole that opened into the drain that ran by the side of the Treasury Building. Tape fastened, the laborer unwound its length along the asphalt for perhaps one hundred feet. Then he began to re-wind the tape into its circular box. As he followed the incoming tape towards the end that was fastened to the manhole cover, winding as he went, he paused for the ghost of a second squarely opposite the little basement door-way in the Treasury Building, where the old watchman stood smoking his pipe on the evening that Storri was told of the gold inside. The old watchman, being on day duty now, was standing in that same door-way, smoking the self-same pipe, and had his ignorant eye listlessly fixed upon the laborer, busy with his measurements. As the laborer paused abreast of the door, he glanced down at the tape.

"The even seventy feet from the center of that manhole," he murmured, as though he thus registered the figures in his mind.

And the old watchman, and the pedestrians hurrying along the pavement, thought the laborer busy with his measurements from the manhole to the little Treasury door had been at work for the public.

That night, had it not been for the moonless dark of it, you might have seen the same laborer who had been so concerned with tape-measures and distances near the Treasury Building, a long shallow basket stoutly woven of willow on his arm, making secretly for the mouth of the drain that once witnessed the investigations of Storri. The basket concealed a short pickax of the sort that miners use, a little spade such as children play with on the seashore, but very strong, and a pinch-bar, or "jimmy," about two feet long. Besides these suspicious implements, there were food, a flask of whisky, another of coffee, and a bicycle lamp, to make up the basket's furniture.

The laborer entered the drain's mouth, and when beyond chance of observation from without, he paused as aforetime had Storri to light his lamp. As the match illuminated his face, you would have identified the features of London Bill, celebrated safe-blower, box-worker, and 'peterman, presently about to begin his first night's work on that thirty-million-dollar job over which he and Storri had shaken hands. Having lighted his lamp, London Bill journeyed on his way until the same bend in the great drain that had hidden Storri shut him out from view.

London Bill splashingly proceeded to the second turn in the drain; from that point he counted the manholes until he stood beneath the one from which you saw him measuring with the tape. As nearly as he might, London Bill, going northward in the drain, slowly paced off seventy feet from the manhole; then he halted and drove two large spikes between the bricks that formed the walls, using the pinch-bar to do the driving. On these nails he hung his basket and fixed his lamp, the latter so as to light the opposite wall. Being disencumbered of the basket, London Bill took the tape and again made his measurements, this time more accurately than might be done by pacing.

London Bill got to work, breast-high and where the lamplight fell, on the wall of the drain nearest the Treasury, and with the point of the pinch-bar began taking out the bricks. Our cracksman worked slowly and surely, laying the bricks in the bottom of the drain so as to form a floor on which to stand. In this way he soon found himself above the water, which thereafter muttered about the bricks instead of his boots, as was the former uncomfortable condition.

After three hours of toil, the last brick was removed; a circular hole four feet in diameter showed in the wall of the drain. Beyond was the earth—gray clay, as Storri had said. Seizing the little spade, London Bill threw a handful into the water; it was instantly dissolved and washed away.

"There's current enough," said London Bill, in a satisfied whisper, "to clear away the dirt as fast as I dig it, which is a chunk of luck my way."

London Bill, being fairly launched upon his great work, crept into the drain every night and crept forth every morning, and the hours of his creeping were respectively eleven and four. Through the day he lay in convenient, non-inquisitive lodgings, which he cared for himself. London Bill did not go about the town, having no wish for company, being of the bloodhound inveterate breed that, once embarked upon an enterprise, does nothing, thinks nothing, save said enterprise until it is accomplished. It was this dogged, single-hearted persistency, coupled with his cunning and his desperate courage, that made London Bill the foremost figure of his old but criminal guild of 'peter-men.

There was a rich man's son who infested the club; and, being a snob with a liking for noble nearnesses, Croesus Jr. had wormed himself into Storri's regards as far as Storri would permit. Croesus Jr., fond of display, bought a little steam yacht—one hundred tons. After two costly months of yachting, Croesus Jr., waxing thrifty and bewailing expense, laid up the yacht in a shipyard on the Harlem River. The yacht's name was *Zulu Queen*. The *Zulu Queen* measured one hundred and ten feet over all, and since she was of unusual beam, her draught was light. In a beam sea the *Zulu Queen* would all but roll her stacks overboard; in a head sea she pounded until one feared for her safety; in smooth water, full steam ahead, she could snap off seventeen knots. She had a twenty-foot launch, equal to fourteen knots, that made no more noise than a sewing machine. Altogether there were worse as well as better boats upon the sea than was the *Zulu Queen*.

Croesus Jr., disliking expense as noted, did not care to keep the *Zulu Queen* in commission. And yet the rust of retirement was eating into her value! A yacht, a horse, and a woman, to keep at their best, should be constantly in commission. Croesus Jr. offered the *Zulu Queen* to Storri for the spring and summer, Storri to foot the bills. This was a sagacious move on the part of Croesus Jr. and meant to kill a brace of birds with one stone. He would keep the *Zulu Queen* steamed up at another's cost, thereby avoiding the wharf rent as well as the rust of her banishment; also he would please a nobleman. Storri accepted the disinterested offer of the *Zulu Queen* from Croesus Jr.; that was just before he met London Bill.

After meeting that eminent bandit, Storri drove to Harlem, and gave orders for overhauling the *Zulu Queen*, as well as for storing and coaling her to the limit of her lockers and bunkers. She was to be made ready for the crew and cruise by May first. Storri was armed with the written order of Croesus Jr., and the shipyard people offered no demur; since they charged all bills in true maritime fashion to the *Zulu Queen*, and neither to Storri nor yet Croesus Jr., the latter provident young person must finally face the expense—a financial disaster which Croesus Jr. never foresaw, albeit Storri was not so blind. As London Bill plies darksome spade and pick and pinchbar, the Harlem shipmen are furnishing and coaling and storing the *Zulu Queen*.

Storri said nothing of London Bill and the *Zulu Queen* to the San Reve. He had well-nigh given up the club, being willing to postpone all chance of meeting either Mr. Harley or Richard, and was, therefore, a more frequent visitor to Grant Place—a social situation that pleased the San Reve vastly.

The San Reve used to dog Storri when he left her; and, inasmuch as she never once traced him to the Harley house or its vicinity, her jealousy began to sleep. But the San Reve, while she haunted the steps of Storri, could not always follow his thoughts, and they went often to the Harleys. Storri had the Harleys ever on his mind; each day served to intensify his hatred for Mr. Harley, and to render more sultry that passion for Dorothy which was both love and hate. Little by little his lawless imagination suggested methods by which he might have revenge on Mr. Harley and gain possession of Dorothy; and the methods so suggested, like the ingenious cogs of a wheel, mashed into that other enterprise of gold which had enlisted the *Zulu Queen* and London Bill. The thought of revenge on Mr. Harley, and a physical conquest of Dorothy the beautiful, grew and broadened and extended itself like some plant of evil in Storri's heart. It worked itself out into leaf and twig and bud of sinful detail until the execution thereof seemed the thing feasible; with that the face of Storri began to wear a look of criminal triumph in anticipation.

The San Reve observed this latter phenomenon and read it for a good sign, holding it to be evidence of the contentment born of their happier relations, and also of clearing skies of stocks. It spoke of fair weather in both love and business, and the San Reve was at considerable care not to disturb Storri with either query or comment.

To show how wrong was the San Reve, glance at this fragment of the thought of Storri.

"What should be better," mused Storri, with that leer which Satan gave him, "than to carry away the gold of these pig Americans, and the daughter of one of them, on the same night? We should be off the coast of Africa in a fortnight, and were I to tire of her I could sell her to the Moors. Who would hear of her after that?"

Thus did Storri rear his sinful castles in the air; and as he brooded his black designs, smoking his cigars and tossing off his brandy in silence, the San Reve sat drinking him in with adoring gray-green eyes, pleasing herself by conjecturing his meditations, and going miles to leeward of the truth. Had the San Reve but guessed them, there might have descended an interruption, and Storri's purposes suffered a postponement at once grisly and grim.

Richard, about this time, troubled the club with his presence no oftener than did Storri—and that was natural enough. He must see so much of Dorothy at either her own house or Bess Marklin's, he was left scanty time for clubs. It is wonderful how love will engage the hours and occupy the faculties of a man.

One evening as Richard was coming from the Harley house he met Inspector Val. Richard, wrapped in visions whereof the constituent elements were roses and music with starlight over all, was careless of routes, and Inspector Val led him past the Treasury Building, across the White Lot between the Monument and the White House, until they stood at the drain's mouth, of which you have heard so much. The stream was rushing forth a clayey gray.

"Do you see?" asked Inspector Val, pointing to the stream.

"See what?" said Richard, waxing impatient, as a man will when roused from loving dreams to consider a question of sewage.

"The color," replied Inspector Val. "That shows our man to be industriously at his task. No, no explanation now; on the twenty-seventh of May we'll come again, and the drain itself shall furnish a solution to the puzzle."

CHAPTER XX

HOW STORRI FOOLISHLY WROTE A MESSAGE

Governor Obstinate being stubbornly and openly for gold, party opinion, disliking concealment and skulking mystery, began to burn the grass of imperious inquiry about the feet of Senator Hanway. Men could understand a gold-bug or a silver-bug, and either embrace or tolerate him according to the color of their convictions. But that monstrous insect of finance, the straddlebug, pleased no one; and since Senator Hanway, whose patriotism was self-interest and who possessed no principle beyond the principle of personal aggrandizement, was on every issue a straddlebug, finance first of all, our sinuous statesman commenced to taste troublous days.

Senator Gruff urged him to declare for gold.

"You will have two-thirds of the better element with you," said Senator Gruff, "and by that I mean the richer element."

Senator Hanway submitted that while the richer or managing element was for gold, the masses might be for silver. If he were nominated following a gold declaration, a silver public might defeat him at the polls.

"But the public," explained Senator Gruff, disagreeing, "are as sheep; the managers of party are the wolves. The howl of one wolf in politics is of graver moment than the bleating of many sheep."

"But the sheep are the more numerous," laughed Senator Hanway, who was amused by what he termed the zoölogical figures of Senator Gruff.

"What matters that?" said Senator Gruff. "Wasn't it Virgil who wrote 'What cares the wolf how many the sheep be'? The wolves, I tell you, win."

Senator Hanway, full of inborn furtivities, still hung in the wind of doubt.

"Would it not be as wise," he argued, "to claim the public's attention with some new unusual proposition? Might not the public, being wholly engaged thereby, forget finance?"

Senator Gruff thought this among things possible; at least it might be tried. Something surely must be done, or Senator Hanway would be compelled to disclose his attitude on Silver versus Gold.

It was the decision of Senators Hanway and Gruff that the former should bring up for Senate discussion the resolution concerning that Georgian Bay-Ontario Canal. Credit Magellan was dead and gone, and had been since the "bear" failure against Northern Consolidated. But no one in the Senate, no one indeed not of the osprey pool, had heard of Credit Magellan. Therefore, Senator Hanway could handle the Canal resolution as a thing by itself. It could be offered as a measure important, not alone nationally but internationally, and to all the world. Senator Hanway would force no vote; but he would be heard, and his Senate friends and allies would be heard. There should arise such a din of statesmanship that the dullest ear in the country must be impressed with the Canal as a subject of tremendous consequence. The public intelligence might thus be made to center upon the Canal. The latter would subtract from, even if it did not wholly swallow up in the common regard, that dangerous query of finance.

"You may be right," observed Senator Gruff. He said this dubiously, for he wasn't as sure as was Senator Hanway of either a public interest or its direction touching the Canal. "It will be a novelty; and the public is as readily caught by novelty as any rustic at a fair. But you might better get to it at once. I had word from the Anaconda people yesterday; they urge definite utterance on the money question. They say that either silver or gold will do as a position; but they must know which it is to be in order to select timber for the delegations. It won't do to name silver delegates if you mean in the eleventh hour to declare for gold."

Senator Hanway brought up his Georgian Bay-Ontario Canal and talked a profound hour. Other Senators followed, and the Canal held the carpet of debate for three full days. Then it was sent back to the Foreign Committee without a vote.

But the object of the discussion had been reached. Canal took the place of Money in the people's mouth, and Senator Hanway, his name gaining favorable place in every paper, particularly in the *Daily Tory*, became a prodigious personality by acclamation. The most besotted of Governor Obstinate's adherents now conceded the superior strength of Senator Hanway, and two or three States which held their conventions about this time instructed their delegates to vote for him as a unit. Mr. Harley and Senator Gruff, being nearest to Senator Hanway, were jubilant; they complimented and extolled the acumen that substituted Canal for Finance as a popular shout.

"You've got it," ejaculated Senator Gruff, slapping Senator Hanway on the shoulder with a freedom cherished by statesmen among themselves; "the ticket is as good as made, with Hanway at the head. Put Frost on for Vice President, and it will be all over but the fireworks."

Senator Hanway was of one mind with Senator Gruff; he could discover no gap in his fences through which defeat might crowd.

"It's as it should be, John," observed Senator Hanway, when one evening he and Mr. Harley were alone in his study. Richard had just left, bearing an elaborate interview with Senator Hanway in which the Georgian Bay-Ontario Canal was displayed as the question paramount and precedental to all others, the interview being intended for the next issue of the *Daily Tory*. "It would be hard, indeed," continued Senator Hanway, "to be wiped out in politics just as we were wiped out in stocks. I can look on present pauperism calmly enough, if it is to be followed by the White House for four years. It would be our turn then to issue German defiances, and use Monroe to milk the Market."

"Yes," assented Mr. Harley, a greedy twinkle in his eye, "a White House should place us on high ground."

Mr. Harley, being thus reminded of the osprey pool, remarked that he received a line that afternoon saying the mysterious builder of the corner in Northern Consolidated had been discovered in Robert Lance Bayard. The old gray buccaneer would at once learn the terms upon which they might ransom themselves.

"If it be so much as three millions for our share," said Senator Hanway, "it will cut us both off at the roots. Three millions would take the last bond and the last share of stock in our boxes."

"The offer will be made for a million a man," said Mr. Harley; "but should Mr. Bayard refuse, there's no help. He holds us at his mercy."

"Absolutely!" assented Senator Hanway, with a sigh. Then in livelier manner: "Still, as I observed, we must console ourselves with a Presidency. That Georgian Bay-Ontario Canal was a fortunate thought. My nomination is certain; and the success of the ticket with the people seems quite as sure. We must offset a loss in stocks by this mighty profit in politics.

"Changing the subject," continued Senator Hanway, "young Storms seems to be the accepted lover of Dorothy. I'm gratified by it; he has no money, but Mr. Gwynn will act the generous part. What surprises me is the submission of Barbara; she was decidedly tragic in her objections one evening."

"Yes," said Mr. Harley, soberly exultant, his conquest of Mrs. Hanway-Harley in the matter of that matrimony being the only battle he had ever won from his domestic Boadicea, "yes, Barbara did object; put it on the ground that Storms was a beggar. Thereupon I expounded her own bankruptcy to her, showed her how it was the pot calling the kettle black, and Barbara, feeling that she hadn't a leg to stand on, surrendered."

Mr. Harley said nothing of that Storri secret between Dorothy and himself.

"When will you appoint the wedding?" asked Senator Hanway.

"Dorothy will attend to that, I take it. Should she come for my advice, I shall vote for expedition. Marriage is so much like shooting a rifle that one ought not to hang too long on one's aim."

Richard received a wire from Mr. Bayard calling him to New York. The next day he was closeted with the ticker-King at Thirty, Broad.

"We have never," said Mr. Bayard, "declared our respective shares in the corner in Northern Consolidated."

Richard insisted on leaving the naming of interests to Mr. Bayard.

"I should say even interests then—half and half," returned Mr. Bayard.

Richard acquiesced.

"Then," said Mr. Bayard, "I must tell you that I'm offered seven millions for the seven members of the pool as it now exists. You remember your friend Storri perished on the first call for margins; we have already taken a half-million from him."

"You won't mind," said Richard diffidently, "if I make an amended proposition?"

"Let me hear it," returned Mr. Bayard, mildly curious; "I'm quite sure I shall prefer your proposal to my own."

"As preliminary then," said Richard, "permit me to give you an informal invitation to my wedding with Miss Harley; it is set for June first."

"I shall be present," said Mr. Bayard, smilingly elevating his brows. "And Miss Harley: who is she?"

"She's Mr. Harley's daughter, and Senator Hanway's niece. Between us, I hardly feel like reducing my sweetheart's family to bankruptcy on the eve of our nuptials."

"I've known it done, however," returned Mr. Bayard, beating down a chuckle.

"I've no doubt," observed Richard. "For all that I'd like to miss the experience. This is my idea: suppose we divide men and not money. Give me Senator Hanway, Mr. Harley, and Storri, and you take the five."

"It shall be as you desire," said Mr. Bayard, "for I see what you would be at. This was not a speculation but a love affair; Miss Harley is your profit."

Richard confessed to Mr. Bayard's reading of the riddle; Dorothy with him had been the prize, and she was won. As for Mr. Harley and Senator

Hanway, Richard would have them released without loss; they were to be restored, plack and bawbee, to what had been theirs on that tumultuous Wednesday when the osprey pool made its initial swoop.

"Adjust the business with them June second," explained Richard. "My wife"—he said "my wife" with a dignity that was visible—"and I will be then on our way to the Mediterranean. Present yourself as the only one in the affair, please; my name is a cat that I don't want let out of the bag."

"And now, my romantic young friend," remarked Mr. Bayard, "you forget Storri. What shall I do with the half-million taken from him?"

"Give one-half to Inspector Val; and with the other purchase an annuity for a gentleman named Sands. I'll send Mr. Sands to you. I want to be out of the country, however, before you arrange any of these matters."

"That's right," declared Mr. Bayard; "I know of nothing more grinding than gratitude. By the way, how old is this Mr. Sands?"

"About thirty."

"He should have at least fifteen thousand dollars a year."

"He has so keen an approval of whisky," explained Richard, "that I don't care to give him the money outright."

Mr. Bayard stated that he would send word to the old gray buccaneer, fixing June second for the settlement and accepting the pool's offer of seven millions.

"And when the day arrives," observed Mr. Bayard, "I'll carry out your financial forgiveness of Senator Hanway and Mr. Harley."

"Not forgetting to hide my name?"

"Not forgetting to hide your name. But Inspector Val and Mr. Sands will have to know."

"It will make the less difference; by that time I'll be three hundred miles off-shore."

"And having," said Mr. Bayard, "so pleasantly adjusted our business, suppose we smoke in confirmation of the adjustment. Also, if you will, please explain the humbug of Mr. Gywnn. Why are you, who are among the world's five wealthiest men, so anxious to pretend poverty and hide your money-light beneath a bushel?"

"Mr. Gwynn is no humbug," returned Richard; "under my thumb, he acts for me in business. I am saved a deal of bother at slight expense and slighter risk. Now and then, of course, I find him absorbing some sly hundreds. When he bought the *Daily Tory*, he substituted a pretended agent between himself and Talon & Trehawke, and in that way sequestered over eleven thousand dollars behind the mask of commissions. But I always discover and rectify these discrepancies. And I forgive them, too; for Mr. Gwynn was educated to a theory of perquisites, and such little lapses as those *Daily Tory* commissions are but the outcrop of old habits too deeply rooted to be eradicated."

"But you present him as your patron—as the head of your house."

"There you're in the wrong," laughed Richard. "When I returned from Europe bringing Mr. Gwynn, society seized upon him for its own. Society went wild over Mr. Gwynn; it discovered in him treasures of patricianism and a well-bred elegance. Since society insisted upon the enthronement of Mr. Gwynn, it would have been impolite, nay narrow, on my part to object. Besides, I recognized in it the essence of democracy and as an American rejoiced. 'By all means,' said I, 'society shall have its excellent way. I can give it little, but I can give it Mr. Gwynn.'"

Richard's old cynicism was for the moment restored, and the laughing philosopher—who is only a laughing hyena in trousers and cutaway—shone out in all a former Abderitish glory. In the brittle case of Mr. Bayard the laughing cynic did not laugh alone; that gray eagle of the tape saw much in Mr. Gwynn and his polite adventures to delight him. He declared the situation to be a most justifiable sarcasm addressed, not against an individual, but an age.

"It was," said Mr. Bayard, "a splendid vengeance upon the snobs. But that doesn't explain," he continued, "why you were sedulous to hide your millions from others—from Miss Harley, for a sample."

Richard braced himself and made a clean breast. He had been educated by musty professors, visionaries, rusty creatures of theories and alcoves; he had come to be as morbid as the atmosphere he was reared in on that subject of his gold. It would corrupt whomsoever approached him. He, Richard, would never know love or friendship—nothing better than a world's greed would he know. Announce his millions, and he would have no existence, no identity, no name; all would be merged in those millions. He would never be given a friendship; he must purchase it. He would never be given a woman's love; he must buy her love!

"Thus was I demon-haunted of my own gold," said Richard. "It seemed to stand between me and all my heart went hungry for. That was my feeling; I was galled of money. I determined to hide my wealth; I would discover what friendships I might inspire, what loves I could attract, with only the meager capital of my merit."

"Well," said Mr. Bayard dryly, "every man at some period must play the fool. All's well that ends well; I shall follow your wishes concerning Messrs. Harley, Hanway, Val, and Sands, attend your wedding, extend congratulations, and salute the bride."

Mrs. Hanway-Harley, Mr. Harley, and Senator Hanway were duly informed of those orange blossoms meditated by Dorothy for June. Bess, who still retained her place as managing angel, pointed out the propriety of such information. Bess said that Richard ought to break the news to the Harleys and to Senator Hanway. But Richard's heart was weak; he confessed his cowardice squarely. In his own defense he pleaded the memory of his former interview with Mrs. Hanway-Harley; it was yet heavy upon him, and he could summon no courage for another. Then Dorothy became the heroine; she would inform Mrs. Hanway-Harley with her own young lips. This she did, bearing herself the while with much love and firmness, since Richard—quaking inwardly, but concealing his craven condition from Dorothy—supported her throughout.

Mrs. Hanway-Harley surprised everybody with the moderate spirit in which she received the word. True, her manner could not have been called boisterously joyful, and indeed she made no pretense of the kind. She kissed Dorothy; she would have kissed Richard had not that gentleman plainly lacked the fortitude required for so embarrassing a ceremony. Having pressed her maternal lips to Dorothy's forehead, Mrs. Hanway-Harley remarked that it was good of the young lovers to bring their plans to her. She realized, however, that it was no more than a polite formality, for the affair long before had been taken out of her hands. Her consent to their wedding would sound hollow, even ludicrous, under the circumstances; still, such as it was, she freely granted it. Her objection had been the poverty of Mr. Storms, and that objection was disregarded. Mrs. Hanway-Harley could do no more; they would wed, and in later years, while being ground in the mills of a dollarless experience, they might justify the wisdom of her objection. In this gracious fashion did Mrs. Hanway-Harley sanction the union of her only daughter Dorothy with Mr. Richard Storms; after which she folded her matronly hands in resignation, bearing meanwhile the manner of one who will face the worst bravely and hopes that others are prepared to do the same.

Dorothy was quite affected, and hung round the neck of Mrs. Hanway-Harley, shedding copious tears. Richard, who felt decidedly foolish and could not shake off the impression that Mrs. Hanway-Harley was somehow the victim of his happiness,—such was the serious effect of that lady's acting,—confessed himself delighted when the interview was over. When Dorothy and he were by themselves, Richard drew a deep breath, and confided to Dorothy that Mrs. Hanway-Harley was a load off his mind, whatever that should mean.

The formalities above recorded having been disposed of, Dorothy, nobly abetted by Bess and extravagantly encouraged by Mr. Harley, plunged into the business of her trousseau with the utmost fury. She became the center of a bevy of dressmakers and milliners, and these artists got vastly in the way of Richard when he called. Richard, being excluded, put in hours in the harmless society of Mr. Fopling, who looked upon Richard, now his wedding day was fixed, in fearful admiration, and said that some day he supposed he must come to it himself. Mr. Fopling spoke of marriage as though it were a desperate creature of citadels and mines and scaling ladders and smoke-filled breaches, to face which would call for the soul of a paladin.

As Dorothy's gown-buying and hat-trimming expanded into a riot of ribbons and flounces and all decorative things, Mrs. Hanway-Harley, attracted by a bustle dear to the feminine heart, was drawn more and more from out her shell of martyrdom until finally she stood in the fore-front of the mêlée, giving directions. She never omitted, however, to maintain a melancholy, and comported herself at all times as should a mother who only bows to the dread inevitable and but dresses her child for the sacrifice.

Storri about this time was excessively and secretly the busy man. He went often to New York, and held conferences with Steamboat Dan. The latter, at Storri's suggestion, began picking up his people; all were criminal, all aquatic, and two were capable, respectively, of discharging the duties of a sailing master and an engineer.

Whenever Storri visited New York, Inspector Val was never far to find; now and then he sent for Steamboat Dan to hear how the plans of Storri moved. Steamboat Dan failed not to respond; for he was stricken of a wholesome fear of Inspector Val. And well he might be. There was that prison cell in Joliet all vacant for his coming; and he must protect the shady peace of the Albion House near James Slip. Altogether, there was no help for it; Steamboat Dan must yield to his destiny of stool pigeon or pay the penalty in stripes. Wherefore he appeared faithfully when called, and told Inspector Val of Storri's preparations. The *Zulu Queen*, rich in stores, her bunkers choked with coal, waited only to be fired up; those men who were to sail her had been secured; her papers and her captain's papers as well as those of her engineer were ready. The one thing now was Storri's signal; and with that all hands would go aboard, get up steam, and point the sable cutwater of the *Zulu Queen* for Washington.

Steamboat Dan informed Inspector Val of nothing which the thief-taker's sagacity or vigilance had not anticipated. But Inspector Val clung to the safe theory that, whether for his facts or deductions, he could not have too much confirmatory proof; wherefore he was prone to put Steamboat Dan to frequent question. One day, however, the stool pigeon gave Inspector Val a surprising piece of information. It related to a talk which he had had with Storri the evening before.

"It was at the heel of the hunt like," explained Steamboat Dan, "an' just as he's about to go, he ups an' makes it known that he's goin' to need a benziner—need a firebug."

"And of course you promised to find one," said Inspector Val.

"I had him ready; one of the gang is Benzine Bob, an' you know as well as I do that when it comes to touchin' a match to a crib, an' then collectin' the insurance, there's nobody nearer bein' the goods than Benzine Bob."

"Yes, I regard Bob as a most gifted incendiary," said Inspector Val.

"Sure; he could teach it. But what do you figger this Russian's goin' to burn?"

"We'll learn in good time. You must have Bob agree to everything this party asks."

"No trouble on that score; settin' fire to things is Benzine Bob's religion. He says his prayers to an oiled rag, and a box of matches is his Bible."

Storri, taking dark and stormy nights for the visits, twice splashed up the drain to see how London Bill came on. Storri was heedful to give the signals agreed upon by rapping on the walls of the drain. He had no desire to be killed in the dark by London Bill upon a theory that he, Storri, was the enemy, and so rapped out the signals handsomely, with a little hammer he had by him for the purpose, while still ten rods from the scene of operations.

London Bill was slowly, yet surely, boring forward with his tunnel. The clay as it was dug must be dragged to the mouth of the tunnel in the willow basket, and cast into the stream; that was a process to require time. However, time there was and plenty; London Bill would have his work in perfect trim against the Friday evening for which the final and decisive attack on the gold was scheduled. The tunnel, as London Bill had said it must be, was about four feet high and three in width, and Storri found that he went in and out very readily by traveling on hands and knees. Storri would have come oftener to observe how London Bill fared with his work, but the cracksman discountenanced the thought.

"There's no sense in comin'," explained London Bill. "You can't do any good, an' you get in the way. Besides, there's the chance of being piped off; some party might see you and catch on."

One day Inspector Val brought Richard a contrivance made of thin rubber. It was circular, and eighteen inches in diameter. If the rubber contrivance resembled anything, it was one of those hot-water bags common in the trade of hospitals. It was hollow, and had a metal mouth shaped like the mouth of a bottle; instead of water, however, the bag was intended to hold air. Pumped full of air, the rubber bag, or rather cushion, exhibited a thickness of about six inches. It looked a little like a life preserver; the more since there was a hole in the center, albeit the hole was no wider than an inch across. The rubber bag or cushion was extremely light, the material being twice the weight of that employed in the making of toy balloons. Inflated and considered as a raft, the rubber cushion would support a weight of twenty pounds, and draw no more than three inches of water in so doing.

"Storri bought four thousand of these from the Goodyear Company," vouchsafed Inspector Val; "had them made after patterns of his own. A mighty tidy invention, take my word for it!" and the eye of Inspector Val glanced approval of the circular rubber raft. Then he showed Richard how the cushion could be inflated in a few seconds with an air-pump; and how, being inflated, an automatic valve closed and kept the air prisoner. "A tidy arrangement, take my word, and does that Russian party credit!"

"What will he do with it?" asked Richard.

"Put the question later," responded Inspector Val, who was a slave to the dramatic and never turned loose his climaxes prematurely.

The San Reve was of a nature too easily the prey of somber suspicions to ever find perfect happiness. Besides she had been saddened, if not soured, by the rougher, harder visitations of life. As nearly as she might be, however, these days the San Reve was happy. And peace came to her more and more as spring deepened into May. Storri was every day to see her; and the most patient investigation only served to make it sure that he had ended his relations with the Harleys. Storri went no more to the Harley house, and if there had existed a least of chance that he would wed Miss Harley, the peril was passed by. The San Reve began to doubt if such a plan had ever been in Storri's mind; she was inclined to think herself a jealous fool for entertaining the belief. She had wronged her Storri; it was as he told her from the first; his relations, those of business, had been solely with Mr. Harley. At this view, so flattering to the loyal truth of Storri, the San Reve's bosom welled with a great love for that nobleman. The gray-green eyes became quietly serene; the strong beauty of her face gathered effulgence in the sunshine of love's confidence renewed.

It was an evening in the early days of May. Storri was saying that he had been commanded, through the Russian Embassy, to report to "His Czar"; he must be in St. Petersburg June fifteenth. The San Reve had begun to believe in the Czar as a close intimate of her Storri.

"Yes, he has called me home, my San Reve," cried Storri. "There is much that he would know about these pig Americans, and who can tell him better than his Storri. When I go, which will be about June first, you shall go with me."

The San Reve's heavy face was in a glow. Russia? yes; and she would see France again! Storri read the pleasure in her glance. Observing that it made the San Reve more beautiful, he was taken of a natural wish to add to it.

"Yes, you shall accompany me; I would not, no not even for my Czar, be separated from you, my San Reve."

Storri was as fond of fiction as Mr. Harley, and of a far livelier imagination. Once started on an untruth, he would pursue it hither and yon as a greyhound courses a hare. Like every artist of the mendacious, he was quick for those little deeds that would give his lies a look of righteous integrity. Thus it befell on the occasion in hand.

"Behold now," cried Storri, as though the idea had just occurred to him, "I will, while the thought is fresh with me, telegraph a friend in New York to select our staterooms for the next ship after June first."

Storri wrote his message; the San Reve watching him, her heart a-brim with love and the happiness of returning home. She would see France, see Paris—see them with the man whom she adored! Storri whirred the telegraph call that was fixed in the hall; presently a gray-coat lad appeared and bore away the message. Then Storri beamed affably upon the San Reve, who took his hand and put it to her grateful lips.

Storri beamed because he was in a right royal humor. The episode had been unpremeditated, and yet it dove-tailed to the advantage of his designs. The maneuver, he could see, had extinguished the final sparks of the San Reve's jealous suspicions; extinguished them at a time, too, when it was of consequence to lull the San Reve into fullest assurance of his faith. And at that he had not thrown away his wire. Storri had remembered that he must send a word to Steamboat Dan in the morning. He decided to forestall the morning; he would dispatch the message at once. Being one of those who suck joy from deceit, it gave Storri a thrill of supremest satisfaction to transact the duplicity of which she was to be one of the victims, in the unsuspecting presence of the San Reve. The Storri vanity owned an appetite for two-faced triumphs of that feather.

Storri had departed; and the San Reve was thinking on her love for him, and how they would return together to the France she was sick to see. The bell rang; it was the messenger lad in need of light. The message did not specify the city; the lad had been told to return and have the omission supplied.

The San Reve took the message with the purpose of writing in "New York." She ran her gray-green eye over it. The message read:

DANIEL LOUGHLIN,

Albion House, James Slip.

Get the men together at your place; I will meet them Friday. They must go aboard at once, and take the yacht to Fortress Monroe. We shall then be sure of having it in Washington when we want it. B.

The San Reve read and re-read until she had every word by heart. Then remembering the boy, she wrote in "New York," and sent him on his way. Boy gone, the San Reve, doubts revived and all her jealous suspicions restored to sharpest life, gave herself to groping out the meaning of that message by the light of those lies wherewith Storri had solemnized its production.

CHAPTER XXI

HOW THE GOLD CAME DOWN

Richard, ever modest and in this instance something timid, was for having the wedding celebrated in Senator Hanway's study. He sought to give the preference an atmosphere of sentiment by saying it was there he first declared his love for Dorothy with his eyes. Bess protested against the study, and insisted upon St. John's Church. Richard was not to wed the most beautiful girl in the world, and then run away with her, making the affair a secret, as though he had stolen a sheep. What! did Richard imagine that Dorothy had been weeks over a trousseau to have it extinguished in the narrow compass of Senator Hanway's study? The marriage must be in St. John's where all mankind, or rather womankind, might witness and criticise. Bess would be bridesmaid, sustained thereunto by four damsels. Mr. Fopling should have his part as best man; it would be good practice for Mr. Fopling, and serve to prepare him for his own wedding, an event which Bess, under the exhilarating influence of Dorothy's approaching nuptials, had determined upon for October.

Mrs. Hanway-Harley joined with Bess for the church. Mrs. Hanway-Harley cast her vote delicately, saying she would have it expressly understood that she only gave it as a view. She hoped no one would feel in any sense bound thereby; she had not been, speaking strictly, a party to this marriage, nothing in truth but a looker-on, and therefore it did not become her to assume an attitude of authority. Mrs. Hanway-Harley would only say that churches were the conventional thing and studies were not.

Richard capitulated; indeed he gave way instantly and at the earliest suggestion of "church." His surrender, made with the utmost humility, did not prevent both Bess and Mrs. Hanway-Harley from demonstrating their position in full.

"When all is said," declared Richard, "the main thing is the wedding."

Mrs. Hanway-Harley would like to know what plans had been laid for the honeymoon. To what regions would the happy pair migrate, and for what space? Mrs. Hanway-Harley wore a look of reserved sadness as though she asked what cemetery had been selected as the destination of the funeral cortège, following services of final sorrow at the house.

Richard explained that, guided by Dorothy, Italy and its mountains had been pitched upon. They would go from Italy to France; then to England.

The length of their stay abroad was to be always in the hands of Dorothy, who would bring them home to America whenever she chose.

Mrs. Hanway-Harley sighed economically, and suggested that Richard's happiness ought not to blind him to the subject of expense. It would cost a pot of money to make the journey intimated. In a sudden gush of hardihood Richard kissed Mrs. Hanway-Harley, and assured her that in all his life, a life remarkable for an utter carelessness of money, he had never felt less like reckoning a cost. From beginning to end he meant to close his eyes to that subject of expense. There the business ended, for Mrs. Hanway-Harley was too much overcome by the kiss to proceed.

Richard went home and, being full of that honeymoon the possible expense of which had alarmed the economies of Mrs. Hanway-Harley, summoned Mr. Gwynn. That austere man assumed his place on the rug in frigid waiting.

"Mr. Gwynn, you will go to London, and from there to Paris, and lastly to Naples, and at each place prepare for our reception. You will meet us in Naples somewhere from the middle to the last of June. I say last of June, for before we reach Naples we may idle away a fortnight in the Mediterranean. Have everything in perfect order."

"Very good, sir," said Mr. Gwynn.

Richard made a slight dismissive motion with his hand, as showing Mr. Gwynn that he might retire. Mr. Gwynn creaked apologetically, but stood his ground.

"What is it?" said Richard.

"If you please, sir," observed Mr. Gwynn, a gleam in the piscatorial eye, "if you please, sir, before I leave for Europe have I your permission to take out my first papers and declare my intention to become a citizen of this country?"

"May I ask what has moved you to propose this compliment for the United States?"

"Why, sir, should you be so good as to sanction it, I have a little plan, sir."

"Indeed; and what may be the plan which results so much to the advantage of this country?"

"I have a plan, sir," said Mr. Gwynn, with a hesitating creak, "always of course, sir, with your consent, to become a Senator, sir."

"Ah, I see," observed Richard with a fine gravity, "your acquaintance with Senators Gruff and Dice and Loot and others, and your study of those statesmen, have encouraged an ambition to make yourself one of them."

"Yes, sir, if you please, sir."

"And what State do you intend to honor as its Senator?"

"That I shall leave entirely to you, sir. I think you will agree, sir, that there are several States where the word of the Anaconda should accomplish what I desire, sir."

"Well," observed Richard, schooling his face to a difficult seriousness, "there has been much in your recent experiences, Mr. Gwynn, to justify the thought. It will do no harm were you to take the steps you suggest towards becoming a citizen, even if it should not end in a seat in the Senate, a place for which I cannot deny you possess many qualifying attributes. However, the great thing now is to get across to Europe with every possible dispatch and have all ready for our coming. We shall be abroad several months; on our return we may again take up this business of making you a Senator."

"Thank you, sir; very good, sir!"

Richard became ingenious; pursuing a bright idea, he took occasion to explain to Mr. Sands that the Hanway report on Northern Consolidated, which he, Mr. Sands, had been so intelligent as to purloin, having resulted in certain Wall Street advantages to Mr. Bayard and others, it was now determined that an annuity should be purchased in his, Mr. Sands', favor.

"The matter," said Richard, "will receive the attention of Mr. Bayard on June second. I am told it will provide you an annual income of full fifteen thousand dollars for the balance of your life."

Mr. Sands did not give way to the least excitement, but said that he was glad. He would hereafter avoid labor, and devote himself to the elevation of the workingman as represented in the union of printers. It is perhaps as well to set forth in this place that Mr. Sands adhered most nobly to his resolution. In the years that followed he flourished the terror of publishers and master-printers, advising many strikes for shorter hours and a longer wage, never failing from his personal fisc to furnish what halls and beer the exigencies of each strike made necessary, and wanting which no great industrial movement can survive.

Word of the coming wedding got about, and the gossipy murmur of it reached the ears of Storri. The news stirred his savage nature to the dregs.

"June, the first!" sneered Storri, as he paced his apartment in furious soliloquy. "Now we shall see! Yes, you little people must first settle with

Storri! A Russian nobleman is not to be disposed of so cheaply! What if he were to steal away your bride? The caitiff Storms must then wait, eh?"

Storri snapped his fingers in vicious derision. He pictured the father and mother and bridegroom, when they arose on the wedding morning to find that the bride had been spirited away. Storri programmed a crime, the black audacity of which went far beyond that dark-lantern enterprise of Treasury gold upon which London Bill was so patiently employed. The design possessed the simplicity, too, which is a ruling feature of your staggering atrocity. The gold would be going aboard the *Zulu Queen* on Friday, Saturday, and Sunday nights. With the first blue streaks of dawn on Monday, May thirtieth, say at four o'clock, the *Zulu Queen*, thinking on escape, must up anchor and go steaming down the Potomac. Now what should be less complex than to have Benzine Bob set fire to the Harley house an hour before the time to sail? A bundle of combustibles soaked in kerosene could be introduced into Senator Hanway's study; the details might be safely left with Benzine Bob, to whom opening a window or taking out a pane of glass offered few deterring difficulties. The Harley house would be instantly filled with fire and smoke. Storri and Benzine Bob, under pretense of saving life, would burst in the door. Storri would seize on Dorothy, who, if she were not already in a convenient fainting fit, might be stifled by muffling her in blankets. Steamboat Dan would be in the street with a cab, himself on the box as driver. Presto! Storri with his sweet prize would whirl away to the river front. The launch would be waiting; the fair Dorothy should find herself safe prisoner aboard the *Zulu Queen* before she knew what had taken place. True, there would be a crowd; the fire people, and what others were abroad at that hour, would rush to the burning house. And yet who would think of questioning Storri, so heroically rescuing life? Who would dream of stopping him who was only taking the rescued fainting one to safe shelter and medical help? In the bustle and alarm, Storri was bound to succeed; there was no least chance of interference.

If Storri could have read the jealous breast of the San Reve, in which kindly soil a wildest suspicion was never two hours old before it had grown to the granite dignity of things certain, his criminal hopes might not have soared so high! Had he known how his every step was shadowed by the sleepless Inspector Val, and that what the latter did not surmise was invariably told him by Steamboat Dan, his horrid confidence would have been less insolent in its anticipations!

Mayhap there be those among you who have "punched" the casual cow, and whose beef-wanderings included the drear wide-stretching waste yclept the Texas Panhandle. If so you have noted, studded hither and yon about the scene, certain conical hillocks or mountainettes of sand. Those dwarf sand-mountains were born of the labor of the winds, which in those distant regions are famous for persistent, not to say pernicious industry. Given a right direction, the wind in its sand-drifting will build you one of those sand-cones almost while you wait. The sand-cone will grow as a stocking grows beneath the clicking needles of some ancient dame. Again, the wind, reversing in the dance, will unravel the sand-cone and carry it off to powder it about the plain. The sand-cone will vanish in a night, as it came in a night, and what was its site will be swept as flatly clean as any threshing floor.

Thus was it with Senator Hanway on a certain fateful day in May, and less than a fortnight before the coming together of the convention which should pass on the business of a Presidential candidate. Compared with that other sand-cone of politics, to wit, Governor Obstinate, Senator Hanway outtopped him as a tree outtops a shrub. In a moment the situation, so flattering to Senator Hanway, was changed disastrously. Those winds which built him into the most imposing sand-cone of all that dotted the plains of party had shifted, and with mournful effect. Senator Hanway, beneath their erosive influence, shrunk from a certainty to a probability, from a probability to a possibility, and then wholly disappeared. And this disheartening miracle was worked before the eyes of Senator Hanway, and before the eyes of his friends; and yet no one might stay the calamity in its fulfillment. The amazing story, avoiding simile and figure, may be laid open in a handful of sentences.

On that dread day, which you are to keep in memory, nothing could have been brighter than the prospects of Senator Hanway. The national delegates, some nine hundred odd, had been selected—each State naming its quota—and waited only the appointed hour to come together and frame the party's ticket. By count of friend and foe alike, Senator Hanway was certain of convention fortune; he was the sure prognostication for the White House of all the prophets.

And because the last is ever the first in the memory of a forgetful age, and therefore the most important, that which particularly contributed to the strength of Senator Hanway was his project of a Georgian Bay-Ontario Canal. There arose but one opinion, and that of highest favor, touching this gigantic waterway and the farsighted statesmanship which conceived it; that is, but one opinion if you except the murmurs of a few railway companies who trembled over freight rates, and whose complaints were lost in the general roar of Canal approval.

At this juncture, so fraught with happy promise for Senator Hanway, what should come waddling into the equation to spoil all, but a purblind, klabber-witted journal of Toronto, just then busy beating the beauties of the Georgian Bay-Ontario Canal into the dull Canadian skull. This imprint, as a reason for Kanuck acquiescence in the great waterway, proceeded to show how its effect would be to strengthen Canada in case of war between England and the United States. Batteries could be planted to defend the entrances of the canal, which might then be employed in quickly sending a Canadian fleet from the upper lakes into Ontario and vice versa. Twenty Canadian war boats, with the canal to aid them, could threaten New York in the morning and Michigan in the afternoon, and keep threefold their number of American vessels jumping sidewise to guard against their ravages. If for no reason other than a reason of defensive and offensive war, Canada should have the Georgian Bay-Ontario Canal. Thus spake this valuable authority of Toronto.

It was Mr. Hawke, among the adherents of Governor Obstinate, who saw the weapon that might be fashioned against Senator Hanway from the Canadian suggestion. Mr. Hawke had long been aware of Senator Hanway's interference against himself in the Speakership fight, and in favor of Mr. Frost. True, he did not know of those four hundred terrifying telegrams that so shook from his support the hysterical little goat-bearded one and his equally hysterical fellows; but Mr. Hawke had learned enough to ascribe his defeat to Senator Hanway, and that was sufficient to edge him with double readiness to do said statesman what injury he could. Besides, there was the native eagerness of Mr. Hawke to move everything for the good of Governor Obstinate.

Mr. Hawke came out in a well-considered interview concerning the Georgian Bay-Ontario Canal, in which he quoted in full the Toronto paper. Mr. Hawke agreed with the Toronto paper; in addition he solemnly gave it as his belief that Senator Hanway's real purpose had ever been to arm England against this country. Mr. Hawke became denunciatory, and called Senator Hanway a traitor working for English preference and English gold. He said that Senator Hanway was a greater reprobate than Benedict Arnold. Mr. Hawke rehearsed the British armament in the Western Hemisphere, and counted the guns in Halifax, Montreal, Quebec, Esquimalt, to say nothing of the Bermudas, the Bahamas, and the British West Indies. He pointed out that England already possessed a fighting fleet on the Great Lakes which wanted nothing but the guns—and those could be mounted in a day—to make them capable of burning a fringe ten miles wide along the whole lake coast of the United States. Buffalo, Detroit, Chicago, every city on the lakes was at the mercy of England; and now her agent, Senator Hanway, to make the awful certainty threefold surer, was traitorously proposing his Georgian Bay-Ontario Canal. Mr. Hawke, being a Southern man, and because no Southern man can complete an interview without, like

Silas Wegg, dropping into verse, quoted from Byron where he stole from Waller for his lines on White:

"So the struck eagle stretched upon the plain,No more through rolling clouds to soar again,Viewed his own feather on the fatal dartAnd winged the shaft that quivered in his heart."

Mr. Hawke closed in with a burst of eloquence, but metaphors sadly mixed, by picturing this country as a "struck eagle," expiring at the feet of England. It then might find, cried Mr. Hawke, how it had winged the murderous shaft that stole its life away with the Georgian Bay-Ontario Canal. Senator Hanway was given his share in the picture as the paid traitor who had furnished that feather from the American Eagle's wing which so fatally aided the enemy in his archery.

To one unacquainted with the tinderous quality of political popularities, what ensued would be hard to imagine. Mr. Hawke's interview was as a torch to tow. A tiny responsive flame burst forth in one paper, then in ten, then in two hundred; in a moment the country was afire like a sundry prairie. Senator Hanway, lately adored, was execrated and burned in effigy. In short there occurred an uprising of the peasantry, and Senator Hanway found himself denounced from ocean to ocean as one guilty of studied treason. It was as much as one's political life was worth to be on terms of friendship with him.

Speaker Frost called, and explained to Senator Hanway that he could no longer hold the delegation from his State in his, Senator Hanway's, interest; it would vote solidly against him in the coming convention. Senator Gruff came under cloud of night, as though to hold conference with a felon, and said that he had received advices from the Anaconda President to the effect that nothing, not even the mighty Anaconda, could stem the tide then setting and raging in Anaconda regions against Senator Hanway. It was the Anaconda President's suggestion that Senator Hanway withdraw himself from present thoughts of a White House. The several States whose conventions had instructed for Senator Hanway, through special meetings of their central committees, rescinded those instructions. Throughout the country every vestige of a Hanway enthusiasm was smothered, every scrap of Hanway hope was made to disappear; that statesman was left in no more generous peril of becoming President than of becoming Pope. And all through the gorgeous proposition of a Georgian Bay-Ontario Canal, and the adroit use which the malevolent Mr. Hawke had made of it! The passing of Senator Hanway was the wonder of politics!

And yet that indomitable publicist bore these reverses grandly, for he was capable of stoicism. Moreover, he was of that hopeful incessant brood, like ants or wasps, the members whereof begin instantly in the wake of the storm to rebuild their destroyed domiciles. And from the first he lulled himself with no false hopes. As one after the other Senator Hanway found his prospects ablaze, the knowledge broke on him, and he accepted it, that the immediate future held for him no Presidency. It would be party madness to put him up; the party rank and file were in ferocious arms against him.

Senator Hanway drew one deep breath of regret and that was the limit of his lamentation. He was young, when one thinks of a White House; there still remained room in his life for three more shoots at that alluring target; he would withdraw and re-prepare for four years or eight years or—if Fate should so order the postponement of his ambition—twelve years away. The public memory was short; within a year his fatal Georgian Bay-Ontario Canal would be forgot. Meanwhile, what was there he might save from the situation as it stood?

Senator Hanway exerted his diplomacy, and as fruit thereof was visited by an eye-glassed gentleman—a foremost national figure, and the chief of Governor Obstinate's management. Senator Hanway showed the eye-glassed Mazarin of party how, upon his own withdrawal, he, Senator Hanway, might put Speaker Frost in his place and endow him with the major share of what had been his own elements of strength. Was there any reason why he, Senator Hanway, should refrain from such a step?

The eye-glassed Mazarin thereupon represented that it would be much better if Speaker Frost were to remain undisturbed in his House autocracy. It was over-late for Speaker Frost and the convention only days away. The die was already cast; Governor Obstinate would be nominated and elected. Once inaugurated, the eye-glassed Mazarin understood that it would be Governor Obstinate's earliest care to invite Senator Hanway into his Cabinet as Secretary of the Treasury. The scandal of the Georgian Bay-Ontario Canal would have blown itself out; also no one—against a President whose hands were full of offices—would dare lift up his voice in criticism of any Cabinet selection.

Senator Hanway was impressed by the hint of the eye-glassed Mazarin. The Treasury portfolio stood within ready throw of a Presidential nomination; he, Senator Hanway, might step from it the successor of Governor Obstinate whenever that gentleman's tenancy of the White House should come to an end. Likewise, the Treasury portfolio was as a thirteen-inch gun within pointblank range of the stock market.

Senator Hanway took a week to consider; he conferred with Senators Gruff and Price and Loot and lastly with Mr. Harley. Then he struck hands with the eye-glassed Mazarin, and published an interview in the *Daily Tory* saying that he, Senator Hanway, was not and had never been a candidate for the Presidency; that he was and had ever been of the opinion that the needs of both a public and a party hour imperatively demanded Governor Obstinate at the Nation's helm. He, Senator Hanway, being a patriot, was diligently working for the nomination and election of Governor Obstinate, and all who called him friend would do the same. Following this pronunciamento, Senator Hanway began laying personal pipes for four years away with pristine ardor.

Friday, the twenty-seventh of May, was dark and lowering, with a slow storm blackly gathering in the southwest. It was four in the afternoon when the *Zulu Queen* came up the river, and under quarter speed crept in and anchored within one thousand feet of the mouth of Storri's drain. Perhaps, of all the folk in Washington, no more than three remarked the advent of the *Zulu Queen*; one of these was Storri, one the San Reve, and one Inspector Val. Storri saw neither of the others; the San Reve saw only Storri; Inspector Val, whose trade was eyes, saw both Storri and the San Reve. Four of Steamboat Dan's men came into town the day before by rail, and for twelve hours prior to the advent of the *Zulu Queen*, and under the lead of Steamboat Dan, had been in the drain giving aid and comfort to Cracksman London Bill in his efforts to reduce the gold reserve.

When Storri observed that the *Zulu Queen* was safely a-swing on her rope at the very spot he had specified, he turned and moved rapidly away. The San Reve, who had seen what she came to see, was already upon her return journey to Grant Place, bearing in her bosom a heart desolate and heavy with no hope. The coming of the *Zulu Queen* had confirmed to her the treachery of Storri. Yes, she the San Reve could see it all! Storri might have quarreled with Mr. Harley; but the loving understanding between himself and Miss Harley was still complete!

Nor was the poor jealous San Reve wholly without a reason, as she beheld events, for her conclusion. Within the past few days, Storri had been several times to and fro in the vicinity of the Harley house. Only the afternoon before he had cautiously studied the premises in company with a couple of suspicious-looking characters, being indeed no other than Steamboat Dan and Benzine Bob. The San Reve kept secret pace with Storri in these reconnoiterings. But she made the mistake of construing preparations to abduct as arrangements to elope. As the San Reve read the portents, Storri planned to meet Miss Harley that very night; they would fly together, the *Zulu Queen* offering a sure means of baffling pursuit.

The San Reve, biased of her jealous fears, had foreseen in the message to Steamboat Dan some such end as this. It was all so plain and sure to the angry, heart-broken San Reve. The false Storri had done what he might to cover his intentions by daily lies as to how and when he, with the San Reve, should sail for France and Russia! Ah, yes; the San Reve saw through those lies! While she listened to his purring mendacities she must struggle to refrain from casting his untruths in his teeth. Bridle herself she did; but she watched and reflected and resolved the wrongful more. Now with the coming of the *Zulu Queen*, the one thing certain was that she, the despised San Reve, would be cast off, abandoned. Those love-lies of Storri were intended to blind her into foolish security; he did not wish the elopement designed by him and Miss Harley to encounter obstruction. Thus did the San Reve solve the problem: while Storri would be for misleading her, Miss Harley was hood-winking the Harleys. For a moment the San Reve thought of notifying the Harleys. Then in her desperation she put the impulse aside. Of what avail would be a call upon the Harleys? It might defer; it could not prevent. No, she must adopt the single course by which both her love and her vengeance would be made secure forever. She would take Storri from Miss Harley; and, taking him, she the San Reve would keep him for herself throughout eternity! The present life was the prey of separations, of lies, of loves grown cold; she, with Storri in her arms, would seek another!

At ten o'clock Steamboat Dan was to show a momentary light in the mouth of the drain. This would be the signal for the *Zulu Queen* to send her launch ashore and begin taking the gold aboard. Storri programmed his own appearance at the drain for sharp ten. As he left the water-front, following the appearance of the *Zulu Queen*, he cast his eye hopefully upward at the threatening clouds; a down-pouring storm would be the thing most prayed for.

Until it was time to start for the drain to oversee the transfer of the gold, Storri would remain with the San Reve. He was none too confident of the San Reve; of late she had been too silent, too sad, too much wrapped in thought. And this was the night of nights upon which Storri must be sure. In favor of his own security, Storri must know to a verity both the temper and the whereabouts of the San Reve.

Five minutes before Storri reached Grant Place, the rain fell in a deluge. The San Reve, more fortunately swift, was home in advance of the rain and came in bone-dry. When Storri arrived, his garments streaming water, she wore the look of one who had not been out of the house for an afternoon. Only, if Storri had observed the San Reve's eyes, and added their expression, so strangely reckless yet so resolved, to the set mouth and that marble pallor of her brow, the result might have sickened his assurance.

Having in mind his soaked condition, Storri called for whisky. The San Reve was good enough to pour him a stiff glass, which he drank raw with the harsh appetite of a Russian. There was the ghost of an odor of sleep about that whisky; but the sleep-specter did not appeal to Storri, who tossed off his drink and followed one dram with another, suspecting nothing. Five minutes later he was drowsing stertorously on a lounge.

The San Reve, white, and wild in a manner passive and still, had spoken no word; she attended Storri's wants in silence. When that sudden weariness came to claim him and he cast himself in slumber upon the couch, the San Reve, from where she stood statue-like in the center of the room, bent upon him her gray-green eyes. She stood thus for a space, then the slow tears began to stain her cheeks. She threw herself down beside Storri, kissed him and drew his head to her bosom, crying hopelessly.

Richard had been requested by Inspector Val to meet him at the south front of the Treasury Building at ten o'clock.

"Do you remember," asked Inspector Val, "how several weeks ago we visited the drain?"

Yes; Richard recalled it.

"Come with me to-night," said Inspector Val; "the drain shall explain the mystery of that muddy water, and why I said our man was hard at work."

When Richard and Inspector Val, water-proofed to the chins, reached the mouth of the drain the storm was at furious height. The rain descended in sheets; the lightning made flashing leaps from cloud to cloud and the ceaseless thunders were as a dozen batteries of big guns in fullest play. As Richard and Inspector Val came to a halt, they were joined by three men. Richard, aided by the lightning flashes, recognized Mr. Duff and Mr. England; the third, being Steamboat Dan, was strange to him.

"Is the Russian inside?" asked Inspector Val of Steamboat Dan.

"I don't know," returned Steamboat Dan. "I've been aboard the yacht since eight o'clock until twenty minutes ago. I came ashore in that skiff. Sure, he ought to be in the drain; they've been sending down the stuff for hours."

"I don't find any of it about?"

"I threw a crowbar across the stream one hundred yards up, and halted the procession. The plan, d'ye see, is for me, the coast being clear, to signal the launch to come ashore for its first cargo any time after ten—which is about now."

"We'll omit the launch," returned Inspector Val. "Go into the drain and give the boys the tip to skip. After that, it's up to all of you to look out for yourselves."

"Remember, Inspector," pleaded Steamboat Dan, "you gave your word that me an' Bill an' the gang ain't to be collared."

"Don't fear; the only one I'm after is the Russian. Jump sharp now, and give them the office to screw."

Steamboat Dan entered the drain while Inspector Val, Richard, Mr. Duff, and Mr. England withdrew to a little distance.

"Everybody goes free except the Russian," was Inspector Val's command to Mr. Duff and Mr. England; "he's to be nailed."

From the drain came booming the smothered report of a pistol.

"That's the signal," said Inspector Val; "the noise of a gun will travel miles in a tunnel. They'll be coming out now."

As he spoke, Steamboat Dan issued from the drain and fled like a shadow. A rattle of anchor chains was heard aboard the *Zulu Queen*; she also had taken fright.

"The others won't be here for a while," said Inspector Val. "They've got a good ways to come, and a pitch-dark drain isn't the Bowery."

Something like ten minutes passed; suddenly, cursing and stumbling and splashing, five men rushed from the drain's mouth and made off into the darkness.

"Close up now," cried Inspector Val; "our party should be hard on their heels."

Inspector Val was wrong; ten minutes, twenty minutes elapsed, and no one to emerge from the drain. Inspector Val, placing his two aids on guard, said that he and Richard would investigate. Bearing a dark lantern, he took the lead and Richard followed. About twenty rods up the drain, Inspector Val stumbled and all but pitched upon his face.

"Look out!" he cried, by way of warning.

The next moment Richard set his foot on something soft and yielding, which exploded with a great noise.

"One of those rubber propositions," explained Inspector Val.

By the light of the lamp, and as far up the drain as his eye would reach, Richard beheld a seemingly endless file of circular rubber air-cushions, mates of the one Inspector Val had brought him. On the six-inch depth of water which raced along the cushions were floating light as corks; in the center of each reposed a canvas sack of gold. As Steamboat Dan explained, this long line of argosies had been brought to a standstill by laying an iron bar across so as to detain the little rubber-rafts while the stream ran on. Inspector Val had tripped over this bar. Remove the detaining iron bar, and the released flotilla would sail downward to the mouth of the drain and deliver its yellow freight of gold to whomsoever waited to receive it.

Richard and Inspector Val continued up the drain, the latter wary and ready for Storri, whom he every moment hoped to meet. There appeared no Storri; the two explorers at last reached London Bill's tunnel, finding nothing during their march but a solid procession of richly freighted rubber rafts—three-quarters of a mile of gold!

"There's four millions of dollars between here and the river," said Inspector Val.

Richard and his guide paused where London Bill's tunnel opened into the drain. Flashing his lamp about, Inspector Val showed Richard where London Bill had built a platform on which to store the rubber rafts before inflating and launching them down-stream, each with its five-thousand-dollar cargo of gold.

"Did you ever see sweeter arrangements!" whispered Inspector Val, in an ecstasy of admiration.

Bidding Richard remain where he was, Inspector Val, revolver in one hand, dark-lantern in the other, bent low his head and disappeared in London Bill's tunnel. He was gone an age as it seemed to Richard. Then he reappeared, and soberly brushed the clay from his garments.

"No Storri," was the sententious remark of Inspector Val; "not a sign of him. But I've thought it out. Do you know why we don't find Storri? The reason is the best in the world; the man's dead."

CHAPTER XXII

HOW THE SAN REVE KEPT HER STORRI

Richard was of a temperament singularly cool and steady. His curiosity had been trained to wait, and he put questions only as a last resort. Throughout the strange happenings of the night—the tryst with Inspector Val—the meeting with Mr. Duff and Mr. England at the drain's mouth—the presence of Steamboat Dan—the colloquy between that unworthy and Inspector Val—the signal pistol shot—the flight of the robbers—he had not spoken a word. While his astonishment was kept to an upgrade, there had not been elicited a syllable of inquiry from Richard. He threaded the drain, encountered the long fleet of little rubber argosies, and finally brought up at London Bill's tunnel, and never an interrogation. This was not acting nor affectation; Richard knew that he might with better intelligence invite an explanation from Inspector Val after having seen and understood his utmost. Moreover, what with the storm and the splashing journey up the drain, there had been scanty opportunity for conversation. Also, when he saw how Inspector Val looked forward to the capture of Storri in the midst of crime, the strain of expectation made silence the natural thing. It took Inspector Val's sudden yet decisive assertion that Storri was dead, to provoke the first word. Storri's death instantly overshadowed all else in the thoughts of Richard.

"Storri dead!" he exclaimed, making as though he would enter London Bill's tunnel, from which Inspector Val had crawled to make his grim announcement.

"Dead as Nero!" returned Inspector Val. "But not there—not in the tunnel!"

"Where then?" asked Richard.

"In Grant Place. You recall the San Reve?—she who wrote the letter about those French shares? Both Storri and she are dead in Grant Place, or I'm not an Inspector of Police."

Richard was for going to Grant Place, but Inspector Val detained him.

"There's no hurry," he said. "Any discoveries to be made in Grant Place will wait. On second thought the death of the Russian is the best solution. But there's no hurry. Besides," continued Inspector Val, his tones betraying that sublime appreciation of art at its utmost which an amateur of bronzes might have felt in the presence of Cellini's Perseus, "besides, I want you to take a look over this job of London Bill! You'll never again see its equal—never such perfection of plan and execution!"

Richard was glad of the darkness that hid the half-smile which the delight of Inspector Val called forth. Protest would be of no avail; it was one of those cases where to yield is the only way of saving time.

Inspector Val re-entered London Bill's tunnel and invited Richard to follow. He showed Richard how truthfully, like the work of a best engineer, the tunnel—begun high above water-mark on the side of the drain—sloped downward until it dipped beneath the Treasury walls. Then it began to climb, heading as unerringly for the gold as though London Bill had brought clairvoyant powers to direct his digging. The tunnel ran to the rear of the vault, and about six feet beneath its floor. Then it went straight upward; and next, the supporting earth and masonry having been removed, the gold, pressing with its vast weight, had forced down two of the floor slabs of steel on one side, precisely as London Bill designed from the beginning. Those five-thousand-dollar sacks spilled themselves into the tunnel of their own motion—a very cataract of gold! As fast as they were carried away, more came tumbling—a flow of riches, ceaseless! Inspector Val flashed his lantern here and there in disclosure of the wonderful beauties of the work. As he did so, Richard heard him sigh in a positive contentment of admiration.

"The most scientific job in the history of the police!" whispered Inspector Val. "London Bill is certainly entitled to his rank as the world's foremost box-worker! It's this sort of a thing that makes you respect a man!"

Richard was driven to smile again as he recalled the sleepy, intolerant exquisite, gloved and boutonnièred, whom he met in Willard's, and compared him with the thief-hunting enthusiast who, dark-lantern in hand and crouching under the low clay roof of the tunnel, was so rapturously expounding the genius of the great burglar.

"But greater still," continued Inspector Val, "greater than London Bill, was that Russian party Storri. And to think this was his first—that he was only a beginner! I used to wonder how he was going to bring out the gold; and I'm free to admit I couldn't answer the question. Sometimes, I'd even think he had blundered; I'd figure on him as the amateur who had only considered the business of going to the gold, without remembering that getting away with it was bound to be the hardest part of the trick. You can see yourself," and here Inspector Val appealed to Richard, "and you no crook at all, that if it ever became a case of lugging out this gold by hand, it would take the gang a week to get away with a half-million. It was when Storri ordered those circular rubber rafts that I fell to it all; it was then I took off my hat to him!"

When Richard and Inspector Val were again at the mouth of the drain, the lashing storm had worn itself out. The night was silently serene; the clouds were breaking, and two or three big stars peered down. There was a moon, and having advantage of a rift in the clouds, a ray struck white on Arlington. Over across, one might make out the tall dark Maryland hills. Far away on the river burned the lights of the *Zulu Queen*; she was holding her best speed down-stream, having reason to think her recent anchorage a perilous one.

"Their hearts will be in their mouths until they clear Point Comfort," said Inspector Val, pointing to the retreating *Zulu Queen*. Then turning to Mr. Duff, who, with Mr. England, had faithfully met him and Richard when they emerged from the drain, and giving him a pasteboard from his case, he continued: "Mr. Duff, present my card to the Chief of the Secret Service, and tell him with my compliments that he and what men lie handy to his call are wanted at this drain. Should he be a bit slow, say that a big slice of the gold reserve has fallen into the drain, and the situation doesn't do him credit. You, Mr. England, will remain on guard until the Secret Service people get here. London Bill might regain confidence, and come back for a sack of that gold."

"Where now?" asked Richard as Inspector Val, taking him by the arm, bent his steps towards the center of town.

"Grant Place," replied Inspector Val. "And on that point, if I may advise you, I'd not go to Grant Place; one of us will be enough. You'd see something disagreeable; besides, this killing may get into the coroner's office, and from there into the courts and the newspapers. Considering that you are to be married in a few days, I should say that you don't want to have your name mixed up with it. No, the wise thing is for me to go alone."

"It's the question of publicity," responded Richard, "that I was revolving in my mind. Here's this bald attempt to rob the Treasury———"

"It was magnificent!" interjected Inspector Val, unable to restrain his tribute.

"And if your surmise be correct," continued Richard, disregarding the interruption, "now come the deaths of Storri and the woman San Reve to cap the robbery. What, may I ask, do you call your duty in the premises?"

"Duty?" repeated Inspector Val. "I've no duty; that is, no official duty. Washington is off my beat. My course, however, must depend upon circumstances. As far as I may, I shall smother every mention of to-night's work. If the papers get hold of one end of it, and begin to haul it ashore, they will bring in yourself and Mr. Harley and Senator Hanway in a manner not desired at this time. Besides, the Secret Service people, goaded by publicity, might pinch Steamboat Dan and his gang. Now I'm not going to lose my best stool pigeon to please these somnambulists of the Secret Service. Also, I've given my promise to Dan, and I never break my word."

"I'm quite anxious, as you may imagine," said Richard, "to bury what we've seen and heard to-night. But how can it be done? You've sent word to the Secret Service Chief."

"The men of the Secret Service will never mention the business unless they have to; it's not to their glory. The danger lies with those dead folk waiting in Grant Place. If there were nothing to hide but the gold in the drain, and the hole under the Treasury wall, it would prove easy enough."

"But are you sure that Storri is dead? It's simply your deduction, you know. You may yet find him very much alive."

"He's dead," reiterated Inspector Val, with deepest conviction. "If he were alive, we would have found him at the drain. That gold would have drawn him there in his sleep. Besides, I saw it coming. I've an idea, however, that the Russian legation people possess as many motives for holding Storri's death a secret as do the Secret Service men for keeping dark the fact that the Treasury has been tapped. Yes, the Russians, with the State Department to help them, will find a way. Everything goes by pull, you know," concluded Inspector Val, confidently, "and it will be queer if the State Department and the Russians, working together, can't call Storri's blinking out by some name that won't attract attention."

Inspector Val related how, step by step, he had kept abreast of Storri.

"When he came out of retirement," explained Inspector Val, "following the loss of his money in Northern Consolidated, I kept close tabs on him. These half-civilized people are only half sane, and some crazy crime would have come natural to this Russian at that time. So, as I tell you, I stayed close to his heels. I could see by his face that he had some big purpose. He began buying maps and visiting the department buildings. I knew then we were getting to the heart of the affair, and, while I couldn't guess the shoot he would take, I had only to follow to find out. The moment he put foot in the Treasury Building, I turned wise. Those visits to the other buildings had been mere 'stalls.' As I followed him through the Treasury I could see that now he was in earnest.

"When the Assistant Secretary showed him the vault that held the gold reserve, I learned all I wanted to learn. His design and the crime he plotted were written on his face. Of course as soon as ever I realized that he meant to try his teeth on the Treasury, I had only to run my eye over the year's calendar to tell when. There was a Sunday followed by Decoration Day—two holidays, and no one on guard worth considering; it was sure that

Storri would hit upon those days to make the play. When I saw how the Saturday before was set apart for a special holiday, the thing was surer than ever. It did not require any deep intelligence to determine when Storri would act. Next I followed him up the drain; and later to Steamboat Dan's. That visit to Dan's so reduced the business that nothing was left but the question of when to make the collar."

"What yacht was that?" asked Richard.

"It belongs to a fat-witted rich young fellow from whom Storri borrowed it. Steamboat Dan is aboard; he went out in the skiff he spoke of. When he's tied her up and his gang's ashore, I'll wire the fat-witted one to come and claim his boat."

Inspector Val never breathed a hint concerning Storri's ebon purpose of abduction, and how he meant to fire the Harley house and then kidnap Dorothy in the confusion certain to be an incident of flames and smoke at four o'clock in the morning. This reticence arose from the delicacy of Inspector Val. The relation could not fail to leave a most unpleasant impression upon Richard, and Inspector Val decided to suppress it for the nonce.

"I'll keep it a year and a day," thought Inspector Val; "then I'll tell him."

Richard adopted the counsel of Inspector Val, and did not accompany that gentleman of secrets to Grant Place. It was the half hour after midnight when Inspector Val climbed the Warmdollar steps, and strenuously pulled the bell. The latter appurtenance was one of those old-fashioned knob-and-wire tocsins, and its clangorous voice was calculated to arouse, not only the house whereof it was a fixture, but the neighborhood round about. Inspector Val's second pull at this ancient engine brought Mr. Warmdollar, something bleary and stupid to be sure, but wide awake for Mr. Warmdollar. Once inside the hallway, Inspector Val told Mr. Warmdollar that he was a police agent, showed that ex-representative the gold badge glimmering beneath his coat, and concluded by informing him that all might not be well in the San Reve's room. Inspector Val did what he could to frighten Mr. Warmdollar. It was necessary to tame that householder to docility, and what should achieve this sooner than a great fright? At the fearful hints of Inspector Val—they were in his manner more than in his words—the purple nose of Mr. Warmdollar became a disastrous gray. Beholding this encouraging symptom, Inspector Val delayed no longer, but bid him beat upon the San Reve's door. This Mr. Warmdollar, nervous and shaken, did with earnestness, not once but twice. Nobody responded; after each visitation of the panel the silence that prevailed was sinister.

"There's no one in," faltered Mr. Warmdollar.

Inspector Val pointed ominously to the hall-rack on which were hanging Storri's hat and waterproof coat. Mr. Warmdollar wrung his hands; his imagination, fretted into fever by the remoteness of his latest whisky toddy,—whisky toddy being Mr. Warmdollar's favorite tipple,—began to give him pictures of what dread things lay hidden in the silence beyond that unresponsive door.

Inspector Val took from his pocket three pieces of steel, each about the size of a lead pencil, and began screwing them together, end for end. The instrument produced was a foot in length and looked like a screwdriver. As a matter of burglarious fact it was a jimmy of fineness and finish. It had been the property of a gentlemanly "flat-worker," who made rich hauls before he fell into the fingers of Inspector Val and went to Sing Sing. Inspector Val applied the absent gentleman's jimmy to the San Reve's door, squarely over the lock. He gave it a twitch and the door flew inward, the bolt tearing out a mouthful of the casing.

"Stand back!" said Inspector Val to Mr. Warmdollar, who having already retired to the lower step of the stair, where he sat with his face buried in his hands, hardly required the warning.

One gas jet was burning in the San Reve's room; being turned down to lowest ebb, it was about as illuminative as a glow-worm. Inspector Val stretched forth his hand and instantly the room was flooded of light. Inspector Val was neither shocked nor surprised at the spectacle before him; he was case-hardened by a multitude of professional experiences, and besides, for full a fortnight he had read murder in the San Reve's face.

Storri was lying upon the lounge, dead—stone-dead. A trifling hole in the back of the head showed where the bullet entered in search of his life. There was a minimum of blood; the few dried drops upon a curling lock of the black hair were all there was to tell how death came. Storri had been dead for hours; the small thirty-two caliber revolver—being that one which Storri had seen on a memorable night in mid-winter—lay on the floor where it fell from the San Reve's jealous fingers. It was a diminutive machine, blue steel and mother of pearl, more like a plaything than a pistol.

The San Reve was on her knees beside the dead Storri, her left arm beneath his head and her face buried in the silken cushion that served as pillow. There was a looseness of attitude that instantly struck Inspector Val; he stepped to the San Reve and lifted the free hand which hung by her side. The hand was clammy and cold as ice. The San Reve had died when Storri died, but there was none of the rigidity of death, the body was relaxed and limp. Inspector Val sniffed the air inquisitively, and got just the faintest odor of bitter almonds. That, and the relaxed limbs, enlightened him.

"Prussic acid," said he.

As Inspector Val replaced the San Reve's hand by her side, a tiny vial—that with a prayer-book—was dislodged from a fold of her dress. The vial showed a few drops of a yellow-green fluid in the bottom. Inspector Val picked it up, and the bitter breath of the almond was more pronounced than ever.

"Exactly!" murmured Inspector Val; "prussic acid! She died as though by lightning;—which is a proper way to die if one's mind is made up. Now why couldn't she have sent Storri by the same route? A drop of this"—here he surveyed the tiny vial with interest, almost with approval—"a drop of this in the corner of his eye, or on his lip, would have beaten the pistol. Ah, yes, the pistol!" mused Inspector Val, taking the baby weapon in his hand; "I suppose the storm drowned the report. Well, they're gone! Storri was asleep, and never knew what hit him; which, considering his record,—and I'm something of a judge,—was an easier fate than he had earned."

Inspector Val made a close examination of the room, rather from habit than any thought more deep, and straightway discovered the sleepy whisky. He put it to his nose as he had the tiny vial.

"Laudanum!" he muttered; "she had mapped it out in every detail. It was the sight of the *Zulu Queen*; she saw that he was about to desert her."

Inspector Val heaved a half-sigh, as even men most like chilled steel will when in the near company of death, and then, stiffening professionally, he called in Mr. Warmdollar, still weeping drunken tears at the stair's foot.

"I want, for your own sake," explained Inspector Val, "to impress upon you the propriety of silence. These deaths will produce a sensation in both the State Department and the Russian legation. If word get abroad through you, it might be resented in the quarters I've named. I shall give the Russians notice, and you must not let a word creep into the papers until after they have been here. If news of this leak out, it may cost Mrs. Warmdollar her situation."

Inspector Val was aware that in Washington the hinted loss of one's position as the penalty of loquacity has ever been the way of ways to lock fast the garrulous tongue. Mr. Warmdollar became a prodigal of promises; neither sign nor sound should escape him of the tragedy. Mrs. Warmdollar, as head scrubwoman, must not be put in jeopardy!

Inspector Val visited the Secret Service Chief, and the two were as brothers of one mind. To lapse into the rustic figures of the farms, on that subject of secrecy they fell together like a shock of oats. Why should the world know of the splendid gopher work of London Bill? The gold had been saved; to publish the dangers it had grazed might inspire other bandits. No, secrecy was the word; that question Inspector Val and the Secret Service Chief answered as one man. And so no word crept forth. When the vault must be restored, it was said that those tons upon tons of gold it sheltered had broken down the steel floor. As bricks by the wagon load went into the drain through the manhole nearest the scene of London Bill's exploits, a pavement idler asked their purpose. They were to repair the drain where the water had eaten into and undermined the walls. Yes, it was a secret stubbornly protected; the tunnel was stopped up, the vault restored to what had been a former strength or weakness, and never a dozen souls to hear the tale.

With the Russians, Inspector Val met views which ran counter to his own. An attaché of the Bear accompanied Inspector Val to the San Reve's rooms in Grant Place. The Attaché was for sending Storri's body to St. Petersburg. Inspector Val objected.

"Why should you care?" said the Attaché to Inspector Val. "I do not understand your interest."

"She cares," returned Inspector Val, pointing to the dead San Reve. "I have made her interest mine. She died to keep this Storri by her side; I will not see her cheated."

The Attaché looked curiously at Inspector Val; a sentimental lunatic was not a common sight. The Attaché, however, was no one to yield. Storri's remains must go to Russia.

"Will you send home then the body of a thief overtaken in the crime?" asked Inspector Val. "This Storri schemed to rob the Treasury. I do not think the representatives of the Czar should oppose me in my whim."

"Who are you?" asked the Attaché. Inspector Val's disclosures were alarming; trained in caution, he did not care to defy them until he was sure of his foothold of fact. "The news you brought so affected me that I failed of politeness and never asked your name."

"I am Inspector Val of the New York police."

"And you declare Count Storri a thief engaged in robbing your Treasury?"

"I say it word for word. More; he had it in train to burn a house and abduct a girl."

The Attaché surveyed Inspector Val with his sharp black eyes. Clearly, here was a man whom it would not be wise—for the honor of the Bear—to oppose!

"And this poor woman loved Count Storri," said the Attaché, shifting his glance to the dead San Reve. "She died, you say, to keep him by her. Yes, you are right; they should not be parted now."

The San Reve, no longer jealous, and Storri, no longer false, were given one grave, and the Attaché of the Czar and Inspector Val alone attended, as though representing rival interests. The San Reve's prayer of passion had been granted; her Storri would be her own and hers alone throughout eternity.

CHAPTER XXIII

HOW RICHARD AND DOROTHY SAILED AWAY

There came but the one name before the convention, and Governor Obstinate was nominated for the Presidency by acclamation. Senator Hanway wired his warm congratulations, and to such earnest length did they extend themselves that it reduced the book of franks conferred upon Senator Hanway by the telegraph company by five stamps. Governor Obstinate thanked Senator Hanway through the eye-glassed Mazarin, who seized upon the occasion to say that Governor Obstinate was more than ever resolved in event of his election—which was among things sure—to avail himself of Senator Hanway's known abilities touching public finance in the rôle of Secretary of the Treasury.

Senator Hanway and Mr. Harley, the Georgian Bay-Ontario Canal still rankling in the popular regard, did not attend the convention. This permitted those gentlemen to be present at the nuptials of Dorothy and Richard, a negative advantage which otherwise might have been denied.

Mrs. Hanway-Harley, basing it on grounds of duty, assumed formal charge of the marriage arrangements in the later hours. She asked Richard to name those among his friends whom he desired as guests at the wedding. Richard gave her Mr. Bayard, Mr. Sands, and Inspector Val. Mrs. Hanway-Harley pursed her lips. Mr. Bayard? yes; but why ask Mr. Sands, printer, and Inspector Val of the police?

"They are my friends," said Richard.

Mrs. Hanway-Harley shook her head in proud dejection as she meditated on the strangeness of things. Her daughter's wedding; and a detective and a journeyman printer among the honored guests! The homely disgrace of it quite bowed the heart of Mrs. Hanway-Harley. She was taken doubly aback when she learned that Mr. Gwynn was on his way to England, and therefore not to attend.

"It would have pleased me," said Mrs. Hanway-Harley mournfully, "had Mr. Gwynn been present. His absence is peculiarly a blow."

"I'm sure," said Richard, putting on a look of innocent slyness, like a lamb engaged in intrigue, "had I known that you might feel Mr. Gwynn's going away, I would have kept him with us."

Mrs. Hanway-Harley elevated her polite brows. Richard would have kept Mr. Gwynn with them! What manner of mystery was this?

Richard's present to Dorothy was a superb, nay a matchless set of rubies, the like of which did not dwell in the caskets of Queen or Empress. Mrs. Hanway-Harley, herself no apprentice in the art of gems, could not estimate their value. They lay in her hands like red fire—jewels above price! Mrs. Hanway-Harley could only gaze and gaze, while Richard's look of slyness gained in lamblike intensity.

Mr. Bayard came down from New York the day before; he must have a business talk with Richard. It would be impossible, in releasing Mr. Harley and Senator Hanway from their obligations as members of the osprey pool, to avoid an explanation. In running over the affair in his mind, Mr. Bayard was convinced that the reprieved pair must be told the truth of their capture and release.

Richard, whose powers of original judgment had diminished in exact proportion as he neared the wedding day, and who now, with the ceremony only hours away, owned no judgment at all, gave Mr. Bayard leave to do as he would. He was to tell Mr. Harley and Senator Hanway, Mr. Sands and Inspector Val, as much or as little as he chose. Richard drew relief from the reflection that, whatever the disclosures, he, Richard, at the time they were made would be safe on the wide Atlantic.

The wedding offered a rich study in expression. Richard was pale but firm, and if his knees shook the aspen disgrace of it didn't show in his face. Dorothy was radiantly happy—beautiful and unabashed. Somehow, a wedding never fails to bring out the strength of your true woman. Bess was splendidly responsible; she showed plainly that she considered the wedding the work of her hands, and was bound to see justice done it. Her supporting damsels, taking their cue from certain bridesmaids who had adorned a recent wedding of mark, wept bitterly. Mr. Bayard was interested in a courteous way; Mr. Harley was patronizing, Senator Hanway benign. Inspector Val, ineffable as to garb, was distinguished by that sleepy, well-bred stare which was his common expression when off duty. Only once did he rouse, and that was when Mrs. Hanway-Harley, deluded by his elegant reserve, over which was thrown just an aroma of the military, addressed him as Captain Burleigh of the English legation. Mr. Sands of all who were there was probably the one most coolly composed; being in profound contrast to Mr. Fopling, whose eye was glassy and whose cheek was ashes.

"Stawms," whispered Mr. Fopling, tremulous with agitation, "if I'm as weak as this at your wedding, what do you weckon I'll be at my own? 'Pon my word, I think I'll have to be bwought to church in an invalid's chair; I do, weally!"

"Bless you, my boy, bless you!" exclaimed Mr. Harley, grasping Richard's hand. Mr. Harley had absorbed the impression, probably from the theaters, that this was the phrase for him. "And you, my child; God bless you! Be happy!" continued Mr. Harley, kissing Dorothy and exuding a burgundian tear.

"I am sorry," said Richard, as Senator Hanway bid him and Dorothy an affectionate farewell, "I am sorry the event of the convention disappointed us."

"It is as one who wishes his party and his country well would have it," returned Senator Hanway, with Roman elevation. "Governor Obstinate is a patriot, and an able man. He will call to his Cabinet safe men—true advisers. The nation could not be in purer hands."

Bess made Dorothy promise to have Richard back for her own wedding in October; Mr. Fopling gave Richard a pleading glance as though he himself would require support on that occasion.

"Stawms, don't fail me," said Mr. Fopling. "Weally, I shall need all the couwage my fwiends can give me. And you know, Stawms, I stood by you."

Mrs. Hanway-Harley supposed the happy ones were to take the B. & O. for New York; Richard explained that they would have a boat.

"In fact," said Richard, "the captain has just sent me word that the yacht is anchored off the Navy Yard, awaiting our going aboard."

"Yacht?" said Mrs. Hanway-Harley. "Oh, I see; Mr. Gwynn's."

"No, not Mr. Gwynn's. Ours."—And Richard looked more lamblike than ever.

Mrs. Hanway-Harley became sorely puzzled. The truth was slowly soaking into her not over-porous comprehension.

As the launch, with the wedding party, rounded the yacht's stern to reach her gangway on the off-shore side, Mrs. Hanway-Harley read in letters of raised gilt: *Dorothy Storms*. She called Dorothy's attention to the phenomenon in a misty way. Mrs. Hanway-Harley, once aboard, went over the *Dorothy Storms*, forward and aft, speaking no word. The yacht, Clyde-built, was a swift ocean-going vessel of twelve hundred tons. Her fittings were the fittings of a palace. Mrs. Hanway-Harley cornered Richard on the after-deck.

"Richard," said Mrs. Hanway-Harley, "what took Mr. Gwynn abroad?"

"Why," responded Richard, with a cheerful manner of innocence, "you see there's a deal for Mr. Gwynn to do. There's the country house in Berks, and the house in London; then there's the Paris house and the villa at Nice, and lastly the place in the mountains back of Naples;—Mr. Gwynn will have to put them in order. The one near Naples—a kind of old castle, it is—has been in bad hands; there will be plenty of work in that quarter for Mr. Gwynn, I fancy. You know, mother,"—and Richard donned an air of filial confidence,—"since this is Dorothy's first look at them, I'm more than commonly anxious she should be given a happy——"

Where the wretched Richard would have maundered to will never be known, for he was broken in upon by Mrs. Hanway-Harley.

"Richard, who is Mr. Gwynn?" This with a severe if agitated gravity. "Who is Mr. Gwynn?"

"Who is Mr. Gwynn?" repeated Richard, blandly. "Well, really, I suppose he might be called my major-domo; or perhaps butler would describe him."

"You told me that Mr. Gwynn had had about him the best society of England."

Mrs. Hanway-Harley's manner bordered upon the tragic, for it bore upon her that she had given a dinner of honor to Mr. Gwynn.

"Why, my dear mother, and so he has had. I can't remember all their noble names, but one time and another Mr. Gwynn has been butler for the Duke of This and the Earl of That—really Mr. Gwynn's recommendations read like a leaf from 'Burke's Peerage.' I myself had him from the Baron Sudley."

Mrs. Hanway-Harley was for the moment dumb. Dorothy and Bess appeared, having completed a ransack of staterooms and cabins. The sight of her daughter restored to Mrs. Hanway-Harley the power of speech.

"Dorothy," she cried, raising her hands limply, "Dorothy, I believe our Richard's rich!" And Mrs. Hanway-Harley wept.

"I shall always love him, whatever he is!" exclaimed Dorothy, all tenderness and fresh alarm.

Dorothy did not understand.

It was ten o'clock; the Potomac lay between its soft banks like a river of silver. There was the throb of the engines, and the talk of the water against her bows, as the *Dorothy Storms* with her two passengers, they and their love, swept onward through the moonlight. Dorothy, her head on Richard's shoulder, and thinking on her mother and Bess and all she had left behind, watched the V-shaped wake as it spread away in ripples to either bank. Now and then a shore-light slipped by, to snuff out astern as distance or a bend in the river extinguished it. Dorothy crept more and more into the Pict arms.

"Dear, when did you name the *Dorothy Storms*?"

"The day after you precipitated yourself into my arms—and my heart."

"I think you were shamefully confident," whispered Dorothy, with a delicious sigh.

Richard the brazen replied to the attack as became a lover and gentleman.

And so they sailed away.

THE END

Milton Keynes UK
Ingram Content Group UK Ltd.
UKHW050034220624
444555UK00004B/384